This compelling novel is the product of imp[...] nates the everyday lives of Civil War soldiers as well as the families [...] were left at home. The plot unfolds with great realism. Guttry shows that wartime did not always produce clean narratives and happy endings. Instead, it was messy and unpredictable. The Brownings grow and change throughout the book. But their faith and values endure, as does the North Florida landscape. *Alligator Creek* is a highly readable novel of historical fiction.

Sean McMahon, PhD

Professor of History
Florida Gateway College
Lake City, FL

Lottie Guttry's account of her ancestors' lives during and after the Civil War is a spellbinding narrative that is written with such care and attention to details of the era that the readers will feel as though they are paging through a diary from that time period. Lottie's attention to the details of everyday life during the 1860s and the use of period-correct verbiage for items of clothing, utensils, animals, or general conversation help to make this work one that truly paints a complete picture of the time, the places, and the people that she so eloquently honors in this worthy book.

Pat McAlhany

Lake City-Columbia County Historical Museum, Inc.
Lake City, FL

The fiction that has been set on the stage of the Civil War can hardly match the realities of what our southern ancestors felt and endured during those harsh years. Author Lottie Guttry, in her novel *Alligator*

Creek, takes one family's story and illustrates the trials and tragedies that can accompany all countries' battleground experiences at home and on the battlefield. In Lottie's story, a single mother with five children faces major challenges—serious illness, the death of loved ones, financial struggles, and the prejudices of her small southern town. Guttry creates realistic scenes from major Civil War battles as well as the physical and emotional difficulties experienced by women on the home front.

Francis Edward Abernethy, PhD

Stephen F. Austin State University
Writer, illustrator, publisher
Texas Folklore Society

The Civil War was more than glory and bugle calls. Based on true events, Lottie Guttry's inspiring historical novel captures the suffering and loving devotion of a remarkable southern family caught up in the tragic events of the 1860s.

Van Craddock

Longview (Texas) News-Journal
Author of *Longview (Postcard History)*,
Historic Gregg County, and *East Texas Tales*

ALLIGATOR CREEK

ALLIGATOR CREEK

LOTTIE GUTTRY

BROWN BOOKS
PUBLISHING GROUP

© 2015 Lottie Guttry

All rights reserved. No part of this book may be used or reproduced in any manner without written permission except in the case of brief quotations embodied in critical articles or reviews.

This is a work of fiction. Any similarity to real persons, living or dead, is coincidental and not intended by the author.

Alligator Creek

Brown Books Publishing Group
16250 Knoll Trail Drive, Suite 205
Dallas, Texas 75248
www.BrownBooks.com
(972) 381-0009

A New Era in Publishing™

ISBN 978-1-61254-241-6
Library of Congress Control Number 2015945293

Printed in the United States
10 9 8 7 6 5 4 3 2 1

For more information or to contact the author, please go to
www.AlligatorCreekBook.com

This book is dedicated to my family and extended family, both ancestors and descendants, who preserved this story of courage and sacrifice.

Contents

Acknowledgments

W ithout the intervention of some special people, this family story would have remained unknown to me; *Alligator Creek* might never have become a historical novel. Two special people brought the family story to my attention. My cousin, Nancy Speck, the King family historian, introduced me to Alexander and Sarah Browning, her great-grandparents and my great-greats. Dr. Francis E. Abernethy, professor of courses in my master's program, taught me the importance of a family legend. Two great friends, Pat McAlhaney and Dr. Sean McMahan in Lake City, Florida, acquainted me with the Columbia County Historical Museum, repository of a wealth of information about the Civil War period, and *A History of Columbia County, Florida,* my textbook for Lake City history. Later, they checked my manuscript for local historical details. A congenial critique group—Vickie Phelps, Donna Paul, Nancy Huyser, Becca Anderson, Pamela Dowd, and I—offered one another constructive criticism during the writing of our books. Dr. Henry McGrede, my knowledgeable friend and gynecologist, answered in detail my questions about childbirth. Many thanks to the team at Brown Books Publishing Group for crafting this book into printed form and to my editor, Sally Kemp, whose keen insight inspired me to finish the book with significant improvements. Most of all, I owe my husband, John, eternal gratitude for accompanying me in my search for information and the far-flung gravesites of my ancestors.

1

You have opened the gates of Hell, from which shall flow the curse of the damned to sink you to perdition.

John E. Call
Former Florida governor,
when told that his state had
seceded from the Union

Lake City, Florida: April 1862

Five-year-old Tommy found a heavy stick and propped it like a rifle on his shoulder. He marched forward and back between wooden benches in front of a bandstand decorated with Confederate flags, his lips tightened in grim imitation of military decorum.

The governor interrupted his speech and pointed to the boy. "That lad's a bit young to serve, but he's sure got the right spirit."

From her seat next to her husband Alex, Sarah Browning watched the marching child with troubled eyes. She hated her young son's war games. Impeded by advanced pregnancy and a baby in her arms, she leaned toward her son. "Tommy! Come sit down now." With her free hand, she patted the space beside her.

Her son's mimicry of a Confederate soldier filled her mind with recurring terror. *War fever's smitten our men with insanity.* Lured by adventure and opportunities for heroism, they turned from their jobs, homes, and families. Even though cattlemen like Alex were exempted from service, she feared he might enlist. Sarah closed her eyes and sent up a short prayer: *Please, God, don't let my husband change his mind and decide to join.*

More than ever, she feared Alex would feel compelled to join the army today, the day Lake City welcomed its hometown infantry company on a well-deserved furlough from their first assignment in Tampa Bay. More than two hundred people had gathered at the town square. Preparations began over a week ago when word came that the soldiers were marching home. The women cooked while the men constructed a bandstand and sawed pine planks to set on barrels to serve as tables. The celebration included a brass band, dignitaries' speeches, and a picnic on the grounds provided by the Ladies' Society of the Methodist Church. Applause at the end of the governor's speech startled Sarah.

A minister stepped forward, an open Bible in his hand. "Brothers and sisters, I know you're proud that these brave men have set themselves apart from the selfish stay-at-homes who make gods of their property and profit. These soldiers haven't remained neutral but have placed their honor on the line in the manner of our Savior. Did Jesus live a life of ease while others perished?" He adjusted his thick glasses and opened a bookmarked page in the Bible. "The second chapter in Joel tells us, 'I will drive the northern army far from you, pushing it into a parched and barren land, with its front columns going into the eastern sea.' Have no fear, my friends; the Lord is on our side."

Sarah wondered how long it had taken the minister to find that scripture. She felt certain the Old Testament prophet had never anticipated *this* war.

The preacher scanned the crowd. "Our courageous men will be comforted to know that everyone here will be praying for a swift Southern conquest." He fixed his gaze on slaves near wagons parked behind the benches. "That includes you bondsmen back there. Raise your hands as a promise you will pray each day for a Confederate victory. Come on now; show your support."

Sarah looked toward the family wagon where their servants Industrious and Hannah stood. They exchanged glances with other slaves nearby. Tentatively, one hand raised, then another. Soon all the slaves had raised their hands, but their hard faces belied their assent.

As the minister stepped from the podium, Tommy aimed his stick down the aisle. "Pow! Pow! Gotcha, you bluecoat devil!" He stopped short when his father bounced him onto his lap. "When are the soldiers coming, Daddy?" He dropped the stick.

Alex gave Tommy a squeeze. "Not long, son. They'll march in by the time you count to one hundred."

"I can't count that far."

"Then count to twenty. Do it five times." He grinned and tousled his son's blond hair.

"OK, Daddy. One, two, three, four . . ."

Sarah studied Alex's handsome profile. She followed the line of his thin nose, which he considered too long, to his dimpled cheeks and ever-smiling full lips. Although he was twenty-eight, many people took him to be younger than twenty. He'd kept his boyish looks—smooth skin, wavy dark-brown hair, guileless gray eyes. His joy of life had attracted her since the first day they met. She smiled as Alex tugged at the stiff collar of his white linen shirt, cuffs buttoned at the wrists above work-worn hands. He preferred faded overalls to the frock coat and vest she'd persuaded him to wear.

Drum beats and the trumpet tune of "Dixie" increased in volume until the audience, now on their feet, clapped in rhythm as they sang—

Then, I wish I was in Dixie! Hooray! Hooray!

In Dixie Land I'll take my stand, to live and die in Dixie;

Away, away, away down south in Dixie!

Shivering, Sarah remained seated.

Tommy pointed past her shoulder. "They're here, Mommy; the soldiers are here!"

Gray-coated men marched double-file between rows of benches toward the stage, sunlight glinting from their muskets and rifles. Under her breath, she counted as they passed, "Two, four . . . twenty, twenty-two . . . one-hundred-ten." She'd heard rumors that the company would soon be fighting. She wondered how many would be dead before the year ended. A knot swelled in Sarah's throat when she noticed Alex staring with fascination at the soldiers.

A colonel, a lieutenant, and twenty enlisted men marched to the stage, their boots thundering against the platform's wooden boards. The soldiers formed two rows behind the speaker, the remaining men surrounding both sides of the bandstand at attention, their eyes focused above the heads of the audience. *Boys*, Sarah thought. *Boys and men playing like boys, looking like so many toy soldiers. Why is it that only the women can see death hanging over them?*

The company commander stepped forward. His words echoed insistent themes of the day: dangers of invasion, the optimism of the gallant Confederate troops, a plea for more able-bodied men between seventeen and fifty. "We'll win out against the Yankee aggressors. We'll show General McClellan and Abe Lincoln how we can fight!"

The soldiers broke from attention and shouted a shrill rebel yell. The crowd echoed their shouts.

Relatives of the returning soldiers swarmed forward. Mothers embraced sons; fathers encircled their boys' shoulders. Little brothers and sisters wrapped their short arms around the soldiers' waists. A young wife held her husband and wept tears of joy.

Alex and Tommy rushed toward the infantrymen in the center of the crowd. Sarah stood and hefted the baby onto her hip. Looking down at her body, round as a bread bowl under her dress, she knew people would disapprove of her appearing in public so near the time of her confinement. She'd convinced Alex that avoiding social occasions during pregnancy would have incarcerated her for most of the past four years. Hannah, Sarah's servant, held out her arms for little Lula, whose face creased into a wide smile. Hannah placed her wide brown hands around the baby's chest and then shifted her into the crook of her arm.

"Thanks, Hannah." Sarah stretched her back to relieve the strain of her pregnancy and lumbered toward the food tables, where a mixture of scents filled the air and teased her appetite—apple pies, baked hams, sweet potatoes, fried chicken. The minister strolled by, examining the food.

"Good morning, Reverend."

Startled, the preacher gazed at Sarah's face. She noticed he avoided even a glance at her ample belly. "You're looking quite well, Mrs. Browning." Discomfort about her condition evident, he focused on the table before them.

She smiled. "Thank you." She knew he expected her to compliment his dreadful speech, but she just couldn't do it. She felt relieved when he turned to greet another of his parishioners.

Margaret Browning, the wife of Alex's older brother Jacob, stood behind the food table assisting a group of women. When Sarah approached, Margaret and the women stared at her belly. Sarah braced herself.

"Oh my," one said to Sarah, "are you quite sure you should be out in this heat?"

"The weather at my house is no cooler, Addie, and I prefer to be here with Alex and my family."

Emma pushed her spectacles against the bridge of her nose. "I'm sure your lying-in cannot be far off," she said, her voice high-pitched and grating. "You know we want to be there to assist."

"We wouldn't miss it for all the world," Pearl said.

The prospect of their attendance at her birthing depressed Sarah, but she lifted her chin and put on a cheery smile without giving the least hint of when the baby might come.

Nearby, a group of soldiers discussed the Union blockade of Florida's ports. "They're trying to strangle us, but by God, we'll be doing the choking from now on!"

Sarah shook her head. *War fever*! Since Hannah was caring for the baby, Sarah fetched a quilt from their wagon and spread it on the grass. She looked back to see her husband returning with Tommy, followed by Jacob.

Jacob's uniform jacket was unbuttoned, his tanned face glowing. He took both of Sarah's hands in his. "How about a sisterly kiss?"

Sarah held his cheeks between her hands and planted a kiss on his forehead. She looked behind Jacob to see his wife.

Margaret scowled. "Sometimes I think he loves you better than he does me. No sooner had he seen me than he started asking about you."

Alex jostled Jacob's shoulder. "You're looking good, brother. I think the army agrees with you."

"Doesn't he look handsome in his uniform?" Margaret said with a wide smile. "I'm so proud of him for serving in this glorious campaign."

Sarah rolled her eyes. "I pray every day that Alex won't become a part of this war."

"Surely you wouldn't want him to look like a coward." Margaret folded her arms and glared.

"Surely I'd prefer him looking like a coward rather than a corpse."

Jacob flicked nervous glances at each of the women, then pointed to the chevrons on his sleeve. "Look here, Alex, would you believe I made corporal?"

Alex laughed, "Congratulations, brother."

Margaret returned to her duties at the food tables.

Tommy pulled on Jacob's pants leg. "Uncle Jake, can I wear your hat? Please."

Jake pushed the soft-billed hat on Tommy's head. Tommy puffed his chest and circled the adults until Sarah stepped into his path.

"It's time for you to sit down and be quiet for a while, young man. We'll be eating soon." She swept the hat from his head and returned it to her brother-in-law. "Go help yourself to some food. We've been cooking three days for you boys. Don't disappoint us."

Alex touched her shoulder. "Just sit yourself down, Sarah. I'll get Tommy's plate and one for you." An irresistible grin spread across his face. "I'll be back soon. It wouldn't be safe to leave a beautiful woman like you alone for long."

Sarah took pride in her dark blue eyes and golden-blonde hair, neatly parted down the center and pulled back into a tidy bun at the base of her neck under her bonnet. She laughed and patted her protruding belly. "Even with this?"

"More to love, my sweet."

A few minutes later, Alex returned with three plates balanced precariously on his hands. He set his on the quilt and gave one to Sarah. Tommy took his plate and sat down with a plate of drumsticks, biscuits, and thick gravy. Jacob had stacked several layers of food on his plate, topped with sliced ham, fried chicken, cornbread, cabbage cooked with bacon, and wedges of various pies.

"This sure beats the grub we've been eating," Jacob said. He sat on a corner of the quilt next to Sarah.

Sarah arranged her plate on her lap. "I heard the army was leaving Tampa Bay."

"We had to pull out of there," Jacob said. "Mostly it was boring guard duty anyhow. Every day we just sat in the sweltering sun and reported every move the Yanks made." He beamed. "Pretty soon we'll get some real action."

"Do you know where they'll send you?" Alex asked.

"We think we'll be joining up with the troops in Virginia. That's where the real war is. All the officers say so."

Sarah stared at Jacob, not able to understand his enthusiasm for something so grim. "I worry about this war. So many more people live up north. Their army would have to be larger." She frowned. "How can we win against so much power?"

"Everyone knows that one Confederate equals ten Yankees." Jacob grinned and puffed out his chest. "Fighting to protect your home fills you up with a strong spirit."

Alex smiled. "I remember how old Stonewall Jackson and his men beat the heck out of them last summer at Bull Run."

"And we'll beat 'em again," Jacob said.

Sarah picked at her food. "Your talk is scaring me to death."

"They're telling us how to run our lives." Jacob emphasized his point with a cleaned-off drumstick. "If we don't fight 'em, they'll take over the South, force us to serve them like slaves, humiliate us, degrade our women . . ."

Sarah laid down her fork and faced him squarely. "Jacob Browning, that is pure hogwash! I've heard it at church. I've heard it on the square. I've read it in the papers." Her voice rose. "You men chose this grand and glorious cause, leaving your women to do your work and take the responsibility of providing for the children you gave us. For what? To risk getting yourselves killed by a Yankee bullet?"

Everyone stared at her.

"Hush now, Sarah," Alex said. "Don't get yourself riled up." He looked at Sarah's plate. "You haven't eaten anything."

"I'm not hungry, Alex. Don't fuss at me. I've got things to say."

"But you need to eat for the baby." He stood.

She let her plate fall to the ground. "After four pregnancies, I don't intend to starve myself, but right now I'd like to finish this conversation."

Sarah watched Alex's expression change and felt a surge of remorse for her unintended reference to the child they'd lost three years before.

Alex looked down at her, his eyes intense. "Sarah Ann . . ."

"Help me up, Alex. This baby has me nailed to the ground." She grabbed his extended hands and stood.

He continued staring at her with a pained expression.

"Thank the Lord . . ." She began hiccupping . . . "You're ex—empt—" She couldn't continue to talk as the violent hiccups convulsed her body.

Jacob stood. "I'll get you some water."

Tommy came up behind her and grabbed her waist. "Boo! Mama! I'll scare 'em out of you."

"Hold your breath," Alex advised.

Jacob returned and held out the water glass. "If you drink it upside down, it'll stop your hiccups."

"In her condition, I don't think she can put herself in an up-side-down position." Alex patted Sarah's back. "Just hold your breath, honey, and drink it down."

Sarah held her breath and swallowed. Soon her hiccups subsided.

Alex took her face between his hands. "My sweet Sarah, always the peacemaker. This war is bigger than you are. You can't stop it. That's our army's job."

Our army?

At that moment Hannah approached with a squalling Lula. "She don't want no more milk, Miss Sarah. I don't know what's ailin' her."

Sarah held out her arms to Lula. "She wants her mama to hold her." Sarah jiggled the baby gently and hummed a song. Sniffling, Lula laid her head against her mother's shoulder.

Margaret approached the group again and laughed. "Sarah, you're amazing." She turned to her husband. "Look at her with a lock of hair slipping from under her bonnet, freckles dotting her face, looking like a young girl. She's just . . . amazing."

Sarah looked away. She never knew how to take Margaret's comments.

Alex put his arm around Sarah's shoulder. "You've no argument with me, Margaret."

"How ever will you manage with three little ones after Alex leaves?" Margaret said.

A shuddering horror shot through Sarah's body. She stared from Alex to Margaret and back to Alex. "What's this about Alex leaving?"

Wide-eyed, Margaret stuttered, "I . . . I felt sure you two had discussed it. Jacob said he was certain Alex would enlist."

So Margaret is only surmising. She doesn't know for sure. Sarah took a deep breath, trying to calm herself. She adjusted Lula in her arms. "I think we should head for home, Alex."

"All right. You wait for me by the wagon with Lula. I'll see that everyone else gets home." He turned to Margaret and Jacob. "Would you two like a ride?"

Margaret nodded toward the tables, now covered with half-empty platters. "I promised to stay and help clean up. Jacob, you go on ahead. I know you and Alex need to talk."

Sarah felt her heart pulse against her rib cage. She wondered whether Jacob had been assigned to convince Alex to enlist. She'd never feel safe from the recruiters until the soldiers' furloughs ended. Rocking the baby on her shoulder, she walked toward the wagon, where Industrious and Hannah helped Alex round up the horses and load Sarah's dishes from the serving tables.

The men took seats beside Industrious in the front of the wagon while Sarah sat behind them on feather pillows Alex had stacked to soften the rough ride to and from town. Hannah sat in the back holding Lula. Standing behind the front seat, Tommy hovered near Jacob, fascinated with his scabbard and knife.

While the wagon bumped along the road to Jacob's house at the edge of town, Sarah placed her hands on her abdomen to feel the baby kick against her fingers. Hearing the garbled voices of the men's conversation, she leaned closer. A few words sifted through the sound of the thumping wagon: "Duty." "Service." "Glory." "Honor." Hogwash! She substituted her own words—*death, violence, injuries, widows.*

The wagon halted and Jacob turned to face her. "So long, Sarah. You take good care of yourself, hear!"

"Come over for supper while you're home," Sarah said. She offered the invitation with reluctance.

"Just say when." Jacob jumped off the wagon seat and trotted down the dirt road toward his home.

As they left town, the road narrowed, curved northeast, and followed Alligator Creek for two miles. They stopped to open the gate. The AC cattle brand painted on a board above the entrance identified the Brownings' farm, named for the stream. Before they reached the barn, their dog Hank, an amiable cur that loved herding cattle, raced across the pasture and greeted the family with vigorous barks. The wagon stopped just past the barn, and while Industrious cared for the horses, Sarah and Hannah carried empty dishes into the kitchen beyond the main house. Benny, a skinny gray tomcat, rubbed his fur against Sarah's leg. Betsy, a tricolor, trailed close behind.

Alex shook his arm. "Shoo, cats! No leftovers tonight. Go catch a rat."

That night, after the children had been tucked in, Sarah and Alex sat in the front porch swing. From there they watched the sun setting across the west pasture and the shallow stream meandering through the middle of the fields. The tails of long-horned cattle swished at flies as they drank from the creek, their red and brown spots blending into the white as the evening darkened.

On the horizon, a mauve thread of clouds covered the setting sun, their edges illuminated with golden-red light. A light breeze chilled Sarah's shoulders through the tent-shaped nightgown she now wore. She'd sewn it from some thin, pink fabric, the perfect material to make clothes later for Lula and the new baby if it happened to be a girl. "Maybe we should go in. I feel cold."

"It seems plenty warm to me."

She began to shiver.

Alex put his arm around her shoulder. "Let's not go in yet. We need to talk."

As much as she'd like to convince him to stay home, she wanted to avoid confrontation for a few more minutes, to enjoy their closeness a bit longer, to pretend their normal life would continue as it always had. "Look Alex, Agothos is out." Sarah smiled at the dark form of a twelve-foot alligator lying immobile on the opposite bank of the stream. The first spring after they bought the farm, she and Alex saw the old alligator, estimated by his size to be about sixty years old. Each year he'd show up after winter hibernation in his burrow. She loved the Greek myths she'd read in school and called him Agothos—the guardian spirit of families.

"I'm gonna have to shoot that old 'gator one of these days," Alex said. "It would be the devil to pay if he killed one of my calves or, God forbid, one of the children."

"You've got a fence for the calves and a gate on our side of the bridge. Leave him alone, Alex. He's been here a long time and never bothered us. Besides, I've grown fond of him." She sometimes thought of Agothos as her personal protector.

"You're a strange one, Sarah." He patted her hand, and they sat silently watching the closing of the day.

In a whoosh of wings, a great blue heron, also a frequent visitor, landed near the alligator, its neck crooked in anticipation of spearing a fish with its sharp beak. Sarah had named the heron Phoenix and knew full well the bird would someday fly away to another place.

Alex cleared his throat. "On the way home, Jacob told me a little about army life."

"He's pushing you to join, isn't he?" Sarah gripped the arm of the swing.

Alex shrugged. "No more than any of the others."

She clamped onto his arm. "Don't go, Alex. You're already twenty-eight. We have two children and one on the way. Claim your exemption as a cattleman."

He squeezed her hand. "Don't worry so much, sweetheart. I haven't said I'd enlist."

Sarah looked into his eyes, glistening in the setting sun. *He wants to go. He feels the call. I can see it in his face. I can almost smell it on his breath.* "You could hire a substitute. If we sold a couple of cows, we could pay someone to fight in your place."

Alex pulled her close and held her across his lap in his arms as though she were a child. "Only conscripts hire substitutes. If I join, I'll volunteer." He smoothed her hair she'd unpinned earlier. "It's not because I don't love you."

She swallowed. "I don't think I could bear losing you. If you love me, you'll stay here to be with me next month when Sallie or Johnny is born. You'll teach Tommy how to be a godly man. You'll repair the fences, harvest the crops next fall. I need you, Alex." He held her close and caressed her back beneath the shoulder blade, but even his familiar touch failed to comfort her.

Her eyes misted. Right now she wanted to crawl inside his stubborn head and turn his thoughts. She reached for his hand and pressed his fingers against her belly. "Please think hard about what's most important to you. I know you love us. Tell me you'll stay here."

His shoulders jerked, but he didn't answer.

She faced him straight on. "Ever since we bought Alligator Creek, you've been looking for an excuse to leave this farm. How can you even consider leaving me here with all this responsibility?"

He pulled his hand back. "You've got it wrong, Sarah. I'd never leave my family except for duty. How can I face myself as a man if I look cowardly in the eyes of my friends? I'd be marked for all my life as a man unwilling to fight for my beliefs. I'm doing this for you and for Tommy, for Lula and our new baby. What kind of life will we have here unless we fight to defend ourselves? I truly believe the Yankees will come here and take away all the freedom we have."

She glared into his gray eyes. "Be honest with yourself for once, Alex. No excuses. You're abandoning us. How in heaven's name will I run this farm by myself?"

"I wrote to Dad and Frances. Since his brother lives nearby, Dad's agreed to leave his farm in Walter's care and move in with you. Then he could go back to Georgia when the war's over. Dad knows everything about farming, and Frances can help you around the house."

She gasped. Now the air felt scalding hot. "You've already asked them without discussing any of this with me?" She knew it took weeks to get mail from Georgia. *He's been planning this for a long time.*

Alex hung his head. "I'm sorry. I wanted to get everything in order before I told you."

She felt anger welling up inside her and threatening to overflow. *How can he even think of going off to war?* When the battle began in 1861, Alex stayed busy raising cotton and cattle, never joining a volunteer regiment or the state militia that guarded the vulnerable seacoast. Why now? Perspiration beaded on her upper lip.

Alex shook his head. "I've got to do it." He took Sarah's face in his hands. "I've got my honor. If Jacob and all my friends are going, I should, too. It's not forever. Bull Run proved the blue bellies don't have enough fight in them to keep it up for long."

Sarah pulled away from the familiar scent of his skin. "You're all misjudging the northerners' strength. Any fool knows they've got more railroads, more factories, more money, more troops."

"Where do you get all that?"

"Not everyone thinks the way you and Jacob do. I've heard men talking down at the store. Ruby and Ellen agree with me. Many of us are against this war."

"Against the war or against your men going to it?" He didn't wait for an answer. "Such talk isn't patriotic. You don't want folks to think you're a Union sympathizer. Even though there's plenty of them in Jacksonville, they're not welcome in Lake City." His face hardened with determination. "The war won't last long. I'll be back by Christmas—maybe even before." Alex put his arm around her. "You'll manage fine, just like your mother did when your father died."

She stiffened in response to his touch. She wasn't so sure about being able to manage the place. Living a pampered childhood, the only child of elderly parents, she'd suffered after their early deaths. "I'm worried sick thinking about those Yankees shooting at you. I love you, Alex— more than my own life. What would I do if I lost you?" Tears of anger streamed down her cheeks. She saw through his transparent clichés of honor and duty. She knew there was more to his leaving. She remembered when he'd left on a cattle drive the week before Tommy was born and was gone two months. He told her the roundup would bring thousands of dollars when they sold the animals. The money they needed for debts never materialized. When Alex got a yen to leave, like a migrating sandhill crane, he flew away. She couldn't stop him any more than she could stop the wind. "Is there anything I can say that would convince you to stay home?"

Alex didn't answer but stood and went indoors. Sarah felt the dog's cold nose pressing against her ankle. She scratched Hank between the ears, and he ambled away. She pushed her toes against the wooden planks on the porch floor. The swing made a clicking noise as it rocked like a clock's pendulum. Worries about her future surfaced in rhythm with the swing's rocking. She had her answer. Alex had already decided to leave. He might be killed. She thought about each of the children— Tommy, Lula, and her unborn baby. Now she'd have enormous responsibilities—supervising the slaves, tending fields, caring for a herd of fifty cattle, harvesting crops, managing money, dealing with the enemy if Florida were invaded, plus all the household duties and looking after the children. She stopped the swing and shut off the crushing flow of concerns. She opened the front door and walked down the long hallway. As she climbed the stairs to her bedroom, she prayed, "Sweet Lord, you alone know the end of the dark path before me. I can hardly see the next turn in the road. Guide me; protect me so that I may protect my little ones. I ask you to watch over my Alex. You are my only help and refuge, Lord."

Later, Sarah lay on her side on the feather mattress and tried to find a comfortable sleeping position. Moonlight poured through the lacy curtains covering her bedroom windows. She listened to Alex's heavy breathing and to a soft growl of thunder like distant cannons firing. The storm blew closer, and thunder rolled in a violent crescendo. Rain pinged against the tin roof. Lightning flashed, illuminated the room, and reflected from the mirror of her dressing table in a surreal scene that disappeared into near blackness in an instant. A small shadow approached.

"Mommy, I'm scared." Tommy crawled into the bed between her and Alex.

She rubbed the damp curls on his forehead. "Mommy's here, Tommy. Don't be afraid."

He stiffened when thunder crashed in a loud boom. She held him closely in her arms while Alex exhaled raspy breaths. Profound sadness saturated her soul like the drizzling rain. In the hall, the floor clock, a relic from her parents' plantation, chimed twelve times. At last, she released herself into sleep. In restless dreams, she chased worries and fled from phantoms. Near dawn, a new solution came to mind, and her slumber deepened into hopeful rest.

2

Both North and South were proving, from their view point the justness of their position by both Bible and Constitution. There was being reared a generation of warriors. . . .

William A. Fletcher
Rebel Private: Front and Rear

April 1862

When Alex sat down at the sitting room table for breakfast, Sarah glared into her husband's gray eyes in a way that usually got her what she wanted. "If I can't persuade you to stay home from this foolish war, grant me one request . . . Take a body servant." She'd rehearsed each day since the celebration, but this morning, her words tasted bitter like quinine. In spite of her bravado, she now doubted her husband would agree to take their slave Industrious away from Alligator Creek to attend him in the army. After all, Alex hadn't heeded her pleas to claim his exemption. He'd already enlisted in the hometown company, which was scheduled to leave tomorrow.

Alex turned to her and grinned. "You look beautiful this morning."

Because she expected company at noon, Sarah had worn her best church dress of cornflower-blue cotton that matched her eyes. Alex's compliments did not please her today. She raised her voice. "You aren't paying attention, Alex. I want you to take Industrious with you."

Alex removed his hat and a shock of dark hair fell across his damp forehead. "You want me to take Industrious? The hometown boys would laugh me out of the army for putting on airs like some rich prissy-pants from Virginia. I'm no plantation owner." He slapped the hat across his knee. "We've only got two slaves, and this old farm can't afford to lose one." Alex looked painfully handsome in his Confederate uniform—trousers and a jacket buttoned to the neck—butternut since factories had already run out of gray dye. His coat, trimmed with epaulets, bore no insignia since he enlisted as a private.

"We're not poor, Alex," she said. Sarah turned her eyes from his uniform to the pump organ, its rack stacked with sheet music. Above the organ hung a framed Currier and Ives lithograph depicting a small boy on his knees with his hands together in prayer. He reminded her of Tommy.

"We're not rich, either, Sarah Ann. If there's one thing I can do without in the army, it's a body servant."

"I'm so scared about this war and . . . something happening to you. If you don't take Industrious with you, I'll worry myself into a state."

"You're gonna fret anyhow. He can't really protect me."

"He can wash your socks and make certain you eat right. He can relieve you of those nasty chores they assign to privates. I'm counting on him to keep you out of trouble."

Alex frowned. "Don't you think I can look after myself?"

Despite her determination not to cry, tears pooled in her eyes.

Alex patted her hand. "Now don't you start up that bawling again. I don't know if I can stand it."

"Then promise you'll take Industrious. He'll look after you, and he'll want to get back to Hannah in one piece just as much as you'll want to return safely to me."

"Hannah will be none too happy to have her man gone. And how will you and one house slave handle the farm? It's not gonna work. You'll need Industrious more than I will."

"What about John and Frances? The last I heard, they're coming in today and plan to stay on." She crossed her arms over her midsection.

His brows arched above his gray eyes. "Dad and Sis can't do field work. An old man and an old maid?"

Angry tears streamed down her cheeks.

"Will you really worry less if Industrious goes with me?" He pulled out his handkerchief and dabbed her eyes.

Sarah bit her lip. "I know you've already decided to go to war." She searched her feelings. "Next week . . . next month, when I'm thinking about you out there fighting, I will feel much better knowing Industrious walks beside you—the way he always does. He'll do anything for you."

Alex spoke so softly she could barely hear him. "I know he will—even go to war with me." Alex turned to her. "Let's ask him together. I want him to know I'm doing this for you."

Sarah nodded, and they walked hand in hand to the kitchen, built separate from the main house to protect the family from the heat. Industrious and Hannah were cutting up chicken on the long worktable. The entire Browning family would arrive later to see Alex and Jacob before they left. The unpleasant smell of raw chicken filled the room. With loud whacks, Industrious cut leg and thigh pieces while Hannah dipped the cut chicken in buttermilk and shook it in a sack of flour. Both slaves stopped what they were doing and turned toward them. Hannah dipped her hands into a pan of soapy water.

The looks on their faces must have given Sarah and Alex away, for Industrious wiped his hands on his apron and drew Hannah toward him. Hannah's head came only to his wide shoulders as she pressed her stout body against his.

Alex stiffened. "Industrious, you'll be going with me tomorrow. Miss Sarah wants you to be my body servant."

Industrious drew himself up and smiled. "Yes sir, Mr. Alex. I be most pleased to go to the army with you. Joey brags all the time about gettin' chosen to go to war with Mr. Stephen. He already thinks he's better'n me because his massa owns that big ol' plantation up the road. Now I got somethin' to tell him about."

Hannah stood frozen.

Industrious moved closer to her and patted her back. "Nothin' to worry about."

Tears squeezed out of her eyes.

Sarah understood Hannah's mood and cleared her throat. "If I had my wish, both of you would stay here together like always. I'm worried sick about Mr. Alex going off to war, about something . . . happening to him. Industrious, you're the only one I trust to look after him."

Industrious nodded. "No worry, ma'am, I look after Mr. Alex real good."

Hannah's silence troubled Sarah. She'd known Industrious would be pleased to travel with Alex, but the depth of Hannah's feelings hadn't occurred to her. "Are you all right, Hannah?"

"Yes'm," Hannah stared at her feet. "I just worry about my man . . . like you."

Sarah had tried to understand Hannah and Industrious, but often when she asked questions, they gave her evasive answers. She never raised her voice nor slapped them the way some of her women friends dealt with servants, and she'd certainly never beaten either one. Her parents hadn't owned slaves even though they could have afforded several. "It's not right for one human being to own another," her mother had often said.

Sarah remembered the horror from her childhood when they'd visited Atlanta, where she'd seen slaves sold at the auction. She shed tears when she heard the screams of slaves being beaten at the workhouse. Her father-in-law had given Hannah and Industrious to them as a wedding gift, but Sarah had never quite learned to be comfortable as their mistress. She lifted her head and spoke to Industrious. She hoped she sounded more confident than she felt. "Take some time with Hannah this afternoon, Industrious."

While Sarah dressed two-year-old Lula, Hannah came to the door of the nursery, her eyebrows knotted together. "I'm finished with the chicken, ma'am. Would you need help dressing the baby?"

"No thanks, Hannah. She's almost ready."

Lula twisted toward the sound of Hannah's voice. A wide smile spread across her cheeks.

Sarah buttoned Lula's shoes. "You're upset about Industrious leaving, aren't you?"

Yes'm." Hannah blurted out her words as if trying to speak her mind before Sarah could stop her. "Mr. Alex wouldn't take him if you told him you need Dustrous here to help you."

Sarah dropped her shoulders. She and Hannah often shared their feelings more as friends than mistress and slave. Once Hannah had asked to stay in her own cabin when her baby was sick, and Sarah had agreed. This was different. Sarah didn't like hurting Hannah, who'd already endured more than her share. Her three babies had died before their first birthdays. She also knew she put Hannah in the very position she despised being in herself. *Alex needs Industrious's protection and help. It's not like he would be going into battle. Industrious would sit on the sidelines. No, I won't back down. I can't.* "I'm sorry, Hannah. It's all I know to do. Alex and I have already discussed things."

Hannah started to reply, then stopped. Sarah tied the pink bow on Lula's ruffled pinafore and admired her two-year-old. "Your aunties and granddaddy will have a fit over my pretty girl."

"Miss Sarah," Hannah said, "Can you come make sure everything's all right for the dinner?" She followed Hannah downstairs to the dining room with Lula toddling beside her. The vase of spring wildflowers Sarah arranged yesterday brightened the center of the large oval table she'd set with her mother's Irish linen cloth and best china. She sat in one of the chairs and pulled Lula into her lap. Sarah loved entertaining here in one of her most formal rooms. Heavy draperies hung over windows, and an ornate carpet covered the wood floor. Crystal glasses gleamed in the sunlight as though they adorned a happy occasion instead of this premature wake for Alex and Jacob. She bit her lip as anger washed over her. *Not only is Alex leaving me, he's choosing to leave. And making arrangements for his father and sister to stay here! How can he fail to consider my feelings about them?* She swallowed hard, recalling John's constant biblical references and Frances's overpowering determination to be right—about everything.

A year after her mother's death, Sarah had blossomed into womanhood at fifteen. When her adoration of Alex overwhelmed her good judgment, she'd faced the wrath of the Brownings over her pregnancy. John had stood like an Old Testament judge before them, directing his rage toward Alex. "The Lord will judge your fornication. The prophet Paul tells us, 'Marriage is honorable in all, and the bed undefiled: but whoremongers and adulterers God will judge.' The only honorable thing, my son, is to take this woman in marriage."

Even though they came from scripture, Sarah hated those words—"whoremonger and adulterer." Giving herself to him seemed right, a fulfillment of their love for one another. Other words from John's tirade had swirled in her head—"woman," "marriage"—grown-up words unfamiliar to her adolescent vision of herself.

Alex's mother and his older sister Frances had insisted on a traditional service in their church with invited guests. She and Alex would have preferred something simple—a civil marriage in the Atlanta courthouse or in the study of their small-town preacher, but the Browning women's concern for appearances overrode the young couple's wishes. Soon after the wedding, Sarah packed the best pieces of her mother's household goods, knowing she might never afford such luxuries during her marriage. After John found a buyer for Sarah's family plantation, he took the newlyweds to Florida, where they invested their money in

Alligator Creek. There they awaited the birth of their first child far away from wagging tongues in Georgia. Sarah and Alex made the 275-mile ride back to Georgia only once—for his mother's funeral.

The sound of Hank's barking outside brought her back to the present. Lula had gone to sleep against her breast. She opened the front door with Lula in her arms to greet Margaret and Jacob with Frances and John close behind. Before Sarah could object, Frances pulled Lula into her arms, and John caught Tommy just as he burst into the room carrying a wooden figure. "What've you got there, young man?"

Tommy held out a miniature horse, carved in intricate detail. "I named him Sammy. Daddy made him for me."

Sarah ushered them into the parlor, and John sat down on the upholstered divan with Tommy. "That's some fine horse, Tommy. Your daddy's always been good at woodcarving. You put this somewhere safe so you won't break it. It'll be worth a lot of money someday."

"I would never sell Sammy, Daddy John."

When Jacob hugged Sarah, she stiffened, still angry with him for urging Alex to enlist.

Jacob grinned. "Don't be mad at me, sister-in-law. We won't be gone long."

She prayed he was right. If the war lasted longer than six months, she might go mad in a house full of judgmental in-laws. She forced a smile.

Frances looked older than she remembered. Her hair—mousy brown streaked with gray—stretched back from her forehead into a tight bun on the back of her head—a style from several years back. Sarah noticed the distinct smell of tobacco clinging to Frances's breath when they embraced and wondered if she dipped snuff.

John, solid and robust for his sixty-one years, a web of wrinkles lining his skin, resembled Alex. Age had softened his features. He gave Sarah a warm hug. "You're as beautiful as ever, Missy. Frances and I are here to help. You just tell us what you need." This man who'd always frightened her when she was younger now seemed like a potential ally.

From their wagon outside, Alex and Jacob unloaded several suitcases, boxes, and two large wardrobe trunks. Sarah directed John to Tommy's room upstairs and Frances to the extra bed in Lula's room. Although she stung from her in-laws learning of Alex's plans to enlist before he informed her, she felt a degree of relief that Alex had brought them here to share the enormous responsibilities of Alligator Creek.

The family gathered around the dining room table. Sarah turned to her father-in-law. "Would you offer thanks, Daddy John?"

Heads lowered and John prayed. "Gracious Lord, we ask your blessings on my boys and protection from enemy guns. Keep them alert to danger. May victory come quickly and bring them back home to their families. Make us thankful for this food and all our many blessings. Amen."

As Hannah passed the last of the serving dishes and Industrious filled glasses with water, Tommy, sitting near the end of the table, raised his voice. "Mommy, is Daddy gonna die in the war?"

Sarah gasped. "My poor baby. You shouldn't worry about such things. Daddy will be fine." She got up from her seat, went to him, and smoothed his unruly blond curls.

"Grandpa talked about guns. Guns can kill." His blue eyes widened in fear.

Sadness poured over her. "Oh, Tommy!"

Tommy's lips quivered as his eyes filled with tears.

She put her arm around him. "Don't you worry about your daddy. Industrious promised to look after him."

"But Hannah told Industrious not to go. She said he oughta run away."

Margaret raised her eyebrows. "Sounds like little pitchers have big ears."

Alex jerked his head around to look at Industrious standing at the door.

"I never gonna run away, Mr. Alex. You know that."

Alex looked stern, but a muscle in his cheek quivered. "I never thought you would." His voice sounded tense.

Sarah stared at Hannah, who'd turned to take a platter out to the kitchen. "Hannah?"

Hannah turned and spoke in a high-pitched voice. "Didn't mean it—I was just talking—didn't mean nothin' by it."

"You really should get control of your slaves," Margaret said.

Frances and John remained silent, without responding to Margaret's criticism.

"Excuse me, please." Sarah ushered Hannah out the door and into the kitchen. "Did you really tell Industrious to run away?" Sarah kept her voice low.

Hannah bit her lip and remained silent.

"I hope you would never leave us. I'll need your help even more after Alex leaves."

"I wouldn't never leave you, Miss Sarah." She clenched her hands together as though praying.

"I believe you, Hannah. Don't fret now." Sarah smiled at her. "Right after dinner, you can go to your cabin to help Industrious get ready. I'm taking Alex and Industrious to the train early tomorrow morning. Tommy's going along with us, but I want you to stay here with Lula."

"What about Mr. John and Miss Frances?"

"They'll take Margaret and Jacob to the train."

"Oh please, Miss Sarah, let me ride along wit you. We can prop the baby on a pillow. I watch her real close. She be all right."

The look on Hannah's face brought softness to Sarah's heart. "I know you want to see your man off as much as I do mine. You can come along." She could do at least that much for Hannah. She rejoined her guests in the dining room.

Later that afternoon, while John and Frances rested, Sarah stood in her dining room putting out leftovers for a light supper. Alex came in carrying his Colt revolver. The sight of it made her sick.

"I'm leaving this gun here, and you need to know how to shoot it." He took Sarah's hand and led her out the back door like a child.

She jerked her hand back. "I don't like guns."

Undaunted, Alex hoisted a lumpy sack and walked out to the fenced-in field.

She followed, arms crossed over her chest. "I might shoot myself if I use it."

"You might need to protect yourself." He removed tin cans from the sack and set them in groups of four or five on pine stumps.

"I could never shoot a person."

"What if someone came in here trying to kill one of the children?"

"All the more reason you should be here defending your family instead of leaving for the war."

He laid the Colt on a weathered table he'd built for the family to use for picnics. Then he removed a flask of black powder, a box of balls, and firing caps from the sack. "Watch me load it." She kept her eyes on his hands as he poured powder and pressed balls into the six cylinders. He inserted the firing caps.

He fired six shots, hitting four cans on the first stump.

"Now you do it." He pushed the gun across the table.

She loaded the cylinders as he'd demonstrated.

"Don't put it down. Use both hands to hold it. Keep your finger on the trigger. Aim at a can." He walked to her side and squeezed her hands tighter around the butt of the gun. "Hold it there. Close your left eye and line up the post in this notch with your target." He indicated the post and the notch then pointed to the cans.

She aimed and pulled the trigger, but nothing happened. "What did I do wrong?"

"Your gun's not ready to shoot. You've got to arm it. Pull back the hammer." He took the gun from her hands, armed it, and handed it back to her.

She fumbled, so he took the gun. The clink of the bullet against tin followed the blast. Her ears rang, and her nose burned from the smelly gunpowder.

Sarah's hand trembled as she gripped the revolver again. She closed one eye and sighted a can through the notch. The discharge jolted her hands upward. She missed the can and fired into the air.

"Try again," he insisted. "You've got four more shots in the cylinder."

She handed the nasty death instrument to Alex and rubbed her hands together. "I really don't want to learn to shoot."

His eyes narrowed. "Sarah Ann, I beg you. Do this one thing for me before I leave. If you don't, I might fly off the handle and get *myself* shot in the war."

Sarah armed the gun, held her hands steady, and aimed again. The bullet hit a stump under the can. She pulled the hammer once more. The next shot blasted a can off the stump. "There, are you satisfied now?"

"You got lucky that time. Keep practicing."

After another close shot and three more that knocked all but one can off the stump, Alex watched her reload the cylinders and shoot another round. Finally, he nodded his approval. "I think you've got the hang of it. I'm loading it, but it's not armed. Don't forget to pull back the hammer before you shoot."

They walked back to the house.

"I'll write you every day," Sarah said. "I'll ask Industrious to remind you to send me letters, too."

"I'll do it. He doesn't need to remind me." His voice sounded curt.

Sarah raised her eyebrows. "I know how you hate writing letters."

"But I'll write you . . . at least twice a week."

Sarah pinned him with a stare. "Every day! Tell me all about your life. I need to see you in my mind wherever you are."

Alex promised, then handed her the revolver. "Put this in a safe place."

She wrapped it in a cloth and placed it behind a metal breadbox high atop a burled wood cabinet in the sitting room.

The next morning, when Sarah opened her eyes, Alex had already dressed and wakened Tommy, who stood by her bed holding a new copper penny.

"Can I put my penny on the train track, Mama?"

Sarah hesitated, reluctant to encourage waste of precious money. "I'll allow it just this once, but remember—if you take care of your pennies, your dollars will take care of themselves."

Tommy rolled his eyes. "It's *my* penny, Mama. Caleb showed me one he'd put on the track. The train squashed it twice as big, and you couldn't even play heads or tails with it 'cause it was smashed flat."

"Keep it in your pocket, son, till we get to the depot." A hollow feeling deep inside followed her thought of the train that would carry Alex away.

In the early morning darkness, Sarah and Hannah rode in the back of the wagon with the sleepy children while Industrious and Alex sat silent on the driver's seat. A lone dog howled from a distant grove, and a sliver of moon hung low in the West. At the station, soldiers clung to wives, sweethearts, parents, and children one last time. Oil lamps hanging on poles cast eerie shadows like ghosts against the depot's boarded wall. Sarah's stomach clenched as she looked around at the boys she'd known since their childhood. She wondered which ones would return.

Most boys arrived in wagons, by foot, or on horseback. Then, a carriage arrived that belonged to the owner of a neighboring plantation. The footman opened the door for a young man she knew—Stephen Winston, followed by his parents and his older sister, Ruby.

Tommy's enthusiasm broke the mood. "I'll put my penny on the track now." He scampered away and placed the copper coin on the closest track. Sarah followed with Lula in her arms.

When they returned, Alex and Industrious were setting down their bags and Jacob's wagon had stopped next to the depot. Sarah moved close to Alex.

When she spotted two boys in uniform she needed to have a word with, Sarah left Alex's side. Max and Lester Cartwright lived on a neighboring farm and had helped Alex with spring planting. Their identical button noses marked them as kin. "I'm going to miss you boys working on our place," Sarah said.

"We'll miss the good cookin' at your house on work days." Max patted his ample stomach.

"You've got yourselves a first-rate boy here." Lester patted Tommy's curly head. "He'll make a good soldier one of these days."

Sarah shuddered. "Surely this war will end before Tommy grows up."

Lester rushed to reassure her. "We think it'll be over by Christmas."

"I'm sure glad we joined up when we did," Max said. "We might have missed it."

Lester rubbed the back of his neck. "I hope you can find some field hands to help you out while we're in Virginny, but like we said, we won't be off for long."

Max beamed. "Never been to Virginny myself, but I heard it's pretty country."

Sarah bit her lip. "I'll be praying every day that y'all will come home safely." She hoped they might be right about the war being over soon. "God go with you, all of you. Look after Alex for me." Having done what she could to protect her husband, she excused herself to go back to him.

While Jacob and Margaret said their good-byes, John and Frances joined Alex and Sarah. John put his thick hands on Alex's shoulders. "Be careful, son. Do your job, but don't even try to be a hero. War is a wicked business, and I want to see you back here with your family at the end of it." Alex embraced his father.

A shrill whistle split the cool morning air. The noise of the steam engine pulsed louder as it neared. Finally, the engine burst into view, black coal smoke billowing into the early morning sky. Sarah put her hand around Lula's head to protect her ears and moved away from the monstrous sounds. The train screeched to a stop.

Sarah moved next to Alex. "I'll pray for you every day."

Alex took Lula in his arms and hugged her. He looked over Lula's head at Sarah. "Write to me. Let me know when the baby comes. I hope it's a boy."

Sarah prayed she'd never have another boy to worry about going to war. She took Lula again and brushed Tommy's hair from his brow. Her hand went protectively to her unborn child.

Tommy pulled at her sleeve. He held the flattened penny in his hand. "I found it by the track."

Alex squatted and held Tommy close. "Look after your mama, hear. You're the man of the family until I return."

Tommy released himself and nodded in solemn agreement. He held out the coin. "You keep the penny, Daddy. It's supposed to be good luck."

Alex stood and dropped the coin into his pocket. Sarah's vision blurred from the tears gathering in her eyes. With the baby between them, he stroked her cheek. *How long will it be before he touches me again like this?* She pushed her face close and pressed her lips against his. He kissed her again and slowly backed away with his eyes focused on her face. Then he reached for his suitcase and turned to board the train.

Hannah stood nearby, her short arms tight around Industrious's muscular torso. He gave her one last kiss on the forehead before he separated from her.

The train blew out a loud whistle and moved forward, slowly at first. The rhythmical chugs came closer together, and the cars creaked into alignment. Sarah imagined that her own heart rode aboard the departing train and yearned to hold it back for at least one more moment of having Alex at home. She stood with Hannah and her children, along with other families, and waved until the lights disappeared into the gray morning.

John extended a hand to help Sarah pull herself into the wagon seat. Hannah settled herself in the back, holding Sarah's sleepy children. In silence they rode home, faces wet with tears. Morning fog had settled over the fields, and Sarah could only see a few feet in front of the wagon as its wheels rattled toward what no longer felt much like home.

3

These marches and campaigns in the hills of western Virginia will always be among the pleasantest things I can remember.

Rutherford B. Hayes

May–June 1862

The train screeched to its last stop in Richmond. Alex and hundreds of other weary soldiers from Florida and Georgia piled out and huddled by the tracks, awaiting their orders. Alex's company commander, Captain Tolbert—bright-eyed in a neat uniform—contrasted with the rumpled, grimy enlisted men.

Industrious stood tall beside his master. "You look plumb tuckered out, Mr. Alex."

Alex took a swig of water from his canteen. At home, Alex would have passed the canteen to Industrious, but not today with the soldiers watching. "I'm thinking some vittles would taste right good."

"Sure enough!"

Industrious rubbed the back of his hand against his cracked lips.

"Attention, men," the captain barked. "We're marching out for camp. Fall in."

Familiar faces surrounded Alex in the marching formation. Jacob walked next to him with Lester and Max behind, Industrious at the rear with other slaves. By noon, many complained of sore feet. When they took a rest stop, Alex noticed a catch in Industrious's step, almost a limp.

"How're you doing?" Alex asked.

"Fair to middlin." Industrious clenched his jaw and sat with a thud. He stretched his legs straight out. Blood oozed from the holes in his shoes.

Alex helped his slave tie thick rags around his feet. "I'll find you some good boots first chance I get."

As the day grew warmer, Alex, like many others, unbuttoned his shirt. That afternoon, they approached a rural community. Merchants and shoppers stepped out of storefronts to take a look at the soldiers. A bevy of young women in ribboned bonnets and full skirts lined the road, waving handkerchiefs and smiling. Alex spied a spirited brunette standing near his side of the road.

She called to her companions. "That's a handsome one. Look at that manly chest."

A redhead smiled. "I dare you to kiss him, Bee. If you do, I'll show my bloomers."

Alex pretended not to hear but inched close enough for her to complete her mission. When the brunette leaned over to peck his cheek, Alex stepped out of line and turned his face so that the kiss landed square on his lips. He laughed along with the other men. The girl jumped back, her eyes wide and her baby-smooth cheeks reddened. She looked too young for such boldness.

Alex winked at Lester and Max and turned back to the girl. "You'd better go home to your mama, little girl, before you get yourself in trouble."

The redhead's boisterous laugh attracted the soldiers' attention. Tossing her red hair, she lifted her skirt and petticoat to reveal white cotton bloomers.

The troops taunted Alex and whistled at the girls. "Show us more, show us more!" The soldiers chanted until officers commanded them to resume the march. Alex licked his damp lips, the kiss lingering in his mind.

When the road took them near a cornfield, the lieutenant assigned Alex and Industrious to foraging duty. While gathering fat ears in a gunnysack, they sometimes stopped to chew raw corn off the cob. That night after the company dragged into camp, they boiled the corn for a long-awaited meal.

A pile of cobs lay on the ground next to Alex. "No mistake," he said while still chewing the corn, "anything tastes good when you're hungry." After he finished eating, Alex found the packet of paper Sarah had tucked into his haversack. By the flickering light of the campfire, he began his first letter:

Near Gordonsville, Virginia, April 25, 1862

My dearest wife,

How I hated leaving you and the children at the station—the hardest thing I ever did. It hurts to think you're angry with me. Please be proud of me for performing my duty and serving my country. This is no pleasure trip, as my story will show.

We got off the train in Madison and marched about thirty miles to our connection in Georgia. A closed-in boxcar got me real close to my fellow soldiers. Due to warm weather, the boys stripped off shirts, then shoes and socks, making a big stink. And the sounds—good Lord—they yelled and sang out patriotic songs, raising a ruckus across the whole state of Georgia. Nigh onto thirty men there, sweating together, singing together, shoved in so tight, I couldn't recollect Alex Browning being a separate person.

We were worn out when the train pulled into Richmond. Right off, they ordered us to march. Not sure how far. We must have marched about eighty to ninety miles over the next few days.

First night Industrious and me slept out in the open. I laid on my blanket looking up at the Milky Way, wondering if you could see it at Alligator Creek. Recollected our plan to look at the Big Dipper on my birthday next month.

Don't worry about me. I'll soon be known as a valiant soldier. Give Tommy and Lula a big hug. Let me know when our baby comes.

I love you,

Alex

He left out the part about the bold girls in the town. No point in stirring up trouble.

An oil lamp cast golden light on the oak table in the sitting room where Sarah knitted baby booties while Frances opened *The Arabian Nights* for Lula and Tommy. With Lula sitting beside her and Tommy at her feet, Frances read "Ali Baba and the Forty Thieves." When she came to the part about Ali Baba opening the cave, she stopped to allow the children to shout, "Open Sesame." As she came to the ending, Lula begged, "Read another one—'Tom Thumb.' I like the part where he tricks the robbers and the wolf."

Sarah looked up from her needlework. "Yes, Frances. Read them one more before you tuck them in. I'd like to write Alex tonight." Sarah opened the cabinet, put up her sewing, and found pen, ink, and some writing paper.

Lake City, Florida, May 5, 1862

Dearest Alex,

I haven't received a letter although I've written every day as I promised. I hope you haven't forgotten about us already. I'll wait a few more days before I get upset. Everyone says the mail is quite slow.

I circled your birthday on my almanac. I'll watch the Big Dipper tomorrow night at 8:30 so we'll be joined in the stars on the day of your birth.

I thank the Lord every day for sweet Hannah. After you left, I was so distraught, I did nothing but stay in bed and cover myself with a quilt. Despite her worry about Industrious, Hannah cared for Tommy and Lula three days while I cried bitter tears on my pillow.

I'm finally becoming accustomed to having extra people in the house. I would have dreaded the quiet, lonely evenings after the children went to bed. I'll have to admit, John and Frances have relieved me of much work. In spite of his age, Daddy John helps a great deal with the farm.

Frances works miracles with the children. I'm trying to get used to her habit of dipping snuff. The offensive odor is a very small thing compared to what you may be enduring. Lucky for me, she was known as the best midwife back home. I'm relieved to have an expert for my lying-in.

Please take care of yourself. I worry about you. Are the Yankees near your camp? How is Industrious? Is he taking care of you? Please write me every tiny detail of your army life, so I can see you in my mind as I love you in my heart.

Your loving wife,
Sarah

The next day, John took Sarah downtown to Flint's Mercantile. She walked through the store past counters where she'd always bought coal oil for the lamps, yard goods to sew clothes, or seeds for spring planting. She passed by barrels of flour and sugar, sacks of corn, and boxes of tools to the back corner that housed the local post office. "Good morning, Mr. Flint. I need to mail another letter to Alex."

Flint smiled. "You're writing him pretty regular. What do you hear from him?"

Sarah looked down at the letter. "I haven't heard from him yet, but I'm expecting a letter soon." After he tore off a three-cent stamp, Sarah dropped three pennies on the counter and fixed the stamp on the upper-right corner. "I'd like this to get off soon, Mr. Flint."

"Next train goes out tomorrow. Your letter will be on it, for sure."

Alex had almost succumbed to the homesickness rampant at camp. Often, he passed the time whittling figures or playing checkers. Wood for whittling had become scarce, and he'd won at checkers too often. The games began to bore him.

Alex shook his head and retired to his tent to pen another letter to Sarah.

Near Gordonsville, Virginia, June 3, 1862

My dearest Sarah,

Rec'd your letter yesterday. Paper is in considerable short supply here. I'm glad you put some in my haversack. On my birthday, alas, it clouded up and hid my view of the Big Dipper, ruining our plans, but knowing I was in your thoughts gave me comfort. Maybe we'll have better luck on your birthday in June.

I've stayed put in camp. Nasty weather left us all feeling gloomy. Lots of boys have come down with the smallpox, typhoid, even the mumps. Our company's lost about ten so far from the smallpox and typhoid—one from a bad case of the measles. Almost everyone has suffered with dysentery as I have from time to time. It's a powerful worriment. Only men with strong constitutions don't get sick.

We're getting anxious about "seeing the elephant." That means facing the enemy and their artillery. Can you remember how us boys used to water circus elephants so we could get free tickets to the big top? We'd never seen more fearsome creatures. Nowadays we fear bullets and cannon balls the way we used to be scared of elephants. In spite of it all, some of the boys are itching to go into battle since many have never seen one before and consider this a great adventure. I admit I'm a bit curious about it, too. I'm eager to see how well I show in battle. We'll all be relieved to move out.

We have a new commander. General Robert E. Lee, a West Pointer, took over the Army of Northern Virginia. He served in the Mexican War. Lee sounds like a strong leader. I'm certain he'll lead us to victory.

Must stop this letter now because the captain is calling us for rifle practice. So far, I proved to be the best shot in my company—which reminds me—you must get that pistol out and practice soon as you can.

Pretty soon you'll need to oil the gun. Dad can help you with that.

Your loving husband,
Alex

4

I scarcely know how I can write to you when I have such heavy tidings to send you.

Susan L. Blackford
Letter to her husband,
Capt. Charles M. Blackford,
March 1862

Virginia and Alligator Creek: July–September 1862

It was late July. Alex gathered firewood for evening mess. He stopped to wipe sweat from his forehead with his sleeve and saw a courier. Fat leather saddlebags flopped across the horse's side as they rode into camp. The thought of a letter from Sarah lifted his spirits like a cool breeze. Five letters came the same day a week ago, but he hadn't heard from her since. He followed the horse and rider to the quartermaster's tent. Soon, a large crowd of soldiers abandoned their various tasks or games and converged on the tent just as the quartermaster and his staff started the mail call.

When he heard his name, Alex took Sarah's letter unopened to a secluded spot under a sweet gum tree. Sitting on the ground, he leaned his back against the rough bark and examined the date she'd written above his address. This one had taken almost seven weeks. He slit the envelope with his knife and held it for several minutes, not wanting to read it too fast. He knew Sarah worried about giving birth without him there. He'd heard of several women in Lake City who died in childbirth.

Lake City, Florida, June 8, 1862

Dearest husband,

We have a beautiful new baby daughter, born two days ago—one month after your birthday and five days before mine. I named her Sallie—the girl name we decided on earlier. With Frances as midwife, I didn't have one bit of trouble. Sallie has dark blue eyes, like mine. Tufts of brown hair curl on her forehead, like yours. You should see her little round pink face framed with Lula's baby bonnet. Were Tommy and Lula ever this tiny? She seldom cries except when hungry. The Lord has blessed us with this precious child. I will await your return for the baptism.

I'm sure you found your Bible I packed with your things. Promise me you'll read it whenever you can. Scriptures will give you courage. My favorite is Psalms 27. "The Lord is my light and my salvation; whom shall I fear? The Lord is the strength of my life; of whom shall I be afraid?"

We miss you, Alex. Take care of yourself. I'll mail this letter as soon as Frances can go to town.

Your loving wife,
Sarah

He closed his eyes and tried to put a full image of the new baby in the space behind his lids—blue eyes, brown hair, tiny pink face. He imagined Sarah sitting on the porch swing holding Sallie, almost two months old now. As well as he remembered, babies began to smile about that age, and so he put a smile on the round-faced infant in his mind's picture and felt a smile spread his own lips as he imagined kissing a soft baby cheek. He tried to picture Tommy and Lula as he last remembered them. He longed to hold them and his precious Sarah.

He stood and stuffed the envelope in his pocket, feeling guilty that he'd never opened the Bible she'd packed. He trudged back to camp for noon mess. With his stomach growling, he filled his cup with thin, gray soup and joined Lester and Max, who sat on a log sipping their noon meal.

"I heard your name at mail call," Lester said. "What's the news from home?"

Alex grinned. "It's good. I'm a daddy again. A girl. Sallie's her name."

Max slapped him on the back. "You're getting a passel of young-uns, Alex."

Alex grinned. "What's the news about moving out of here?"

"Some of them was discussing a big battle up at Manassas," Lester said.

Excitement tingled down Alex's spine. "Wasn't that where we beat the Yankees last year?"

Lester nodded. "Same place. Maybe we're going back. Who knows? They never tell us anything until we're ready to move."

Max made a face. "I don't know how they expect us to fight when they don't feed us enough to live." He slurped the last drops of his soup.

That night, Alex lay awake in his tent wondering what lay ahead. He hoped he'd find a way to distinguish himself in this battle. If he got the opportunity to save the lives of any men, Sarah would realize that his leaving was worth the sacrifice. Unable to sleep, he dug a pencil and paper out of his knapsack and went out by the campfire. He began another letter to Sarah.

Sarah stared at the fog through her bedroom window with Sallie nestled in her arms. Her first child, Mariah, had died on a damp, dismal September evening, and each succeeding September filled her with dread. Today, she fretted over the dense clouds. It was said they brought down infectious vapors, spreading diseases to innocent children. Over twenty in Lake City had died during the past year—sons and daughters of friends and acquaintances—children not long ago laughing and playing in the churchyard struck down by smallpox, diphtheria, or whooping cough. When she conversed with other parents, their hollow eyes reflected her fears. Which mother's arms would be emptied next?

She moved Sallie closer to her breast. Last week, Sallie had begun coughing after each nursing. Dr. Taylor gave Sarah a small bottle of liquid to quiet the baby's cough. Dark lines under his kind, blue eyes revealed his exhaustion. As he instructed her on its use, he placed a tender hand on Sallie's cheek. When he shook his head, strands of rumpled gray hair fell over his eyebrows. He told Sarah to keep cold compresses on the baby's forehead if she developed a fever.

Early this morning, Sallie began to cough and then started screaming. The coughing had become more frequent by afternoon. Sarah spoke soft words into Sallie's ear and gently pressed the baby's mouth against her heavy breast. But Sallie pulled back and turned her head away. Sarah dipped a clean cloth in water and held it to Sallie's lips. The baby sucked a few drops of water and coughed again. Sarah reached for the medicine on the washstand and drew out a dose. She inserted the dropper in the baby's mouth, but Sallie refused the medicine.

Sarah looked down at Sallie, whose face burned red with fever, each breath a stuttering rasp or a weak cough. She prayed a familiar scripture: "I will lift up mine eyes unto the hills, from whence cometh my help. My help cometh from the Lord, which made heaven and earth."

Tears wetting her cheeks, she pleaded, "Lord, you have always been faithful to me. Spare this baby. I cannot bear to lose another child. I am at the limit of my endurance. Please, Lord."

Still cuddling the feverish baby in one arm, she picked up a recent letter from Alex and reread it.

Near Gordonsville, Virginia, August 25, 1862

My dearest Sarah,

From what we hear, I reckon we'll be on the march in a few days—maybe tomorrow. Don't know if we'll have a quick victory or long, drawn-out defeat. I still believe in the cause of defending my state and the Confederacy from the evil of the North. And I know there's a chance I might die for my beliefs.

Sarah pressed her lips together, and tears squeezed from under her lids. *How much more can I bear?* She exhaled and continued to read:

Please, my dear Sarah, don't worry. The South will prevail because we're fighting to defend our own land. I believe the old saying—a rooster fights best on his own hill. After all this is over, I hope to be remembered as a man of courage, willing to stand up to the enemy.

Your loving husband,

Alex

She put the letter down. Sallie's even breaths, although still raspy, told Sarah she was sleeping. Sarah laid the baby in her crib, praying that her fever would break before she awoke. Sarah covered her with the light quilt she'd made for Mariah before she was born. Each of the children had loved the quilt, its corner frayed where they'd cut their teeth on the soft material.

Sarah read the letter again, but the questions plaguing her remained unanswered. Did Alex march to Manassas? The newspaper reported over eight thousand Confederate casualties in that battle. Was Alex one of them? While Sallie slept, Sarah planned a letter to Alex, not knowing whether he'd ever see what she wrote. *I don't want to upset him, but Alex needs to know. He's Sallie's parent, too.* She began the letter:

Dearest Alex,

I'm sorry to write that Sallie has whooping cough and I fear for her life . . .

As she addressed the envelope, Frances entered the room and tucked a loose strand of hair into the bun on the back of her head. "Hannah is feeding the children their meal. May I bring you something? You haven't eaten since yesterday. "

The thought of food made Sarah nauseous. "I don't have an appetite. You go ahead and eat. I'll stay with Sallie." She knew what Frances would say next, and so she added, "I'm going to take care of myself. Don't worry."

Frances adjusted her reading glasses and leaned over the baby's crib. Sallie lay like a lifeless doll. Frances felt the baby's forehead. "She's still hot. I'll bring a fresh washcloth and a pan of cool water. Undress her, and we'll give her a bath."

Sarah unbuttoned the cotton dress and removed Sallie's diaper, still dry since this morning. Sallie's skin glowed bright pink against the white cloth beneath her.

Frances put the pan on the marble-topped table. When Sarah laid the baby into the cool water, Sallie let out a yelp. Frances drizzled water over the baby's head, across her chest, up and down her thin arms and legs.

Frances wiped Sallie's forehead with the cloth again. "She's a little fighter."

Sallie didn't even wiggle.

Sarah blinked back her tears. "Do you think she'll come through?"

"We'll pray."

Sarah took the cloth and dripped more water on the baby's skin. "Hasn't she soaked long enough?"

Frances touched Sallie's cheek. "She's still too warm. Wait a few more minutes. You might try again with the cough medicine."

Sarah drew out what remained into a dropper. She watched in desperation as the last drops of the medicine dribbled down the baby's chin.

Frances felt Sallie's forehead and frowned. "Not much change, if any. You can dry her now. We'll try again later."

Sarah lifted the baby and patted her dry. She held a wet cloth to the baby's mouth and watched but could see no signs of sucking.

Frances gripped Sarah's shoulder. "John and I will go for Dr. Taylor. Hannah will check on you while we're gone." She put a light kiss on Sarah's cheek.

"Be sure he brings us more medicine." Sarah picked up her letter to Alex. "While you're in town, would you mail this?"

Frances took the envelope and left Sarah praying to God to spare her child.

5

*I have heard the sound of muskets being fired and know
it was the death-knell of some . . . deserters who were
executed on the hill.*

Capt. Charles M. Blackford
2nd Va. Cavalry,
August 1862

September–December 1862

With Sarah and Frances watching, the doctor held his stethoscope to Sallie's chest. He put his hand on her forehead and cheeks. "Her chest sounds better, and her fever doesn't seem to be quite as high as Frances described." Holding Sallie's head, the doctor inserted a dropper of medicine inside her mouth. The baby's lips puckered, and she sucked the liquid out. Sarah felt a shred of optimism grow inside her.

The doctor looked up. "Has she nursed at all or taken any liquids?"

Sarah grimaced and shook her head. When she thought of her baby nursing, circles of milk soaked through her dress.

Frances stared at the stains. "Maybe you could gather some of that nourishment in a cup and feed her with a spoon."

Dr. Taylor smiled. "A suggestion I was preparing to offer."

Sarah handed the baby to Frances and stepped into the hall. She massaged some milk into a cup and brought it back into the bedroom. Frances dipped a teaspoon into the milk and held it to Sallie's lips. The baby took a few drops.

Sarah shook her head. "Two drops. That's not enough to sustain her."

"For a little baby, a tiny drop helps more than you'd think." Dr. Taylor said. "You might try giving her water or milk in a baby bottle. Sometimes a sick baby takes it better that way."

Sarah shook her head. "My babies have all taken breast milk. I don't have a baby bottle."

The doctor pursed his lips. "You can find them at Flint's. There are several types of nipples available, but the rubber ones work best."

Frances touched Sarah's arm. "Father and I will go back to the store. If they have a baby bottle, we'll find it."

Dr. Taylor put his hand on Sarah's shoulder. "I'll be back to check on her. Keep up what you're doing. This is a critical time."

Through the rest of that day and the day that followed, Sarah stayed by Sallie's bed or held her, following the doctor's directions. After Frances returned from Flint's, they tried coaxing Sallie to suck the baby bottle filled with Sarah's milk. Sallie refused the bottle. When Sallie slept, Sarah sat by her side and touched her chest every few minutes to see if she'd stopped breathing. The afternoon of the second day, Sallie began to nurse—weakly at first then more vigorously as she gained strength. Despite her exhaustion, Sarah felt renewed in spirit as she at last allowed herself to hope.

Three weeks later, she received another letter from Alex and was relieved to hear again so soon. Sarah perched on the aging settee that had survived their wedding trip from Georgia. She slipped a finger under the seal.

Near Manassas, Virginia, September 15, 1862

My dearest Sarah,

Well, we stomped the Yankees again at Manassas. If we show our colors like we've been doing, this war will be over with before you know it. Most of us gave it our best—with a few horrible exceptions.

Some of the new recruits turned tail! I couldn't believe my eyes. They ran like crazy men and threw away their guns, packs, and coats—anything that was loose. The officers hollered at them to hold up, but to no avail. It was like they tried to stop a raging river. They caught two of them. Officers kept them bucked and gagged for a day—tied their hands over their knees, with a stick between their arms and legs and a bayonet tied in their mouths, both of them a bloody mess. Then they decided to make an example of the deserters. The court martial sentenced them to death. The firing squad shot them in front of everybody. A terrible thing for those men to die in shame when we need soldiers. As much as I hate skulkers, the scene made me sick.

Your loving husband,

Alex

Alex pondered what he had written before he sealed the letter. He questioned whether he could stay the course if Sarah had a problem she couldn't handle.

Sarah folded Alex's letter with the realization that Alex had not yet received the news of Sallie's illness. A lump in her throat almost choked her when she learned the harsh penalties for desertion. *Would her letter cause him to desert?* She dashed off another note and told him of Sallie's recovery. She hoped that by some miracle it might reach him before— or at least soon after—the earlier one made its way into his hands.

In mid-November, the day before Alex's company marched toward Fredericksburg, he received Sarah's letter written during Sallie's illness. *Have I already lost another child without knowing? Oh dear God. Don't let our baby die.* Examining the date on the letter, he realized he might be praying too late. The baby might have already died. After Mariah's death, Sarah had clung to him and cried herself to sleep for months. *What will she do without me to soothe her? If the baby dies while I'm gone, she'll hate me forever.*

Jacob rushed into the tent. "Hey, brother, are you packed up for the march?" He sat down on the cot beside Alex. "What's wrong? Get moving."

Alex swallowed and handed him the letter. "It's the baby. I think she's dead."

Jacob read the note and frowned. "She didn't say Sallie died. I'll bet she's well by now." He handed Alex's letter back. "That's the trouble with this wretched mail. It takes a lifetime to get any news." He put his hand on Alex's shoulder. "Let's hope she's well by now."

Alex hung his head as he held back tears. "I feel certain the baby's dead. I've got to go home to be with Sarah."

"You don't *know* that."

Alex stood. "I'll talk to Captain Tolbert."

"The troops are marching out tomorrow morning. He won't let you go now. You could request a furlough for this winter."

Alex stood. "I have to go *now*. Winter's too late." Alex lifted the tent flap and walked out with Jacob following close behind.

When he reached the officers' quarters, a guard stopped him. "What do you want, soldier?"

"I need to see Captain Tolbert."

The guard pushed him back. "The captain is in a meeting with the other officers. You'll have to wait until we start the march."

Alex gripped the guard's arm. "This is important. I can't wait that long."

The guard removed Alex's hand and spoke as though reprimanding an unruly child. "Look, soldier. I don't know anything important enough to bother the captain right now. We'll be heading north before dawn tomorrow."

Alex observed the well-armed guard. Then he turned back toward Jacob.

Jacob grabbed his elbow. "Calm down, Alex. There's nothing you can do about Sarah right now. Try to put home out of your mind."

Alex kept his voice low. "I'm going home. I'll wait until dark and sneak out through the woods."

"You're not that stupid. I know you're upset, but use your head."

Max and Lester caught up with Alex and Jacob. Max looked from one to the other. "What's going on?"

Jacob spoke in a quiet voice so that no one around could hear. He told them about the letter and Alex's reaction. The three surrounded Alex as they accompanied him back into the tent. Jacob pushed him onto the cot and sat next to him. "You know what happens to deserters."

Alex glowered at his friends. "That's only if they catch me."

Lester leaned nearer. "Even if you get away, your name will be ruined. The folks at home would find out."

"They've got home guards all over the South," Max added. "You'll get caught or shot somewhere along the way."

Jacob gave him a look Alex recognized from his childhood. The look said, "Don't ever let me hear you talk about this again."

Alex hung his head and pushed his sadness down. "You're right. I'll be on the march tomorrow." He wouldn't talk about it, but he knew he'd look for opportunities to escape.

After five hours of marching, the captain called a halt for the men to eat. Instead of sitting with Jacob and his friends, Alex sat near some newcomers to the company.

One recruit made a sour face. "I'm sick of eating these nasty, dry biscuits."

Another man stared at his biscuit. "It's harder than a rock. I'm gonna chunk it at that squirrel over yonder." He swung his arm back.

Alex grabbed his arm. "Wait. Don't throw away that biscuit. I'll take it." Two others offered Alex their biscuits, which he put inside a tin in his haversack.

The first recruit studied him. "How come you're stashing biscuits, Browning?"

Alex shrugged. "Don't want to waste good food." That evening, he packed in a tin of sardines from his ration, then another one the next night. After five days, his pack bulged with his stash.

Jacob, marching next to him, nudged the pack. "What you got in there, brother?"

"It's just a bulky scarf Sarah knitted for me." Alex grinned.

On the sixth day, after dinner, Industrious brought Alex the haversack he'd left by the creek when he filled his canteen. "This here bag's mighty heavy, Mr. Alex, like you maybe put rocks in it." When he loosened the strap, Alex lunged at his bag. "Don't worry about it. I'll take it. We're only a few hours from camp now." He slung the pack over his shoulder and walked away.

As they continued marching, the strap on the haversack dug into his shoulder, but Alex straightened his back and quickened his step. He thought ahead to his guard assignment that night.

Just after sundown, Alex reported for picket duty. One of the guards stomped his boots to warm his feet. "I've had my fill of that sticky blue beef they feed us. Ain't it almost Thanksgiving time?"

"I can just see it in my mind," another guard said. "A great big table stacked up high with turkey and dressing."

"And don't forget the pumpkin pies."

"I like pecan pies, myself."

Alex coughed. "How come y'all can't talk about anything but food?" He grabbed his belly for the third time this picket. "I gotta go to the woods again. This dysentery is getting the best of me."

The men gave him a sympathetic look. "Go on, but get far enough away so you won't spoil our appetites."

Alex hid behind a tree where he could hear the men continue to complain about food.

"There's not even any place to forage in this God-forsaken country."

"I ain't seen a planted field nowhere."

Alex rejoined them just as the second shift for picket duty arrived. "See anything?" the new guard asked.

"Not a thing. Quiet as a mouse."

Alex moved aside and groaned. "You boys go on back to camp. I need to head for the woods." As they ambled away, he hurried in the opposite direction toward a clump of scrubby cedar bushes where he'd hidden his haversack earlier in the day. A sliver of a moon shone in a dark sky. Cold air gusts cut through his pants and jacket. It seemed early for such a chill, but after all, it was almost December far north of his home in Florida. He felt his way past a dark forest until he touched limber cedar branches and found his pack. In his mind, he reviewed its contents—several biscuits, some hardtack, and six tins of sardine—not the makings of hardy eating, but enough to sustain him if he could find apples or berries along the way. The many streams along the road would offer a water supply. He slipped the haversack over his shoulders and walked parallel to the road leading south.

Concern about Sallie urged him onward. He took one last look at the campfire's glow in the clearing and listened to the muffled voices and the occasional whinny of the cavalry's horses. Too early now for them to miss him, but tomorrow morning, scouts would search the woods for their most recent deserter.

He wrapped the hand-knitted wool scarf around his neck. He measured his steps into a moderate pace he thought he could sustain, but the exertion soon heated his body. With the north wind at his back, he removed the scarf and unbuttoned his jacket. The quiet woods and the hard dirt turnpike magnified the sound of his lone footsteps.

A noise behind him caused his heart to lurch. He stopped. *It's just a squirrel or a bobcat scurrying about.* He resumed his pace, and this time he heard what sounded like footsteps. He stood still. The sounds grew louder and closer together. Whoever followed was running, not walking. Alex left the road to watch from behind a tree. He strained to see through the faint moonlight. The feet beat like drums. He made out the shape of a large man much taller than himself breathing in loud huffs. The figure stopped, but the loud breathing continued. *Have they already sent a scout after me?* Alex held his breath, not daring to move. He exhaled a quiet, slow breath. *Maybe the scout will turn around if I wait long enough.*

The figure spoke. At first Alex couldn't understand what he said, but the second time, the words became clear. "Mister Alex. Don't leave me, Mister Alex. I'm goin' wit' you."

6

. . . on the first day of January, in the year of our Lord one thousand eight hundred and sixty-three, all persons held as slaves within any State or designated part of a State, the people whereof shall then be in rebellion against the United States, shall be then, thenceforward, and forever, free . . .

Abraham Lincoln
Emancipation Proclamation

December 1862–July 1863

Industrious took a deep breath. "I come to take care of you, Massa Alex. I gotta stay with you."

Alex's heart sank. "There's no way on God's earth I can make it through four Southern states with you in tow. They'll have us both in chains—or dead. Why did you follow me?"

"You was goin' off without me. What you think I gonna do in the 'federate army all by myself? Nobody but you would of cared about ole Dustrous. They'd a shot me through. And you just left me!"

Alex couldn't see Industrious's face in the darkness but imagined his heavy features contorted in pain and fear. He swallowed. "I figured Jacob would take care of you. All I thought about was Sarah grieving over another dead child and blaming me for not being there. I just wanted to go home. Now we've got to go back to the army."

"I don't rightly know what you got on your mind, but I'm stickin' right by your side."

"Hush talking. We're turning around. I don't want them to know I tried to leave."

"I ain't never tellin' nobody."

"Shh!" He pulled the big man over to the grassy side of the road to muffle their footsteps. "The pickets are up ahead," he whispered. They made a wide circle through the woods around the guards. Firelight silhouetted the campgrounds ahead. They hid in bushes nearby until someone walked toward the woods with a lantern that afforded enough light for Alex to locate his tent. Industrious turned toward the place where the slaves slept under the stars.

Inside his tent, Alex lit a candle to write a letter to Sarah—what she would want to hear:

Near Fredericksburg, November 8, 1862

My dear Sarah,

I received your letter about Sallie's illness. I'm praying that she's gotten well. If there were any way, I'd come home. I tried to get a leave, but no luck. I thought of men who'd left the army with much less reason than mine. I could never leave even though I'm worried to death about you and the children.

My company has shrunk by half. Some of them went home due to sickness and lots of them died. My clothes are ragged with holes wearing through, my jacket's dirty, but holding out. Please sew me another pair of trousers—a couple of inches smaller in the waist.

Tell the children I love them. Coming home for Christmas is doubtful. Look forward to another letter from you at winter camp. I pray it will bring good news of Sallie's recovery.

Your loving husband,
Alex

Sarah unlocked the secretary and opened the wooden box holding Alex's letters. She added the latest one to the stack. She should have known he'd handle his worry in a manly fashion.

She took a piece of wool she had long ago set aside for a winter cloak for herself. Using an old pattern and adjusting for the smaller waist, she sewed until midnight. Before she wrapped the folded trousers, she slipped Tommy's Christmas drawing into the pocket. She dreamed of Alex that night—thin but still handsome in his new trousers.

The next morning, she took the package to Mr. Flint. "I hope he'll get this by Christmas."

Flint examined the package. "Not a chance. Even if the train comes this afternoon, it'll be three or four weeks."

On Sarah's first Christmas Eve without Alex, a small crooked pine tree in sad need of decorations stood in the sitting room. Their dog Hank and the two cats warmed themselves before the rock fireplace. Sarah sat in a lounge chair wrapping her gifts. She had sewn two dolls from scraps she'd saved for a quilt. She'd made a pillow for Frances and a new apron for Hannah. She knitted a scarf for Daddy John and made some marbles from clay dug down by the creek for Tommy. She could have easily bought gifts a year ago.

Tommy and Lula burst out of the hall into the sitting room with shiny garlands looped over their arms. Tommy jumped up and down. "Look Mama, Auntie Fran found this these decorations in the attic. Lula and me strung popcorn and berries." He laid the strands on the oak table.

"Lula and I." Sarah corrected his grammar, more out of habit than interest, because her thoughts lingered on Alex. She hoped he'd receive his new pants before his old ones fell apart.

While Frances shooed away the curious cats, Daddy John helped the children string garlands on the little tree and light a candle near a manger scene on the mantle. Tommy pulled Sarah's sleeve. "It's time to read the Christmas story, Mama."

Sarah rubbed her eyes and sighed. "Daddy John, would you read the story? I'm exhausted."

Tommy pouted. "No, Mama. You're always supposed to read the baby Jesus story."

Sarah smiled. "We don't have to do everything the same way every year, Tommy."

"Yes we do! If we don't do it the same way, St. Nicholas might not fill our stockings." He looked as though he might cry.

Daddy John retrieved the heavy family Bible from the bookshelf, opened it to the second chapter of Luke, and laid it on Sarah's lap. "Here you are, Missy. Like the boy said, 'You're supposed to do it.'" He smiled. "It'll give you the Christmas spirit."

Frances, holding Sallie, moved an oil lamp to a stand near Sarah's chair. Tommy and Lula sat in their pajamas at her feet.

After she finished the story of the shepherds' visitation by the angel, she laid the open Bible on the table. "God gave us his Son this very night so we might know He's always with us. Even though Daddy's gone, we're not alone." As she opened her arms, Lula crawled onto her lap and Tommy snuggled against her. Frances brought Sallie over and squeezed her into Sarah's arms to complete the circle. Sarah hugged them close. "My children, how I thank the Lord each day for you." She held them a few more minutes, savoring their closeness and connecting with the joy Mary must have felt when she held her firstborn. She got up and carried Sallie as she walked them upstairs to their bedroom. "Close your eyes, little ones. St. Nick won't come until he knows you're sleeping." She kissed their squeezed-shut eyes.

In early January, Sarah and Frances took the wagon into town to buy a few staples. While Frances drove the wagon, Sarah looked over the list—molasses, syrup, baking soda—things their land couldn't provide. Prices had risen so quickly during the war. She knew these necessities would cost at least twice the amount she'd paid last time. She prayed their money would hold out until the crops came in next summer.

They turned off the road that meandered next to Alligator Creek and drove past the square toward Flint's store. Pungent wood smoke drifted from chimneys into a cold, blue sky. Old men, shivering in heavy jackets, huddled on the boardwalk outside the general store. Sarah recognized the bank president, William McArthur, beside Charles Flint. Mr. Flint read in a loud voice from a newspaper. He stopped reading as Sarah and Frances pulled alongside them.

"Good morning, ladies."

Sarah managed a weak smile. "News from the war?" Her pulse quickened as she considered how many men had died.

"There's news all right," the white-haired banker said, "but not from the war. Most soldiers are in winter camp now."

"President Lincoln's done it again," Mr. Flint said.

"Done what?" Sarah asked.

"Freed the damned slaves."

Sarah frowned in confusion. "How can he do that?"

"It's nothing new. He warned last September that this proclamation would take effect in January. Nobody thought he'd carry through. But it's not legal. He even admitted it himself."

She gathered from the men that the President had declared slaves free for the Confederate States—but not in northern or border states. While she and Frances shopped, Sarah pondered what she'd heard. What would the slaves think about the proclamation? Had they even heard of it? Fearful thoughts flooded her mind even as she paid the cashier. *What will happen to Industrious? Or Hannah?*

They loaded their supplies into the wagon, and Sarah climbed into the seat. "What do you think, Frances?" she asked as Frances moved in beside her. "Will Hannah know about Lincoln's proclamation?"

Frances took out her snuff box and tucked a pinch into her cheek. "Even if she does, it won't make any difference now."

Sarah wrinkled her nose at the offensive smell. "What do you mean—now?"

"If the Yankees win this war, they'll all go free. No chance of that. Look what would happen. None of us would be safe. You may think Hannah would stay loyal, but I'm telling you—you can't trust any of them. You remember what happened in North Carolina."

Sarah remembered the story an acquaintance had told her about the elderly woman murdered in her bed by house servants. Such tales caused panic, but Sarah suspected some stories were exaggerations. "Hannah would never hurt any of us."

Frances shrugged. "I don't think so either, but if she's free, she won't have to stay."

The next morning, Sarah walked outside and into the kitchen. Hannah stood patting flour into a thick, doughy oval on a breadboard. John sat in a straight chair drinking a dark, steamy mixture that passed for coffee. He looked up from a folded newspaper. "I'm studying this proclamation Lincoln made."

Sarah looked over his shoulder at *The Florida Sentinel.* A preface warned readers that the disgusting words of Lincoln would strip the South of its rights to property and self-determination. It also attacked abolitionists for stirring up insurrection among slaves. Sarah wondered how northern newspapers reported the event. "What do you think, Daddy John?"

"Old Abe's got something up his sleeve. It looks to me that if our slaves make it to the North, they won't send them back like they did in the past. I think Lincoln's clearing the way for an invasion of the South so their soldiers can free slaves wherever they win a battle. But that's not our worry. So far, the Yankees have turned tail after all the Virginia battles."

Sarah noticed Hannah holding a rolling pin suspended above the dough, her back toward Daddy John. She'd surely heard their conversation. How much did she understand?

That evening, Hannah brought up the subject while setting the table for dinner. "I hear Mr. Lincoln ordered slaves be freed."

"His laws don't apply to us in the South . . . I don't know what I'd do without you," Sarah said almost in apology.

Hannah pursed her lips and lifted her shoulders. "It's no never mind, Miss Sarah. I don't have nowhere to go anyhow—not till Dustrous come back from the war."

A week later, Sarah found a letter waiting for her at Flint's store. She stepped behind a rack of clothes and tore open the envelope.

In camp near Gordonsville, December 30, 1862

My dear wife,

Will now tell you about the battle at Fredericksburg. Some day when the children are older, they can read about what happened. From our position above the Rappahannock, I watched Federals cross a pontoon bridge and form battle lines. They kept coming at us—rank after rank—but our position was strong. I couldn't stand to listen to the wounded Yankees hollering so pitiful for someone to help or bring water. Wanted to go out there, but couldn't. Whenever anyone tried, Yankees shot at him. Next morning, the plain between us and them was filled with bodies of Federals. Some of them dead, others all twisted up in pain. I could have walked all the way across that field stepping on corpses and wounded men.

On Monday the enemy cleared out, leaving the dead behind. The smell was awful. But Jacob and Lester and a mob of other boys collected boots and weapons from dead Yankees. We're no longer barefooted. And we've got equipment.

Kiss the children for me. Industrious sends his love to Hannah.

Your husband,

Alex

Sarah shuddered. She'd save the letter but could never read such horror aloud now for their young ears.

Because she was accustomed to snowy winters during her childhood in Georgia, Florida's balmy February days always surprised her. Still, the chance of occasional freezes delayed the job of planting for another month.

Along with worries about Alex and her children, Sarah remained preoccupied with the family's financial requirements. She looked for ways to stretch the Confederate dollar's decreasing value and possibilities for making more money from farm products—selling eggs, smoking hams, or making berry jelly. A soft knock at the door interrupted her thoughts.

A petite young woman with carrot-red hair and green eyes stood outside the door.

"Hello there. I'm Megan McLoughlin, and I wondered if you'd be so kind to rent me a room." She spoke with a thick Irish brogue

Sarah's eyes brightened as she considered the boarding income. She invited Megan into the parlor. Daughter of Irish immigrants, Megan had married a Floridian she'd met in Boston. At the first opportunity, her husband had enlisted in the Confederate Army. A few months ago, she'd received news that he'd been killed at Antietam.

"With my teacher's salary, I can't afford to keep my house, so I sold it and started to look for a room." Her eyes filled with tears. "Please let me stay. No one wants to take me in because I'm from the North, but I can't go back. I can pay you well. The boarding houses are asking thirty dollars a month, but I'll pay thirty-five. My salary's sixty dollars, and my needs aren't much. I'll help around the house, too."

The extra thirty-five dollars would go a long way for the family. *Thank you, Lord.*

By March, planting crops consumed every daylight hour for several weeks. Despite the exhausting work, Sarah loved planting season. Unlike the dreariness of pulling out old stalks in the fall, the excitement of dropping the tiny seeds into the loamy soil lifted Sarah's heart with new hope for life.

Six-year-old Tommy studied the corn kernels Sarah had dropped into his hand. "How can a big corn stalk grow out of these little bitty seeds?"

Sarah smiled. "It's God's miracle, son. He's put everything inside those seeds to grow tall stalks with big ears of corn."

"How do you know they won't be beans or flowers or oak trees?"

"I know because each plant grows its own seeds." Sarah guided his hand toward a furrow. "Plant your seeds in this corner so you can remember where they are. In a week or so, you can come out and watch them grow."

Tommy buried his kernels in a deep ridge and covered them with loose, brown dirt. He sat staring at them for a few minutes as though he expected immediate results.

When Sarah took him out to the field a few weeks later, he knelt to examine the tiny plants that had popped through the soil. "It's already happening, Mama. God kept his promise."

Sarah enfolded him in her arms and prayed that fulfillment of God's promise for strength in these hard times would be so obvious.

Each July morning, Sarah arose at four and dressed by candlelight so that she could beat the brutal sun to the cornfields. The heat, the worst she could recall, was all anyone could talk about. Frequent rains steamed the atmosphere but failed to cool the air. The cattle stood in the shade of wilting trees.

Sitting at her dressing table on the wall between two west windows, Sarah moved the candle closer to the mirror and noticed brown freckles on her face and hands where the sun had found her vulnerable skin. She pulled on a faded, long-sleeved gingham dress, a wide-brimmed straw hat, and gloves.

She cinched her well-loved sidesaddle onto her horse and rode to the field, where the two hired field hands, Lou and Harvey, looked up, wiped the sweat from their eyes, and then waved their damp bandanas at her. They dropped plump ears of corn into burlap sacks and emptied them into wicker baskets at the ends of the rows. Sarah squinted at the strange sight of corn being harvested in Alex's cotton fields. When the market for cotton had been cut off by the Union blockade around Florida, they'd switched crops.

After two hours of picking corn, Sarah rode to the other end of the field. The sun had risen just above the horizon, already a scorching blaze. A man rode up, with Hank yapping at the horse's heels. Ignoring the dog, the man dismounted and removed his hat.

Sarah turned her horse toward him. "Hush, Hank." The dog trotted back toward the pasture.

"Miz Sarah Browning?"

Sarah recognized the Southern uniform. "I'm Sarah Browning."

"Isn't your husband serving in the Confederate army?"

She sucked in a deep, hurried breath. "Has something happened to Alex?"

"I'm sorry, Mrs. Browning, I have no word of your husband. I'm here about state and wartime business. I'm Corporal Ruford Sanders."

She nodded and waited.

"Here's the thing, ma'am. General Lee's men are desperate for food."

Sarah recalled Alex's letters about their bad food and the weight he'd lost.

The corporal unbuckled his saddlebag and removed a stack of papers. He licked his index finger as he turned the pages. "How many cows do you have on this farm, ma'am?"

Sarah stiffened. "Why do you want to know about our cattle?"

"Ma'am, I'm the Confederate agent authorized by the war department to collect your Confederate tithe."

"I don't understand." She'd only heard of tithes connected with church—*voluntary* contributions.

The agent seemed annoyed. "We're here to collect ten percent of your cattle and your crops according to the Impressment Act of March 26 of this year and the General Tax Act on April 24. It's a tax in-kind of one tenth of all agricultural products."

Sarah shook her head. "How will you make sure that this corn and these cattle of mine will reach Virginia?"

"We'll collect foodstuffs at the commissary depots for the army. We'll send the cattle to the front where they'll be butchered." The corporal breathed a sigh. "We'll count what you have here and round it up. And if you don't mind, we'll have your man here fill our wagon."

Sarah narrowed her eyes. "I don't think Alex and the other soldiers would be happy to know that you're taking away our living. We barely make ends meet. I'm supporting three children and two other adults besides myself—in addition to all our workers." If she could, she'd pack up everything in the fields and send it straight to Alex. But she didn't like being forced to give away hard-earned crops. *What authority does this man have? He isn't even an officer. How do I know he's telling me the truth?* "Let me see your papers."

"I have my orders, ma'am. You need to sign a release." Corporal Sanders held out his papers for Sarah.

The legal language of the order confused her. "I can't sign these now. I should talk it over with my father-in-law."

"Trust me, ma'am. This is for the good of our soldiers."

Sarah gripped the saddle with her knee and gave the horse a firm kick, turning down the corn row.

She heard the corporal's horse behind her. "Ma'am," he yelled. "Stop, ma'am. In the name of the Confederate States of America, halt!"

Giving the horse another hard kick, Sarah galloped down the row, corn leaves slapping her on either side until she heard the gunshot.

Her startled horse skittered sideways, throwing her down into a corn row. Dazed, she raised herself to her hands and knees in the dirt. The man dismounted a few feet away, his face dark, determined.

The corporal moved toward her. "Are you all right, ma'am?" He leaned over to help her up.

Choking down the bile rising in her throat, Sarah ignored his offered hand and stood. She removed her dirty gloves.

He handed her a sheet of paper and pointed to a heavy black line at the bottom. "Sign there, ma'am."

What could she do against a man in uniform with a gun? "I really don't want our soldiers in Virginia to starve. It's—it's just hard making ends meet here."

The corporal smiled. She held her breath for a moment then signed her name on the order. She turned to the field boss. "Lou, give the man ten bushels of corn and round up five cows for him."

Several days later, when Daddy John took the family for a trip to town, the wagon passed by the depot. Beside the railroad track Sarah saw corn rotting in large barrels. She remembered the agent who had impressed her corn and cattle. *How dare they waste our precious food!* She hoped the cattle had survived the long train ride to Virginia.

7

Four score and seven years ago our fathers brought forth on this continent, a new nation, conceived in Liberty, and dedicated to the proposition that all men are created equal. Now we are engaged in a great civil war, testing whether that nation, or any nation so conceived and so dedicated, can long endure. We are met on a great battlefield of that war. We have come to dedicate a portion of that field, as a final resting place for those who here gave their lives that that nation might live. It is altogether fitting and proper that we should do this.

Abraham Lincoln
Gettysburg Address

The Battle: July–September 1863

After two weeks of marching northward, in spite of hot weather and sore feet, Alex's excitement grew, fueled by his comrades' noisy enthusiasm. This battle could turn the tide and end the war for good. Perhaps this time, he'd find an opportunity to show his bravery.

He looked across the line at the uniforms. Not one of the Confederate uniforms matched another. Uniform pants and shirts ranged from varied shades of gray to butternut or even light blue. Their hats were different, too, and most wore farm work boots—if they had any boots. Alex remembered his surprise at Second Manassas when the Yanks' spiffy blue uniforms charged the scruffy rebel picket line.

At mid-morning, Alex rolled his shirtsleeves up past his elbows.

"We've whupped them damn Yankees three times now," Lester said.

"And we're gonna whup 'em agin. This time in their own stompin' grounds," another young soldier shouted. Alex hoped they were right.

"Let's hear it, men," the captain called out.

At the captain's call, the men began chanting in time with their footsteps:

> We whipped 'em once and twice and three.
> Nothin' can stop our General Lee,
> Down the valley and up the hill,
> Manassas, Fredericksburg, Chancellorsville.

The shrill rebel yell echoed through the ranks. "Whoee! Whoee!"

Alex joined the yelling. It helped calm his nerves, which always became jittery before a battle. So far, Sarah's prayers had protected him, and Industrious's sharp eye had saved him more than once when he pointed out Yankee sharpshooters aiming rifles his way. He touched Tommy's penny in his pocket. He'd never discounted luck, either.

He twisted around and smiled at Industrious, marching just behind him today instead of at the back of the troops. "Hey, you're keeping up real good now."

"I marches lots better in these here new boots."

Alex winced when he remembered that Jacob had yanked them from a dead Yankee's stiff feet in Fredericksburg.

"You deserve them," Alex said. "Everyone agrees you're a better cook than the mess sergeant."

"Thing about Industrious," another soldier spoke up, "he's a man we can trust, not like the Negroes others brought. You know who I mean— that traitor Joey. He went running for the Yankee lines the minute he got a chance."

Alex flicked his eyes back toward Industrious, who gazed into the distance clenching and unclenching his hand, something he did when he was upset.

The soldier continued. "Did your master name you 'Industrious'?"

"No suh, my mama always called me that. Wanted me to work hard and do good."

Alex grinned. "The men even trust you with their ammunition, Industrious."

By late morning, the soldiers reached the Potomac River, which lay flat and wide near Williamsport. The men removed their shoes and trousers and carried them on their shoulders atop their cartridge boxes as they waded across the shallow water. Lester slipped on a rock, dousing himself to the ears. "Never thought I'd get myself baptized on the Mason and Dixon line." The men roared with laughter and splashed water on one another.

Goosebumps rose on Alex's damp legs. Even after he pulled on his dry trousers and shoes, he felt shivery. He wrapped himself in his blanket and waited on the Maryland bank, unable to stop worrisome thoughts of Sarah and their children.

After everyone crossed, Industrious helped the mess officers pour each man two ounces of whiskey. The whiskey tasted good. Alex drank slowly and allowed the golden liquid to slide down his throat, warm his stomach, and ease his edginess.

Jacob, sitting near him on a rock, held his tin cup in front of him. "I'm saving mine. It'll be my treat after today's march." He emptied water from his canteen and replaced it with the whiskey. Alex thought his brother must be crazy. Water was a necessity while they marched.

Long before they were ready, the officers ordered the men to resume the march. Alex stretched his stiff legs and moved back into formation for the fast journey north. Toward noon, the sun burned through the rain clouds and reflected off the greenest fields he'd seen since he left home. A wooden road sign announced their entrance into Pennsylva-

71

nia. Lush foliage, sleek cattle, and well-dressed people contrasted with ragged, war-torn folks in Virginia, where he'd fought the past year.

In one small town, a group of women sold cakes, yeast bread, and butter. When Alex dropped out of line and asked the price, a young girl answered in a strange language.

"They're Dutch," a soldier shouted. "Can't speak English."

A Yankee walked past going the other direction. "They're not Dutch, they're Deutsch—Germans!"

The first soldier replied, "They sure ain't from Florida!"

Alex rejoined the line. In another town, a housewife approached Industrious. "Are they treating you well, servant?" she asked. Her Yankee accent irritated Alex's ears.

Industrious nodded. "Yes'm. Can't complain."

"Wouldn't you rather live here?" She arched an eyebrow.

Industrious hesitated, glancing at Alex. "It's mighty pretty, ma'am. But there ain't no place I'd rather go than back home."

Seeing so many men not in uniform surprised Alex. The Yankee civilians walked along the streets gawking as troops marched through. A Southern soldier spoke to one of them. "You don't need to worry about your women and children. We won't make war on them like you did in our country."

The troops exited the town into the countryside again. Alex passed whitewashed fences and limbs heavy with crimson berries hanging over. Boys ahead threw cherries back to their comrades. Alex caught one in mid-air and put it between his teeth. When he popped the tight skin, cherry juice sweetened his mouth. Men broke off branches and ate cherries while they marched.

When three enlisted men jumped the fence and began milking cows into their canteens, the lieutenants commanded the men to stop foraging. The officers reminded them of Lee's orders to abstain from injury to private property in enemy territory—except from requisitions of the quartermaster or the commissary, who'd pay for acquired supplies with Confederate money. A wave of resentment poured over Alex as he considered the horrors the North had inflicted on Virginia civilians and their property. The Confederate general seemed to want to set a rightful example for the enemy in spite of their wrongs. He sometimes questioned Lee's strategies, but Alex always admired his character.

That night, when they made camp, Alex ate with his friends. Jacob winked as he opened his canteen. "You fellows enjoy your fresh milk. I'll have a drop of whiskey." He turned up the canteen and drank two swallows.

Alex smiled. During the hot march he'd been glad for his water, but now, sitting under the stars with a light breeze cooling him, he almost wished he'd saved his whiskey.

He heard the one-two rhythm of a horse trotting up the road. The uneven timbre of the beat told him the mount was missing a shoe. He watched as the messenger rode past and wondered, as he had many times through the last few days, about the cavalry. In other battles, they'd seen them when they returned from scouting the enemy or bringing recent news to the company's commanders. He wanted to call out to this lone rider to hear the news direct, but the man looked sullen and tired and the horse's legs were marked with dried rivulets of sweat. Alex kept still.

"We'll camp in Gettysburg tonight," the captain told them the next morning when they started their march.

As his company wound through the country towns, Alex noticed sutlers following the troops, pulling wagons loaded with merchandise. In spite of their high prices, the sutlers provided the men with items not available in the army. They were always a welcome sight. During rest stops, soldiers could spend their money buying the sutlers' wares. Alex found a quarter in his pocket and purchased a pair of socks. Others bought tobacco or coffee.

When they neared Gettysburg, Jacob stopped and stared at the distant hills. "What's that out there? Cannon fire?"

Faint but distinct sounds came from a distance. "It's gunfire. The battle's already begun."

Jacob rubbed the back of his neck. "How come our regiment always brings up the rear when we go into a fight?"

"Patience has never been one of your virtues, brother." Alex shook his head and realized he, too, became jumpy waiting for battle. "I saw one horse a ways back but haven't seen the cavalry. Aren't they supposed to be out there getting information about the enemy's position?"

Jacob scratched his head. "You're right. I haven't seen hide nor hair of 'em."

Alex shivered as they climbed a small rise. From two miles out, the town appeared below them, lying in a valley surrounded by rolling hills. The gunfire they heard earlier had stopped. Except for his apprehension, he found the scene quite lovely.

Early the next morning, Alex looked over a stone wall into an open field on the edge of the woods. The troops waited all day, fidgeting, trying to remain calm. Alex's shoulders twitched each time cannons boomed and echoed across the valley. Alex breathed slowly during a short, silent period. Spates of gunfire followed. His physical reactions fragmented into contrasts—one second he shook with panic, and in the next second, fear paralyzed him; in one his heart raced, in the next it seemed frozen. While he waited, a minute lasted a hundred years.

Finally, the captain gave orders to advance. Alex shrugged his haversack from his shoulder. It fell onto the stockpile of arms and ammunition the slaves would guard during battle. He looked up into Industrious's steady gaze.

"You take care of my stuff while I'm gone now. When I get back, it best all be here." Alex gave a nervous laugh and jostled Industrious. He turned to look toward the battlefield. There'd be no Industrious there today, just him and the other soldiers with Yankee devils trying to shoot them down. He turned back to his servant.

"Just you come back in one piece, Mr. Alex, and your stuff'll be here sure 'nough."

Alex nodded as he swung the cartridge box over his shoulder. He gripped his rifle and followed his unit into the field. The grass gave little cover, and Alex bent low as he ran to gain what shelter he could. Around him, he saw the other soldiers doing the same. Artillery fire blasted his eardrums as bullets rained around him. Sulphurous smells burned his nostrils.

Straight ahead lay their defined goal, rising like a knife-edge into cloudless sky. The captain had called it Cemetery Ridge. Spindly trees spiked up, outlined against the skyline, giving the knife a jagged blade. It looked like an easy target. The men around him moved faster, and Alex raced to keep up. He joined their screaming. It felt good after staying quiet so long. The sound of his own voice pumped up his courage as he charged. No telling how many Yankees hid behind the trees. No knowing what the future held. He only knew to keep running up the hill until they either won or he died.

When a cannonball exploded into the dirt fifty yards away, men and body parts flew into the air. Dense smoke rose from the hill ahead, and still the troops advanced. Alex's feet stumbled over the rough ground. Wiry grass grabbed his trousers as he passed. Sweat dripped into his eyes and down his chest. He pushed ahead with new energy. The ridge now within range, he fired his rifle. Reloaded and fired again.

Ahead, the color bearer, a boy barely sixteen, jerked, then sagged to his knees. The pole of his standard jammed into the earth and teetered for a moment, its colors drooping like the sleeve of an amputee as the boy's lifeless eyes sought heaven.

Alex rushed on toward men falling all around him. He wanted to tear off enemy heads, to stomp them to death to avenge the horror. He could see their blue uniforms. Their faces. Their guns. Without thinking, without fear, he reacted as trained. Returning fire. Reloading cartridges. Bullets and cannon fire came from everywhere. The coppery smell of blood filled his nostrils.

Then he heard the captain yell, "Retreat!"

As he turned back, a horrifying thought stopped him. *What if they shoot me in the back?* Again he faced the Bluecoats, this time walking backwards until out of their bullets' range.

That night, at camp, Alex and other survivors collapsed on the ground, their faces blackened with gunpowder. Overwhelmed with fatigue, Alex lay prone on the grass. He lifted his head to sip water from the tin cup Industrious held to his lips.

Industrious patted Alex's shoulder "I been prayin' for y'all, massa. Praise God, you're OK. Mr. Jacob, too!"

When the patting continued, Alex moved Industrious's hand aside and waved a tired arm at Jacob. His brother winked and grinned.

"I feel like the devil," Lester said, "aching all over."

"Who all got kilt besides the little color bearer?" Max asked in a flat voice.

"I saw Gerald and T. J. fall," one soldier reported, "but we lost way more'n that."

"I feel like I've been trampled by a bull," Lester said.

Alex rubbed his sore limbs. "Maybe this'll be the end of it."

"Hell, no," said a young recruit. "We'll get 'em tomorrow."

That night, Alex slept fitfully. His legs cramped with sharp pain. He turned on his side and massaged his calf. Through the silence, faint chimes of a clock in town struck three. He shifted into a more comfortable position and listened to his own breathing. The thump of his beating heart felt like the steps of marching men.

In a low voice, a messenger repeated at each tent, "Meeting in ten minutes."

Still dressed, Alex pulled on his socks and boots. Near the campfire's light, he stood next to Industrious and Jacob with the remnant of his company. Many wore bandages on wounds sustained in yesterday's battle.

Moonlight washed their ragged, filthy uniforms to their original gray. The captain stood before them, haggard as his men, unshaven, unwashed. "This time we'll make it through," he said, his voice deep with conviction and authority.

Alex wanted to believe the captain, needed to believe him. If it weren't true, his own death waited on the hill like the bodies from yesterday's battle.

The captain stared at Industrious. "I'll need you as a stretcher bearer today. Wait over there with the others." He pointed out a group waiting at the edge of the woods

Industrious hesitated and shot a look toward Alex. He saw wild terror in those eyes. Industrious had never been out in the thick of battle. Alex put his hand on Industrious's thick arm and felt it tremble. "It's my turn to protect you, Industrious. I'll be watching for you and keeping an eye out for the enemy."

Alex and Jacob took positions behind the stone wall. Soon after, General Lee rode through the lines. The men, instructed to remain quiet to conceal their location, didn't cheer but rose, removing their hats in reverent, silent devotion. The General seemed more worried than they'd seen him before. "Hold your positions, men," he said as he passed through the dawning light.

For the rest of the day, Alex and Jacob lay flat behind the wall, sweltering in the sun as bullets flew through the air inches above their heads. He looked back at Industrious waiting behind the line with the stretcher bearers. Forbidden to speak, Alex fidgeted, eager to get started again, to get it over with. Rivulets of sweat seeped from under Jacob's hat onto the limp collar of his shirt. He could tell from his brother's tight grip on the musket that they shared a common fear.

A year and a half of battles—Second Manassas, Fredericksburg, Chancellorsville—had taught Alex a hard lesson: kill or be killed. The first time he took aim at a man, his hands on the gun shook like a flag in the wind—pure luck another soldier's bullet hit true. Now, he could take a bead on a Bluecoat and squeeze off a round, cool and steady. He'd concocted a formula, however false it might be, that for each Yankee he shot, he earned another day of staying alive. Here he sat, war-hardened, battle-worn, another man entirely from the one who had pulled on his butternut jacket and gone to war.

When they finally received their orders, Alex crawled over the wall and advanced across the valley. Alex squinted through the smoke at the silhouette of trees and recognized the ridge they'd charged yesterday. As ordered, Alex fixed his bayonet and marched shoulder to shoulder with Jacob, in step with the men on his right and left as though performing a drill.

As far as Alex could see to his left, gray lines moved forward. The crunch of thousands of feet across the fields and the jangle of weapons beat a quick rhythm for their advance. Surely, this spectacle would inspire fear in the Yankees on the hill. Gaps appeared in the line. Alex kept his pace steady. The grim truth soon became clear—Yankees were picking off gray soldiers like birds on a rail fence. Screams of agony rose across the valley. Stretcher bearers hurried by to pick up the injured, rushed them back toward safety, and returned for more. Corpses, contorted into grotesque poses, littered the field.

Alex charged forward through relentless gunfire, smoke, and confusion. Alex became oblivious to his own body—feeling no hunger, no thirst, no fatigue. Violent energy charged through him.

Officers moved among the lines calling, "Halt! Close the gaps! Dress the line!"

A sudden realization burst through Alex's mind—*we've changed places.* At Manassas and Fredericksburg, the Yankees had sent in rank after rank against the Confederates' solid entrenchment. Not this time. Commanders were sending him and his fellow soldiers to be massacred. Alex stole a glance to his left and saw Jacob's determined profile. Just ahead, he recognized Industrious running in front of an empty stretcher. The crack of a rifle. Industrious fell. His heart lurched. Alex struggled to breathe. The captain yelled, "Retreat!"

Alex ran to Industrious and turned his head to the side, not sure whether his servant was breathing. Then, he felt the wide back move—

or did he? Around him the company retreated, falling back to safety. He tried to lift the big man. Dead weight. He gripped him under each arm and exerted all his effort. He only moved a few inches. He couldn't lift Industrious. The massive slave outweighed him by nearly half. And he couldn't drag him over the rough ground. The knot in Alex's stomach tightened and twisted. He'd promised Industrious he'd protect him. *How can I abandon him now?*

"Come on, man!" a passing rebel soldier tagged Alex's shoulder. "They're almost on us!"

Alex bent down and spoke into Industrious's ear. "I've got to go now. I don't want to, but I've got to." He kissed the back of Industrious's head and stood. "Please, God, let someone find him." He left Industrious lying in the dust of Gettysburg.

He reached the wall and leaned over to retch in dry heaves.

He later inquired of the ambulance drivers, but no one had seen his slave. Grief welled up inside him. He knew Industrious was dead. With no other choice available, Alex marched on.

The army began its retreat over the southern route they had traveled less than a week before. To Alex, the jubilant march northward seemed years past. The green fields, with their whitewashed fences and the heavy-branched cherry trees dripping rain, depressed him. Thoughts of Industrious brought sickening emptiness inside him. Memories of their childhood games, their pranks and jokes. Times when Industrious's simple but profound faith had lifted him out of despair. "When I's feelin' down, massa, I just try to imagine Jesus sittin' down beside me holdin' my hand." Alex couldn't talk about his sadness. No one could understand his grief over a slave. Too many men had lost friends or brothers.

The ragged troops around him, depleted by casualties and heads lowered in desolation, moved along the turnpikes toward Virginia headquarters. Families of sightseers rode out in carriages to witness the rebel retreat. Some women cried, showing tenderness—even sympathy—for the bedraggled men limping down the turnpike. Others raised eyebrows or even smiled. A few soldiers stopped to pose for photographers along the roadway.

Yankee sharpshooters hounded the retreating troops. Forced to defend themselves, the soldiers continued their retreat in a circuitous path, attempting to avoid further conflict. What should have been a six-week march extended to more than two months.

Arriving at camp at last, Alex struggled to compose a letter to Sarah about Industrious's death. The words looked clumsy and crude, unable to relay his sad message except in the same manner. After shredding two attempts, he'd wasted the only paper available. During the rest of his days in camp, he spent long hours between scanty meals playing checkers or cards with Lester and Max. At least the games drew him away from his depressing thoughts of the lost battle and of Industrious. When the notice of his furlough arrived, he scratched off a short note to Sarah on a borrowed scrap of paper. He decided to tell Hannah about Industrious in person when he went home in mid-February.

8

February 1864

The army had furloughed the men at different times. Most had already left and come back before Alex's turn came in mid-February. He wore his uniform, packed extra shirts and pants, and carried his gun and ammunition. Such items often disappeared in the owner's absence.

The first leg of his journey took him through Richmond, where he changed trains for a four-day ride through North Carolina, South Carolina, and Georgia. Many times during the trip, he took out a darkening daguerreotype of Sarah's face. His memory of her features had dimmed during the two years since he'd seen her. At the end of the line in Georgia, Florida soldiers had to march thirty miles to the train station in Madison. Sarah's last letter said she'd meet him there to ride the last miles of the trip to Lake City together.

He arrived at the station tired and dirty from walking and spotted her standing on the platform. She ran toward him, slim as a reed, her dress swirling in the wind. She wore a black wool cape and a bright yellow scarf draped around her neck.

With a joyous smile, she enclosed him in her arms. "Alex, is it really you?"

He nuzzled her hair and sniffed its sweet fragrance. Closing his eyes, he held her delicate face between his rough hands. He kissed her eyelids, the tip of her nose, each rosy cheek, and her soft lips. When he felt damp tears, he pressed her against his chest. "I thought I'd never see you again. So much, so many things have happened. I should have listened to you."

"Shh," she whispered. "We're together." She leaned her head against his shoulder and tightened her hold. "Our time is too short to talk about war. Let's pretend we live in a place where just you and I and our children can raise corn and cows, read books and play, and have plenty of milk and food."

"It's a pretty picture, Sarah." He tried to imagine the scene she described. Alex felt a knot in his stomach and lowered his head. "Do they remember me? They must have grown in these past two years."

Sarah nodded. "Tommy's seven—the girls, two and four. Mariah would have been ten next August."

He'd kept up with the ages, but in his memory they remained as he'd left them. "Little Sallie's already two! No more sickness?"

Sarah smiled. "The Lord has spared them all. He knows I couldn't bear to lose another."

"It must have been so hard for you," he mumbled into her hair.

Sarah cleared her throat and hesitated before she answered. "We miss you very much—but we're getting by."

He could tell she was holding back. He still remembered the letter about Sallie's illness, but she'd never complained about difficulties running the farm.

Sarah stood back a few inches. "I left the children with Hannah and Frances so we could spend a night together. We have a room at an inn. We'll leave for home tomorrow. I hope you're pleased."

He saw the question in her dark blue eyes. "How could I not be happy for such a gift? But how could you afford to pay for the room or the train tickets?"

"I saved back some money. I've been sewing for a few wealthy women in town."

He pulled back and rubbed his whiskery face. "I must look wretched."

"Dirty or clean, I'm happy to see you." He felt her hand on his ribs under his jacket. She pushed him away and frowned, studying him up and down. "Your coat is hanging off your shoulders and your pants are loose. You're as gaunt as a ghost, my poor darling. You need something to eat."

After a short walk, they entered an airy second-floor room. Thin, white curtains rustled in a cold breeze that seeped through the cracked window. The walls, covered with a pattern of tiny pink rosebuds, held daguerreotypes of solemn-faced women and men who may have been present or past owners of the hotel. Alex picked up the razor and clothes Sarah had brought for him from home and stepped behind a curtained area where a wall mirror hung over a table holding a wash bowl. When he came out, clean and shaved, Sarah sat on the bed with an opened picnic basket beside her. He sat down and removed the cloth from a plate of cold fried chicken, cheese slices, and deviled eggs. His stomach growled as he struggled not to seem hoggish.

Sarah chewed a small bite and set her chicken on her plate. "I suppose you left Industrious with Jacob."

He nodded, unable to answer with a mouth full of food.

When he finished his plate, she handed him her half-eaten food. "I've had enough. Please eat mine, too." After he'd cleaned the plate, she unwrapped two large slices of apple cake, his favorite.

Sarah sat on the side of the four-poster bed. She raised her chin and pointed her finger at his chest. "Take off your clothes."

"But I just put them on." He exhaled a stream of air in a blast. "Sarah . . . I . . . I don't want you pregnant again."

Sarah burst into laughter. "You crazy fool. I only want to see your feet, your chest, legs, and arms, and make sure you still have all your parts." She jumped off the bed and unbuttoned his shirt. He removed his pants and stood naked before her. She looked him over, up and down. She turned him around and checked him. "Except for calluses and a few blisters on your feet, you're unscathed. Not injured anywhere. I'm satisfied."

As he remembered his dead comrades, hundreds of walking-wounded amputees, and more hundreds stricken by disease, Alex recognized his good fortune. He also knew the guilt of the unscathed.

Sarah stretched out each of his arms, ran her fingers down his back and from behind him, touched his legs, and moved her hands up his torso.

He responded to her caress just as he always had. He lowered his eyes. "You may as well take your clothes off, my sweet. I can't stop now."

She'd never resisted his touch, unlike many women he'd heard about from friends and fellow soldiers—women who feared sex or found it distasteful. Her body arched against him, her breasts soft against his chest. Her fingers stroked the hair on the back of his neck.

Later, as they lay snuggled together, Sarah slept as contented as a child, Alex wide-eyed, alert, delighted in the touch of her warm, soft flesh against his body, memorizing the smell of clean sheets, pacing the rhythm of her even breaths, sinking into the softness of the pillow and mattress. He'd slept too long on hard dirt or sagging cots. He couldn't remember how many days, weeks, or months had passed since he'd slept in a real bed. He wanted to savor it now.

After a hearty breakfast at a café, Sarah and Alex hired a carriage from the inn to the train station. On the way, Sarah turned to Alex, freshly dressed in a clean uniform. "When we get to Lake City, let's gather the children and run away from this terrible war." She squeezed her hands into two small fists and tensed her shoulders. "I mean it, Alex; we could take a boat to Mexico or Cuba. Even Texas would be a better place to live."

Alex's mouth went dry as he remembered how close he'd come to being a deserter in Fredericksburg. He thought of traitors at Gettysburg who'd crossed to the enemy line when they were fighting face to face.

"Come over to the side of the Lord," the Bluecoats had taunted.

Alex had felt a strong impulse to surrender along with them. He paused before answering. "Running would be cowardly."

The conductor looked at their tickets. "Lake City." He paused. "We should be there in a couple of hours unless there's a delay."

"What kind of delay?" Sarah asked.

"Word came from Jacksonville that Union forces are marching west toward Lake City. We've got over a thousand soldiers on board heading to the area. They're fighting pretty near the town, last I heard."

"Alex, I'm frightened," Sarah said as they found their seats in the car. "What will the Yankees do? Board the train and take us hostage?" The train lurched forward toward the next station.

Alex scanned the other passengers. "Look around at the Confederate uniforms. You'll be well protected." He hoped to inspire confidence although his heart hammered against his chest.

Sarah straightened her skirt and adjusted to the narrow seat. "I can't help being scared. I've never been this far away from my children. Who will care for them if something happens to us?" She paused then frowned. "They may not even be safe at home. Alex? Alex!" She seemed near tears.

He leaned close to hear over the loud clacking of metal wheels against the rails and put his arm around her shoulders. "Relax; the Yanks are miles from here." He stood in the aisle. "There's a captain sitting up front. I'll see if I can find out what's going on." Swaying and grabbing the backs of seats along the way, Alex proceeded up the aisle toward the captain.

After a hasty conversation, he returned to his seat. "Here's what's happening. General Seymour's Union troops landed in Jacksonville three days ago and are marching west. They're close to Baldwin by now. We'll get to Lake City in a few hours, days before the Yankees could get there even in double-quick time. We'll have time to take the children to Cousin Arthur's house in Tampa."

A Confederate colonel entered the car from the rear and spoke in an authoritative voice. "Attention, please. You're all safe at this time. Now follow my instructions," the officer said. "All civilian passengers must disembark at Lake City."

Alex felt Sarah's fingers digging into his arm. Panic grew in her eyes. He patted her hand while he focused on the officer's voice.

"I'm herewith assigning all military to remain aboard after we stop in Lake City," the colonel read from a yellow sheet of paper. "You will continue to Olustee, where you will join General Finegan's reinforcements."

"Dear Lord in heaven, you'll have to go fight!" Tears trickled down her cheeks. "What about the children? How can they take you from them before you've even seen them?"

Alex didn't answer but squeezed her small hand. "Be strong, Sarah. Find a safe hideout for yourself and the children. If things get bad, Dad can take all of you to Tampa. Keep faith. I promise you; we'll turn the Yankees around in their tracks."

She clenched her teeth and nodded.

An hour later, the train began to slow. Sarah turned to Alex. "Hannah keeps asking about Industrious. Is he all right?"

He sucked a deep breath. "I'll be home in a few days. When this battle is over, I'll talk to her then." He was glad there was no more time for questions.

He watched her from the window. Sarah, red-eyed and tense, stood waving to him at the platform while the train gained momentum, blew its shrill whistle, and left her behind.

His thoughts turned to his early childhood. Whenever he anticipated a new battle, Alex calmed himself by retrieving early memories of warm summer days in Georgia, of sitting in his mother's lap, hunting with his father, swinging on a rope, and of leaping into the creek. The train's brakes screeched. Now, he would have to face a new and unknown battle.

"Off the train, off the train!" Officers herded enlisted men out the doors before the train had even stopped.

Alex picked up his weapon and leapt to the ground. He marched double-quick through late afternoon shadows with a line of Georgia Confederates. The soldiers entered a thick grove of pines that grew so close together their stubby limbs offered no support for climbing. A thick mat of golden brown pine needles muffled their footsteps. A sudden spate of gunfire erupted from behind the trees. Artillery boomed in the distance. "Take cover!" the captain shouted.

The men positioned themselves behind narrow pines, where they could search for the enemy hiding behind trees a hundred yards ahead. Alex took aim at a blue sleeve that appeared from behind a tree. Nearby, a rebel soldier screamed in pain as a shot hit his leg. Moving forward from tree to tree, rebels took cover behind a line of earthworks. Above, in the limbs of occasional live oaks, rebel sharpshooters fired at men ahead in the bluecoat line.

Acrid smoke filled Alex's nostrils and burned his eyes. When the captain gave orders, he climbed out of the trench into his position in a straight line with fifty or more men. He moved forward with the line of soldiers, their feet shuffling through pine straw. He entered a clear field, and less than five hundred feet ahead of him, he saw at least seventy-five men in dark blue uniforms with rifles and muskets aimed directly at him. His heart pounded as he forced his feet to step forward. Cannons erupted with deafening booms from behind the Yankee line while the Bluecoats' rifles cracked in rapid succession. The Confederate captain ran back and forth behind the line. He called out, "Fire, fire" again and again. One Yankee after another twisted to the ground, and as Alex reloaded, three rebels fell to the enemy bullets. Alex dropped back into the woods as another line of the killing machine took their place. Just as he took aim at a blue uniform in the left flank, a rebel sharpshooter's body dropped out of an oak tree onto the ground near him. He froze, his eyes fixed on thick red blood oozing from the soldier's chest, staining his tan shirt. *Will I never get accustomed to the sight?* Alex shifted to study the boy's youthful face. A surprised look around the eyes and mouth made him wonder what thoughts the bullet had forever interrupted. What would happen to his own thoughts if he died? His knowledge of animals, his ability to read and solve problems, his love of Sarah—erased forever or stored in another place?

A scant hundred yards across the way, Bluecoats made a move. Alex picked his target and fired, and a man fell sideways. His stomach clenched as he added one more to his list. He looked around for the men in his unit. *Where are they? Have they left me here alone?* In the lengthening evening shadows, black specters appeared. At Gettysburg, he'd seen Negro soldiers in the Union Army, but never this many nor this close. His hot breath dried his mouth. His tongue stuck to his cracked lips. *Dear God, is this it? Is this my time to die?* His mind jumped backwards to other battles he'd fought, to his lovemaking with Sarah in Madison. If he died here now, how would she know? A shiver rippled through his sweat-drenched body.

Blue-coated soldiers with menacing black faces moved toward him.

9

Well, Papa, I performed my maiden operation about three days ago. I amputated the upper third of thigh.

Cuvier Lipscomb
Cpl. CSA,
hospital steward,
letter to his father, 1864

February–March 1864

Hank's persistent barking awakened Sarah from deep sleep. Darkness outside obscured clues to the disturbance. She heard loud pounding. A woman's voice called her name. Sarah lit a lamp, hurried downstairs in her housecoat, and opened the door for Ruby, her neighbor.

Sarah had spent two restless nights at home after Alex left for Olustee. Still only half-awake, she hugged Ruby and brought her inside. "What's happening?"

Wide-eyed and breathless, Ruby settled in a chair. "Get dressed, Sarah. They need everyone downtown to tend wounded soldiers. A trainload of them unloaded a few hours ago."

Sarah shook her head, trying to grasp the situation. "What do you mean? What wounded soldiers? Where did they come from?"

"The Yankees attacked Olustee."

Sarah was awake now. "Of course. Alex went there two days ago. How many wounded?"

Ruby shook her head. "I really don't know. In the hundreds, I'd guess. They've asked everyone who's able to help tend their injuries. Mother and I have been up all night, but they sent me to find more help. I hope Frances can come, too?"

Sarah gasped. "Alex was . . . is . . . in that battle. Alex might be wounded . . . or dead."

Ruby stared into her eyes. "How can you *not* go?"

Sarah shook her head. "This is all such a shock, too much to understand . . . But . . . but of course, I'll go." She hugged her arms across her chest. "Frances, too. I'm sure she will."

Ruby took a breath. "They need bandages—old bed sheets, whatever you have."

"Anything else?"

Ruby shuddered. "Sharp knives and saws."

After Ruby left to recruit more nurses, Sarah wakened the family. She assigned Daddy John and Hannah to protect the children.

With a satchel full of sheets and a few implements, Sarah and Frances reached downtown within the hour. In the early dawn sunlight, a chaotic scene greeted them. Men and women carried stretchers holding men drenched in blood and scurried to find space for the wounded in one of the larger houses being used as a makeshift hospital. As they passed, Sarah searched from one patient to the other, looking for Alex. But in the dim light, she knew she'd never identify him among the bandaged men. Mr. Flint directed Frances to park the wagon and helped them carry their supplies into a house.

Screams and vile smells assaulted Sarah when she entered.

Inside, old Dr. Taylor, wearing a white apron saturated with blood, instructed his new volunteers. "You'll see both blue and gray uniforms here. Nonetheless, they all bleed red."

Faces tensed at the word "blue."

An agonized scream erupted from the back of the house.

Dr. Taylor continued. "We'll tend to the blue as kindly as we do our own boys."

Beds, tables, even the top of a grand piano provided operating space. In the dining room, a local carpenter in a bloody apron acted as surgeon. He dripped ether into a cloth-filled funnel covering the man's nose and mouth. Across the room, Emma and Addie, Sarah's acquaintances from church, wide-eyed and pale, watched the procedure, apparently waiting for instructions. The patient thrashed his head as he counted backward from twenty. His voice faded at sixteen. The carpenter looked up. "He's out." He instructed his nurses, "This man took a bullet in his limb. Pine trees protected their bodies but not arms and legs." He pointed to Sarah. "Mrs. Browning—you soak blood from the wound while I work." He told Frances to hold the man's arm still.

Holding a small towel, Sarah stood close as the carpenter-surgeon probed the bullet wound with a sharp, pointed instrument. Blood oozed around the metal tool. Sarah reached forward, but he stayed her with his left hand. "Not yet." He continued to probe—up, down, to either side. The patient's arm jerked from Frances's hold. "Grip that arm firm. I want him still." Frances's knuckles whitened as she pressed the man's wrist against the table. The carpenter probed again. "Found it! Give me that small knife." He slit the skin wide open. Sarah braced herself and blotted blood. Then, he inserted what he called an extractor. Seconds later, he lifted out the bullet, dripping blood down his arm. Emma dropped to the floor with a soft moan.

After the bloody metal clinked onto a plate, he handed an assistant a bottle of ammonia. "Hold it to her nose, then take her out of here. Give her something else to do."

Orderlies lifted the patient to a stretcher and then brought in another with bright red blood dripping from a thick layer of bandages on his leg. He screamed, "God save me! I'm dying . . . Can't stand this pain."

The carpenter clenched his teeth and unwound the bandages. A gaping, oozing wound appeared that was almost as large as the patient's leg. Blood pulsed from his thigh in a short fountain. "This one's bad. We'll amputate."

Nausea swept over Sarah. Just then a scripture came to mind: "Inasmuch as ye have done it unto one of the least of these my brethren, ye have done it unto me." Even as the scripture stilled her fear, she knew she'd twisted it with her own meaning. She was doing this for Alex.

"No . . . no!" the man yelled. "Don't take my leg!"

"Sorry, fellow, it's your leg or your life. Be thankful we still have ether."

Frances gripped the man's head as anesthetizing fumes filled his lungs.

His patient finally quiet and motionless, the surgeon quickly sliced through the soft thigh flesh and then sawed through the bone. An orderly threw the amputated leg outside the back door as though it were a cow bone. By the time he returned, the carpenter had tied off two blood vessels. From the stump, he extracted one vessel at a time with a sharp, hooked instrument then tied each one off with catgut. After smoothing the femur's rough edges with a rasp, he sutured the skin over the stump. The orderlies lifted the man onto a stretcher.

The surgeon dipped his hands into a bowl and shook reddish water off his fingers. He nodded at Sarah and Frances. "If I hadn't smoothed it, that rough bone would have given that poor fellow terrible pain later."

The next patient lay still. The surgeon briefly probed his massive chest wound and covered the man's face with a piece of a sheet. "Take this one to the cemetery."

One after another, wounded patients were brought in. Some were treated; others were already dead. The grim images she had witnessed that day followed Sarah home that night, disturbing her thoughts and keeping her awake for several hours before she could sleep.

The next morning, Sarah, her muscles aching from tension, reported again to the house. Although sick with worry about Alex, she focused her mind on her job in the "hospital." Her heart reached out to each injured man as though he were Alex. She prayed that if he were injured, someone would care for her husband as she had for these others.

Emma opened the door. "They assigned me to running errands and visitation. I can't stand to watch the operations." A horrendous scream pierced the air. Emma winced and shuddered. "They ran out of anesthetic last night."

Sarah patted Emma's arm and returned to the dining room, where the carpenter-surgeon was extracting a bullet from a patient's calf. After he examined the next patient, he prepared for another amputation. Patient after patient lay on the dining table with Sarah assisting as she could.

When the day finally ended, Dr. Taylor entered the room. "Good news. We've finished the surgeries. Now, we must care for these men until they're able to go home, back to the army, to a hospital or . . ."

In her mind Sarah finished the sentence. "Or until they die."

"You ladies can still help—changing bandages, writing letters, or reading to them."

Sarah stepped forward to volunteer. If she visited every patient during the next week, perhaps one of them would remember Alex. *Maybe he's even here.*

The next day, she started at another home volunteered as a temporary hospital. She looked at the soldiers' faces in each room. "Did you meet a Florida soldier named Alex Browning?" she'd ask. No one had heard of him. She didn't expect to find him easily since he'd been recruited on the train into a company of men he'd never met.

At the next house, a boy of about sixteen lay moaning, unattended. "What can I do for you?" Sarah asked.

He groaned and closed his eyes. A vile odor overwhelmed her when she lifted the blanket covering his legs. The black skin above the bandage indicated that gangrene had already set in. "A letter. In my haversack. Over yonder." His halting words told her his pain was intense.

When she located the letter, he lifted his arm and pointed to it.

"Do you want to see it?"

He shook his head and pointed to Sarah.

"You want me to read it to you?"

A faint smile crossed his lips and he nodded.

Sarah began reading:

> My dearest darling William,
>
> Since your daddy died, you and Clement fill my heart with more love than I can tell you. I pray every day that you won't meet your brother face to face in a battle. Last I heard, Clement was fighting with General Sherman in Georgia. Take care of yourself, William. What would I do without my brave boys? I ask God to end this terrible war and bring you back home to me.

Sarah stopped and looked at William, his face peaceful and still. She felt for a pulse in his wrist and reported another death.

A commotion outside took Sarah to the door. Shouting and waving Confederate flags, a group of men and women marched down Lake City's Main Street. Her heart quickened. *Is the war over?* "The South beat the Yankees at Olustee," someone shouted.

After a few weeks, all but a small number of the patients had left Lake City, along with the need for hospital volunteers. When they'd gone, Sarah felt bereft. If Alex were wounded, she'd have found him, but still the possibility of his death haunted her. Since he was a stranger to the officers in Olustee, they wouldn't have known his name. *What if they buried him? I'll never find him.* Sarah stayed busy with the children and tasks around the farm, but her unanswered questions disturbed her thoughts and sleep.

A month after the battle, Daddy John brought in a letter from Alex. Her hand trembled so much she could barely open it. She flattened the letter on the table in front of her. The children, Frances, Daddy John, and Hannah hovered over her. "Read it. Read it to us, Mama."

Winter camp, March 4, 1864

My dear sweet Sarah, Dad, Sister, and children,

I know you've been worried sick, not knowing what happened to me at Olustee. At one point, I thought sure I'd be dead. I got separated from my men and the Yankees started coming at me. But at that very moment, like an act of God, I heard a train behind me gaining speed and saw a Confederate general, standing behind an enormous cannon on a railroad flatcar, blasting shots at the Union soldiers every five minutes. Then another miracle—the enemy retreated, a few at first, then in large numbers, heading east. An officer on horseback rode up hollering, "Hold fire, men. We've stopped them."

After the victory, I thought they'd let me finish my furlough. I planned to take the train back to Lake City to be with you all. But the train kept on going past Lake City, carrying me non-stop to Madison. We marched back to Georgia. It was a long train ride to camp. Which is where I am now.

I've got something real bad to tell you, Sarah. I've tried at least a dozen times to write. But couldn't find the right words. Intended to tell you during the furlough, but didn't want to spoil our time together. Then thought I'd tell you after the battle when I got home.

Sarah looked up at the faces huddled around her, their eyes wide in anticipation of what she'd read next. Sarah turned the page over and read the last words to herself.

Tommy's voice interrupted her reading. "What did he say, Mama?"

Frances moved closer and looked over's Sarah's shoulder. "What is it?"

Sarah crushed the letter to her chest. "I'll tell you about it later." She hurried to her bedroom and shut the door.

10

In the present civil war it is quite possible that God's purpose is something different from the purpose of either party.

Abraham Lincoln

March–May 1864

Sarah read Alex's terrible words again. "I lost Industrious at Gettysburg." Her stomach churned, and heavy sadness enveloped her. She'd always imagined Industrious and Alex marching home together, rejoining the family—whole again as before. She walked back into the hall, the ordeal of telling Hannah looming before her.

Hannah was working alone in the kitchen when Sarah opened the door. As Hannah mopped the varnished hardwood floor, Sarah touched her shoulder. "Sit down, Hannah." She motioned toward two chairs pushed against the whitewashed kitchen wall.

Hannah hesitated.

Sarah swallowed. *How can I do this?* "It's all right. Sit down."

Hannah lowered herself into the chair, her eyes fixed on Sarah's tense face.

Sarah placed her hands on Hannah's plump brown arm. "Mr. Alex told me he lost Industrious."

Hannah looked confused. "How could he *lose* Dustrous, big as he is?"

She couldn't soften the message any longer. "What he meant was—Industrious got shot down."

Hannah sat frozen in shock. "Dustrous dead? My Dustrous dead? No, no, can't be, I'd a knowed it. Him and me know these things when one of us is in trouble."

Sarah stood and opened her arms. Hannah hugged her and leaned her head against Sarah's shoulder. "How come you make him go off? Dustrous didn't never do anyone no harm. He didn't know nothin' 'bout war. He could a stayed here helping you out on the farm." Then, she sat down again and laid her head on her arms. A high moaning sound like the saddest song filled the room.

Sarah ached with guilt. *Will Hannah ever forgive me for sending Industrious with Alex?* She sat grieving beside her until Hannah finally dried her face on her apron and walked out the door toward her cabin.

Early on a Sunday morning in May, Sarah stood on the front porch. The air carried the heavy sweetness of honeysuckle blooms that clung to the picket fence. At that moment, the bubbling of the creek outside the fence sounded more like sobbing.

Sarah made her way across the bridge and through wet grass toward the barn, her lantern lighting the path. The barn door squeaked open to her push, releasing strong scents from within. Boards groaned as two horses shifted their weight against the stalls. Sarah entered Chloe's milking stall, removed the bucket from a nail, and set it under the cow. Chloe chewed hay as Sarah massaged milk from the udder in a feeble stream. She lifted the lantern above the half-filled bucket. Awaiting the usual drop of milk Sarah no longer dared to waste, Betsy mewed pitifully.

Sarah directed her disappointment at the cow. "Not enough, Chloe. You were my last hope—the only one that hasn't dried up. Now you're giving out. It's time to get serviced."

Too bad womenfolk couldn't be certain of their fertile time. She'd read women's manuals but didn't trust the information. One book claimed that the only safe time fell two weeks after a menstrual cycle. The last time she'd seen her monthly bleeding was in February, just before she'd met Alex in Madison. She counted on her fingers—March, April, May—a sure sign. Most women she knew dreaded pregnancy and feared the dangers it posed. She nurtured the new life inside her. The realization brought Sarah a vitality she'd not felt since the war began. Yet, the uncertain future brought a shiver of fear. God had protected her thus far, but she knew of many women who had died of childbirth.

Sarah walked carefully over the bridge that crossed Alligator Creek with the cats rubbing against her ankles. In the pre-dawn light, she recognized the motionless form of the old alligator, Agothos, on the opposite bank of the stream. The creek split the land into two large triangles. The cattle and the barn occupied the land west of the creek; the cornfields, gardens, and orchards filled the area behind the house to the east. Leaving the stone walkway, Sarah followed a dirt path to the kitchen beside the house.

Hannah, a kerchief wrapped around her bushy hair, stood at the kitchen door. Her brown face perspired in the heat, and her fists disappeared in the folds of her hips. She took the milk pail from Sarah and frowned at its meager offering. "This here milk won't last your children two days, Miss Sarah."

"I know, Hannah, I'm taking Chloe and the other cows out to see the bull this afternoon."

"Hell's bells, Miss Sarah. That old bull couldn't mount a runt nanny goat. Looks to me like it's time that old boy got turned into some beef steaks."

Sarah smiled. For the first time since she'd learned of Industrious's death, Hannah joked as she did before. "You're right, Hannah. I'll talk to Mr. Winston about taking our cows over to his place. Maybe he won't charge us too much to use his bull."

"Shoulda done that six months ago."

Sarah sighed and left the kitchen. While Hannah cooked breakfast, Sarah went upstairs to the children's room and gathered her sleepy brood for their Sunday morning family devotional. She sat the three children in chairs around the oak table in the center of the sitting room.

Already in his usual spot, John Browning, looking all of his sixty-three years, doctored his "ersatz coffee" brewed from roasted corn meal. He poured a drop of milk into his cup and sweetened the bitter brew with a heaping spoon of wild honey. "This coffee tastes like . . . "

Sarah interrupted. "Careful, Daddy John. The children are listening."

Frances dipped a wad of snuff into her cheek. "I guess we're lucky to have what we have, Papa. At least, we're not starving like some folks who don't have a farm." She gave the lump below her lip a poke with the stick.

Sarah lugged the huge family Bible from its stand and laid it before her on the table. "Would you like to lead the service, Daddy John?"

He took a sip of his coffee. "No, Missy. You do it. You're the head of this household."

Sarah cleared her throat to signal the beginning of the devotional. "Let's begin with the Lord's Prayer, 'Our Father which art in heaven . . .'"

At the "amen," Megan McLoughlin, Sarah's boarder, crossed herself and bowed her head. Dressed for Mass in a black cotton skirt and a white high-necked blouse, her bright red hair tied back under a white bonnet, she slipped into a seat between Tommy and John.

Frances frowned. "Why don't we just attend services at the Lake City church instead of going through this family-worship rigamarole every Sunday morning?"

John swatted a bee that lit on the edge of the table. "Because Sarah doesn't like the preacher's sermons,"

"You shouldn't have done that, Daddy," Frances said. "A bee in the house is a sign a visitor's coming. If you kill it, the visitor will be disagreeable."

"Nonsense!" John said. "Let Sarah get back to her church service."

Sarah looked over at Tommy. With eyes squeezed shut and hands under his chin, he seemed to be praying already. "What are you praying for, son?"

"I want God to bring my daddy back home."

"We all want that, Tommy," Sarah said gently, "but before we ask God for anything, let's begin by thanking Him for our blessings. Would you start the thanksgiving, Frances?"

"Thank you, Lord, that the blue bellies haven't invaded our town."

Daddy John cleared his throat. "We praise your name that we haven't gotten sick this year."

Megan crossed herself. "Thank you, Father, precious Lord Jesus Christ, and Mary the Mother of God, for these lovely people who have taken me in although I'm from a different country and a different church."

Sarah turned to her son. "Tommy?"

"I thank you, dear God, for our food and clothes and for our Mama and Daddy John and Aunt Franny." He paused and lifted his eyes. "And thank you for loving us and sending us Jesus."

Her son often amazed her with spiritual wisdom far beyond his seven years.

When two-year-old Sallie began to whimper, Sarah set the child in her lap. She continued the prayers. "We give our thanks for bringing us Megan, who taught us the goodness of those who help little children to learn."

Frances smiled. "And she also brought us that good Irish tea from Boston."

"I thank you for each of my precious children," Sarah continued, "for Hannah whose help I couldn't do without, for our food, our health, our lives, and most of all, the gift of your Son Jesus Christ." She paused. "Now let us confess our sins."

"I hate this part." Four-year-old Lula pouted.

"Lula, why don't you begin?" Sarah said.

"Do I have to?"

Sarah narrowed her eyes.

"OK, then. I'm sorry I told on Tommy yesterday."

Tommy frowned at his sister. "What did I do?"

"Shh." Sarah put her arms around both.

Megan began her confession. "I'm having great difficulty forgiving my enemies—those dreadful school boys who hoot and call me terrible names because I'm from the North."

Sarah prayed for Megan's perseverance, that she wouldn't leave town because of such rudeness. Sarah had seen citizens deliberately run their carriages through puddles to splash mud on Megan.

"That commandment, love your enemy, gives me a heap of trouble, too." John said.

Lula gave a loud squeal.

Sarah glared at Tommy, sitting next to his sister. "OK, then, young man. It's your turn."

Tommy bit his lip. "I'm sorry I pinched my baby sister—but I promise I didn't pinch her hard."

Lula lifted her chin. "I'm not a baby!"

Sarah raised her eyebrows, questioning her earlier thoughts about Tommy. She sighed. "We may now tell the Lord of our needs, which he knows before we ask. Frances, will you begin? "

Frances spat a stream of tobacco into a tin cup. "Lord, we ask that you protect Alex and Jacob from the guns of our wicked enemy."

Megan's green eyes clouded.

Sarah gave her an embarrassed smile but said nothing. She turned to her son. "Tommy, I know you have something you want to ask for."

Tommy folded his hands in a steeple under his chin. "Lord, please, please, let my daddy come home soon. Keep him safe."

Megan cleared her throat, "Precious Lord, we pray that this bloody war will end and that all Americans will someday live in peace with one another."

"I pray for this family," John said, "that we can live through this war with food and clothing and money enough to keep our house and farm. Give us strength to do the work if our field hands leave us. I pray that the sick cows will get well and that the others won't catch it."

Lula folded her hands under her chin. "Dear God, I'd really like a new dolly."

Hannah brought Sallie back to her seat at the table and put a biscuit in front of her.

Sarah sighed and bowed her head. "Lord, you have heard our honest prayers. Bless this family, keep Alex and Jacob safe, and, Lord, I offer a special prayer for a new baby I'm carrying now. Let it be born safely and give me the wisdom to raise my child to become a Christian with a loving heart in a world full of hate and bloodshed."

Frances gasped, "My God, Sarah. You're expecting another one?"

Sarah smiled, "The Lord has blessed me once again, Franny."

"It was that trip to Madison. If you'd stayed home like I told you, it wouldn't have happened. Didn't you take precautions?"

Sarah knew what "precautions" Frances referred to. With a twinge of embarrassment, she remembered how Frances had passed on her advice about using vinegar after Sarah's third child was born. But Sarah had misunderstood. For several weeks, she'd drunk a full cup of vinegar each time she and Alex had intimate relations. Sarah complained to her sister-in-law when the bitter liquid caused severe vomiting. Too amused to offer sympathy, Frances had laughed and then explained how to make a vinegar douche.

Sarah bit her lip. "Since I lost my darling Mariah to whooping cough, I'm grateful for each child and each pregnancy." Even the briefest thought of Mariah brought a lump to her throat. Her voice quavered. "Enough talk, now. Our breakfast is ready." She bowed her head. "Thank you, Lord, for the food we're about to partake of. Amen."

Hannah walked through the door and dipped out bowls of corn meal mush she'd prepared in the outside kitchen. She laid a piece of bacon on top of each and placed biscuits and orange slices on a platter in the center of the table. Just as they began eating, someone knocked on the back door. When Sarah opened the door for Jacob's wife, she tried to quell the annoyance she always felt when she saw Margaret.

Dressed in her finest pre-war silk, Margaret gave a sour-faced glance at the adults in their work clothes and the children in pajamas. "Everyone's been asking about you. We've been missing you in services."

Sarah stiffened. "Brother Deihart frightens the children with his ranting about the devil. We have family services here."

Margaret gazed upward. "I hope the Lord understands." She dropped her head and began trying to unbutton her reticule. She removed an envelope. "I received this letter from Jacob yesterday. He mentioned Alex. I also brought a paper from Charleston." She took the newspaper from under her arm.

Sarah smiled, ashamed of her ill feelings. "You're very kind, Margaret. Won't you sit down? Megan brought us some tea. Would you like some?"

Margaret stiffened. "I'll leave the letter and the newspaper, but I'm not sitting at the table with that—*Yankee* woman." She tipped her head toward Megan. "And I'm certainly not drinking her tea. I'd rather starve, thank you very much."

"Stop it, Margaret," Sarah said, eyes blazing. "Megan is a friend, a guest in our home."

Margaret sneered, "Well, pardon me—and all this time I thought she was paying rent." Margaret slapped the newspaper and letter on the table and walked away, slamming the door behind her.

Tears welled in Megan's eyes. Sarah reached across the table and took the girl's hand. "I'm so sorry."

"No, I'm sorry I'm causing trouble in your family," Megan said. "I try to understand because my friends in Boston aren't fond of southerners, either."

"Just what faults do those high-falooting Yankees find in us?" Frances spat tobacco juice from her snuff into her cup.

Megan didn't answer. John got up and walked out on the porch.

Sarah gripped the edge of the table, her fingers white with tension. "OK, let's eat our breakfast and stay quiet for a few minutes while we all cool off."

"I'm leaving for Mass now," Megan said. She brushed by Sarah's chair and touched her extended hand on the way out.

They ate in hostile silence. Sarah sipped her tea in an attempt to dislodge a dry lump of biscuit that had filled her throat. She covered her lips with a napkin and left the table for her bedroom, where she coughed the sticky wad into a clean chamber pot. A light tap on the side of the open door caused her to turn.

Frances came in. "Are you feeling ill, darling?"

Sarah sat down on the bed. "Oh, Franny, I'm making such a mess of things." She squeezed her arms across her chest and rocked back and forth. "I try to conduct a proper religious service, and the children misbehave. Then everyone starts trading insults. Why can't we worship without arguing? What did I do wrong?"

Frances sat beside Sarah and hugged her. "Sweet Sarah, no one tries harder than you." She paused. "Why are you so critical of yourself? You're managing the farm, keeping the children clothed and fed, even putting back some money—working from sunup to sundown. But . . ."

Sarah's eyes watered. "But what?"

Frances paused and looked at the ceiling. "I don't want you to take this the wrong way."

"Tell me."

"Well, sometimes, you try to bend everyone to your own peculiar views." Frances continued talking as she circled the room, looking behind the furniture for something. "The rest of us look at the world as black and white, but you see it in shades of gray." She folded her arms across her breast. "It's us and ours against them and theirs. We're in a war, honey, struggling for our very existence."

Sarah gulped and looked down at her hands, her fingers interlaced in a tight grip. "I can't help it, Franny. It's always been either my gift or my curse to see the good in people's hearts and to try to understand why they do things and say things, whether they're on our side or not. Like when we tended the Yankee soldiers. That doesn't mean I like everything about people. For instance, I love you like the older sister I never had, but I really hate that snuff you dip."

Frances laughed and reached for the chamber pot to spit a stream of tobacco juice. She looked down into the pot. "What is that disgusting white glob? I hope it didn't come out of you."

"It's my biscuit, Franny." Sarah sighed. "Do you think I should quit trying to have Sunday devotions?"

Frances shook her head. "You know, that's just one job you may have to leave up to the Lord and the good old church down the street. You can't change other folks' convictions about the war, at least not for now. Maybe someday the wolf shall dwell with the lamb and we'll beat our swords into plowshares, but not yet, my sweet. Not yet. The children are too young and the old folks are too stubborn."

"So you think we should go back to attending the services?" She squeezed her hands into fists and beat them against her thighs. "Brother Elias makes me so angry when he starts talking about how God's on our side! As though God planned the war for His own purposes." Sarah sneezed.

"God bless you," Frances said.

Sarah laughed. "Do you think I have the devil in me?"

"Better to be safe than sorry." Frances lifted her chin. "Don't laugh. You saw what happened after Daddy killed that bee."

Smiling at Frances, Sarah shook her head.

Frances patted her shoulder. "Let's go back to the table now and read the letter from Jacob."

Sarah nodded and followed Frances downstairs to the sitting room. Sarah sat in her chair, slid the letter out of its open envelope, and began to read:

My dearest wife Margaret,

I hope this letter finds you well and not suffering. I was relieved to hear from Alex that our boys in Olustee turned the Yanks on their tails, and you won't have any fighting in Lake City. We're now camped in Verdiersville. We'll march tomorrow to join the Southern troops in the Wilderness. Our spirits are high. We should reach them in time to save the day and give the Yanks another whipping. Such be the case, we'll be home soon. But before each battle all of us pray He will take care of our families if we don't survive the enemy's fire. Alex is also writing Sarah a letter. If I don't return, please know that I'll love you always and we'll meet again some day in heaven.

Your dear loving husband,
Jacob

"Did you get a letter from Alex?" Frances asked.

"Not yet," Sarah said, "but often it takes several weeks before the letters get here from Virginia."

Sarah studied Hannah, her watery eyes, her fidgety hands. She rose and circled an arm around Hannah's shoulders. Sarah recognized a strong connection with Hannah's grief for her husband and her own fear for Alex's life. Sarah kissed Hannah's forehead.

Hannah unclasped her hands and put an arm around Sarah's waist, tears spilling from her eyes.

"Let's see what the *Charleston Courier* says about the battle," Frances said. She adjusted her glasses and ran her index finger down the front page and read. "Latest from the Battle Field: General Lee's Dispatch from Spotsylvania Court House."

John leaned forward. "Read us what General Lee said."

Frances squinted at the small print on the page, "He wrote a letter to the paper. 'After a sharp encounter, Gen. R. H. Anderson with the advance of the army repulsed the enemy with heavy slaughter, and took possession of the Court House. I'm the more grateful to the Giver of All Victories that our loss is small, signed: R. E. Lee, General."

"Where's Spotsylvania?" Tommy asked.

"Let's find the map in the newspaper." She turned several pages. "Yes, here's one." She laid the open paper flat on the table. With a dinner knife, she pointed to the area where Alex had camped and moved the knife to an area labeled "Wilderness," then right to a tiny dot called Spotsylvania. "Look how close it is to where Jacob said they were going. I feel certain they were there and helped General Lee win the battle of Spotsylvania."

All of them nodded in agreement, though their faces held concern. Even a victory costs lives.

11

We went to the wilderness in Va. There we had orders to stand dead or alive.

Alexander Browning
Cpl CSA,
letter to Board of Pensions,
1910

May 6–12, 1864

A spring breeze gusted through the tent flap, chilling Alex's bare chest. Startled, Alex opened his eyes. Above him, his brother Jacob stood fanning him with his blanket. "Happy birthday! It's May 6, 1864. How old are you now, old man?"

Alex shook off heavy sleep. "Older than the hills but not as old as you. Thanks, though, for remembering." *Thirty years old today and lucky to be alive!* "Do you think the captain will give me a day off?" He smiled at his own joke.

Jacob rolled his eyes.

Alex threw his legs off the cot and, by a lantern's dim light, pulled boots over his smelly socks. "What's for breakfast? Ham and eggs?"

"Brother, you're spoiled rotten. But I forget; you were Mama's favorite. She always made your special food on your special day. See you at mess." Jacob bent his head and walked through the tent opening.

Alex put on his butternut jacket, now with corporal chevrons roughly sewn on the shoulders. He removed the bowl, cup, and spoon from his haversack and walked into the early morning darkness. Lured by the smell of fresh coffee and hot bacon, he grouped with his company around the skillet wagons.

The cook filled their bowls with corn meal mush topped with a small chunk of bacon. "We've got real coffee today, lads. Captain ordered it special since we'll be on the march all day."

Alex took his food and sat on a log. The air smelled of fertile earth and spring flowers. Barely visible in the lights of the campfire, a road meandered into a dark meadow toward a place known only as the Wilderness. The Orange Plank Road, a narrow track with a wooden strip down the middle, spanned the distance between Orange and Fredericksburg.

Alex caressed the smooth, flat penny still in his trouser pocket and hoped it would bring him good luck in the new battle they were facing. He joined thousands of soldiers lined in columns for the march, haversacks packed with rations and muskets and rifles on their shoulders. The band played a merry tune as they proceeded northeast along the plank road, which grew narrower as they approached the dense woods. A small, dark stream with steep embankments soaked the soil into swamps matted with bushes.

Alex stayed next to Jacob on the long marches. He felt responsible for his brother and knew Jacob felt the same responsibility for him.

"What do you think this will be, Alex?" Jacob asked.

"It couldn't be worse than what we went through at Gettysburg. General Lee knows what he's doing."

"Have you heard from Sarah?"

"Yeah, I got a letter at Verdiersville. She told me she might be having another baby."

"Again? Good heavens!"

Alex ignored the jibe. "It's hard for Sarah with three children, even with Hannah and Frances helping. I missed the birthing of the last one, and who knows where I'll be when this one's born?" He pressed the lucky penny. The next battle might give him opportunity to prove himself.

"You didn't have to join up," Jacob said. "You know you'd rather be out here marching than working on the farm."

Alex wondered if he'd have made the same choice knowing what he did now. Memories of his farm, his family, even his sweet Sarah paled in the too-familiar, sickening sights, smells, and sounds that had become his normal life.

The division chaplain moved into the line and put his hand on Alex's shoulder. "You look worried, Alex. Can I help?"

He couldn't recall even one of the hundreds of questions he'd wanted to discuss with the chaplain. Alex shrugged.

"What about your soul, Alex?"

Such questions made him squirm. "I don't know. I guess we're all going to hell for our killing, if the Bible's any truth."

"A man who does his duty can't be judged for obeying orders."

"You think there's a difference? I don't feel anything. I used to feel more sympathy for my cows than I do for those Yankees. I think the devil may have got my soul."

The chaplain remained silent for a moment. "The Lord loves an honest man. Do you have a Bible, son?"

Remembering the Bible Sarah had packed in his haversack, Alex nodded.

The chaplain handed Alex a small slip of paper. "Here's a verse for you to read."

Alex stuffed the paper in his pocket.

By early afternoon, the soldiers met up with another Confederate division resting at the crossroads. Alex, Jacob, and his hometown friends took seats by the road. A sergeant from another company joined the group. "Mind if I sit down?"

"Hey, Sergeant," Alex said. "Tell us what you know. We heard about a terrible fight over here."

"It's been an enormous ordeal." The sergeant pointed to the thick woods across the road.

Alex stared at the twisted trees clumped so closely that shadows between them were dark as night. Vines tangled between dense growth.

"Those trees stretch back for miles with Yankee soldiers hiding all through them. Our soldiers couldn't form lines or even see in there. Couldn't tell who the enemy was. Mostly, we were shooting blind. In spite of that, our men had just about claimed a win. When General Longstreet got shot, they ordered the men to pull back."

"Is he dead?" Alex asked.

"He'll recover, but it'll take hours to replace him and to reorganize these men into attack positions. The Yanks are still in there—and some of our wounded, too. You just can't see 'em for the trees. Don't even think about crossing the road. You'd never come out of there alive."

At sunset, the men camped by the roadside and took out their rations. Between bites of food, everyone stared across the road, where smoldering coals lit the forest with an eerie glow. A sudden wind gusted and torched the embers into blazing fires. Alex watched, stunned with horror as dried trunks of pine trees burst into flame. Wounded men screamed as the fire trapped and engulfed them in sure, gruesome death. Popping sounds punctuated their moans when cartridge boxes in their pockets exploded. Alex recognized the odor of burning flesh. A wave of nausea swept over him.

The division chaplain stood before the group and sang out in a clear baritone voice, "Though like the wanderer, the sun gone down, darkness be over me, my rest a stone. Yet, in my dreams I'd be nearer, my God, to Thee." A few deep voices joined in; then fifty, one hundred, and more than a thousand sang the words. Some voices from the Northern camp across the road echoed, "Nearer, my God, to Thee, nearer to Thee!" Alex bowed his head. *How can God allow such horror?*

Later that night, word passed from rear to frontlines that Grant was on the march.

A wide grin smeared Jacob's face. "Hey. We scared 'em off. They're running home with their tails dragging."

A weary soldier next to him spoke. "The captain said Grant's army is headed southeast, not north."

"What does that mean?" Alex asked.

The company captain moved up beside him. "It means they're marching for Richmond. We've got to head them off. Get your butts moving."

Alex grabbed his haversack and weapons and ran to catch up with his company. After the first mile, his lungs burned and his side ached from the running.

"Come on, brother," Jacob said. "We gotta hurry if we're gonna catch 'em."

A few hours after dawn, they dropped into one of several hastily built trenches that guarded the tiny settlement of Spotsylvania Court House, located on the direct route to Richmond.

In the dark of the night, Alex stood watch in the U-shaped entrenchments called the "mule shoe." He stared through an opening in a log barricade into an opaque forest. A loamy fragrance filled his nostrils. His feet, swollen from over a hundred miles of marching, pressed against the inside of his boots. His body ached with fatigue. He craved sleep but dared not shut his scratchy eyes. Lester, rifle aimed and ready, stood on his right and Jacob on his left. The quiet woods around him lacked birdcalls or even wind in the trees.

That afternoon, the captain had crawled into the ditch next to Alex and Jacob. "Get ready for a scouting expedition." He explained the information he wanted them to gather. "Calvary can't get through the woods without causing a commotion. Be careful!" He gave them a hand-drawn map.

Alex listened closely, proud to be chosen for such responsibility. A few minutes later, the map tucked in his pocket, he and Jacob crawled out of the trench. They moved past the pickets and plunged into thick undergrowth where stunted pines grew intertwined with vines and creepers. After a mile or so, the musty odor of moss-covered ground rose from a riverbank. They followed its twists and turns to a road shown on their map as leading to Fredericksburg.

Alex stiffened his arm against Jacob's chest. "Shh."

Jacob halted, sniffing as though trying to catch the enemy's scent.

Alex spotted wagons lumbering up the road toward them and yanked Jacob down behind a clump of bushes. A blue-coated cavalry leading a wagon train rumbled past a few hundred yards away going northeast.

"Looks like the federals are moving out." Jacob's voice sounded hopeful.

They stayed hidden until the wagons passed. Alex reached inside his trouser pocket. He felt the folded map, but he didn't feel his lucky penny. He dug deeper and pushed a finger through a small hole. He shrugged it off. How much luck could a penny bring, anyway? But he wished he still had it.

"Let's go back to the river," Alex said. Staying within the shadows of the trees, they crept back toward their entrenchment. Sounds of movement in the woods stopped Alex.

"What's happening?" Jacob whispered.

"I can't see anything, but it sounds like troops moving near our right flank."

Jacob paused. "I hear metal clanking—probably men with guns. Do you think it could be our own men?"

Alex unfolded the map. "We should be about here." He pointed to a spot on the map. "The sounds are coming from over there."

They returned to camp and reported the Yankee wagon train headed northeast and possible troop movement near the right flank. As the sun set, Confederate soldiers hitched horses to the twenty-two guns that guarded their forward position.

Settled next to Alex in the trench, Jacob whispered, "I hope we were right about Grant's move. If they attack us now with the artillery gone, we're dead."

Alex didn't answer, worried their report might have given insufficient information. Could the wagons they spotted have been ambulances carrying Yankee wounded to Fredericksburg? Would the Yankees attack the apex of the "mule shoe" again as they did two days ago? The guns had definitely run them off then. How could soldiers armed only with rifles and bayonets defend the trenches against a large attack? Bone tired and worried, Alex dropped into fitful sleep.

Raindrops tapping on the stiff canvas tarpaulin wrapped around him gave him a start. He pushed up to sitting position and shoved his cover back. Mud from the sides of the trench oozed through his jacket.

Someone whispered, "Alex, they're out there."

Alex struggled into wakefulness. "Who's out there?"

"Can't you hear them?"

Alex strained to filter out sounds of rain, wind blowing, men grunting and wheezing. "I hear something, but it's probably thunder."

Jacob leaned closer. "It's not thunder. Something out there is moving."

Alex held his breath, his heart thumping like a jackrabbit's leg. "It can't be. We saw them leaving this afternoon."

Jacob coughed and cleared his throat. "We *thought* we saw them. I think we'd better pray."

Alex began with a shaky voice. "Yea, though I walk through the valley of the shadow of death."

Jacob loaded his rifle. "I will fear no evil." The rain turned to mist and the woods became still as a dead man.

Seconds later, Jacob hissed, "Someone's marching toward us."

Alex tightened his grip on his rifle and focused his attention to faint sounds from the woods.

The drizzle became pelting rain, plastering Alex's hair to his head and streaming down his forehead into his eyes. The rumble before him now sounded like a roaring steam locomotive, but he'd known battles enough to recognize the sound. This was the noise of marching men. A great many men.

Alex pointed his rifle into the unseen enemy in the dark wilderness. He tried to calm himself by recalling events from the past five days— the long march, the face-to-face battles in the Wilderness, the race to Spotsylvania. All blurred into a single unending horror that he expected to recall as his thirtieth birthday for the rest of his life. The days had melted into evenings then blended into mornings, sunlight and rain, and back to nighttime again.

He wondered what would at last bring this nightmare to an end. A surrender by South or North? Would the Yankee bullet fire true this time and bring his life, however mean or fine, to its end? Thunderous marching interrupted his thoughts.

Lester, crouched on Alex's left with his finger tense on the trigger of his rifle, nudged Alex. "What do you think? Are they attacking or retreating?"

Jacob exhaled a heavy breath. "It's getting louder. They've gotta be advancing, but I don't know if they're on our right or left."

Alex prayed that someone would replace the artillery before the blue onslaught. "If they go left or right, they'll miss us. Make ready for the worst. I wish we had those cannons guarding us."

The stomping boots grew even louder. Then, from the fog-shrouded woods, came a deep-throated growl of advancing Bluecoats—a sound totally different from the high-pitched rebel yell. Throngs of close-packed Yanks with fixed bayonets luminous in first light broke out of the mist, coming for the direct center of the U-shaped trench. Alex, Jacob, and Lester fired reflexively at point blank range.

"I got one of 'em," Jacob shouted just as Alex missed his target. Alex's next shot rang true, the bullet blasting the center of the man's face in a bloody explosion. Alex blanched but reloaded as fast as he could.

On and on they came, line after line, man after man. Alex and his comrades loaded cartridges and fired until their ammunition ran out. Someone yelled, "Fix your bayonets." Alex snapped his into place. When a Yankee jumped onto the parapet above the trench, Lester sliced his throat. Blood squirted into their faces, mingling with the rain. Max flung his bayoneted rifle like a javelin and pierced the body of an invader. The hammering rain transformed the floor of the trench to muck. Alex dared not look down—he knew he stood on bodies of the dead and wounded, trampled deep into slimy, bloody mud. No one spoke or yelled; they reacted. They used anything—guns, logs, shoes, shovels—to beat off the relentless enemy. Numbed by horror, he became a machine, neither angry nor fearful.

"We can't keep on," Jacob gasped at their captain.

A quick answer came back: "Your orders are to stand dead or alive."

Alex put his hand on Jacob's shaking arm. When a bolt of lightning flashed, the look in his older brother's eyes frightened Alex.

"I found another cartridge." Jacob pressed it into his rifle. He gripped the slippery side of the trench and jumped onto the parapet, laughing and screaming obscenities as he fired on the enemy below him.

"Jacob, come back. Have you lost your mind?" Alex shouted.

Jacob's manic laughter stopped short as enemy fire cut him down. He fell ten feet in front of Alex.

The sight of his brother's body sprawled on the mud before him launched Alex into action. *My brother will not be stomped underfoot on this hellish battlefield.* Placing his hands on the log barrier at eye level, Alex dug his feet into the side of the muddy trench. He lost his footing and slid down, coating his ragged clothes with mud. Determined, he planted his feet again, climbed up and over the parapet toward Jacob, grabbed his ankles, and slid his body into the trench.

Something hard pressed against the center of Alex's back. A voice with a northern accent spoke, "OK, we've got you, Johnny Reb. If you don't make a fuss, you stay alive. I'd love to shoot you, but the captain said take prisoners. Move along."

Alex yelled down the trench, "Get my brother." He climbed out of the muddy hole and stumbled through thick woods toward the enemy lines with the Yankee gun in his back.

When Alex reached a ditch, the soldiers shoved him in along with hundreds of other rebel soldiers. Too tired to resist, Alex fell asleep across the hip of a fellow infantryman. He finally awoke, dazed, his stomach aching with hunger.

A new prisoner fell into the ditch beside him. "We won the battle at Spotsylvania," he said. Alex groaned, wondering what marked the difference between victory and defeat.

12

In peace, sons bury their fathers; in war, fathers bury their sons.

Herodotus

June 1864

The floor clock struck six. As soon as sunlight filtered through the west window of her bedroom, Sarah sat down at her sewing machine to finish a black dress for Jacob's funeral. She needed to hurry before her houseguests awakened.

Arriving yesterday, the three Browning cousins had interrupted her sewing. By the time she moved the children to pallets and Megan into Frances's room, there wasn't enough light to stitch by.

Sarah released the handle on the wheel and squinted at her seams. Even in bright daylight, the black thread often disappeared into the black fabric. If not for the quickly approaching funeral, she'd have hand-woven the cloth with a loom retrieved from the loft, but weaving required too much time. She rubbed her finger across the smooth, close-woven cotton fabric with a twinge of guilt. When Mr. Flint told her the price, she'd taken a deep breath and told him to put it on her account. Somehow, she'd find a way to pay the bill. Luckily, her sewing basket still contained a spool of thin black thread she'd bought before the war. Coarse, homemade thread would tangle and fray in the Singer.

She checked the expandable waist she'd inserted in the skirt—a practical measure, since she might need this dress for another funeral. She shuddered at the thought and prayed it would be for someone else, not for Alex, that she'd next shroud herself. Guilt swept over her until she reminded herself that praying for her husband's safety wasn't wishing harm to another.

Last Friday, Margaret had received the official letter informing her that Jacob had died by enemy fire at Spotsylvania. Each time Sarah heard a knock at her own door, her throat had closed in fear. She needed good news—a letter from Alex. She hadn't heard from him since the letter about Industrious. She wondered what battle Alex faced today. Forcing her thoughts back to sewing, she added a ruffle made of the same fabric to either side of the buttonhole panel on the bodice. She also decided to sew the hem with the sewing machine to save time.

After knotting the thread on her last seam, Sarah put on the dress. She pinned back her hair under a hat she'd created earlier from black material, adding a bow on one side. Studying herself in the mirror, she admired the way the dress billowed over the crinoline and the soft drape of the bodice over her breast. This was the first dress she'd made for herself in over a year. A memory of Alex materialized behind her so real she almost felt his hands touching her waist and his lips kissing the back of her neck. He loved to watch her model new dresses.

The creak of the back door closing alerted her that Hannah had arrived from her cabin. *It must be nearly seven. Plenty of time until the funeral at ten.* She walked downstairs to the dining room.

"Look, Hannah; I finished the dress."

"Lord, ma'am. I don't see how you did it so quick. That's some pretty dress!" She wiped her hands and came closer. "Turn 'round now and let me look at you." She picked at the material on the back. "You got a pucker right here." Hannah lifted the hem and examined the stitches. "Looks like you machine-stitched this here hem."

Sarah sighed. "No one will notice."

"I sure hope not. I'd 'a done it by hand."

After breakfast with the family, she and Hannah dressed the children.

Hannah shook out a pinafore of thin, blue cotton with embroidered pink flowers and pulled it over Sallie's head. "I sorry Dustrous ain't here to pay his respects. He loved Mr. Jacob almost as much as Mr. Alex. I sure do miss Dustrous. If any of my babies had lived, I might not of been so lonesome." Her voice held no self-pity. She mentioned the three babies who'd died in the same tone as she might discuss carding cotton.

After Sarah squeezed Tommy's feet into his shoes, the children were finally ready. The family group proceeded down the front porch steps— Sarah in her new dress holding Tommy's hand, Hannah in a black smock and white apron carrying four-year-old Lula, and Frances with baby Sallie in her arms. Sarah had enlisted Lou, one of the field hands, to drive them to the funeral in a buggy borrowed from her neighbor, Mr. Winston. Looking uncomfortable in Alex's white linen shirt, Lou helped the ladies and children into their seats. Lou and Hannah had loaded food bowls and pies into the old wagon driven by John. The relatives had already left in their carriage.

The measured rhythm of horses' hooves clopped along the dirt-packed street through the middle of town. Not since her mother's funeral had Sarah felt more eyes appraising her, as though she and her family acted upon a stage an unrehearsed display of their grief. As they passed the square, several men stood in respectful attention, hats over their hearts. A Negro man with thick white hair shook his head and held his palms together under his chin in prayer.

Friends and neighbors were already filing in when Sarah's group arrived at the small frame church. They waited in the back until an usher directed them down the aisle past crowded pews. Sarah surveyed the church while the organist pumped out sad hymns. Spring flowers cascaded out of vases at the altar as though their bright colors might divert attention from the lack of a coffin.

Margaret, sitting in front of Sarah, turned and squeezed Sarah's hand. She sniffed into a handkerchief throughout the service. Sarah pitied Margaret today and offered a prayer for her strength and endurance, which led to another prayer for Alex's safety and finally for all the poor widows of this horrible war. *Where was Alex when Jacob was shot? Where is he now?* Sarah sighed. She opened her hymnbook to the first hymn, "Rock of Ages."

Brother Elias looked with sympathy toward the Browning family. "It is never easy to give up a loved one. Yet, just as God gave up his son Jesus Christ for us, the life of our own son, Jacob, serves as a sacrifice for the high moral principles of the South. Just as Christ rose from the dead, these brave soldiers will also see the face of God in their own resurrection. Just as Christ set himself at war with the Anti-Christ, they have set themselves against the devil's representative on this earth— Abraham Lincoln and his Godless apostles in the North."

Sarah closed her eyes to control her anger at the minister's twisted fusions of politics and religion. *I'm glad I conduct my own church service at home!*

After the funeral, the family procession wound its way back to Margaret and Jacob's house not far from town. While Hannah corralled the children, Sarah and Lou took food into Margaret's dining room. Their offerings joined others on a large table set up to feed those who came to pay their respects.

As she cut her lemon chess pie into wedges, Sarah felt someone grasp her right elbow. She turned to see Brother Elias. "We've been missing your family at services, Miz Browning." His eyebrows rose in sharp angles above wire-rimmed glasses that magnified his brown eyes to the size of walnuts.

"We're doing our best, Brother Elias."

"You need to set a good example for those youngsters of yours. As the good book says, 'Just as the twig is bent, so is the tree inclined.'"

"In what book of the Bible might I find that scripture?" Sarah asked.

The minister pushed a fat finger into the tight collar of his shirt. "I'm pretty sure it must be Proverbs."

"Hmm," Sarah said. "Could it be from Alexander Pope instead?"

"My goodness, woman, what a blasphemous thought that a Protestant minister would quote a Pope."

Sarah choked back her laughter. "Excuse me, Brother, I think my sister-in-law needs my help in the kitchen." Sarah pulled Margaret aside. "Why don't you go back to your bedroom and rest awhile?"

"I can't," Margaret said as she directed friends with cakes to the dining room table. "There's too much to do, and I'd rather stay busy." She found a knife and laid it next to the cakes. "What did you think? Was the funeral all right?"

"You planned it quite well," Sarah said.

"I loved Brother Elias's words," Margaret said. "He has blessed our church with his holiness and wisdom."

Sarah restrained herself and touched Margaret's shoulders. "Are you all right, Margaret?"

Margaret bit her lip and raised moist eyes toward the ceiling. "It's hard, Sarah, but I'm very proud of Jacob. I've always known he could be killed, but on that terrible day they brought me the letter, I realized it had actually happened. I'll never see him again on this earth." She removed a handkerchief from her sleeve and dabbed her eyes. "Have you heard from Alex?"

Sarah shook her head. "I haven't heard anything for awhile. I'm sick with worry—but I'm sure they'd have written me if he'd been killed or injured. Would you like me to help you in the kitchen? Frances is taking care of my children."

Margaret sniffed and shook her head. "Not now. The ladies at the church are taking care of everything."

Sarah began to perspire as more people crowded into the house. "If you're sure there's nothing I can do for you, I'll step outside for a few minutes." She walked outside onto a porch stretching the length of the home. Toward the end of the porch, she spied her neighbor Ruby in a circle of young people, which included a man Sarah did not recognize.

Ruby caught Sarah's eye and waved her over. "Sarah, I want you to know Bart Benedict." She turned to him. "Bart, this is my neighbor, Sarah Browning."

Sarah nodded and smiled.

Bart took her hand in his. "My pleasure, Miss Browning."

"Mrs. Browning," she corrected.

He smiled, "But of course, such a beautiful woman would already be claimed. Is your husband here?"

"My husband is fighting the war." She withdrew her hand. "Were you acquainted with Jacob?"

His eyebrows knotted over intense eyes. "No, ma'am. As a fellow soldier, I came to offer my condolences to his wife."

One of Ruby's friends, a young brunette, moved into the circle. "Bart moved here recently to start a new business."

Another young woman leaned forward. "Bart's also a war hero, but he's too modest to tell you that."

Sarah gave him another look. She noticed a missing earlobe just below his thick, dark hair. *Had he been wounded?*

The brunette answered the unspoken question. "The enemy shot his horse out from under him at Fredericksburg. Then, he single-handedly advanced on enemy artillery, saving his entire company."

Bart lowered his eyes and shrugged. "Anyone would have done the same."

"That's doubtful," Sarah said. "My husband fought at Fredericksburg. He wrote a letter about the terrible conditions."

"It wasn't so bad," Bart said.

"Perhaps your company was better equipped than the Florida boys."

He ignored her implied question. "I was a captain with the 10th Georgia under General Longstreet. I hated like sin leaving those boys out there. But after my injuries, they sent me home." He touched his ear.

She noticed he said "injuries" and wondered what other wounds he'd sustained, because the loss of an earlobe would hardly have kept him from battle.

"I must pay my respects to Miss Margaret," he said, "if you will excuse me." He took Sarah's hand and flashed a beautiful smile. His smooth skin, dimpled cheeks, and the dark curls tumbling over his forehead gave him an almost adolescent youthfulness. A tailored, black suit hugged his slim physique. "I'm delighted to meet you, Mrs. Browning."

After he left, Sarah turned to Ruby. "Have you and Bart been keeping company?" Sarah hated that her hard work had kept her too busy to enjoy long conversations with her young friend. Even when they were nursing the injured soldiers, they never had time for small talk.

"This is the first time I've seen him since last summer. There's someone else, now." She smiled and squeezed Sarah's hand. "We must visit soon so I can tell you about him. Bart and I were never serious, anyway. He could have his pick of anyone in town. All the single women are swooning over him."

Sarah turned and admired Bart's elegant good looks. "I can certainly see why." She left Ruby with her friends and looked for her family. After gathering a few dirty plates from the tables and stacking them in the sink, she prepared a plate for herself and sat down in the parlor.

Bart came in and sat beside her. "Hello again, Mrs. Browning." He gave her a long look. "By the way, you look stunning in that dress. Have you been shopping in Jacksonville or Macon?"

She looked down. "I sewed this dress myself."

"You are a talented woman . . . By the way, how did you know Ruby?"

"Alex and I bought our farm from her father when we moved here right after our marriage."

"It must be hard running a farm by yourself."

"It's not so bad," she said. "Ruby's friend said you are starting a business in Lake City." Sarah ate a bite of her turkey dressing.

"That's true." Bart turned to her and smiled. "Through my contacts, I have access to European imports and supplies from the North. I hope to establish a place to sell these items."

Sarah was shocked. "How can you do that? I thought the North had blockaded all the Florida ports." Sarah took another bite of turkey from her plate.

"There are infinite ways around the blockades. I own part interest in a lucrative business in Nassau with boats capable of getting through the federal ships."

Her eyes widened. "That sounds dangerous."

"Not if we're careful. Our cargoes come from Europe through Nassau to Florida's east coast, then return with cotton and tobacco to sell in Europe."

The information stunned her. "Then why have you come to Lake City? We're miles away from the coast. Why didn't you settle in Jacksonville or St. Augustine?"

"This is the perfect place. Many boats come right up the Suwannee River within a few miles of Lake City. I can offer your people the opportunity to buy European merchandise. I'll also encourage local farmers and plantation owners to continue growing cotton and tobacco that we can export."

Sarah squirmed in her seat and laid her plate on the end table next to her. "Is this legal? Alex and I used to grow cotton, but we were told to grow crops that would help feed the hungry in this area."

Bart took her hand and turned his intense black eyes on her. "I know you're having a difficult time managing that farm all alone. Please let me know if I can do anything to help you."

Sarah was uncomfortable with his touch and worried that she had been with him too long. He seemed to be flirting with her, but, then again, perhaps he was only being a gentleman. She released her hand

and stood. "Thank you, but we are managing quite well. I must leave now; it's been nice talking to you."

Bart stood and took a slight bow. "My pleasure, ma'am."

Sarah was unsettled by his attention. She took her leave to seek her children. The funeral and her conversation with the young man had stirred up her longing for Alex. She ached with loneliness.

13

They captured us . . . May 1864 and they carried us back to the rear and put us in a bottom to keep us there 11 days without any rations but what we had in our haversacks and some of us had none. We got to Point Lookout about 18 of May we got a small piece of beef and that was the last we got and we stayed there 3 or 4 months.

Alexander Browning
former POW,
letter to Board of Pensions,
1910

May–July 1864

Alex wiped his eyes and surveyed the scene. Confederates, their uniforms ragged and dirty, sat shoulder to shoulder in a shallow trench at the rear of the Union lines. The Bluecoats stood above them on the rise, rifles aimed down at men in the ditch. A new group of rebels staggered in from the battle, Union soldiers prodding them along with rifles. The captors pushed them into the trench with Alex. He recognized two men from his company, one lanky and the other squat—Lester and Max.

His empty stomach aching, he felt for the strap of his haversack and pulled it into his lap. Inside he found two pieces of bread and a chunk of yellow cheese wrapped in brown paper. As he anticipated the taste of the bread and cheese, saliva flowed into his mouth. He put the cheese between the two pieces of dry bread, took a bite, and washed it down with a swallow of water from his canteen.

Two prisoners leaned toward him, wide-eyed. They nudged one another, and, without a word, one snatched his food from his hand. The other grabbed for it, tore off a corner of the bread, and devoured it like a ravenous animal. Alex sat with his back pressed against the wall of the trench, too weary to argue.

After a few minutes, he pushed his haversack beneath his body and sat on it, remembering a piece of bacon, a biscuit he'd saved from an earlier meal, and two apples purchased at an outrageous price from a sutler hawking his wares to the troops. He'd wait until dark to try eating again.

The Union soldiers set up a table and filled their plates with meat, beans, and cabbage served up from a tent. "Hey, Rebs," a corporal said, "Would you like some pork ribs and beans?" He waved a rib bone toward the prisoners.

A prisoner pleaded, "Oh dear God, I'm so hungry. Don't taunt us."

The soldier laughed, and the others at his table joined in.

"This grub ain't for any dirty Reb."

"Shut yer mouths and stop the whining."

Each night, Alex nibbled the small rations left in his haversack, and during each day, he sat in the May sunshine, his pants rank with urine, wondering whether he'd die in this ditch. He reached in his pocket and removed the Bible verse the chaplain had given him. He tucked it inside the Bible in his haversack. Would Sarah ever find out what happened to him? Each morning, he gouged a mark on the side of the trench to help him remember how many days had passed.

On the eleventh day, Alex awoke to the sound of horses' hooves. A Union courier delivered an envelope to a soldier wearing captain's bars.

The captain motioned to two guards. "We've got orders to move these filthy animals out today."

"Where are we taking them?" the guard asked.

"Point Lookout, Maryland." He turned to the prisoners. "Rise and shine, Rebs; we're on the march."

Alex and the other prisoners crawled out of their trenches and brushed dried mud off their clothes as best they could. Alex straightened, stiff and unsteady. Guns of the walking guards prodded the prisoners into shuffling columns as the rifles of mounted cavalrymen aimed down at them. Alex followed the swelling, stinking horde of bedraggled prisoners pouring from the woods onto the turnpike. In dejected silence, they marched toward their fate in a Maryland prison.

When a young boy fell from formation onto the side of the road, a Yankee private kicked him. "Get up, you lazy slob." The boy retched and moaned. The private tried to force him back on his feet at rifle point. The boy rose to his knees then slumped forward on the muddy turf. The Yankee left him there by the side of the road.

Alex boiled with hatred toward the Yankee. Did war create such evil or merely offer opportunity? The Yanks he'd met often claimed they were more humane than the South. *Dear God, I treat my cattle more kindly than these "humane" Yanks treat us.*

On the third day, just when he thought he couldn't march another step, Alex's column stopped at the Maryland coast. Ahead, a steady stream of men boarded a government transport.

Alex sat on the deck of the ship pressed between other prisoners. He opened his haversack and removed his Bible and some letters from Sarah. He took out an early letter, well-worn from rereading. In closing Sarah wrote, "I love you in our absence with constant yearning desire, with admiration for your strong character, and pity for myself that I'm separated from the love of my heart. I'm doing as well as I can. We have enough to eat and clothes to wear. I pray that God's love will sustain you, Alex, and keep you from harm, so that whenever this dreadful conflict ends, we may continue our life together." She then quoted from "To My Dear and Loving Husband," written by Sarah's favorite poet, Anne Bradstreet.

She'd signed the letter: "Your faithful, loving wife and companion always and forever." Alex wiped his misting eyes with his jacket sleeve and opened the Bible.

He felt a light tug on his arm. "Hey, buddy."

Alex looked to his left to see a thin, ashen-faced man with sparse, matted hair. "What can I do for you, fellow?"

The man answered with a raspy cough. "I'm dying."

Alex looked more closely at the man next to him, his skin drawn across his cheekbones and his hair patchy and dry. "Would you read me a scripture from your Bible before I go?"

"What's your name, soldier?"

"Charley—Charles Horton."

Alex quaked. *I can't do last rites for this man.* He looked around the deck for a familiar face and, not finding one, said, "Charles Horton, I will abide by your last wishes." He flipped through his Bible and tried to remember a scripture that had comforted him. Stuck between the pages he found the note from the chaplain—"Revelation 21:4." He finally found the chapter and verse in the last book of the Bible:

"And God shall wipe away all tears from their eyes; and there shall be no more death, neither sorrow, nor crying, neither shall there be any more pain: for the former things are passed away."

Charles Horton exhaled a rattling breath as his body relaxed onto Alex's lap. This reminded Alex of times when Tommy had fallen asleep in his lap in the wagon after he'd taken him fishing. Pondering the words he'd discovered in Revelation, he turned the boy on his back, closed his eyelids and stroked his rough whiskers. *God forbid that my son ever has to fight in such a war.*

After the ship docked at Point Lookout, a huge mass of prisoners piled off. Alex blinked at the blazing sunlight reflected on the flat beach and stumbled forward, propelled by the crush of miserable men oozing like mud from a creek bank toward a group of buildings enclosed by a heavy fence at the peninsula's end. A heavily armed federal battleship, guns trained on the walls, commanded a critical position out in the bay. *There will be no escaping this prison, at least not alive.* Yet, he knew he must find a way to get out or at least to stay alive.

He crossed into the prison grounds through heavy gates. Trenches divided the yard into narrow roads. Reeking sewage proved the trenches unsuccessful for providing drainage. The guards directed him to a tent where twenty-five bare cots were lined up side to side on the sand. He put his haversack under one of the cots. He lay down and immediately fell asleep.

He awoke from dead sleep to Max shaking his shoulder. "They told us to go outside and line up."

Alex forced his feet off the side of the cot. "Where are we going?"

"Roll call and inspection," another soldier said. "Move fast. There's no telling what they'll do if we're late."

They hurried out to a wide beach surrounded by a fourteen-foot parapet. Alex quickly found himself crushed between the sweaty bodies of several thousand prisoners. At the guards' prodding, they spread out into formation across the yard. A gentle breeze brought the smell of salt water from the ocean, but when the air calmed, the noxious stench of urine replaced it.

"See that line, Rebs?" a captain yelled at the mob. A length of twine stretched between stakes marked off an area ten feet inside the wall. "We call it 'the deadline.' You cross it and you'll never see Dixieland again." He nodded at a tower where a soldier sat pointing his rifle toward the yard. Beyond the deadline stood a tall wooden fence pitted with gaping holes at its base where boards had rotted above the sand. "Don't think about approaching that fence even to peep out. They have orders to shoot anyone crossing that line day or night. Do you understand, prisoners?"

Alex sucked in a huge breath. No one spoke.

"I didn't hear you answer, Rebs." He repeated his question in a much louder voice. "When I ask you scum a question, you answer me, 'Yes, sir.' I repeat, 'Do you understand?'"

"Yes, sir," boomed the formation.

"OK, men. Strip off those nasty clothes. It's laundry time."

Alex removed his shirt, trousers, and boots as the others took off whatever remnants of Confederate uniforms remained on their bodies. Alex followed as his line marched naked past an enormous washtub and dropped their clothes into boiling water. The sun seared his bare skin like a torch. *What more will they think of to humiliate us?*

"Back into ranks," the captain yelled. "One other piece of information, in case you're thinking of getting out of here legal. Colonel says no more prisoner exchanges for the duration."

Alex stared at the wall, the guard tower, and the deadline. *I'll never escape this place. But I'll survive no matter what!*

The sound of horses' hooves rolled toward them. An officer on horseback galloped past. "It's Benjamin Butler," Lester whispered to Alex. "A fellow who's been here awhile told me about him while you were sleeping. They call him 'The Beast.'"

"General Butler will review the prisoners," the captain said.

Butler reined in his horse at the front of the formation and burst into maniacal laughter. "You pitiful, miserable excuses for men. What would your General Lee say if he saw you now? I'll tell you who you are. You're Lee's miserables!"

Howling in laughter, the general whipped his horse and plunged straight into the formation, which split like a wheat field in a windstorm. Alex jumped out of the way. Butler lashed at the bare backs of any men unable to move fast enough.

The Yankee captain, still grinning, yelled, "Attention, men. Back into ranks!" Alex looked to his left; he found the rudiments of a line and tried to adjust his position to straighten it. The captain walked to the last row. "Follow me. Others, fall in."

134

The hot sand burned Alex's feet as he followed other naked men past the tented area where they slept. When they entered a long wooden building, the smell of meat made Alex's mouth water. Fifty or sixty tables stood end to end in rows with low, rough wood benches lining them on both sides. As he passed a serving table, a Negro man in a blue uniform smirked as he slapped a piece of cold meat into his cupped hands. Several men started to eat but stopped when the captain yelled, "You'll eat when I tell you to." Gripping the greasy beef, Alex and the other captives stood at attention behind the benches until the captain shouted, "Sit!" He surveyed the men for several seconds. "Now you can eat."

Many men gnawed greedily, consuming their meat in less than a minute. As hungry as he was, Alex knew the food would stick in his throat and haunt his empty stomach if he ate too quickly, and so he paced himself with small bites. His mouth felt dry, and he yearned for water to wash it down. Intermittent sounds of retching filled the room, but Alex kept chewing, refusing to give up one morsel of nourishment that could help him survive.

The captain resumed his position of authority. "We sincerely hope you appreciate our kindness in serving you this good beef. Eat heartily, Rebs. This will be the last meat you'll see while you're at this place. After today, it's bread and water. We'd intended to serve you coffee, but your comrades at Andersonville cut the coffee ration for our fine men. So you'll pay the price—no coffee at Point Lookout."

The men groaned and turned back to their last supper.

A few minutes later, they were lined up to leave. On the way out of the mess hall, each man was allowed to dip his hands into a barrel containing grayish water with swirling sediment beneath the surface. Alex held his breath to stop the stagnant smell and dipped his hands down into the barrel, bringing the brackish liquid to his lips.

The next morning, still naked on his bare cot, Alex awoke to a skinny Negro guard emptying a sack full of clothes on the gritty floor. "Ya clean uniforms, men," he said with a sarcastic note to his voice then reached deep into the laundry bag and turned it inside out. He hung the bag over his arm and sauntered away. Alex wondered if it gave the Negro soldiers pleasure to control Southern white men.

Alex crossed to the wadded pile of shirts and trousers. Not finding his own uniform, he chose clothing he hoped would be near his size and carried it to his cot while other prisoners rummaged through the rest. Damp and stiff, the clothes already smelled sour. *Probably washed in our drinking water.* The shirt fit pretty well, but the pants were baggy and loose. Perhaps he'd find a rope or string to use as a belt. He looked under the bed. *Someone has removed my haversack.* A pang of loss cut through him like an icy wind when he remembered Sarah's letters and the Bible. *One way or another, I'll get out of here.*

After darkness covered the camp, Alex fell asleep minutes after lying on his cot. A loud crack, the unmistakable sound of gunfire, set Alex's body quaking. Drenched in perspiration, he lay listening. *What's this?* In the dim glow from flares outside the tent, Alex made out an armed soldier pacing between the beds. He heard another shot explode in a nearby tent. The soldier in his tent continued snaking through the cots. Suddenly, he stopped beside a prisoner sleeping several beds over from Alex. He aimed the rifle at the cot and fired. *Dear God, he doesn't even know who he killed. It could be anyone.*

Each night, Alex jerked awake every few minutes to watch for a guard entering the tent. A week later, during a wakeful interval, he heard boots scrunching on sand. Someone brushed by his side. He held his breath. The shadow stopped at the next cot. A cracking explosion was followed by a shriek. A few minutes later, another shot. Then silence.

During the next weeks, the crack of a rifle set Alex shaking, wondering if he'd be next. Sometimes, a man would moan in pain from illness. A shot often followed. After awhile, Alex slept through the night as if the sounds were firecrackers popping.

Despite the meager rations, the combined stench from the marshes and trenches removed any remnant of Alex's appetite. Others sought relief to their desperate hunger. Some had eaten soap scum and orange peelings found in the yard. Every night, men sneaked out to catch rats in improvised traps. Others checked the sand that had washed under the stockade, looking for dead fish. Alex once watched a hungry prisoner hurriedly eat a seagull that had washed up on the shore before others took it away from him.

Eventually, routine began to make the unbearable bearable. After breakfast—a thin slice of stale bread and two scoops of stagnant water—Alex congregated in the yard with a few fellow prisoners, including his Lake City friends Lester and Max. The guards, always in sight, stood far enough away that the friends' conversations couldn't be heard.

Alex and his comrades also discovered that when sitting on the west side, their tent blocked the glare of the blazing mid-summer sun for an hour or more. Yet, nothing could block the sewage stench from the thousands of prisoners crowding into Point Lookout or stop the clouds of mosquitoes swarming above stagnant water.

"I wonder what's happened to all our home boys." Lester slapped a mosquito on his cheek. He wiped away the blood with his ragged sleeve.

"I ain't seen my old friend Henry in forever," Max said. "We used to have twenty, thirty boys from home right after Alex joined up. I guess some of 'em got shot at Spotsylvania along with Jacob."

Alex looked away. "There's some of 'em shamed us. Charley and Joseph shot themselves in the hand when we were in winter quarters. Got themselves a long furlough. I suppose old Henry took the oath of allegiance." Alex turned toward a former sergeant from Jacksonville. "What are you thinking over there so serious and quiet, Jackie?"

"I've been considerin' takin' that loyalty oath. 'Specially if it would get me outta this hellhole alive." Jackie rolled up his frayed gray trousers. "Lookie here at my legs."

The four men in the group leaned close to the sergeant's thin legs, spotted with red blemishes around the hair follicles. Alex and Lester inspected their own legs and found similar raised red spots.

"That ain't nothing. Look at this." Max held out an arm blotched with red and black bruises. "What do you suppose is causing this?"

"It's scurvy," said Bruce, a prisoner from Tampa. "I went down to the infirmary with pain in my knees and elbows and heard the doctors talking about us all getting scurvy from not having any fruit and vegetables. They've had us on bread and water for six weeks now."

"How long does it take to die from it?" Alex asked.

"Takes awhile," Bruce said. "More likely we'll die from typhoid or dysentery. The other day, I passed by a stack of bodies waiting to be buried."

"For what it's worth, I'd rather die than to take any oath to the Feds," Alex said. "I've seen what they've done, and I'm proud to be fighting against their evil ways. They killed my brother in Spotsylvania. There's no way I'd join 'em."

"I don't know how come I ever signed up," Jackie said. "Everyone in Jacksonville got so wrought up over this war. I never wanted to go, but they made me feel like a low-down skunk if I didn't join the cause."

Bruce nodded his agreement. "I never wanted to join up, neither, but some soldiers came down to Tampa and forced me."

"Do you think there's any way out of here?" Alex asked.

Lester, his brow furrowed, looked across the yard as though he could see the ocean through the tall fence. "Max and me have been studying it, but it's damn discouraging. We saw it the day we got here. We've got water on three sides of us, guards with guns up in the towers, a gun boat out in the Chesapeake." With a stick he drew a crude map of the peninsula in the damp sand. "The only thing we've come up with is to escape when they transfer us out."

Max nodded. "They're gonna have to move some of us. It's getting too crowded to move around."

"I reckon they've shoved a couple or three thousand a week in here since we came in May," Lester said.

"I overheard something pretty interesting the other day."

Max scratched swollen bites on his bare feet. "What's that, Bruce?"

"Promise not to talk about it, or it won't happen." They raised their hands as if taking a vow.

"OK, I heard that Lee's planning a raid on Washington this month. They're gonna crack open Point Lookout and release us prisoners to help 'em fight."

"That sounds like prison talk to me," Alex said. "Wishful thinking. When is this supposed to happen?"

Bruce picked at his head and squeezed an insect between his thumbnails. "Somewhere about the middle of July."

"What day is today?" Max stared at the sky as though it might be a giant almanac.

Alex counted on his fingers. "Today's Tuesday. It's July 7. I've been keeping up since my birthday."

Three days later, after breakfast, Alex found Max and Lester sitting on the sand in the shade of the tent. Bruce sat down beside them. "Jackie took the oath."

"That traitor! I didn't think he was serious," Max said. "What about the raid?"

Bruce looked grim. "Haven't heard any more about it. The Feds probably found out."

Alex choked down his disappointment. "Do you think Jackie told 'em?"

Bruce shrugged.

"The raid wouldn't have worked anyhow. I don't know anyone around here fit to fight," Lester said.

Bruce leaned forward. "Captain told me they're shipping us out to Elmira next week."

Max grimaced. "What's it like there?"

"I don't know much. It's a new prison in New York. It should be cooler up there and maybe not so crowded. Couldn't be worse than here," Bruce said.

"I know enough about Yankees to know this much: it will be another hellhole." Lester slapped his thigh. "I'm going to escape on our way. I'll do it. Any of you want to join me?"

14

That ye may be the children of your Father which is in heaven: for he maketh his sun to rise on the evil and on the good, and sendeth rain on the just and on the unjust.

Matthew 5:45

Summer 1864

Early on a June morning, Sarah tiptoed downstairs to the parlor with a carved wooden box. The family seldom came into this tiny formal room in the front of the house. They preferred the comfortable, often-messy sitting room. But Sarah enjoyed its privacy, the floral wallpaper, its thick carpet and heavy drapes, and her mother's many knickknacks that brought memories from her childhood home. She sat down at the secretary and opened the box containing items she held dear or preferred to keep private. She kissed a thin stack of letters tied with a yellow ribbon and returned them to the box. As was her habit, she read some scriptures from her Bible. Afterwards, she opened a small volume by Anne Bradstreet, a poet who came to colonial New England with her husband in the seventeenth century. She closed the book of poetry and opened her diary, where she recorded the events of the previous day—the funeral and the conversations with the minister, with Margaret, and with Bart. After replacing the diary in the box, she took an accounting ledger from the shelf and copied the amount for the black fabric. *I shouldn't have spent so much money.* A light cough in the hallway interrupted her thought.

Her father-in-law opened the door. "You're up earlier than usual, Missy. I'll start a fire in the sitting room." With the ledger under her arm, she joined him at the oak table.

He placed a pine knot under the wood in the fireplace and set it ablaze. Then, he scooped a cup of parched corn meal into the tin kettle. Adding water, he set it on the hearth. "Would you like some coffee?" he asked.

"No, thank you." She wrinkled her nose. "When you finish, I'd like some help with the ledger. I can't seem to make it come out right."

After the "coffee" had boiled and settled, John poured a cup and sat down. "Let me see the books, Missy." He adjusted his wire-rimmed glasses, flipped back several pages, and frowned at the figures she'd entered. "You've got everything down as far as I can see—Alex's salary and sale of eggs, milk, canned goods. Course, that's all in Confederate money, which isn't worth the paper it's printed on since the fools in Richmond keep on printing more of it. Last I heard, the exchange was thirty cents to the US dollar. Your best income is your rent from Megan for her room."

"If I don't get us run out of this town for renting to a Yankee."

John continued muttering as he ran his finger down the ledger.

"So how are we doing, Daddy John? Do we have enough money to keep the wolves from the door?"

"Well, first off we need to go over our expenses."

"I feel guilty about charging that material at Flint's."

"Don't you worry about that, Missy. It's the first money you've spent on yourself since the war started."

She looked at the frayed sleeves of her housedress with patches sewn in several thin spots. She knew the new, black mourning dress would be her last for a long time.

He turned back to the books. "Things are getting mighty expensive these days."

"I know," she said. "When I was in town, I looked at a pair of shoes for Tommy selling for a hundred dollars. It's a good thing the children can go barefoot all summer. Maybe next fall I can swap some bacon or eggs to the cobbler for shoes."

John got out of his chair and removed a rusty metal box from a top shelf. Walking back toward his seat, he continued talking to Sarah. "We're better off than the poor town folk, Missy. We still have some hogs we can kill. We can count our lucky stars we don't have taxes."

He opened the box. "Look here. We've got about two hundred in Confederate and two-fifty in US right now."

Sarah frowned at the two thin stacks of currency. "Maybe next week I'll ask Frances and Hannah to help me can peas and tomatoes. Mr. Flint pays good prices for my canned vegetables. I'll look for some sorghum or wild honey to sweeten the berry jelly and wild orange preserves. Folks buy those as fast as I can make them."

John nodded. "Why don't we set up a stand next time they have market day in the square? No sense in you giving Flint a cut of your money when you can sell them for full price. Maybe someone will buy our smoked hams, too."

Sarah felt better as she returned the ledger to the desk in the parlor.

A month later, on a Saturday in July, the sun reddened the clear eastern sky, promising a hot, humid day. Only a few gray clouds banked on the horizon. Clippings from *The Lake City Press* advertising market day lay on the kitchen table. While Sarah and her helpers cooked and canned, other ladies in town sewed, old men whittled, and grandmothers embroidered doilies, pieced quilts, and crocheted throws to sell at their booths in the courthouse square. Sarah heard talk of so many offerings that she prayed for enough customers to buy her goods.

Suspended between two poles on either side of a wooden counter, a sign painted in red and blue letters on a strip of cloth read, "Sarah's Sweets and Succulent Victuals." John and Lou had constructed a wooden booth and spread a canvas roof over it for shade and for protection against rain. Mason jars filled with bright red tomatoes, green peas, and pickled corn relish sat in rows on the right side of the counter. The left side displayed berry jelly, strawberry and wild orange preserves, along with several pound cakes. She'd sliced a loaf of sourdough bread to allow for samples of her jellies and preserves.

While they waited for the first customers to arrive, Sarah smoothed her apron hanging loose over her growing belly. She tucked a strand of hair under her bonnet. When Frances dug into her apron pocket and brought out her silver snuffbox, Sarah intervened just as she opened the lid. "You know, Frances, our customers might be offended by tobacco." She didn't want anything to make a customer turn away. She had hopes for earning some much-needed money.

Frances snapped the lid of the snuffbox.

Sarah knew Frances couldn't last the entire day without her snuff. "After awhile you might walk down behind the courthouse to the lake."

Frances gave a tense shrug. "I don't need it." But a few minutes later, she strolled away toward the water.

Dressed in green, her favorite color, Megan sauntered around the booth to make certain the sign she'd drawn hung in a prominent and readable position.

John and Tommy worked at the back of the booth assembling paper sacks to package the sales. In the back corner, John watched over the cigar box, holding a stack of Confederate one-dollar bills for change.

The first customers were lookers—freed slaves with a little money jingling in their pockets. An old Negro woman with a cane limped around the square studying the offerings at each booth.

A little later in the morning, two ladies carrying ruffled parasols alighted from a fancy carriage. Sarah recognized Mrs. Pettigrew, who lived in the finest mansion in town, a white frame house with dormer windows and verandas on the second floor. Magnificent oak trees with drooping swags of Spanish moss shaded the grounds surrounding the mansion. She guessed that the younger woman was Tillie, her daughter, who attended a boarding school in Georgia.

Head erect, back as straight as a poker, Mrs. Pettigrew proceeded directly to Sarah's booth. "Tell me, Miss Sarah, do you have any of those wonderful smoked hams you're famous for?"

Sarah smiled. "Yes ma'am, I have a few today. Would you like a whole ham or a half?" John brought out several sizes of hams wrapped in newspapers and laid them on the counter. The air filled with their smoky aroma.

Mrs. Pettigrew selected two whole hams, which John wrapped and sacked. Then she chose four cakes and a box full of canned goods. "It's so hard to find goods these days with those dreadful Yankees blockading our ports." Sarah added up the bill. Twenty-five dollars for each of the hams, five dollars each for the cakes, and a dollar apiece for the canned goods, a total of seventy-five dollars. Sarah smiled in anticipation of a profitable day.

"Hand me my reticule, Tillie," Mrs. Pettigrew said to her daughter. With the crocheted bag hanging over her arm, Mrs. Pettigrew removed a fat coin purse. Just as she put her fingers on the clasp, a strong wind blew in from the west, strewing newspapers and paper sacks over the grass in the square. Megan and Tommy scampered after the blowing papers and gathered them under their arms.

A Negro woman and her little boy, about eight years old, crossed the street toward the square. The child squealed when he saw Megan and ran straight to her, wrapping his short arms around her waist. Megan kissed the top of his curly black hair.

From the other direction, Emma, Addie, and Pearl came close to the booth. Emma extended a gloved hand and pointed toward Megan and the little boy. "That's the one," she said, her voice raised, "the Yankee girl who came down here to stick her nose in our business."

"She's the one," Addie screeched. "She's a boarder at Sarah Browning's house."

The three women stared at Megan and the child. "I heard she was teaching some pickaninnies in that school the abolitionist lawyer set up next to his office," Pearl said.

Sarah tried to hide her shock at this revelation. Even though Florida had no laws forbidding education for Negroes, most white citizens opposed teaching them. She gave the ladies a nervous smile and hoped they might buy some of her wares. Suddenly, with no warning, rain fell out of the sky in a giant splatter, drenching the square. The ladies unfolded their parasols. The wind gusted again even stronger than before, turning their parasols inside out. The women scampered across the street and took shelter in a dress shop. In the meantime, Mrs. Pettigrew, who'd observed the scene with a stern frown, had buttoned her reticule. She made a stiff about-face. With her selections still lying on the counter, she proceeded to her carriage, her head held high and her daughter a few steps behind. Their manservant assisted them into the carriage then jumped into the driver's seat, clucked the horses, and set the buggy rolling toward the Pettigrew mansion.

Megan and Tommy, soaking wet, rolled dripping papers in a pile inside the booth. Sarah looked at John, her eyes filling with tears. John shook his head and held out his hands in surrender to the disastrous turn of events. Sarah put her arms around John in despair. "We'll never be able to make any money now, Daddy John."

"There, there," he said and patted her on the back. "Failure is never fatal unless you give up. The good book says, 'Blessed is the man who perseveres under trial.'"

Over John's shoulder, Sarah saw a man with dark, curly hair striding through the rain. When he came closer, she recognized Bart Benedict.

He leaned across the table that held the wares. "What's going on here, Miss Sarah?" After she related the unfortunate incidents, he removed a roll of Confederate bills from his pocket. "I'd like to buy all your merchandise. Does one thousand dollars sound like a fair price?"

15

As I went over to the first hospital this morning early, there were 18 dead bodies lying naked on the bare earth. Eleven more were added to the list by half past eight o'clock.

Anthony Keiley
Ward Assistant,
Elmira Prison,
September 1864

July–November 1864

The plan was simple. They'd worked it out before they left Point Lookout. On the train from New York City to Elmira, Alex would chat with the guard. Just after the third stop on the way to the prison, Alex would tell the guard that a man in the back of the car had threatened other prisoners with a knife. While the guard investigated the incident, Alex, Lester, Max, and Bruce would jump off the train with high hopes of making their way south.

When Alex actually entered his assigned car on the train, he joined fifty other men. Sour prison smells clung to their bodies. Guards stood at the doors that slid shut and locked them from the inside. As soon as all were aboard, two Bluecoats walked the entire distance outside the train. Stopping at each door and jamming a heavy crossbar through two loops, they secured the doors from the outside.

Alex observed the security procedures with a heavy heart. He nudged Lester. "What are we gonna do about that?"

Lester surveyed their assigned car. "Maybe they'll forget to bolt 'em shut at one of the stops. Go ahead and chat with the guard. At least, we'll be prepared if we have a chance to get out." Lester, Max, and Bruce squeezed into a seat by an open window near the front of the car while Alex sat farther back next to the aisle.

The guard on their car, a very young corporal with red cheeks and a shock of corn-colored hair, bit his lips nervously and flicked baby-blue eyes across the prisoners inside the car.

Alex caught his eye and smiled. "Where are you from, Corporal?"

In reflex, the guard returned the smile then stiffened his body as though to impress the prisoners with his toughness.

"Not allowed to talk, I reckon."

The corporal nodded seriously and forced his shoulders back.

"Hey, it's gonna to be a long trip—maybe four or five hours with all the stops we make. Your officers aren't in here, and we won't tell them you talked to us."

"It's more like three hours with five stops," the corporal said in a northern accent.

"Sounds like you've made this trip before. Are you from New York?"

The corporal's mouth clenched shut.

"You been in the army long?"

The guard ignored Alex's questions and, with his hands behind his back, walked down the full length of the aisle. Alex wondered whether he'd be able to engage this disciplined soldier in a conversation before the end of the trip. He kept his eyes straight forward, and, after several minutes, he heard the guard's boots clicking. The corporal assumed parade rest position next to Alex's seat. Alex smiled at the guard then looked away as though ignoring him.

"What's your name, soldier?" the corporal asked after a few minutes.

Turning toward him, Alex thought he saw a hint of a smile. "Alexander Browning. I'm from Florida, originally from Georgia."

"I went to Georgia when I was a boy. My grandmother lives in Atlanta."

"We know some folks in Atlanta. What's her name?"

"Burkley, same as mine, but she's Betty; I'm Billy after my father William."

If Billy Burkley hadn't been a Yankee soldier, Alex thought he might have liked the lad. He could see his friends five rows ahead looking back and grinning at him. He turned to the guard. "Tell me about your family, Billy."

But Billy's attention moved to his duties as screeching brakes announced the train was slowing. When they stopped, sympathetic women from the town pressed in on both sides of the train and handed bundles of clothing as well as boxes filled with cakes, cookies, and pies through the open windows. The guards also opened the doors to allow some good-hearted people to come aboard to distribute their contributions down the car's aisle.

After the visitors got off, the officers locked the doors, the conductor clanged a bell, and the train resumed its journey. When they neared the second stop, prisoners leaned out the windows in anticipation. Corporal Burkley bent over them. "Get your heads back in those windows, Rebs. Right now! Are you deaf?" He tramped down the aisle and jerked the men back into their seats. Finally, he unholstered his pistol and waved it around. "Don't make me use this thing!"

The laughing prisoners slowly settled into their seats. When the train stopped, the guard leaned across the rows of soldiers and tried closing some windows. Several jammed.

Outside the train, an elderly man, formally dressed in a topcoat and hat, waved his cane at the train full of Confederate prisoners. His voice carried through the windows that were still open. "If I had it my way, they'd shoot every last one of you Rebs and send you off to everlasting hellfire and damnation for what you've done to this country. Damn you all. Damn you all."

The soldier sitting next to Alex frowned. "Where did that old grouch come from? I liked the ladies with the cakes a whole lot better."

"Enough! Settle down," the guard said as the train started up again.

This guard is an easy touch. Alex started a new conversation when the train approached its third stop. "Do you have relatives in the army, Billy?"

"Sure do. My daddy's a colonel stationed in Washington, and my brothers both fought at Gettysburg." Billy took an empty seat facing Alex.

"No kidding? My brother and I fought at Gettysburg, Chancellorsville, and Second Manassas."

"I haven't had a battle yet," Billy said.

As he and Billy continued trading stories, Alex felt the train slow for the third stop. The smell of burning coal wafted through the windows. With doors secured inside and out, Alex saw no way for the planned escape to work, but he continued the conversation. The train stopped in another small town with neat little cottages surrounded by tree-covered hills.

"Where are we now?" Alex asked.

Billy leaned over and looked out the window. "This is Owego, a little old town—not the same as Oswego. We shouldn't be here long."

The train backed up, and metal banged metal as new cars hooked onto the train. Fully aware of the train's motion, Alex kept up his small talk with the guard. As the engine began its slow chug forward, he saw his friends standing in their seats, but he continued talking not daring to look at them directly.

Out of the corner of his eye, he saw his friends crawl out the window and leap to the ground. Suddenly, Billy stood and twisted toward the front of the car. He pulled his pistol. "What's going on?"

Alex stared at the empty seat where his three friends had sat. The window stood fully open.

Corporal Burkley marched up the aisle. "Who was sitting here?" he demanded from prisoners sitting behind the empty seat.

"I didn't know them," one said.

"They jumped out the window when we started taking off."

"I didn't know them, neither," another said, but Alex knew he wouldn't tell even if he did.

Billy Burkley's eyes widened, and he raised the pitch of his voice to a screech. "Do any of you know the names of the men who escaped?" He pulled the chain to alert the engineer to stop. "If anyone in this car moves, you'll be shot."

Like angry wasps, blue-coated officers swarmed the car, interrogating each man. Through the windows, Alex saw federal cavalry galloping past the train, probably searching for his friends, and he started a prayer for their safety. They could tell Sarah he was alive—all he could hope for now. Finally, a colonel boarded. He opened a cloth-bound book and called roll. Then, he questioned the remaining prisoners.

Alex worried through how he'd answer the questions sure to come. If Billy Burkley found out Alex knew the escaped prisoners, he'd figure out that Alex's conversation was a ploy. Then again, Billy might not want to admit his negligence to his superiors. It wouldn't take much checking to find out that the Cartwrights were from Lake City same as Alex. He shivered, fearing he might be shot for aiding in the escape.

A Yankee lieutenant took the vacant seat across from Alex. "Do you know any of the prisoners—Lester Cartwright, Max Cartwright, or Bruce Danielson?"

Alex's mouth went dry and his tense shoulders ached. "I knew who they were," he said. That was the truth. He only hoped that other prisoners wouldn't reveal how often the four of them had met and talked in the shade of the tent. As far as he knew, no one paid close attention to them. Alex kept his jaw stiff to keep his teeth from chattering.

The lieutenant glanced out the window. "We're almost at Elmira." He narrowed his eyes at Alex. "You'll be answering a lot of questions very soon, soldier."

When they arrived at Elmira, Alex and the other captives entered the prison through the lower gate in the stockade. A pond, the backwash of the Chernung River, filled the lower part of the prison yard. Slime oozed between their toes as they plodded barefoot across swampy ground. The guards directed them up a hill toward the army barracks. Alex followed his group into his assigned barrack, where he found bunks along the entire length of the structure crowded two deep on both sides. Alex took a lower bunk near the back of the windowless building.

"Browning. Alexander Browning," a rough voice shouted from the door. Alex stood as a federal officer approached.

"Come with me," the officer said.

Alex threw his hat and a sack of clothes on the bed and followed the officer to the adjutant's office. His heart hammering against his ribs, he prayed, *Dear God, don't let them shoot me.*

Alex stood at attention before the adjutant, who wore captain's bars on his shoulders. Sucking the fumes of a fat cigar, the captain examined a page of handwritten notes lying on the polished top of a wooden desk. Alex gritted his teeth while the captain continued to read without speaking or lifting his eyes.

Finally, the adjutant looked up from the paper, his eyes drilling through Alex's skull. He flicked a clump of ashes from the cigar onto the floor. "Don't lie to me, Browning."

"No, sir!"

"How well do you know the escapees?"

"Sir?"

"You know what I'm talking about. Answer the damn question."

Alex stalled. He needed to find out how much the Feds already knew. "You're talking about the fellows that jumped the train this morning."

Not speaking, the captain continued to stare. He exhaled a cloud of cigar smoke, his mouth curling into an irritated snarl.

"Lester and Max are from the same town as me," Alex said.

"What about Bruce Danielson?"

"I met him one time at Point Lookout. He's from Tamp—"

"You're wasting my time. I know where they're from. I want to know how you were involved with helping them escape." He sucked on the cigar butt.

"I didn't even know they were gone until the commotion started."

The adjutant blew a cloud of smoke in Alex's direction. "Did you intentionally try to distract Corporal Burkley's attention? Don't lie to me, Browning. I already know you were talking to the guard. Another prisoner's already told us."

"We just talked a few minutes."

He held the cigar between two fingers and picked a piece of tobacco from his lip.

"What did you talk about?"

"Places we'd been and stuff about our families."

"Do you make it a practice of making friends with the enemy?"

"Sometimes."

The captain turned to guards standing nearby. "Manacle this prisoner, and throw him in the dog pen."

Cramped into a low outbuilding uphill from the barracks, Alex leaned against one of two plank walls four feet apart on either side of the enclosure. In the dim light filtering in through a thin crack above the door, he could barely make out the contours of the tiny room: to his left, a wooden door heavily reinforced with iron bars; to his right, rough stones formed the end wall. Above he saw log ceiling supports and felt grimy dirt beneath him. A ray of light glinted off the curved surfaces of a pewter chamber pot and a tin food bowl. Endurance, not a speedy escape, could get him out of here, he figured.

His army training in Virginia included instructions about what to do if captured. Officers who had lived through imprisonment passed on their methods of avoiding physical and mental deterioration during solitary confinement. "If you think too much about your hunger and thirst, you'll go crazy," warned a sergeant imprisoned early in the war. "Focus on happy events from the past, recite the books of the Bible, count to one thousand—anything to take your mind away from there."

Alex thought of Sarah and their night in Madison. He tried to imagine how each of his children might look now. Then, he allowed his mind to wander back to his own childhood. On a late summer afternoon, when he was twelve, he set out for the creek with a fishing pole over his shoulder.

"Be careful," his mother warned. "Remember; don't ever go to the swimming hole without Frances."

"I'm just going fishing, not swimming."

He met Industrious on the path wiping gritty sweat off his face with his sleeve. He'd spent the day picking cotton with the field hands. "Come on, Alex. Let's go swimmin' and cool off. I'm hotter than a teapot on a wood fire."

"Can't. I promised Mama I wouldn't go without Frances."

"She just don't want you out swimmin' by yourself. You and me can look after each other."

They followed the bank of the creek to a widening in the stream where leafy oaks drooped and a cliff jutted above the deepest part of the water. The boys scrambled up to a rock platform twenty feet above the pool.

"Watch me, Industrious," Alex said. He gripped a long rope just above a thick knot. "You've got to get a running start then kick off from the rock. Swing to the middle of the hole and let go of the rope. If you hold on too long, you'll run into that hill over yonder and hit a rock or a tree." Alex kicked off with a whoop and released the rope just above the deepest part of the pond. As he fell downward, he wrapped his arms around his bent knees and hit the water with a stinging splash. He made his way to the surface and looked up the cliff where Industrious held the rope, ready to go.

"Jump, Industrious," Alex shouted.

Industrious ran a few steps, leapt off the cliff, and swung wide over the water.

"Let go! Let go!

Industrious squeezed the rope even tighter as he arced out. Then, he reversed toward a cypress tree jutting out of the bank near the platform where they started. When his head hit a sharp limb, he tumbled down the hill into the pond and disappeared beneath the muddy water.

Alex paddled furiously to where Industrious fell. He inhaled a huge breath and dove deep beneath the surface. He opened his eyes, but the muddy water blocked his vision. He swam deeper, making a circle. Soon his aching lungs forced him to the surface. He dived again a short distance from his first exploration and felt something kick his side. Grabbing Industrious's thick hair, Alex pulled him onto the bank, where they lay side by side, panting and unable to speak.

That night, twelve-year-old Alex marched behind his father for his punishment—the red paddle.

At the barn, his father began questioning. "Didn't your mother tell you not to go swimming without Frances?"

"Yes sir, she did." For the first time in his young life, a calm assurance replaced his usual dread of punishment. How much could it hurt? He could stand it.

"And what is the commandment about obeying your parents?"

"Honor thy father and thy mother . . ."

"And the rest of it." John slapped the red paddle against his thigh.

Squinting his eyes, Alex tried to remember. "That thy days . . . uh . . . I can't remember."

"That thy days may be long upon the land which the Lord thy God giveth thee."

Alex wondered how the last part applied to him.

"Why do you think your parents made the rule about swimming?"

"I guess 'cause y'all didn't want me to drown."

"Because we love you, son. It's our job to keep you safe."

Without being asked, Alex lowered his pants and lay over the well-worn stool, ready to get it over with and determined to withstand the pain. Through ten burning whacks, he clenched his teeth and fought the urge to cry out. When the spanking was done, Alex, still proud of rescuing his friend, squared his shoulders and grinned at his father.

A blinding light interrupted his memories. A guard stuck his head through the opening of his cell. "Chow time. Where's your bowl, prisoner?"

Alex scrambled for the tin bowl. The guard filled it with water then handed him a chunk of dry bread. He was already eating the bread when the heavy door slammed shut.

Pain started the next day. Alex directed his mind toward happy memories to block his awareness of his throbbing back and legs. He fortified himself with his endurance of the red paddle and determined to survive this punishment as bravely. For several days, a pain in his chest grew more intense. Then, he developed a headache and a dry hacking cough. Chills wracked his body, and a sore throat progressed to congestion that made breathing nearly impossible. Ignoring his pleas for help, the guard pushed in crust after moldy crust that Alex left untouched. Finally, two Union guards released him from the dog pen.

As the guards carried him across the grounds, he noticed two men hanging from the limb of a strong oak. They were bound by their thumbs with their toes barely touching the ground. When he came closer, he recognized Max and Bruce. His eyes filled with tears at the agony of his friends. "Where's Lester?" He burst into a spasm of coughing.

The guards carried him to a pavilion where only tents sheltered patients from the weather. They stopped at a rusty metal bed devoid of a mattress. An orderly removed Alex's clothes and covered him with a blanket.

When a doctor finally arrived, he put a dry hand on Alex's burning forehead. Then, he placed the ends of two metal tubes in his ears and pressed a cold, bell-shaped rubber object against Alex's chest. The doctor smiled when Alex recoiled. "You've never seen a stethoscope. I'm listening to the sounds in your lungs. Take a deep breath and hold it." The doctor frowned. "You've got a bad case of pneumonia, soldier. Unfortunately, we haven't received our medical supplies, but we'll put compresses on your chest to try to clear up the congestion." The doctor gave instructions to an orderly and moved to the bedside of another patient.

After two weeks, the fever and the pain in his chest subsided. He could breathe more easily although a cough lingered. Alex had observed the hospital routine. Negro soldiers performed most menial tasks—cooking, emptying bedpans, bathing patients. Some also acted as guards.

Each day, more beds, more patients, more deaths. The unmistakable stench of diarrhea. One morning, when he awoke early, he counted eight dead men in his tent. As soon as orderlies removed the bodies, new patients took the beds. Bone thin with hacking coughs, they screamed with pain and begged for opium.

Alex wanted out. He feared he would contract another disease if he stayed there. "Why can't I go back to the barracks?" he asked an orderly who brought soup.

"We gotta hold y'all in the beds till we get some pantaloons. We burned all the old clothes so as not to spread the sickness."

The Negro orderly's voice sounded familiar. "Industrious?"

"The name's Luke . . . but there's a man named Industrious working here. I'd never forget a name like that."

How can that be? Alex could not imagine that Industrious survived Gettysburg. He yearned to see *this* Industrious to be sure. "I'd like to see him."

The orderly shrugged. "You can't miss him. He's bigger than anyone here. You watch."

The next morning, Alex awoke to see Industrious dressed in a Yankee blue shirt and trousers. The big man was studying him. "How ya doin'?" He grinned at Alex but showed no recognition.

Alex stared, wide-eyed. "I—I thought you were dead."

Industrious's eyes widened. "Mr. Alex! You don't look like yourself no more. But I knowed that voice."

Incredulous, Alex felt Industrious's muscular arm. "You're really alive. I can't believe it. How did you get here? I thought you died."

Industrious put a strong hand on his shoulder. "I got work to do now, but I come back and take care of you. I help you get better." In long strides, he walked away.

Seeing Industrious stunned and troubled him, reopening an unhealed wound. The raw grief and guilt that had hounded him after Gettysburg had diminished but never quite disappeared. The blue Yankee uniform Industrious wore grated him like a rasp on an axe blade. Many questions formed in his mind.

Late one night, Industrious returned. "I come back to talk wit you while nobody's listenin'."

Alex awoke with a start. He wanted to ask his questions before Industrious had to leave. "How did you get here—from there?"

"The bluecoat soldiers, they take me to the hospital and cut that bullet outta my shoulder. I thought sure I gonna die, but the Lord, He wasn't ready for me yet."

Alex whispered. "My God, Industrious, how could you join up with our enemy? After all we've been through together! How come?"

"They told me if I took the oath, I could be a sure 'nough army soldier and after that—a free man. Can you imagine? A free man. Praise the Lord."

"But you were happy with the Brownings. We always treated you good."

"You was my best friend, Mr. Alex. There wasn't nothing I wouldn't do for you. I won't never forget how you save me at the swimmin' hole.

I thought 'bout that while I laid out there on that battlefield. I thought I gonna die without ever being a free man."

Alex turned on his side away from Industrious to hide the tears welling in his eyes. "I would have carried you out if I could. The captain ordered us to retreat. The bullets came too fast."

"The Yankees fixed me up real good. My heart flew like a bird when they told me I be free. It just ain't right for one man to own another one."

Alex looked at his former servant's face. He thought he'd known Industrious, but clearly he didn't know his heart. Industrious had spoken the one truth that had made being a slave owner uncomfortable—*It's not right for one man to own another.* A tickle in his throat induced a spasm of coughing.

Industrious put his hand on Alex's forehead. "You OK, Mr. Alex? I go get you some water."

A few minutes later, Industrious held Alex's head in his big hand and pressed a cup of water to his lips. "I gotta go and work now, but I be back. If any clothes come into here, I grab you a shirt and some trousers."

A few days later, Industrious visited Alex again with bad news. "We got a whole load of trousers and shirts, but the boss man say we can't give 'em to the prisoners 'less they be gray."

"What did they do with all those clothes, Industrious?"

"Burned em."

"How stupid! Why would they destroy good clothes?"

Industrious shrugged. "I dunno."

Alex spoke under his breath. "I'll never understand these damn Yankees." He sat on the side of the bed and then stood. After Industrious wrapped a sheet around him, he clutched it to hide his scrawny body and walked outside the hospital tent to relieve himself. He thought about his former slave in the blue uniform. It still didn't seem real. Then, he remembered the letter he'd sent to Sarah. *Hannah still thinks he's dead.*

In mid-August, while orderlies carried sick men on stretchers, Alex and other ambulatory patients wrapped themselves in bedding and shuffled to the newly built hospital. A pile of gray shirts and trousers awaited them.

While Alex dressed himself, a doctor approached a group of patients. "We're short-handed here in the hospital. We need some of you to work as nurses and cooks."

Clustering around the doctor, prisoners begged for assignments. Alex moved closer. He wanted the doctor to assign him to hospital duty. Anything was better than digging trenches in the mud. Five men were chosen but not Alex. Maybe his reputation for aiding escapees kept him from receiving such privileges. Guards escorted him back to his quarters—now a tent. Another prisoner had long since occupied his bunk inside the barracks.

A few weeks later, Industrious came into the tent. "Would you help me, Mr. Alex? A soldier brung this message to me." He unfolded a sheet of paper with a US Army insignia at the top.

Alex took the letter addressed to Industrious Abraham. *Where had he gotten that last name?* Before the war most freedmen in Lake City had taken the names of their former masters. He went on to read the contents of the letter. "Congratulations, Industrious. You've been promoted to Corporal." He looked up. "We're the same rank now."

Industrious grinned. "Thank you for reading my letter, Mr. Alex. I didn't want the captain to know I couldn't read. Did it say anything else?"

"They said you served the army well."

"Now ain't that nice!" He grinned again.

"Industrious Abraham?"

Industrious laughed. "When I woke up in the hospital, they asked me my name. I tole em 'Industrious.' Then they wanted my last name and tole me I could take any I wanted."

"So you chose Abraham—from the Bible?"

"Oh, no suh. After Mr. Lincoln. From what folks said, he's the man who made us free. I hoped he wouldn't mind me borrowin' his name."

Alex grimaced. "I'm sure you're not the first slave that took that name."

Industrious looked down. "You still mad at me for going over to da Yankees, ain't you?"

Alex felt confused, unable to connect this man in the blue shirt with the boy and the man he'd loved. "Just tell me. How could your life be better now than it was in Florida? They make you wipe up vomit and clean nasty bedpans."

"It's better bein' free even with all the nasty jobs in the world."

"What are you going to do *after* the war?"

Industrious shook his head. "I tell you one thing. I ain't working in no hospital."

"What then?"

Industrious turned his dark eyes across the prison yard as though seeing something beyond it. "Hannah and me talked lots of times 'bout what we do if we was free. I'd make me some money then put some of it down on a piece of property. We could work the land, build us a little house, and live offa the crops. Might even get us a couple of cows and horses." He frowned and shrugged. "That's probably just foolishness, but I do it if I getta chance."

"So you'd come back home?"

"Right now, I'd get shot for sure if I went down south." He pursed his lips. "If the Yankees turn me loose some day, I come back for Hannah." His lips widened into a big smile.

Alex's thoughts wandered back to Gettysburg, and he tried to imagine how Industrious had felt, wounded and left to die. "I'm glad you didn't die, Industrious."

Things had changed since his sickness. The stench of ammonia wafted from sewage flowing into Foster's Pond. The din of prisoners, rumored to number over ten thousand, roared from the barracks, tents, and the open yards. It took more than three hours for them to eat in shifts.

In September, he noticed several of the strongest prisoners had disappeared. He asked a sickly, fellow prisoner with a festering sore on his arm, "What happened to Sam and David? They were healthy as horses."

"They got exchanged," the soldier said. "I heard they're swapping rebel prisoners for some Yankees imprisoned in the South. You have to get checked by the doctor to see if you're healthy enough to make the trip."

The next week, Alex saw the doctor who attended him at the hospital. The doctor weighed him, examined his skin, and listened to his chest.

"I'm feeling much better doctor. Can't you put my name on the list?"

The doctor shook his head. "Not yet. They don't want anybody who might die going back."

So Alex endured, day after day, praying to be sent to the South.

By November, a cold spell had brought winter frost to the prison yards where men answered roll call, their bare feet turning blue from the cold. Prisoners who'd come in recently wore only rags. Many broke down from exposure. Alex's friend Bruce from the Maryland prison had died of smallpox, and Alex had found two more of his bunkmates stiff in their cots one cold morning. He knew he'd never survive a winter in this God-forsaken place. "Hellmira," they called it.

16

Prices are very high, but money is plentiful and becoming more so.

Catherine Ann Devereaux Edmondston
Journal of a Secesh Lady,
1860–1866

October 1864

From the front porch, Sarah watched gray fog spread over the pastures and diffuse the morning sunlight. Even the outside walls of the house were turning gray where paint had peeled off the wood planks. Earlier, she'd noted the date, October first, on the almanac in the kitchen and counted forward three months—the time she expected the baby. She stroked her growing belly with a light caress and felt sad. What a miserable time to be born!

After Frances and Tommy joined her, they walked across the bridge to meet John, who had prepared the wagon for a trip into town. As the wagon turned parallel to the stream, Sarah stared at the bank where the large alligator reclined.

"Penny for your thoughts, Missy," John said.

"Funny you'd mention money." Sarah touched the roll of bills in her bag. "That's exactly what I've been mulling over. I've never known or even imagined prices as high as now. Pretty soon, we'll need a wagonload of Confederate bills to buy anything."

"Not much we can do about it, though." John stared at the rear of the horse pulling the wagon.

"Maybe there is. I've been holding onto that Confederate money Bart Benedict gave me for my goods in July. The way prices are going up, that money won't be worth anything in a few months. If we buy something we could sell later, we'd be better off. Do you have any ideas?"

"Smart girl." John cocked his head and paused. "Hmm, something other folks need, like farm equipment or such."

"First, Tommy needs a pair of new school shoes." Sarah remembered how he'd limped in the old shoes that pinched his growing feet.

Frances touched Sarah's shoulder. "Don't forget; I helped can those tomatoes and beans. While we're out shopping, I could use a can of snuff."

Sarah grimaced.

When they reached the block of Flint's Mercantile Store, John patted Tommy's leg. "I'll hitch the horse, and you help your mama out of the wagon." Tommy leapt from his front seat and held his mother's hand. Sarah eased herself down holding her purse close to her body, fearful that somehow the money might escape.

As soon as Sarah's feet touched the ground, Tommy raced down the planked walkway to the store and reached it before the others. "There's a big sign on the door. I think they're closed."

When she caught up with him, Sarah read from a poster plastered across the locked front door: "CLOSED. OUT OF BUSINESS." She stood facing the door as though staring could change the words. She'd shopped at this store since 1853, the year she and Alex had moved to Lake City. Mr. Flint had always let her charge to her account when money was tight. She wondered what happened to the post office.

Tommy pointed across the street. "Look, Mama, there's another store."

A huge banner read, "Bartholomew's Bounty: Mercantile, Sundries, Foodstuff, European Collectibles."

"Well, this is a fine state of affairs!" John said as they crossed the street. "I hate to see an honest businessman like Flint close his doors. I'm going down the block to look at farm implements. Maybe someone will know what happened to Flint." He left them at the door.

"Good morning, ladies," Bart greeted them with the smile Sarah remembered. "Please come in. We opened just a week ago so things may not quite be in order. We're applying to move the post office here. We'll be handling the mail within the month." He glanced around the room. "Please feel free to browse, but let me know if I can be of assistance."

Sarah felt her anger rising. She felt certain that Bart's opening had hurt the business of her friend Flint. What good would it do to lose her temper? Clearly, Bart now owned the only store in town. "Tommy needs new shoes," she said. "He enters second grade next week."

Bart laid his hand on Tommy's shoulder. "I'll help this young man find some shoes while you ladies shop." Bart led Tommy to the back of the store.

Sarah and Frances roamed the aisles. Fascinated, Sarah inspected English china cups and marveled at how the imported items had come through the blockade. She could only think of three or four people in Lake City who could afford to buy such things. She admired a doll with a fine-featured porcelain head and dressed in an elaborate miniature dress. "Lula would love this doll," she told Frances. "I wish I could afford to buy it for her."

Frances, who never showed much interest in fancy things, shrugged and wandered to where food items were displayed. "Sarah," Frances called, "you have to see this."

Sarah gasped when she saw what Frances had found—a shelf crowded with canned tomatoes, peas, and beans priced at five dollars each, every jar newly labeled "Canned vegetables from South Carolina farms." A package, identified as Craig's Virginia Smoked Ham and priced at fifty dollars, hung from a ceiling hook. "He bought those goods at my stand." Sarah whispered, "He relabeled them, but he paid dearly. I suppose he can do as he pleases."

Frances gripped Sarah's arm, "Look at how much profit he's making."

Bart entered the aisle, a pair of boy's black leather shoes in his hand. "A perfect fit, and I'll make you a special price. They're selling for a hundred and fifty dollars—"

Sarah gasped. "A hundred and fifty dollars?"

"Don't get riled up, Miss Sarah. I'll sell them to you for fifty dollars. I guarantee you'll not find them for less."

She had already checked with the cobbler. His price was seventy-five dollars. She inspected the shoes and gulped. "I'll take them." She unrolled a one hundred-dollar bill from the thousand dollars in her pocketbook and handed it to Bart, who gave her fifty back.

While she waited for Bart to wrap the shoes, John sauntered to the counter. "Don't spend all the money, Sarah. Remember our agreement about investing it."

Sarah put her arm through the handle of her pocketbook and handed Tommy the package. They followed John down the street to the farm supply store to look at a used wagon. A few steps along, Tommy peeled back the brown paper wrapping his shoes. "Hey, what's this?"

Sarah took the parcel and slipped her hand inside. A small item enclosed in thin, white paper snuggled alongside the shoes. Sarah unwrapped the porcelain doll and read a note pinned to its skirt—"For Lula," written in fine Spenserian script. Her earlier annoyance with Bart dissolved into the warm fall breeze.

When they walked into the farm store, a salesman sat behind the counter reading the inside pages of a newspaper with bold, startling headlines. "Sherman's Troops Attack Atlanta." This recent war news so close to home made Sarah ill with worry. She forced herself to take interest in the wagon.

"We already have a perfectly good wagon, Papa," Frances said.

Sarah walked around the wagon and eyed it from every side. "We could use this wagon."

"Sarah, don't forget your decision. We're buying this wagon with the idea of selling it next spring to preserve the value of our money," John said.

"How much is it?" she asked.

"Five hundred," said the salesman. "It's barely used. The wheels are in great condition."

John rubbed his chin. "I'll think about it." He pulled Sarah aside and whispered, "How much do we have?"

"The shoes were fifty dollars. We've got nine-fifty left."

"What do you think?" John asked.

"We'll pay you four hundred," she told the salesman, who shook his head.

"Four-fifty."

Sarah unbuttoned her purse and removed the bills. "We'll take the wagon."

"And that new cultivator you priced me at two hundred," John said.

"Remember; you got me down from two-fifty."

After Sarah paid for the farm equipment, John hitched the new wagon behind the old one. "Six-fifty Confederate won't be worth three hundred in a couple of months," she told him on the way home.

In late October, Sarah and John came in from the fields. Sarah noticed an unfamiliar paint horse tied to the fence. She touched John's arm. "We have a visitor. I'll see who's here."

Lester Cartwright sat in a rocking chair on the front porch. His gaunt body and thinning hair made him look older than his twenty years.

"Lester," Sarah said. "I thought you were in Virginia with Alex and Max."

"It's a long story, Miss Sarah." Lester stood and enfolded her in a strong hug. She felt his bony arms press her back.

John shook Lester's hand. "Have you heard from Alex? We haven't had any word of him in months. Is he all right?"

"As far as I know, he's in prison at Elmira. When I was out on the road, I heard something about Elmira prisoners getting exchanged in Savannah. Maybe he was one of them." He stopped and looked Sarah over. "Another baby? When's this one due?" he asked.

"Next month." She pointed toward two rocking chairs on the porch. "Lester, you and John sit down. We want you to tell us everything. Hannah will bring us some lemonade."

Lester related a long story about the battle at Spotsylvania and their capture by the Yankees. She wept when he described conditions at Point Lookout and laughed when he came to the part about the Yankee ladies who came aboard the train with cakes and pies for the prisoners. She could hardly bear the suspense in the story of Lester's escape.

By this time, Frances and Tommy had joined them and listened intently to Lester's story. Hannah brought lemonade and distributed the glasses to everyone.

He continued his story. " . . . and Alex, bless his heart, sat behind us with the door bolted shut on two sides talking friendly-like with the guard so his buddies could jump out of the window when the train slowed up."

"I wish he'd escaped with you," Sarah said.

He patted her arm. "Soon as we hit the ground, Max and Bruce and me started up running fast as we could with no idea which way to go. We figgered the best chance was staying outside of town, so we cut out 'cross a field and headed south toward what appeared to be a forest. About that time, we seen four horses galloping like the devil was chasing 'em. But soon we saw it was them chasing us. Bruce stumped his foot on a berry vine and fell flat on his face, but Max and me, we kept on running, never looking back to see if poor Bruce got caught."

Lester stopped to take a swig of the cool lemonade. "This is delicious. How'd you make it, Hannah?"

Hannah smiled. "Started out with well water and squeezed some lemons, then put in honey for sweetenin.'"

Tommy's eyes were wide with excitement. "Don't stop. Tell us more."

"We didn't stop till we came to a thicket. We rested ourselves there, and took turns sleeping and watching for Yanks. That afternoon, I saw three Bluecoats tramping through the woods. I jostled ol' Max to wake him up and took off running again with Max right behind me. Then they caught Max, but I just kept on running. You know, one of us boys had to get back home to find Ma and Pa and tell 'em our story."

"New York's a long way," John said. "How'd you get home?"

"By walking south, sleeping during the day and following the stars by night. Finally, I made it to Maryland and some sympathizers fed me pork ribs and taters. After Virginny, I took to the road. I grabbed a ride on a wagon when I could and slept over at farmhouses along the way. In North Carolina this nice farmer and his wife give me some food and this here painted horse to ride. I couldn't have made it without them kind folks."

"How long did it take you to get here?" Frances asked. She spit a stream of snuff juice off the edge of the porch.

Lester scratched his head. "About two months, I reckon."

Sarah gripped his thin wrist. "Tell me more about Alex."

"If he's still living, he's probably at Elmira. Haven't heard anything from Max after he got caught, either. If I hear something, I'll let ya know. Him and Bruce were strong last time I saw 'em in spite of all the bad stuff we went through at Lookout."

"What about you, Lester? Will you stay here? Do you have to go back?"

"I can't go back, not after what I been through, Miss Sarah. More than anything now, I wanna stay alive and find my brother dead or alive. It would just about kill Ma if both of us died." He looked off toward the creek. "I can't stay at home. The regulators and home guards are out to kill deserters. I'm headed up to Savannah to see if I can find Max and

Alex. Maybe I can land a job somewhere—picking crops or maybe doing a little carpenter work."

When Lester paused, Hannah walked closer. "Tell me 'bout Dustrous, Mr. Lester. Was you with him when he died up in Pennsylvany?"

"I saw him once carrying a stretcher. After the fight, the captain yelled 'retreat,' and we started back. Alex came back alone."

Hannah folded her arms and sighed. "You never seen him after that?"

He shook his head. "There was thousands of us out there. When we started marching on the Yanks, soldiers were falling dead all 'round. I never saw him." He gave Hannah a sad smile. "I wish I could tell you more."

A tear rolled down Hannah's cheek. Sarah stood and took her hand.

Lester got out of his chair. "I'd better be going."

Sarah wrapped her arms around his thin body and kissed his cheeks. "God go with you, dear friend. And keep you safe from harm."

"I'm needing all the help I kin get. But I'll be back. You'll see." He mounted his horse and rode away.

17

I was transferred to Elmira, N.Y. and about the middle of November exchanged. They kept us on the Ohioan Steamer about 25 days.

Alexander Browning
former POW,
letter to Board of Pensions,
1910

November–December 1864

Late in November, guards came for Alex. "You're gonna be exchanged," one told him and directed him to join a group of soldiers marching toward the train. Men with pale, gaunt faces and eyes without luster shuffled through the prison gates never looking back. Their tattered clothing hung loosely on their skeletal bodies.

While prisoners filed into the cars, the guards joked among themselves, paying little attention. Most men headed for freedom wouldn't try to jump train in New York even if physically able to do so. Alex took a seat, impatient for the train to leave and to move even an inch closer to Lake City and his family. Even as he yearned for home, he feared facing Sarah again. After horrendous battles and two prisons, he was not the same man she'd known. As soon as the train got underway, he stared out the window at the bleak countryside and the snow-covered roofs of scattered farmhouses with smoke puffing from their chimneys.

At Baltimore, the prisoners crowded onto an Ohio steamer in Chesapeake Bay. On the floor of the lower cabin, Alex sat pressed against his fellow prisoners for several hours before the captain blew the horn and cast off. He overheard two men describing their experiences in an early battle. Their conversation reminded Alex of the maimed bodies twisted on the fields of Gettysburg. The horror of his memories made his head throb and his heart pound against his chest. Gasping for air, he made his way to the upper deck.

Later, as he returned down the gangway, he heard a familiar voice. He stumbled toward the stooped back of the speaker. "Max . . . Max Cartwright, is it you?"

Max unfolded himself off the floor and wrapped his arms around Alex. "My God, Alex. You old sonofabitch. You're still alive. I thought sure you'd die from the consumption."

"I did almost die, but, hey, fellow, the last time I saw you, you were hanging by your thumbs in the prison yard."

Max held up his disfigured hands, the thumbs hanging useless against his palms. "I can't hardly stand to think about it. I fainted a couple of times and nearly yanked my thumbs out of their sockets. Two days we stood out there. Dear God, if we'd only known what lay ahead."

Alex blew out a long stream of air as if he could exhale all the evil, putrid smells and sights he'd endured during the past six months. He patted his friend's back. "I know. I know. I just want to get out of this damn place. Have you heard anything about Lester?"

"As far as I know, the Bluecoats didn't shoot him," Max said.

As he had for several weeks, Alex slept fitfully. He dreamed about Jacob when he climbed out of the trench. He awoke in the dark hold of the ship amid the grunting snores of his fellow passengers, his heart beating wildly.

"What's wrong?" Max mumbled.

Alex didn't answer.

In the following days, the routine of the ship settled in on him—eating the same food twice each day and watching without a grimace when sailors hoisted dead bodies overboard. Alex and Max speculated about how many days they'd been at sea.

"At least twenty-five," Alex surmised.

"It just seems like it to you, Alex. It's less than that."

"Five bucks says twenty-five."

"My guess is twenty. You can pay me when we get to Savannah." Just then a sailor walked down onto the lower deck and passed out rations.

"How long have we been on this boat?" Alex asked him.

The sailor stopped for a minute. "We left on November twentieth and today's the eighth of December. Let's see." He counted on his fingers. "Eighteen days."

"You owe me, Alex. I'm closest," Max said.

The steamer entered the mouth of a river and docked at Point Genesis, the location of Fort McAllister, a Confederate fortification on the Ogeechee River. The prisoners piled off and passed through openings in thick earthworks guarded by large canons into a rectangular, mud-colored building.

A sergeant stood, beefy arms crossed, and examined the newly released prisoners assembled before him. "If any of you boys feel like fighting, we could sure use your help to protect Savannah from the Yankees. Sherman's on his way here." Alex listened with mounting fear as the sergeant described how Sherman burned Atlanta to the ground and with his hordes of bummers had foraged fields and ransacked homes across Georgia. It had been seven months since Alex had heard news of the war. Three men walked forward, but the captain dismissed them. Alex didn't think the bone-thin, ragged prisoners looked capable of military service. He and Max didn't move a muscle.

The sergeant took a seat behind his desk and motioned to Max to come forward. He squinted at Max's deformed hands. After a few questions, he dipped a quill into an ink well, scribbled a note, and handed it to Max. "Take this down the hall to the door marked 'Medical.' The doctor will decide whether you should be discharged." The sergeant peered at Alex. "What kind of problems you got, soldier?"

Alex bit his lip, trying to choose the right words to describe the way he felt. "I been feeling real bad—kind of numb—everything goes blank."

The sergeant made a steeple of his fingers and stared over them.

Alex touched his hand to his chest. "At night my heart starts galloping like a wild mare." He detected a faint shrug in the sergeant's collarbone.

The sergeant made a note on Alex's form. He pointed toward the medical office. "Take this down there. Tell the doc about it."

Alex waited outside the door until Max came out with an official-looking paper. "Looks like I'll get me a discharge," Max said. "I'll wait for you outside."

The doctor leaned back in his chair. "So you're having heart palpitations."

Alex nodded. "Every day or so, it starts beating real fast."

"Anything else?"

"Sometimes, Doc, I don't know what day it is or even what year."

"Yeah, well, that's common among recently released prisoners. You have problems sleeping?"

"Stay awake all night—afraid the nightmares will come." Alex studied the man in front of him trying to determine his level of sympathy.

The doctor narrowed his eyes, and his mouth turned down. "What kind of nightmares?"

"Same one mostly. Everything's dark and rainy just like that night in the 'mule shoe.' I smell gunpowder and blood. Then Jacob starts hollering." As Alex relived the dream, his heart began to palpitate. Perspiration broke out on his forehead.

"Jacob?"

"He was my brother. The pictures keep running through my head over and over." His voice became shrill. "I try to stop 'em, but I can't."

"Not unusual. I've heard similar stories from soldiers who fought in rough battles. They can't forget about it. Sounds like 'irritated heart.' Some call it 'soldier's heart.'" He put his hand on Alex's shoulder.

The small gesture of kindness gave Alex some relief. "I thought I was going crazy."

"You're a long way from crazy, soldier. I've seen many worse than you—ranting, screaming maniacs they were. Had to take them to the insane asylum." He stood and walked toward Alex.

"If you'll give me a discharge, I can get over this. I'll get better for sure." The prospect of commitment frightened Alex.

The doctor pressed a stethoscope on Alex's chest. "Take a deep breath. Now exhale." The doctor frowned and moved the instrument into another spot. "Heartbeat's rapid, but your heart sounds healthy. Just a little bronchitis. After you rest awhile, you'll be good as new. I'm recommending a sixty-day furlough for you, soldier. Take care of yourself."

Alex's stomach clenched with disappointment.

Alex and Max checked out with the commandant, who signed Max's honorable discharge and handed Alex a furlough order.

"Go home for a time, Corporal Browning. Report for duty with your company in Richmond on February eighth."

Alex stared at the commandant in despair. "I'm not a well man."

The commandant shrugged. "If you have further medical problems, you can apply for an extension to the furlough." He shuffled some papers on his desk. "Dismissed," he said without looking up. "Stop by the purser's office on your way out."

After pocketing fifty Confederate dollars each, Alex and Max boarded a small boat that took them to the harbor of Savannah. It was swarming with gunboats. A forty-foot bluff rose above the Savannah River, topped by a long row of brick buildings painted a patchwork of colors.

After they walked past huge stacks of baled cotton on the dock, they climbed a steep stairway and out onto Bay Street under the cloudless blue sky of a crisp December afternoon. Max ran leaping and whooping down the boardwalk and caught the attention of Confederate guards stationed at various intervals. Out of breath, Alex followed behind as they ran past offices and government buildings into a residential area where roofs of houses, cupolas, and church steeples peeped out of thick live oaks draped with Spanish moss.

Abruptly, Max stopped. "We're free. We survived." He ran back and laid his hands on Alex's shoulders. "Nobody can tell us where to go and what to do. Never again. Praise God!"

Alex lowered his head wishing he could share Max's exuberance. He attempted a smile and blinked away tears. Max stared. "What's the matter? You look gloomier than a bloodhound."

Alex shook his head. "I don't know what's wrong with me."

Max looked at Alex more closely. "Are you sick?"

"I can't shake off this feeling like something bad is about to happen."

"Hey, friend, nothing bad's gonna happen to us. We're free."

"Easy for you to say. You got a discharge. I gotta go back in February."

"Maybe not. The war might be done by then."

Alex really didn't care who won now, but he knew he didn't want to go back into battle. He thought about Sarah and the children and the new baby. A tear rolled down his cheek. He wanted to go home, yet he feared going there. Maybe he'd remain in Savannah for a while until he felt more certain and less afraid. "You wanna stay here a few days?"

Max looked puzzled. "I thought you wanted to go home."

"I don't know. It's a long way from here to Florida," Alex said.

"If you're sick, I'll stay here with you till you get well."

"If you want to go on . . ."

Max shook his head. "I'm not leaving you here feeling bad."

Alex looked down at his filthy shirt. He scanned the city street. "We need to buy some clean clothes."

After a few blocks, they came upon a square planted with magnolias, live oaks, and mulberry trees. Lining the squares, magnificent brick mansions reflected an earlier era of wealthy owners, perhaps cotton factors, bankers, or ship owners. They turned west into a run-down neighborhood and found a booth sheltered by a striped awning. Clothing lay in messy stacks on a long table. They bought trousers, shirts, socks, and jackets from an old woman, who threw in used canvas satchels to hold their purchases. Further on they saw a sign offering rooms by the week hung askance on an unpainted, sprawling, three-story clapboard house. Two shutters hung loose against the outer wall.

A sallow-faced man, gray-bearded and leaning on a cane, opened the door. His once-white shirt hung loose over a sunken chest, and suspenders prevented his trousers from falling around his bowed legs. "I'm Cory Lanagan, the landlord," he told them with a smile, revealing wide-spaced, rotting teeth. "You fellers looking for a room?"

"How much?" Max asked.

"If you pay a week in advance, you got yourselves a room and two meals a day—five bucks a week. Follow me."

Max nudged Alex. "You pay for my week since I won the bet."

"What bet?" Alex asked. But he paid the landlord ten dollars.

He led them down a hall where they passed a dining room containing a large rectangular wood table. A musty smell pervaded the hall and the rickety stairway they climbed to the second floor. He opened the door to a room, barely large enough for its one double bed. A faded quilt, leaking tufts of cotton filler, sprawled over the mattress. Sunshine seeped through the trees from outside the room through an open window.

"This is it. You want it?"

Max agreed, and Alex, accustomed to sleeping with his brother as a child, nodded his assent. "Supper's at six-thirty." Cory clumped down the stairs.

An hour later, Alex and Max washed up, changed into their new clothes, and went downstairs to eat. Six men of various ages and two young women occupied benches on either side of the table. A brown-skinned woman with a bandana tied around her hair set down a large pot of rice and a plate of boiled fish. Alex figured the fish came from the river and suspected the rice was harvested from one of the plantations he'd seen in the lowlands approaching Savannah. A young man reached across and spooned a generous helping into his bowl.

Most of the men had fought battles in Virginia. A tall man with bushy eyebrows growing across the bridge of his nose explained. "Our men are dying quicker 'n flies. We had no food, no ammunition, our shoes were falling apart. In every battle, we lost as many men running the other way as were shot dead." Alex suspected some of these men had deserted.

A former university student with a red, blotchy face agreed. "Only a fool would stay on to fight now. Unless he had a penchant for suicide."

Max elbowed Alex and whispered, "Nobody would say that in our regiment—except for the stragglers."

When Alex dipped out a spoonful of rice, his hand trembled, spilling some grains on the table. He tried to eat the fish, but it was bony and he couldn't swallow it. He spit a clump into his spoon and laid it beside his bowl. He turned to see Max gripping his spoon against his palm and twisting his chin to bring the food to his mouth. *I should feel lucky to have come through the war unscathed.*

The red-faced man unfolded a newspaper and read silently from the front page.

"What's the news about Sherman?" Max asked.

The man continued looking at the paper. "I'm reading about him now. He's got near about sixty thousand Yankees on the march since they burned Atlanta last month." He ran his finger down the column of print. "Last week the Yanks shot some old men and boys—about six hundred in all—outside Milledgeville. Then the dirty blue bellies went on to the state capital and tore up everything they could get their hands on."

The man with the bushy eyebrows cleared his throat. "My sister wrote me about how they come through Macon stealing food and poking ramrods in all the flowerbeds."

"Why ramrods?" Alex asked.

"They're looking for silver and jewelry the ladies had buried to keep 'em from finding it. My sister's scared out of her mind that they're gonna steal her stuff or burn her barn or worse—"

A fear shivered through Alex as he imagined Yankees invading his own home and doing hideous things to Sarah and the children.

"We heard that Sherman might be headed here," Max said.

"From what I'm reading, General Grant doesn't even know where Sherman is much less where he's headed. Listen to this. Grant says he's like a ground mole that disappears under your lawn. You never know where he will come out until you see his head."

Everyone laughed. Alex smiled, amused—not at the joke but at Grant's confusion between moles and gophers.

The red-faced man continued. "In my opinion, Sherman's headed straight for Savannah."

"Why are you so sure?" Bushy-eyebrows asked.

"Because every chance that devil gets to talk to a newspaper reporter, he threatens to burn or starve Savannah."

Alex shivered again at the disturbing war news.

The two young women walked around the table, stopping behind Alex and Max. Alex felt the warmth of their presence, but the honeysuckle waft of their perfume made him nauseous.

"We're going into town. You boys wanna go with us?" the redhead asked.

Max wiped his mouth with a stained napkin. "Sounds good to me. Alex?"

"Nuh uh. I'm beat. You go ahead. I'll stay here and sleep." The disturbing news had shaken Alex into numbness. His meal half-eaten, he excused himself and trudged the creaking stairs to his bed. He stripped down to his long johns, covered himself with the tattered quilt, and fell asleep immediately. In his dream, he yelled for Jacob to come back to the trench. Alex grabbed for Jacob's leg, and a muddy boot slipped off in his hands; then, Jacob stood and laughed that crazy laugh as bullets riddled his body. He awoke to the sound of screaming—his own.

Alex stumbled out of bed to the open window and breathed the night air. Myriad sounds rose out of the cool, damp night: people laughing, horses' hooves thumping, carriage wheels rattling on sandy streets. When he looked down, he saw a familiar figure, his arm around a red-headed woman and another taller man following behind. When they reached the circle of light under the gas lamp across the street, he heard them speak. He recognized Max's and Lester's voices.

"Good night, Rosy," Lester called. Moments later, Alex heard two pairs of boots stomp up the stairs. When his friends entered the room, Alex crushed Lester against him. "My God, man, you're a ghost from the past. How did you find us?"

"I been looking for you and Max ever since October when I heard they was exchanging the prisoners in Savannah." His smile waned as he stared into Alex's eyes. "I been home and seen Sarah."

Alex sat down hard on the bed. Lester and Max, for lack of chairs, sat down on the rough wood floor. Alex was breathing hard. "Tell me," he said, "How is she? How are the children?"

"Sarah's got steel for a backbone. She's gonna figger a way to take care of herself and them kids no matter what." Lester clapped his hands on his knees. "She asked about you. She lives for the day you come home to her. I expect she's already had herself a new baby by now."

Eyes tearing and lips pressed together, Alex felt desperation mixed with longing welling up inside him. "If there was any way, I'd go to her."

"Hell's fire," Lester exploded. "I went all the way from New York to Florida. Then, I made it back here to look for y'all. The word is the Yanks are mighty sure to attack Savannah. You need to get out of here—and soon."

Alex's voice was barely audible. "I can't go. Not yet." He didn't want to see Sarah until he felt better. He worried about his tiredness, his headaches, his inability to sleep, and his heart palpitations.

Alex returned to bed as soon as Lester left. Max blew out the candle and climbed in beside him. Alex squirmed, wakeful and anxious as Max began to snore. Giving up, he went to the window and watched dark clouds swirl over the moon. Then, he lay on the plank floor and fell into deep sleep until bright morning sun blazed in his face.

He awoke with his head throbbing and his heart beating rapidly. *What's wrong with me?* He stared at his trembling hands. Still dead tired and craving more sleep, he flopped on the bed again, yet fearing the terrible dreams that haunted him. When he finally slept, he didn't dream about Jacob, but Industrious lying unconscious and bleeding. Bullets exploding around him in the dream, Alex put his hands under Industrious's arms and tugged, but the body wouldn't move. A loud voice yelled, "Retreat, retreat." Alex awoke wet with perspiration, the unfinished dream still vivid as though it had happened moments earlier.

18

How soon, my Dear, death may my steps attend, / How soon't may be thy lot to lose thy friend . . . And when thy loss shall be repaid with gains, / Look to my little babes, my dear remains.

Anne Bradstreet
"Before the Birth of One of Her Children"

November 1864

As November approached, Sarah's body grew heavier. Numbing fatigue settled over her. Hannah and Frances took on the house chores, and John directed the hands in making repairs to the barn and the fences. On warm days, Sarah sat in a rocking chair on the porch waiting for John to finish his work.

Each day, he brought her more disappointments: "We lost another cow today . . . I had to let the hands go . . . The bean crop's dying on the vine . . . We're getting short of money."

Even in her exhaustion, Sarah wished she could do something to relieve the hopelessness.

One day, Margaret came by with newspapers folded under her arm. She sat down in the swing.

"Bad news?" Sarah asked.

"Nothing but." She unfolded the papers. "Sherman's burned down Atlanta."

Sarah winced, imagining the city she'd visited as a child with its beautiful mansions in ashes.

"Early's surrendered in the western valley," Margaret continued. "They think Lincoln's going to win the election next week. He's promised to keep on fighting until they wipe us out."

A week after the election, Sarah noticed a few spots of blood on her garments. She thought little of it since her delivery was due in about three weeks. The second time, she asked John to bring the doctor. Dr. Taylor prescribed bed rest. If she didn't do as he said, she'd risk her health and the baby's. That evening, she copied into her diary an excerpt from Anne Bradstreet's poem "Before the Birth of One of her Children," which told of the poet's fear of death in childbirth. The words spoke to Sarah's dread of possibly dying and leaving her children orphaned. She'd formed a strange friendship with this seventeenth-century Puritan woman whose poems looked outward at God's glorious creation and inward at her own doubts and fears.

A few days after Sarah had gone to bed, Frances sat beside her applying a cold compress to her burning forehead. Sarah moaned, "I'm so hot. Take off the covers."

"The doctor said you had a little infection, but he said you'd likely be fine and have another healthy baby."

"Where are my children?"

Frances gently wiped her neck and arms with rubbing alcohol, cooling her skin as the medicinal smell filled her nostrils. "Don't worry, darling. Hannah takes good care of the girls, and Tommy's still at school. After school, Tommy will walk to Margaret's house. You just rest easy now."

"And John? Where's Daddy John?" She turned restlessly.

"Stop fretting. Everything will be fine. Papa has taken the cultivator into town. He thinks he may have a buyer. If he can get US cash, we'll make it through the winter. We've got plenty of meat in the smokehouse and a crib full of corn. We're going to be all right." Frances stood and walked toward the bedroom door.

Sarah pulled at the quilt tucked around her. "Don't go, Franny. Talk to me. Tell me the truth. Am I going to die?"

"All of us die . . . someday. But I don't think you'll be leaving us anytime soon."

"If I die having this baby, I want you to take care of my children."

"Sure, darling, but—"

"Promise me you'll do it. Don't let Margaret take them. Please!"

"I promise."

Sarah sighed and relaxed into the pillow for a few minutes. Then, she raised her head. "Franny, are you still there?"

"I'm here, honey. I won't leave you."

"Do you think I'm going to hell for not going to church?"

"I'm not going to let you die, Sarah."

"I want to know what happens after." She craned her neck toward Frances. "The Bible says that if we love the Lord, we'll be with him in heaven. But not one soul has ever come back to tell us what happens. I'm afraid of living in the dark, under the ground forever."

"Listen to me, Sarah. Every time I help a baby into life, I know that little person was created for eternity." Frances stroked Sarah's forehead gently. "A loving Lord wouldn't have created those innocents to exist only for this short, brutal lifetime." As Sarah relaxed, she continued stroking her face. "Of course, there's a heaven. Your mama, your daddy, and your darling Mariah live there. Many years from now, you'll be there, too."

Sarah felt a sharp pain in her abdomen. She sucked in a breath then gasped.

"What is it?" Frances asked.

"I think the baby's coming. I recognize this pain. It's always like this at the beginning. You'd better get everything ready. It's not supposed to come yet, but I recognize this pain."

"I've delivered babies early—little bitty cusses—but they grew up fine." Frances walked to the bureau and removed a clean sheet.

Another painful surge wracked Sarah's body. "Oh, Franny. I want Alex." Tears squeezed out of her eyes. "He ought to be here with me. Where is he, Franny? Where is he?"

"Only God knows that, darling. You hush now and rest up for the birthing."

She sat by the bed and held Sarah's hand. From time to time, she wiped her forehead with a wet rag. She poured more warm water in the ceramic bowl on the washstand and dipped the rag in the water again.

"How long have my pains been going on?"

"About an hour, honey. This is your fourth child so it should come quicker than the others, but you probably have a few hours to go." She squeezed excess water from the cloth and continued bathing her face and encouraging Sarah. Time, marked in quarter hours by the clock's chimes, moved in interminable slowness through the afternoon into the dark of evening. Sarah's pains lapsed and then resumed in full force. She began trembling, drenched in perspiration.

Frances patted her arm. "I won't be gone long. I'm going to boil some water and get some clean cloths." Frances left for what seemed an eternity as the pains came closer and closer together and increased in intensity.

When she returned, she propped Sarah's legs on boxes covered with clean white cloth.

"Bear down, honey," Frances said.

Sarah screamed and gripped two strips of sheeting that Frances had tied to the posts on the brass headboard. "Alex, Alex," she repeated until his name became a chant.

Hannah cracked the bedroom door. "How is Miss Sarah? Is there somethin' I could do?"

"Sarah will be fine, Hannah. It's taking a long time. Just tend to those children, and keep them occupied so they won't bother us. Get

Megan to help you when she comes home from her school. You might get some supper for Mr. John."

"I already fed him and the chillun. I go put the babies in bed." She shut the door softly, but after it closed, Sarah could hear the girls running up the stairs laughing and Hannah shushing them. The impending birth drove a new, even more intense pain like a pick through Sarah's body. She pulled hard on the sheeting tied to the headboard.

Frances felt Sarah's pulse. "Push, Sarah. Push as hard as you can."

Sarah exerted enormous effort, pressing on the huge weight in her abdomen. She felt determination grow like a storm inside her. *I can do it. I'm going to live and so is this baby.*

Frances leaned forward. "Oh my God in heaven," she cried, "I can see the little foot." She yelled for John, who appeared at the door almost instantly. "Go for the doctor quick. It's a breech birth, Papa. And tell Hannah to come . . . now!"

The sound of a galloping horse faded into the distance as John raced out into the night for help. Hannah opened the door.

Frances turned. "Hannah, bring me a clean knife, a whetting stone, a lighted candle, a needle and some strong thread . . . and some whisky . . . and hurry!"

When Hannah brought the items, Frances sharpened the knife with the stone and held the blade over the flame of the candle until the metal turned red. When the knife cooled, she laid it on the clean cloth next to the hot water. "Stay with me, Hannah. I'm going to need some help."

Sarah screamed again and strained her body to push the baby into the birth canal. She lost consciousness for a few moments. Frances lifted Sarah's head and tilted a glass of straight whisky into her mouth until the strong yellow liquid ran down her throat. She coughed violently.

"We may have a wait for Dr. Taylor. I can give you more whisky if you need it." Frances said.

Sarah shook her head. "No, no more. Do it. Do it now, Franny. Get the baby out."

"I can't. It's a breech. It's too dangerous."

Sarah screamed again and squeezed her eyes shut.

Frances examined the birth canal. "O my God, dear Jesus!" she gasped.

"What's wrong?" Sarah asked.

Hannah sputtered, "The cord—the cord's hangin' out. Very bad sign!"

Sarah gasped. *What is happening? Please, God; don't let me die.*

"Hush, Hannah," Frances whispered. "Don't say things that will upset her."

Frances placed a wooden stick between Sarah's teeth. "Bite down when the pain starts, honey." Frances reached inside Sarah. "I'm pushing this cord back up and getting a hold on its little feet. When I tell you, bear down hard."

Sarah felt a sharp pain and a sensation of something moving in her abdomen. She clamped her teeth on the stick.

"It's coming," Frances said. "It's coming now. Hannah, get ready to hold this baby while I cut the cord."

Sarah heard the baby's soft cry, like the bleat of a lamb, and fell unconscious.

Each day afterwards, Frances came into the room to bathe Sarah. Later, Hannah lifted the tiny baby from its crib and laid her in the bed beside Sarah for her feeding. Sarah stroked the little head while she nursed. Some evenings, Megan came in and knelt beside her bed, praying with her rosary. Gradually, the pain of the birth subsided, as did the chills and fevers that wracked her earlier.

Several weeks later, Sarah awoke to the muffled cries of the baby and, wincing slightly, made her way to the crib. "Good morning, Lena," she said, and lifted the tiny bundle. She returned to the bed to nurse her.

Frances opened the door. "How did Helena get out of her crib?" she asked.

"Let's call her Lena. Helena is too much name for such a tiny little girl."

"You must be feeling much better," Frances said.

"I'm alive, Frances, thanks to you."

Frances took a torn envelope from her apron pocket. "It looks like Alex wrote you a letter."

19

I long for home, long for the sight of home. . . .

Homer
The *Odyssey*

December 1864

During the next week, Alex grew to fear the moods and strange visions that overcame him. News from the war added to his worries. Dinner conversation at his boarding house centered on Sherman's capture of Atlanta and his march through Georgia toward the Atlantic Coast.

On December fifteenth, a newspaper from Charleston appeared on the table at breakfast with huge headlines: *SHERMAN TAKES FORT MCALLISTER.*

"How far is that from Savannah?" Max asked.

"Twelve or fifteen miles." The red-faced student picked up the newspaper. "They attacked the fort two days ago. Some US warships have also entered the harbor bringing supplies . . . Here's a quote from Sherman. 'I shall make little effort to restrain my army, burning to avenge the national wrong which they attach to Savannah in dragging our country into civil war.'"

The word "burning" fixed in Alex's mind. He left his breakfast unfinished and imagined flames licking at the rickety stairs as he climbed to reach his room.

Max entered just after him. "What is it, Alex?"

"We've got to get out of here. They'll burn us alive." Alex gasped for air.

"I don't think Sherman meant it that way."

"Why not? He burned Atlanta."

Max pulled the ratty quilt over Alex and felt his forehead. "You seemed better this week, but something set you off again. Was it the war talk?"

Alex considered. "I haven't felt normal since we got here—can't sleep. If I do, the dreams are terrible."

"What kind?"

Alex shook his head vigorously. "Can't talk about it."

Max looked frustrated. "You've got to forget about the war, Alex. There ain't no sense in you living it over and over when it's all past."

"I wish it was that easy."

Each day, each night, he prayed to forget. Visions and nightmares came on him and exploded in his brain like mortar shells, leaving him mentally dismembered. He often lay awake at night, in fear of the distorted memories that emerged in his dreams. With his quilt pulled to his neck, he often spent the entire day in bed.

The night of December twenty-first, Alex awoke to the blast of shells rocking the city. Beside him Max arose, fumbled with the latch, and threw open the window. "Sherman's attacking. It can't be far away."

Feeling numb, Alex turned away from the sounds and bright flashes coming from the window. His body twitched at each explosion. Later that night, loud voices in the hallway awoke him again. "They sunk the *Savannah*! Right there in the harbor." Alex finally realized they meant the warship, not the river.

Two days later, Lester entered Alex and Max's room. "The siege is already over. Rebels are marching out of the city on every street. We're going home, fellows, leaving today." He sat down beside Alex. "Max tells me you're still having those spells."

Alex nodded.

"Look, there's no good reason for you to stay here in this seedy boarding house. You're not getting any better. Max and me are taking you home where Sarah can look after you. Get your things together."

Wearing two layers of clothes to protect their bodies from the damp cold of winter, the three friends began their trip home. They made their way through a near-empty city. Many people had abandoned their houses and businesses, and looters were breaking into buildings, carrying off food, furniture, expensive lamps, and clothing.

A few miles out of Savannah, a sutler headed south with his wagon of commodities offered them a ride. He dropped them off at the cross-road to Valdosta, where he was headed. A few miles down the road, Alex and his friends found a clapboard house where a farmer and his family welcomed them and gave them food, extra clothes, and beds for the night. The next morning, the husband told them where they might find some mules. Warmly dressed in castoffs, they followed the farmer's directions. Lester stopped. "Max, you and Alex stay here. I can probably strike a better bargain by myself."

After a long, quiet spell, Max nudged Alex. "I been noticing something. Since we left Savannah, you ain't had none of those spells."

It was true. Even at the beginning of their trip, Alex had felt stronger, his head clearer. The open road, the fresh air, even the old sutler had lifted his spirits. Also, his friends had carefully avoided talk about war. He pointed down the road. "Look, here comes Lester already, pulling a couple of mules."

"Did you strike a bargain, brother?" Max laid his hand on back of one mule, which turned a lazy eye his way. "At least, he's not mean."

"Fifty bucks for both. Seems like they wanted to get rid of 'em. But I can sell 'em for more when we get home."

With Alex riding single and the brothers double, they proceeded at a slow pace, stopping often to let the mules graze. Along the way, hospitable farmers offered food and allowed them to sleep in their barns. On the day after Christmas, just after they crossed into Florida, a bearded man on horseback stopped them. "Home guard." Dark, beady eyes stared from under a black felt hat. "Lemme see your papers."

They dismounted the mules, and Max presented his discharge papers. The guard examined them for what seemed like a long time. "Where you headed?"

"Going home, sir. Lake City."

Alex exhaled. Lester's expressionless face gave no hint of concern as he walked back to his mule, removed the saddlebag, and pulled out a shirt and an old letter.

"Never mind," the guard said. "Go on your way. I can see you're not deserters. Sorry to trouble you." He turned his horse and rode away.

Alex smiled and took a breath of warm Florida air. "We'll be home tomorrow."

When they turned down the road that paralleled Alligator Creek, Alex became impatient with his mule's sluggishness and jumped off and ran ahead. Reaching a widening of the creek, he removed his clothes and leapt into the clear, cold spring water. He submerged himself then splashed water in his face and ran his fingers through his wet hair.

Both grinning, Max and Lester appeared above him, each one straddling a mule. "What are you doing down there?" Lester asked

Max chimed in. "Aren't you scared that old alligator is gonna eat you up?"

At the side of the bridge, Agothos kept guard and blinked his slitted eyes in the bright sunshine. Phoenix, the blue heron, stood on one leg beside him on the creek bank.

Alex nodded at the alligator. "He doesn't usually come out of his burrow this early in the season."

"They'll do that some days in the winter when it's warm," Lester said.

Laughing, Alex emerged and put on his clothes. "I'm ready to go home, fellows." Knapsack over his shoulder, Alex climbed back on the dirt road and walked toward the house.

Max yelled at him. "You all right, Alex?" When Alex waved them on, Lester turned his mule back with Max following.

The setting sun cast a golden aura over the house, where Sarah sat in a rocking chair on the front porch nursing a tiny infant. Tommy, Lula, and Sallie knelt in a circle around her playing a game. Sarah's golden hair hung loose around her shoulders reflecting sunlight like a halo around her face. The scene took Alex's breath. He paused, wishing to frame the picture and to hold it in his mind forever.

Tommy saw him first. Amidst screams, he and Lula sprinted, their short legs flying down the path toward him. "Daddy, Daddy . . . Daddy's home." Hank ran ahead of them and leaped on Alex.

"Hey, fellow. You still remember me!" He patted Hank and pushed him down.

Sallie toddled down a few steps then plopped down on her rump. Sarah wrapped the baby Lena closer in her blanket, and, holding the bundle against her shoulder, waited beside the rocking chair. Alex thought his heart would burst. His family was safe. He picked up Sallie and held her above his head. "Thank you, Lord," he whispered.

With Sallie in one arm, Lula holding his other hand, and Tommy close behind, he walked toward the porch and set the girls down. He enclosed Sarah and the infant in his arms.

Tears streamed down her cheeks. "I thought I'd never see you again, my husband."

Alex looked closely. A faded dress hung loose over her thin body, its sleeves frayed above her sun-darkened hands. When she smiled, he noticed tiny wrinkles at the corner of each eye.

His sister and father appeared and hugged him. Finally, Hannah walked out. She stopped cold and stared at him. "I wanta know more 'bout how you lost Dustrous?"

"I have a lot to tell you, Hannah, some good things—he's not dead."

Hannah's eyes widened. "Praise the Lord. I knowed it, I knowed it!"

Sarah moved closer. "Tell us. Tell us what happened."

John raised his hands into the air. "It's a miracle."

"Let's go inside and sit down." Sarah led the way to the sitting room and laid the baby in her cradle. A few Christmas decorations still remained on the mantle.

Alex took his usual chair at the end of the table, and the family, including Hannah, sat in wide-eyed attention while Alex related the story of Industrious's rescue by Yankees, his recruitment into the army, and his job at the hospital.

"When Dustrous comin' home?"

Alex shook his head. "He can't, not while the war's on. The home guards might kill him."

"You think he *ever* come back here and git me?"

"I know he wants to—if he thinks it's safe." Alex shook his head. "He wouldn't want to put you in danger."

Tears flowed down Hannah's cheeks. "I waited so long, thinkin' he's dead, but knowin' in my heart he was out there alive some place. I gotta believe the Lord will find a way we get back together. Some day. Somehow."

Several days after Alex's arrival, the family sat talking after they finished supper.

"If the weather holds out tomorrow," Sarah said, "we'll all go for a picnic at the lake."

"Can I go fishing, please, please? Can I invite Barrett?"

"Sure, Tommy," Alex said, hugging his son.

Alex noticed how Sarah had taken charge of the household. He wondered where he'd fit into the pattern of daily living when the war was over and he finally came home to stay. Soon after sundown, Sarah and Frances put the children to bed. At Sarah's suggestion, Alex went upstairs to Tommy and Lula's room and led the children in their evening prayers. They were so much older and wiser than the children he remembered from two years ago. He shut the door softly and tiptoed to the bedroom he shared with Sarah. He stood above little Lena asleep in her crib beside the bed. He studied her smooth baby face, her tiny hands, and her chest moving up and down as she breathed. As he adjusted her blanket, he felt Sarah's arm around his waist.

"She's a miracle child, Alex," Sarah said.

"Yes, I remember when I first saw Tommy."

"This one especially so. She and I nearly died during her birth."

Alex considered the horror. "I didn't know. Oh, dear God, how I wish I could have been with you. What day was Lena born?"

"November twentieth."

"That's the day I found out I'd leave prison and they'd take me to Georgia."

Sarah stiffened and her voice grew cold. "When did you get to Georgia?"

"December eighth," Alex said. "We landed in Savannah that day."

Her blue eyes flashed anger. "Why did you take so long to get here? Savannah's not *that* far."

"It's a hard trip."

"So when did you leave Savannah to come home?" She stared into his eyes.

Her questions surprised him. "That first week I was sick and didn't feel like traveling." He hated himself for his weak answer. "I came as soon as I could."

". . . and why didn't you write when you got there?"

"I figured I'd be home to tell you myself sooner than the mail would come."

"I wrote you at least four times every week. Did you get my letters?"

Alex sighed. "I got one telling me the baby was coming. Then, I wrote a letter to mail to you, but someone stole it in prison." He reached for her. "Don't be angry with me, Sarah."

"That explains it."

"Explains what?"

"The empty envelope addressed to me in your handwriting. I received it in November right after Lena was born."

Lena woke and began to fuss. Sarah ignored her for a moment and wrapped her arms around Alex. "I thought of you every day and wanted to know where you were, if you were well. Whenever I could find a newspaper, I looked for news of your company."

The baby let out a yowl.

Alex kissed her. "I'm very tired. Let's go to bed now."

"Go ahead. I'll be there after I nurse Lena."

He sank into the bed and pulled the quilt up to his neck. He could hear soft noises of the baby's suckling. Soon, Sarah climbed in beside him and pressed her warm body against his.

He awoke from a grotesque dream—the Jacob dream again. But when he grabbed Jacob's leg to pull his brother back down into the slimy trench, Jacob scrambled loose and crawled up on the bank. Alex looked down at his hands, still holding Jacob's leg—detached from his body.

"What's wrong, Alex?" Sarah said in a sleepy voice.

"Nothing, darling. Just a dream. Go back to sleep."

But the nightmare had stolen Alex's sleep. He wrapped himself in a blanket and padded barefoot out to the porch. He dozed in snatches the rest of the night while he sat up straight in a rocking chair.

He awoke to see Sarah come through the door holding tiny Lena in her arms. "What are you doing out here?" she asked.

"I've been sleeping on the ground or hard cots so long that I'm not used to such finery." He stood and allowed Sarah to sit in the chair.

She opened her gown and held the baby's face against her breast. "Tell me . . ."

Fascinated with the familiar sound of Lena's eager suckling, Alex missed the question. "What?"

"I asked what was happening in the war."

Alex felt a large lump in his throat. "Can't we talk about something else? I really don't want to talk about it."

"I know you couldn't sleep last night," Sarah said. "My father had nightmares for years after he fought the Indians."

Alex remained silent, unwilling to speak of his dreams and aware only of his pounding head.

Sarah raised her face toward the sky where wispy clouds whipped in the wind. "It's really warm for January—a pretty day for our picnic. I'll feed Lena again at ten, and she'll last for three or four hours at home with Hannah."

Alex felt better after she switched to a lighter subject.

Later that day, they spread a quilt near an opening in the ferns and cypresses that framed the shallow spring-fed Alligator Lake. After Frances set a large picnic basket in the center of the quilt, she took charge of three-year-old Sallie. John had cut cane fishing poles and dug worms for Lula, Tommy, and Barrett, Tommy's school friend. The young fishermen baited their hooks and threw their lines into the clear water.

Alex and Sarah took a walk down a path through the woods. Sarah squeezed his hand. "Hannah has been a new person since she found out about Industrious. In a way, she and I have shared the same experience."

"How's that?"

Sarah stopped. "You know, for most of last year I feared that you'd been killed. I haven't heard from you for a year."

"Please don't start that again, Sarah."

"And why not? I know it wasn't your fault for not writing. But now that we're together, you refuse to talk about what has happened to you the past three years. How can I understand if you won't talk to me?"

Alex changed the subject. "I know things have been hard for you. Do you have enough money to get along?"

"I'll tell you the truth. We've had a very hard time. Right now, we're almost at the end of our money. If our crops don't come in this year or if they put any more taxes on us, we're in deep trouble."

Alex looked at Sarah, amazed at her knowledge of operating the farm. "You've never told me any of this."

"I've never had a chance. I didn't know you were in prison until Lester told me last fall."

"Don't you worry, Sarah. I know my corporal's pay is only a drop in the bucket, but soon as the war's over, I'll make some money for us."

"Are you going back?"

"I have to. My papers order me to report on February eighth, but I'll leave before then."

She sighed. "We'll have little more than a month together."

They walked in the silence of the pines and returned on the looped path that led back to the picnic grounds. Just as they came to the clearing, they heard the shrill sounds of children playing.

"Bang, bang, pow, pow. I gotcha." Bored with fishing, Lula and the boys were chasing one another with sticks they pretended were guns.

Alex froze. He felt a wild fury explode inside him. Tommy came from behind a tree with his stick pointed toward his parents. "OK. Stay where you are. I've got the enemy covered." He turned and pointed the stick toward Lula. "Kaboom!" Lula melted to the ground in a dramatic pretense of being shot.

Alex rushed toward Tommy and snatched the stick out of his hands. "Stop it!" he screamed. "War is no game for children to play." He shook Tommy's shoulders until his head wobbled. Lula got off the ground. Like wide-eyed statues, she and Barrett watched Alex scold Tommy. "All of you, drop those guns. End your stupid game this instant." They dropped their sticks to the ground. Alex picked up the sticks and slung them spinning into the woods.

Sarah caught Alex's shirtsleeve. "What are you doing? They're only children. They meant no harm."

He shook her off. "You stay out of this. I'm their father." He caught Tommy by the arm and dragged him toward the picnic area. "I'm the head of this family, and my word is law around here."

"Evil demons have possessed you, Alex Browning!"

20

What a cruel thing is war: to separate and destroy families and friends, and mar the purest joys and happiness God has granted us in this world. . . .

Robert E. Lee
letter to his wife,
1864

January–February 1865

A lex released Tommy's arm and stood dead still. Sarah bit her lip and wished she could take back what she'd just said. She wrapped her arms around her husband. "I'm sorry, Alex. Those words flew out of my mouth before I could stop them. The children have no idea why things that remind you of war make you react like this. When did all this start?"

"In Savannah . . . no, it was on the ship, I first . . . Sarah, sometimes I . . ." He paused for a long moment. "I think I'm losing my mind."

Almost every night during the next week, Sarah awakened to Alex's screams. His yelling also upset Lena, whose shrieks added to the bedlam.

"I'm moving to Father's room," Alex said after one horrendous night. "He can sleep through thunder. I don't want to disturb you and the baby any more."

One morning, Sarah walked with Alex through their fields and pointed out where they'd cut some trees for a new pasture. Across the meadow, John repaired a fence and Lou cleared the fields of withered corn stalks and dry shucks. With planting time still two months away, lighter winter chores offered opportunities for odd jobs left over from busier seasons.

"I want you to get rid of Megan," he said abruptly.

"The extra money has helped us survive. I know how you feel about Yankees . . ."

Alex interrupted. "You have no idea of the cruelty they've inflicted on me."

"OK, maybe I said it wrong, but keep your mind open. She's a kind-hearted person and a great friend of our family."

Alex stopped and faced her. "Margaret told me folks around town are angry about her being here and teaching the Negro children."

"I've told you, Alex, we need the extra rent money after all we've lost." Sarah's firm voice accentuated the words. "Every year the Confederate army took our best cattle along with ten percent of our crops. I wouldn't have minded that so much if I thought my crops would feed soldiers. But when I saw those bushels of corn and cabbages rotting by the side of the railroad track . . ." She picked a tall stalk of grass and pointed it at Alex. "I've told you about the inflation. Confederate money's worth next to nothing now. So you see why I must have the rent money."

Alex took the grass from her hand and leaned next to her face. "Before long, you'll find yourself in real trouble . . . Get rid of her. She can find another place to stay."

Sarah raised her voice. "We can't afford it, Alex. Perhaps if you would stay home to help us make ends meet instead of going out to fight in your stupid war for a paltry twenty-five dollars a month in Confederate money, I could have choices about whether or not to take a boarder, to sell my canned goods, or make dresses for wealthy ladies." Sarah felt her pent-up anger exploding. "I've worked like a dog trying to keep this place and put food on my children's plates."

"Other women have done the same. My life hasn't been a bed of roses, either."

"You had a choice! You were never conscripted. You could have stayed here and kept the cattle business going."

Alex stopped and raised his hands to the sky. "Dear God above, I did what I thought was right."

"What you thought was right? What about us? What's right about deserting your children in their early years? And look at you now! What has your glorious war done for you? It's turned you into a ghost of a man, reliving the horror every day and every night of your life."

She forced the air out of her lungs. "Don't go back to the war, Alex. Surely there's a way for you to get a discharge. Stay here with us. You've gone through too much already."

Alex clinched his fists. "Don't you understand? I signed up for three years in April of sixty-two. Two and a half months is all I have left."

Sarah gritted her teeth and faced Alex. "No, I don't understand. My world vanished into the flames of hell when you signed up!"

A few days later, Sarah returned from a trip to town. When she came into the house, she found Frances and John sitting at the table with glum faces. "What's wrong?"

John wiped his hand over his cheek. "It's Alex. He's locked himself in my room."

Frances shook her head. "He's been talking crazy. Said they were coming after him. When I asked him who was coming, he gave me a wild look, grabbed his rifle, and went into his room."

"His rifle!" Sarah screamed.

"Don't worry; we disarmed it earlier and hid all the cartridges."

Sarah ran up the stairs and knocked on the locked door, choking on fear. "Alex, let me in so I can help you." With no response, she pounded the wood panels. Finally, she retrieved a skeleton key. The door opened on an empty room. She walked to the center, made a complete turn, and took in the bed's tumbled sheets and quilts, Alex's clothes flung over a chair or lying hodge-podge on the floor. Sarah ran to the open window and looked out on a ladder leaning like a drunk man against the eave of the house.

"Alex," she screamed out the window. *Alex must have sneaked out the back door and leaned the ladder against the house.* She headed back downstairs. "I think he's on the roof," she told John and Frances. They rounded the house to see Alex dressed in his Confederate uniform and sitting on the ridge of the roof, his rifle propped across his bent knees.

"I have to get away," Alex yelled at his family. "The Yankees are coming after me."

Sarah froze. She felt sick with guilt when she recalled her tirade. Had she caused him to lose his mind? *No, this is none of my doing. The war has taken away Alex's sanity. What will become of him? How will I care for him?*

John clamped his hand on Sarah's forearm. "Let me handle this." His confidence reassured her. She knew she couldn't risk climbing on the roof to get Alex down. If she were to fall . . . She took a deep breath and prayed.

John walked closer to the ladder. "Stay where you are, son," he said in a stern voice.

Alex became quiet at the sound of his father's voice.

John climbed a few rungs of the ladder. "It's safe to come down. The Yankees have gone. Take it slow; make your way down to me. Careful, careful."

Still seated, Alex inched his way down the steep incline toward his father.

From below, Sarah watched his progress and prayed under her breath, "Dear God, help us to help him. I want my Alex back, Lord— the way he was."

Leaning on John, Alex made his way back to their bedroom, where John removed his boots and laid him down on the bed.

Standing in the doorway, Sarah tasted salty tears drip into the corner of her mouth. When John tiptoed out of the room, Sarah took his arm. "We've got to take him to a doctor."

John nodded.

While the children ate their breakfast the next morning, Sarah sliced bread and some ham for Tommy and Lula to eat at school.

"Where's Daddy?" Three-year-old Sallie asked, her mouth full of porridge.

"Sallie, you know better than to talk with food in your mouth," Sarah scolded.

Lula slid out of her chair. "I'll go wake up Daddy."

"Be careful, baby sister. He might yell at you," Tommy warned.

"He only yells at you 'cause you're a wise acre. He gives me hugs and kisses." She smiled angelically, spread her skirt, and curtsied.

"You make me sick, Lu-Lu!!" Tommy said.

Lula scampered upstairs, but Sarah chased after her, propelled by uncertainty about what Alex might do. "I'll go with you."

They returned to the sitting room with Lula pulling her father by his hand and Sarah following close behind. Alex, hair still rumpled, grinned at Tommy and gave John and Frances a stiff smile. "What's going on so early in the day?"

Sarah set Alex's food before him. "When John returns from taking the children to school, we're all going to town to see the doctor." She turned and scraped off the other plates into a pan.

"Who's sick?" Alex asked.

John gave him a serious look. "Sarah and I think you should let Doc Taylor look at you."

Frances inserted a wad of snuff into her cheek and nodded agreement.

While Hannah cleaned dishes, Sarah sent Alex back to dress and took the pan of food out for the dog.

When John stopped the wagon at Dr. Taylor's office, Sarah turned to Alex. "I want you to talk to Dr. Taylor, Alex. I think you may have some problems related to the war. Maybe he can recommend that the army extend your furlough."

Alex's shoulders twitched. "I told 'em I wasn't a well man."

Sarah put her arm around him. "That's right. Dr. Taylor can help you if you'll tell him about your problems."

The doctor checked Alex's heart and reflexes, and he took notes while Alex ranted about the enemy digging holes to bury him.

"What else, Alex?" the doctor asked. "Problems sleeping? Trouble concentrating? Nightmares?"

"All of those, Doc. My hands get numb and, sometimes, they shake something terrible. I can't hold 'em still."

The doctor looked at Sarah for affirmation. She nodded.

"Sounds like soldier's heart. I've been studying on it. There's a lot of this going on with the veterans. Sedatives have helped in most cases so I'm going to give you some laudanum. One teaspoon before bedtime and another one about noon—no more no less. And no alcohol. You follow my directions exactly." He turned to Sarah. "You'll see that he does?"

"Of course," she said, relieved at the diagnosis and the simple treatment. Dr. Taylor handed her the bottle of laudanum in a paper sack.

"What about getting a discharge?" Alex asked.

The doctor shook his head. "You'll have to go to an army doctor for that. I'm sorry."

Alex's shoulders slumped.

When they got home, Sarah gave Alex his first dose of the sedative. He began yawning during the noon meal then retired for a nap.

The final weeks of the furlough passed quietly. Relieved that Alex seemed so much better, Sarah began to relax. On the second day of February, Alex packed his bag for his trip back to Richmond.

That night at supper, the family gathered around the table for their last time together. Alex showed Tommy the pocket watch his father had given him. "I've missed having my watch so I'm taking it back with me. When I get home, I'm going to give it to you, son." Sarah prayed Alex would come home safely with the watch.

She brought out the Bible for a family prayer time, her mood resigned but grim. "I don't think God wants any more petitions about the glorious Confederate cause, so aim your prayers toward Alexander Browning."

After each of them, including the older children, had spoken their prayers for Alex, in unison they said, "Amen."

Sarah locked eyes with Alex, whose cheeks were wet with tears. Love for her husband poured over her in an unexpected torrent.

The next day, Alex boarded the train that would take him north. Beginning three weeks after Alex left, John went by Bart's store each afternoon before he took the children home from school. Sarah rushed out when his wagon stopped at the gate. Each day, he shook his head and dashed her hope for a letter that never arrived.

21

February 1865

A lex's trip from Lake City to return to the Confederate army took him through several towns in southern Georgia in a northeasterly direction toward Savannah. Before their scheduled arrival, the train began to slow and creaked to a standstill. Alex looked out the window onto flat marshlands rather than the town he expected to see.

A Confederate captain came into their car and announced to the enlisted men. "We'll get off here and march into Savannah. Sherman destroyed most of the railroads in Georgia, so we don't want to take a chance on damaged rails."

Alex and a group of soldiers he'd met in Valdosta gathered up their belongings and got off the train. "How far is it to Savannah?" Alex asked.

Hiram, whose thin face sported a handlebar mustache, surveyed the landscape. "These flat rice fields look like coastland. It couldn't be too far."

A short, quiet young man called Martin shrugged. "It sounds like we're going to be stuck in Savannah till they fix the tracks to Richmond."

Alex reached in his jacket pocket and examined his military orders. "I'm supposed to report to my company in Richmond on February eighth."

"How do you think you'll get from here to Richmond with the railroads all tore up? Walk? Ride a mule?" Martin asked.

A soldier wearing captain's bars on his jacket examined the paper and sneered. "Grant and Sherman have run our armies all over Georgia and Virginia. Your company might not even be in Richmond. It could be most anywhere. Good heavens, man, you may not even have a company any more."

They walked a few miles without talking until Hiram pointed out a steeple, dim on the distant horizon. "Look, there's St. John's Church. We're almost there."

Alex quickened his step, encouraged by the visible sign of their destination. An hour later, they reached Savannah. The town looked different now. Everything seemed whiter. The Bay Street warehouses and even the trees lining the street had been whitewashed up to seven feet.

He noticed a woman approaching with an empty basket. "Excuse me, ma'am. Who whitewashed the trees?"

"The Union soldiers did it to prevent yellow fever." She made a face to show her distaste for Yankees.

"Are they still here?" Martin asked.

"Thank the Lord the devils left here January fifteenth. We've been cleaning up their mess ever since."

The three men began interrupting one another with questions, but the woman ignored them. "Pardon; I must be on my way to the harbor. I heard there were ships from New York with some food supplies." She scurried away.

A few tents and Union flags remained on the streets. Evidence of recent violence included broken fences, windows, and doors. A few blocks farther, they entered a saloon on Johnson Square, where they took a table among several other soldiers and civilians.

Hiram rolled a tobacco-filled paper into a tube shape. "What's the plan? Are we going to try to go to Richmond?"

Martin shook his head. "It's useless and probably too dangerous."

Hiram picked up an empty whiskey bottle someone had left in the center of the table. "If I was to spin this bottle, I'll bet you money when it stops going around, it would point at someone considering leaving the army." He gave the bottle a whirl.

The bottle came to a slow stop, its neck pointing toward Alex. He glared at the open end of the container. "No matter! I'm no drone in the beehive." Alex remembered his brush with desertion when he thought Sallie was dying. After that, he swore to God he'd never do that again.

Hiram jabbed him with his elbow. "Ha! Better a live drone than a dead worker bee."

"If I deserted, I couldn't live with myself."

The captain ignored him and stood. "If everybody chips in, I'll buy us a bottle of whiskey at the bar." The other three men emptied their pockets of change. Martin rose to go with the captain. They returned to the table with a bottle and four whiskey glasses. Alex remembered his doctor's warning about drinking alcohol but decided he'd be safe with one small drink. Martin poured everyone a glass. Hiram struck a match on the underside of the table, lit his cigarette, and inhaled.

"I'll take one of those, Hiram, if you don't mind," Alex said. Hiram removed a paper from his pack and sprinkled it with tobacco. He handed it to Alex, who licked the edge, rolled it, and leaned forward for Hiram to light it. Alex took a deep draw and coughed. He took a sip of the whiskey.

"What battles were you in, Alex?" the captain asked.

Alex gave an abbreviated version of his war and prison experiences, but his heart began to race. He sipped again from his glass. "Let's talk about something else—not the war!"

"It's not right them making you go back after all you've done!" Martin said.

"Come on, Alex," Hiram said, his voice rising. "Aren't you sick of it? I've had nightmares and laid awake half the night shaking and sweating." He laughed. "I've even had day-mares."

Alex recalled his own dreams and memories. The tobacco and whiskey had made him dizzy and slightly nauseous.

Hiram continued talking. "Lord, I'm sick of blood and gore. Let someone else finish it up."

Martin gave a melancholy smile. "I'd like to go back home to my sweetheart."

"You can't go back to Florida, Martin," Hiram said. "The home guards would hunt you down and shoot you like a dog."

"Why in the name of all that's holy should we be the ones to get killed? No one else seems to care," Martin said.

Alex knew he couldn't face another battle. *I'd make a fool of myself. Wouldn't it be more honorable to start work to support my family?* "Why don't we just stay here in Savannah?" The words coming out of his mouth surprised him, but he kept talking. "I lived here awhile, and I know a cheap boarding house. We could work a few months till the war's over; then, we could split up and head for home."

"Sounds good to me," Hiram said.

"Me, too," Martin said.

When he stood to leave the saloon, Alex's knees sagged. Hiram and Martin held him up and helped him out the door with the captain close behind.

"He just had one glass," Hiram said.

Martin put his arm under Alex's other shoulder. "Alcohol affects some folks more than others, I guess."

After walking a few blocks, the cold air cleared Alex's head. He walked more easily now and led the group to the rambling boarding house where he'd lived in December.

Cory Lanagan answered the door, his beard matted with crusts of dried egg. He pointed his cane at Alex's chest. "Don't I know you from somewheres?"

"I stayed here three weeks in December," Alex said. "My friends and I need rooms."

Lanagan, toothless now, moved his lower jaw forward so that it almost touched his nose. "I got two empty—a room for three at five dollars each and a single for ten. That's by the week."

"I'll take the single," the captain said.

The men paid Cory and followed him down a long hall to the triple room. A double bunk covered one wall, and an army cot sagged under an open window. Alex, Hiram, and Martin chose their beds while Cory took the captain to the single room on the third floor.

"You think that captain will report us for desertion?" Alex asked.

"Nah! He didn't seem opposed to the idea." Hiram dragged his chair across the floor to the window. "Anyone wanna smoke?"

The next morning, Alex and his new acquaintances went out looking for work. They found some construction workers who were finishing the last two in a row of cotton warehouses. The crew boss crossed to meet the three men. "This job's nearly done, but we need men to repair a sorghum plant across town." He gave them directions. "You're going to end up working with darkies freed by Sherman," he told them.

The imposing frame of the plant rose at least thirty-five feet into the sky to the ridge of a steep-angled roof. Mules pulling wagons loaded with syrup cans cut muddy ruts around the side of the building. White supervisors directed two crews consisting of both white and Negro workers. Because Alex had experience in roofing, a boss sent him with a bag of shingles over his shoulder, hammer and nails in a belt around his hips, up a shaky ladder that leaned against the building.

Alex climbed about twenty feet rung by rung, struggling to balance his heavy load. As he climbed higher, the ladder swayed, but he dared not look down. He kept his eyes focused upward at the roof, his hands firmly on the ladder. Only seven more rungs to the top. When he reached the eave, a heavy Negro man in a blue jacket and ragged trousers put out a hand and pulled him onto the roof. Two other Negro workers raised their heads and squinted at Alex then turned back to their work. Alex laid his shingles on the roof and adjusted his feet against the roof's steep slant. "My name's Browning."

"I'm Murphy," the heavy man said. He pointed to a tall, muscular man wearing a red-plaid flannel shirt and a stocking cap topping a blue-black face. "That there's Thomas. He'll take you over to the back side of the building and show you what to do . . . Hey, don't forget your bag of shingles."

Without speaking, Alex fetched his bag and followed the plaid shirt over the high point of the roof. Reaching the top, he allowed his eyes to scan the ground where lumber lay stacked behind the building.

As they made their way across finished rows of shingles, Thomas stopped. "Have you ever worked with freedmen, Browning?"

Alex remembered his strolls through Savannah and his surprise at the large number of Negroes—more than he'd ever seen in Lake City. "I worked all the time with my man Industrious. He was a good man—even went to war with me."

Thomas looked surprised. "Confederate army?"

"Of course, Confederates. I'm from Florida."

Thomas pointed to another Negro man who was hammering nails further down the roof. "Yonder's Jasper. He fought with the Federals till he got shot in the shoulder. They gave him a blue uniform just like the regulars."

"You tell me what to do, and I'll get started."

Thomas held out his hand. "Give me your hammer."

Alex removed it from his belt and handed it over.

Thomas leaned over a shingle row and gave each one little light taps with the hammer. One tap produced a dull, hollow sound. "This one's rotten." He pulled it off with the hammer's claw and threw it over the roof's edge.

Puzzled, Alex watched the procedure. "Why not replace them all? They'll be bad in a year or so."

"Owner can't afford it. Told us just replace the rotten ones."

Thomas handed back Alex's hammer. "If you find loose shingles, just tack some nails to hold 'em down." He started climbing up the roof then turned around. "You have any trouble, holler for Thomas."

Alex waved him off. He knelt above the shingles and replaced the one Thomas had removed. Then, he crawled across the row, tapping until he found several more to replace. He worked his way to the edge of another section of roof. As he moved back and forth, he finished rows toward the edge of the roof. He kept his eyes on his work, afraid to look down. After he'd replaced shingles for an hour, he stood to stretch his aching back and turned to look at the other roofers. Two workers, a Negro and a white man, were ripping rotten wood off the hipped-on section.

Alex began tapping shingles on the lowest row of the roof's edge. He heard a hollow sound, but the shingle didn't look rotten. He tapped again and decided to remove it. He put the claw under the wood and pulled, but it held fast. He jerked harder. No luck. Unwilling to ask Thomas for help, he stood above the shingle, inserted the claw, and leaned back using his body weight as leverage. The wood cracked, and Alex fell backwards. His feet slipped forward, and he began sliding off the steep roof.

He grabbed for a handhold but continued falling, unable to stop his downward motion. Alex tried to catch himself, but he slid off the edge. As his body fell free of the eave, he looked down into a lumber pile and extended his arm to stop the fall that would likely kill him.

22

The savage in man is never quite eradicated.

Henry David Thoreau
"Journal"

February 1865

Sherman's relentless march pushed refugees from Georgia and the Carolinas across Florida's northern border to search for food or an abandoned house. Pitying the starving wanderers, Sarah often fed them or allowed them to sleep on her porch overnight.

On a dreary afternoon, when Hannah had already left for her cabin, Sarah and John walked out to the front porch. Cumulus clouds were gathering on the western horizon. "Lotsa clouds, but nothing ever comes of them. I sure hope we get some rain in March. If we ever needed a good crop, it's this year. We've about used up all our reserves except for our emergency savings, but we don't want to spend that for our daily sustenance."

Sarah shivered in the cold wind. Then, she noticed dust rising off the road past the creek. "Looks like someone's headed our way."

"Probably more refugees," John said.

Sarah squinted into the distance. "There are two—no three—all of them men."

"Your young eyes are better than my old ones," John craned his neck to see. "We'd best lock our door. Pretend we're not home. I don't mean to be unfriendly, but we can't afford to be generous. Pretty soon, we'll be the ones starving."

"Oh, John." Pity welled up inside her.

"It's root hog or die!" John's voice implied he'd take no other stand. He opened the door for her and let Hank inside.

Reluctantly, she followed him and made straight for the sitting room where Frances sat reading a fairy tale to the children. "Keep the children quiet, Franny." Sarah explained John's decision not to feed the refugees. She walked over to Lena, who was lying in her cradle, eyes closed and arms outstretched. She was beginning to stir from her afternoon nap. Sarah carried her to a rocking chair and lifted Lena to her breast. The sounds of her child's nursing filled Sarah with love that almost smothered her worries.

In the next instant, gunfire cracked, followed by angry male voices and Hank's frenzied barks. Her heart beat in a rapid staccato, but she continued nursing. She feared that Lena would yell if separated from her food source now. Another shot from a gun then another. The glass in the sitting room window cracked, and a bullet slammed into the opposite wall. Holding Lena tight against her, Sarah bent low and crept out of view into the hallway.

John came toward her holding two rifles. "Put the baby in a safe place and take this gun. Whoever is out there sounds desperate. We've got to protect ourselves."

John followed as she wrapped the baby in a blanket. Praying that Lena wouldn't cry, she went upstairs and slid the baby under the bed in Megan's empty room.

"Are Franny and the children still in the sitting room?" she asked John as she took the rifle to the hallway.

"I sent them to Tommy's room."

A man's hoarse voice resounded from outside the front door. "Y'all can't lock us out. We're bustin' in right now." Pounding blows were followed by a loud crack like a tree splintering from a woodsman's axe. Hank barked louder, whimpered, then suddenly stopped.

Sarah worried that they'd killed Hank, but she had to protect her children.

Three men in tattered gray shirts and heavy boots burst through the door at the opposite end of the hall. The man in front wore a greasy felt hat with a snakeskin band. He pointed a rifle at John then Sarah. "Jest throw them guns at my feet real gentle like, and ya won't get hurt."

They laid both guns on the floor. Keeping his rifle trained on Sarah and John, the man slid the guns across the floor to his comrades, who put them outside on the porch.

Sarah summoned her courage. "Do you need food or clothes? You don't have to hurt us to get what you need."

The man's smile revealed rotten teeth. "We don't want no food and clothes, lady. We're looking for money and stuff we can sell." The front man spoke to the men behind him without turning around. "Garrett, you and Willie start in the dining room."

"Sure, Jack. Looks like she's got some pretty dishes and knickknacks in that other room we passed."

"That's the parlor, Willie. Don't you know nothin'?" Jack said, still aiming his gun at Sarah and John huddled together against the wall. With his free hand, he pulled a plug of tobacco from his shirt pocket and stuffed it in his mouth.

Soon after the men disappeared into the parlor, Sarah heard china clattering and cabinet doors slamming. She felt a stab of helpless anger that these renegades dared to steal treasures her mother had left her. She wanted to check on the dog but dared not go to the door.

John spoke to the man they called Jack. "Who are you people? Where did you come from?"

"We fought for the Rebs up in Georgia till it got hopeless," Jack said with a chilling smile. "It's a long trip down to Tampa, where we're from. We figure on making the trip fruitful, so to speak." He spit tobacco juice on Sarah's clean floor.

"You're Confederates! You're supposed to be on *our* side." Sarah said in disbelief.

Jack laughed. "Not no more, honey. We didn't join up, neither. A recruiter got us drunk, and when we come to, we was in the army and couldn't do nothing about it. Didn't figger on getting kilt, though." He fingered his snakeskin hatband and nodded toward the parlor. "When Willie and Garrett finish sacking up the silver and china, they'll go through your other rooms, too."

Cold fear poured over Sarah. *What will they do if they go upstairs and find the children?* If she ran to protect them, this creature in front of her would probably kill her.

Garrett and Willie came back into the hall, their gunnysacks rattling with her possessions. They laid their sacks against the wall and climbed the stairs with Jack following. Sarah and John waited a minute and crept upstairs behind them. Willie opened the door to the first bedroom. The second man pushed into the room then returned to the hall. "Ain't nothin' in there except clothes and stuff."

Sarah watched in terror as Garrett turned the knob to the bedroom where Franny and the girls hid. When the door didn't open, he rattled the knob again.

Good! They locked the door. Without thinking, Sarah yelled out, "Just more clothes and stuff, like the other room."

The man called Willie ran his fingers through his long, stringy hair. "I think she's hidin' somethin'."

"No doubt." Jack leered at Sarah.

Willie gave the door a powerful kick, and they entered the bedroom through the shattered door. Frances's screams, joined by Lula's and Sallie's, pierced the air. "Don't you touch these children," Frances yelled. A thud followed.

The two men emerged from the bedroom. The long-haired man held Sallie by her upper arm. The other man gripped Lula across the chest.

Fear drenched Sarah like a sudden shower. She tried to pray, but all she could do was repeat the words of a Psalm: "The Lord is our rock and our salvation from which cometh our strength."

"You want these kids back, you do as we say," Jack said.

Sarah felt anger bursting inside her. "If any of you hurt my kids, I'll hunt you down and kill you. I swear I will!"

Jack pointed his rifle at Sarah's face. "Simmer down, lady. You'd better behave yourself."

Sarah looked at her children's terrified faces. "Let the children go, and I'll give you anything I have."

Jack raised his eyebrows and nodded to his accomplices. "Turn 'em loose."

The men released the children. Lula and Sallie scuttled fearfully toward Sarah.

She held out her hands to halt them. "Go back to Aunt Franny."

"But Aunt Franny's hurt. The man hit her—hard," Lula said between whimpers.

Sarah stared at the barrel of the gun pointing at her. "You hurt an innocent woman, you devils, you . . ."

Garrett shrugged. "She tried to hit us with a chair. We didn't hurt her bad."

Frances appeared at the bedroom door with an angry red blotch on her cheek. "Aunt Franny's all right now. Come on back, children."

John gave the girls a gentle shove toward the bedroom.

"Where's your money?" the leader asked.

Sarah looked into John's narrowed eyes. "I'll get it for you," she said and walked, her back straight as a plank, down the stairs and toward the sitting room.

The scroungy leader and his men followed close behind. He stopped and told his men to take their sacks outside. Sarah prayed the robbers wouldn't find Lena in Megan's bedroom. The clock chimed the quarter hour. Sarah suddenly realized that Tommy would be walking home from a neighbor's house by 4:30 p.m., probably in the next fifteen minutes. Her teeth chattered with fear. She had no way to warn him of the danger. The smashed front door hung open on broken hinges. Hank had disappeared. *Maybe he ran away.*

Standing on a chair in the sitting room, Sarah took the rusty metal box that held their spending money from the top of the burled wood cabinet. As she removed it, she saw the gun Alex had given her when he'd left. "This is all we have," she lied, handing Jack the money.

Scowling, Jack counted the Confederate bills and threw them on the table. "You've gotta have more 'n this, darlin'."

He put his dirty hands around her throat. His breath, reeking of tobacco and alcohol, made her nauseous. Although she trembled inside, Sarah looked straight into his shiny black eyes. "Like I said, that's *all* we have."

He continued to hold her neck for a long moment. Then he released her and pocketed the money. "Let's go see what we can find outside." He yelled out the door, "Garrett, Willie, go put the stuff in the wagon."

Through the sitting room window, Sarah watched the men heave the gunnysacks into the wagon. Down the road, she saw Tommy walking home with Hank trotting by his side. She climbed back on the chair, retrieved the revolver from the shelf, and pushed it between her breasts. When John entered from the hall, she gripped his arm. "Tell Frances to keep the kids safe. I think those men are through robbing the house and are headed for the barn. I've got to warn Tommy."

She ran past the men, who'd stopped to hitch the horse to their new wagon.

"Where do you think you're goin'?" Jack yelled.

In a burst of energy she sped toward her son. "Tommy, hide in the woods. Quick. Those men will hurt you. Run. Run and hide, baby."

Tommy sprinted behind some bushes and disappeared from her sight for an instant, but Hank's yapping revealed his location. Then, she saw Tommy's red and white knit hat bobbing as he ran deeper into the woods. Her heart stopped when she saw Jack turn to chase after him. Without a thought, she took the revolver in her hand, pulled back the hammer, aimed a tad ahead of the moving target as Alex had taught her, and squeezed the trigger.

The gun jolted her arms upward. Still gripping the gun, she ran toward Tommy. Her heart lurched when she saw the only person she'd ever shot lying facedown in the grass, blood seeping from a hole in the back of his shirt. Steeling herself, she ran past him toward the spot where she last saw her son. She yelled for him to stop. Together, they sprinted through the woods across from the farm and made their way toward the barn. Soon, acrid smoke filled their lungs, and as they drew closer, orange flames licked toward them from the burning barn roaring like a locomotive. She took aim at Garrett, who was chasing her hog, but her bullet missed its target.

He continued chasing the hog toward the bridge. When the hog took a left turn and headed out toward the pasture, Garrett came face to face with Agothos, the twelve-foot alligator, on the bank of the creek. "Let's get outta this place," he yelled.

Willie looked across the field. "Where's Jack?"

Jack staggered toward them. The men jumped on the loaded wagon and drove away. Several shots exploded from the front porch, where John had picked up one of the rifles the men had left, but the wagon took a turn and disappeared from sight.

A voice from behind startled Sarah. "What's going on?" Megan had returned from her teaching.

"I've got to see about the children." Sarah turned and stormed past John into the house with Megan and Tommy close behind. She retrieved little Lena, who lay squalling under the bed. Frances tiptoed into the bedroom with Lula and Sallie.

Hannah appeared at the door. "I heard all the commotion and came quick as I could."

Sarah handed the baby to Hannah and stood like a general in front of her troops. "Frances, stay in the house with Hannah and the girls. Megan and John, you've got to help me put out the fire."

"Let me help, too, Mama," Tommy begged.

"All right, but be careful, son. You can bring us wet sacks and blankets to put out the grass fires. We'll never save the barn the way it's blazing. We've got to keep the fire from spreading to the house. Everyone grab a blanket and wet it in the creek. Hurry! Double time."

Following her directions, they flailed with wet blankets at the little snakes of fire that shot through the grass from the burning barn. Within an hour, neighboring farmers who'd spotted black smoke rising above the trees formed a line from the creek to the barn and passed buckets of water from hand to hand until the water finally hissed into steam on the blazing flames.

"Megan, there's another grass fire. To your left!" Sarah shouted.

Megan swung the blanket above her head and beat the fire until only black cinders remained.

The roof of the barn crashed into the loft, and the sides crumbled into charred splinters. The fire continued to blaze intermittently. Finally, convinced that the flames wouldn't spread to the fields, Sarah sat on the ground and wept.

John sat beside her, his arm across her shoulders. "We can rebuild the barn, Missy. Just be thankful we're safe. We didn't lose any animals except for the hog."

"But they carried off our new horse and wagon," she said.

"God has blessed us, Missy. We've still got the old wagon and an old horse that can pull it."

Sarah wiped her eyes. "You're right, Daddy John. And they didn't get our hog. I saw him running away."

At that moment, Tommy squealed and ran across the field toward the hog that was rooting under the fence. He wrapped his arms around its fat, muddy body.

John hugged Sarah. "You see, Sarah, the Lord was taking care of us."

"What about our savings we hid in the barn?"

23

The pain of the mind is worse than the pain of the body.

Publius Syrus

February–May 1865

When Alex regained consciousness, horrible pain throbbed in his cheek and wrist. Two men carried him on a stretcher. "Where am I?" he asked the man he recognized as the construction supervisor.

The man looked at a sign on the building they approached. "We're at the Southern Army Medical Hospital. We found military papers in your pocket, so we brought you here."

"No!" Alex screamed, "Don't take me to the army hospital. They'll send me back to the war."

The stretcher bearer looked down at him. "Not with a broken arm!"

"I've fought with people hurt worse than this. They'll patch me up and send me out again."

The men lowered his stretcher to the ground. "You fell over twenty feet off that roof, and your arm's got a bad break," the supervisor said. "You want to go to a civilian hospital?"

He tried to turn his body. "I can't pay for a hospital. Get me off this thing. I can walk." He noticed someone had wrapped several layers of dirty cloth around his left arm. Alex maneuvered so he could sit, and as he did, a severe pain shot up his arm as though someone had stabbed him and hammered in the knife. He lay back until the pain subsided. After unwrapping the cloth, he examined the hand, twisted back at a right angle to the forearm. Even his greatest effort couldn't make his fingers move. Blood dripped on his shirt from a wound on his face. He moaned in agony. "Take me to my boarding house."

That afternoon, his landlord brought a friend, Mack McGee, to Alex's room.

"Are you a doctor?" Alex asked the sunburned man with matted curls and thick eyebrows.

Mack set down a black leather bag and washed his dry, cracked hands. Even after he'd washed up, Alex detected an unpleasant odor about the man. "I done some doctorin' in the army at the first of the war."

"What do you do now?"

"I run a little fishing boat, but folks around the docks call me all the time to set broken bones and such. They say I've got a talent."

Alex looked at his swollen, distorted wrist. "Can you fix this?"

Without answering, Mack cleaned and bandaged the wound on Alex's face then lifted his arm to study the contorted wrist. "Looks like a nasty fracture of the wrist." He removed two boards about fourteen inches long from his bag and wrapped them with gauze. "Do you have a pair of clean socks?"

"Socks?" Not sure Mack knew his business, Alex directed him to his bureau. "Look in the second drawer."

Mack placed the rolled-up socks in Alex's palm and wrapped gauze firmly around his hand. Then, he laid Alex's arm flat on one of the boards and placed the other board on top of it. "Brace yourself. This is gonna hurt." He pressed down on the top board.

A horrendous pain accompanied the sound of bones scraping against one another. Alex screamed as tears streamed down his face.

Mack touched Alex's twitching shoulder. "Hold on. I'm almost done."

With Alex's hand between the two boards, Mack wrapped more gauze around the makeshift splint, trapping the lower arm into a rigid position. Then, he tied the corners of a baby diaper together, constructing a sling for the arm.

"How does it feel?"

Alex couldn't remember ever suffering such pain. "It hurts like the devil."

Mack removed a bottle from his black bag. "This laudanum should help the pain until you get better."

A few doses of laudanum each day eased Alex's pain. After a week, with his arm in a sling, he even felt like strolling around the city with his landlord, who took leisurely walks down the streets each afternoon. The elderly man's slow pace didn't bother Alex, who found that walking faster jarred his injured arm.

Cory liked to tell Alex about the old days when coachmen drove rich homeowners down the sandy streets in handsome carriages. He also related the more recent events of Sherman's peaceful capture of Savannah. "We all felt sure he'd burn us down like he did in Atlanta. Some say the general's conscience kept him from destroying a place as pretty as this. Others say the mayor made a deal with him, sold us out to the Yankees. Just as well, though. We're better off. I heard Sherman sent a letter to Lincoln about Christmas time like he was giving Savannah to the president for Christmas."

Alex admired rambling homes built before the war, the great oaks draped with Spanish moss, and the stately fountain in the park. He tried to imagine how Sherman must have felt when he saw the same sights.

Cory pointed his cane at a two-story red stucco house with an ornate wrought-iron entrance. "That house was built by Mr. Charles Green, a rich cotton merchant. He let Sherman stay in his house during the siege. The general stood right there on the front porch and read

Lincoln's Emancipation Proclamation. I don't think the darkies here knew about it before then. Then, he told 'em they were gonna get forty acres and a mule when the war was over."

When Alex removed the splint from his arm, his hand bent at an angle as though he were bracing for another brutal fall. Although he could use his thumb and forefinger, the awkward bend in the wrist severely limited movement in his left hand. Whenever Alex viewed himself in the mirror in his boarding house room, the long scar on his cheek and the deformed arm made him nauseous with self-hatred. *How could my beautiful Sarah ever love me?* He avoided thinking about her or the children.

Whenever the laudanum wore off, the wrist pain increased in a gradual crescendo until it consumed his body. He began to take three or four teaspoons a day. Then, he used a tablespoon. When the sedative ran out, Mack supplied him with more.

After a month, Alex gulped the medicine straight from the bottle and spent most of his days lying on his bunk in his room. One day, as he lay in a stupor, a cool hand touched his face. He blinked at the man standing over him. "Max?"

"No, Alex, it's Martin, a friend you met at the train station. We're worried about you." He held up a half-empty bottle of laudanum. "You're taking too much of this stuff. It's got a hold of you, fellow. You're gonna have to cut back."

Alex turned his face into the pillow. "Let me be. I need to sleep."

"No. It's time for supper. You haven't eaten for three days. And I'm taking charge of this bottle." Martin read the label on the outside. "I'll give you your doses."

Alex stumbled out of the bed and followed Martin downstairs. He took several deep breaths, which cleared his head before he sat down.

Sitting at the head of the table, Zach announced, "It's all over. Lee's surrendered at Appomattox."

The words stunned Alex into alertness. He felt sad for the wasted years, for all he'd lost.

"You feeling all right, Alex?" Martin asked.

"I feel terrible."

For the next week, Martin doled out the doses, unresponsive to Alex's pleas for more. "Does your arm hurt?"

Alex looked at his deformed wrist. The pain came not from the hand but from something deep inside him, a craving like a hungry animal greedy to be fed. Yet, food repulsed him. Even a small amount produced violent nausea and vomiting.

Nighttime in the boarding house was the worst. One night, as he flipped from one side to the other, perspiration gathered on his forehead. Struggling to breathe, he got out of bed and lit a candle. While his roommates snored in their bunks, he scoured the room for the laudanum. He looked in bureau drawers, inside Martin's suitcase, on the windowsill. Still holding the candle, he finally crawled next to where Martin slept and looked under the bed.

A strong hand clamped his shoulder. "Get back in the bed, Alex. You're not getting more medicine until tomorrow."

Alex crawled into his bunk and finally dozed off.

He blinked his eyes in the early morning daylight and jerked awake to see Martin and Hiram folding clothes into their suitcases. "Where are you going?"

"War's over now. We're going home," Hiram said.

Martin sat down on the bed by Alex. "I'm leaving your laudanum, but I won't be here to tell you when to take it. Promise me you'll get off of this stuff. You can do it, Alex. But it's gonna be hard, real hard." He put his arm around Alex's shoulder. "I'll be praying for you, fellow." He set the bottle on the bureau, paused, and scribbled a note. "I'm leaving my address. Write me every week and tell me how you're faring."

For an hour after his friends left, Alex sat staring at the bottle as though it could speak to him—his friend, beckoning him to partake. *No, he's my enemy plotting to destroy me.* When he heard someone clumping up the stairs, he hid the bottle in the drawer with his socks.

"Well, Browning, your buddies have gone. When are you leaving?" his landlord asked from the door.

Alex shrugged. "I'm planning to stay on."

"You owe me ten dollars back rent."

Alex fumbled through the drawer for his wallet—only twenty dollars left. He took out two fives and handed them to Cory. If he didn't get a job soon, Cory would throw him out on the street.

Cory smoothed the bills into a money clip. "I should be bringing you some new roommates pretty soon—'less you wanta pay fifteen and be left alone."

Alex didn't answer, and Cory clumped back down the stairs.

For the entire day, Alex talked to his seductive companion but didn't succumb to the bottle of laudanum. He turned over and faced the wall, alternately suffering chills and fevers, nausea and cramps along with visions of insects or reptiles climbing the walls of his room. He grabbed the bottle by its neck. "I'll kill you, you devil. I won't let you ruin me." Continuing to strangle the glass container, he walked to the window, flung it into the yard outside, and watched the bottle break against a wooden walkway. He breathed a sigh of relief, which quickly turned into yearning for his friend. He restrained himself from going outside to sop the liquid from the ground. "You're *not* going to destroy me," he yelled into the evening air.

After a week of fitful nights, he awoke into alertness he hadn't experienced in months. He decided to go to the construction company and ask for his job back.

The construction supervisor must have felt sorry about Alex's injuries. He offered Alex a new job apprenticing as a master craftsman. In the poor economy, few of Savannah's citizens could afford to build new homes, but some wanted to repair damage and wear to their older houses. A few even eked out the funds to add rooms to their homes.

In spite of his injury, Alex managed to hold the wood with his left hand while he carved with his good right one. He enjoyed the job, especially carving repairs for elegant columns, stair railings, or crown molding, but he slept very little. He still craved the sedative. He didn't expect the return of the war nightmares that the medicine had stilled. Two weeks after he'd thrown the laudanum out the window, he awoke screaming from the Jacob dream. Afterwards, he lay staring at the dark ceiling of the room wondering which demon was worse. With no sedative to soothe him, he lay waiting for daylight to flood the windows. At 8:00 the next morning, he planned to lose himself in a piece of pine yielding to his knife as he repaired the moldings of intertwining fruits and vines that adorned a decorative ceiling.

Daytime passed in a flash, leaving him to face endless hours of dark. When Alex refused to take a sedative for sleep, fatigue bore down on him as he worked then lay awake at night fearing the hellish nightmares. The roommates Cory promised had never come. Maybe he knew no one would want to share a room with Alex.

One night, he awoke from a bloody dream of the Wilderness battle in which he became a walking corpse, a dead man unable to take the final step to oblivion. *I can't live this hell any longer,* he thought once he was awake. His mind flitted from one method to another and narrowed his choices between shooting his brains out with his pistol or getting enough laudanum to put him under for good.

He took his pistol from the bureau drawer, cleaned it, and oiled it. He didn't want a botched attempt. He inserted black powder and pressed in a ball and cap. It could be over in the flash of a second, his misery and his nightmares. *Shouldn't I tell someone?* Thoughts of home flickered in and out of his mind. His family would be better off without him. He thought of Martin, his last friend, and dug the address out of his drawer. He located the pocket watch his father had given him when he was sixteen and held it tightly for a moment. His promise to give the watch to Tommy worried him, but he saw no way to fulfill that promise. He wrapped it in tissue and pressed it into a cartridge box. Then he wrote Martin a letter on a page from a tablet:

Martin—

You were a good friend to me when I was in trouble. You'll be glad to know I haven't touched the medicine since you left. I know now for absolute certain I have only a short time to live, so I want you to have this watch that belonged to my father. When you look at it, remember your friend who appreciated you for the kindness you gave me.

—Alex

He folded the letter, placed it alongside the watch, and tied the box with a piece of twine. He wrote Martin's address on the outside.

24

The time is near at hand which must determine whether Americans are to be free men or slaves.

George Washington

April 1865

When the South endured the humiliating final days of the Civil War, citizens of Southern states approached the end with varied attitudes—from resignation to acceptance, from bitterness to hope, from fear to relief. Many Southerners viewed the "Defenders of the Cause" as tragic heroes, especially in Florida, whose governor retired to his home in Marianna on the first day of April and shot himself in the head. "Death would be preferable to reunion," he wrote in a note to his legislature. Two weeks later, news of Lincoln's assassination electrified the country.

On the last day of April, Sarah and John gathered up a week's worth of eggs and the last of the bacon from the smokehouse to barter in town for flour, molasses, and yard goods. Before they even reached the square, they heard loud voices. In the middle of town, they found a crowd of Negro men, women, and children shouting and singing. The women circled, holding out their skirts and dancing in the street. Sarah recognized Lou, their field hand, in the crowd. As they moved closer, she heard their song:

> Mama, don't you cook no more,
> You's free! You's free!
> Rooster, don't you crow no more,
> You's free! You's free!
> Ol' hen, don't you lay no more eggs,
> You's free! You's free!
> Ol' pig, don't you grunt no more,
> You's free! You's free!

As they passed the square, Sarah craned her neck at the demonstration. "What's happening, Daddy John?"

"It may not be safe here." John turned the wagon onto the street that passed in front of Bart's store.

Bart leaned against the outside wall talking with Paul McGinnis from the farm supply store.

John stopped the wagon in front of the store. "What's the commotion downtown?"

Bart walked close to Sarah's side of the wagon. "Word just arrived that Lee surrendered at Appomattox. The darkies are going crazy— leaving their plantations in droves—as if they think they can run off and take care of themselves."

Sarah smiled. "So the war's finally over. I'm glad. When did Lee surrender?"

"It happened three weeks ago." Bart touched her arm. "My store's open if you're out for some shopping, Miss Sarah."

Sarah turned to John. "I think we'd better go home now."

"It's always a pleasure to see you, Sarah. Please come back," Bart said.

Sarah gave him a half-smile. "Another day, Bart—Good-bye."

Bart squeezed her hand just as John snapped the reins to goad the horses forward. John gave her a quizzical look. "I think that young man's flirting with you, Sarah."

"Don't pay him any mind, Daddy John. It's just his manner."

He shrugged. "Does Hannah know about this—that the slaves are free now?"

"I'm sure she's heard by now. Hannah knows everything that affects the slaves."

When John and Sarah arrived back at the house, Frances told them Hannah had left. They crossed the bridge and walked down to her cabin. Hannah, dressed in her Sunday clothes, stood outside tying her bonnet.

"Where are you going, Hannah?" Sarah asked.

Hannah twitched and flung her hands at her sides. "Oh, Miss Sarah, I just heard the news. Now, I's really free. Right now, I's goin' downtown and see my friends. The day of Jubilee is come to pass."

This wasn't the way Sarah had imagined the end of the war. She'd intended to give Hannah her freedom, to embrace her with tears and words of gratitude—certainly not this abrupt and joyous leave-taking, as though they'd never shared thirteen years together with the birth of babies, raising children, suffering heartaches, laughing and crying together. "Are you coming back?" Sarah's voice trembled.

"I be back about sundown. No worry."

Sarah swallowed and allowed her relief to show.

After she and Frances had washed the supper dishes and put the children to bed, Sarah sat in a chair beside the window, staring across the pasture at deepening dusk.

Frances walked up behind her. "Why do you think Hannah will come back to us when she doesn't have to?"

"She promised." Sarah immediately recognized the flimsiness of such a promise in the face of this crucial event. She continued looking out the window. After another hour, she heard sounds of laughter and saw torches moving up the road toward the bridge. Her heart pounded. She turned to John, who'd fallen asleep in his chair. "John—Daddy John. I think some Negroes are coming."

John leapt out of his chair and reached above the cabinet for his gun. "You and Frances stay here with the children, Missy. I'll see who's out there."

Sarah and Frances snuffed the candles and sat in the dark by the open window. Snatches of conversation wafted into the house.

"You been drinking, Lou?" She heard John ask.

Then Hannah said, "We be having Jubilee."

Sounds of laughter died. Then John burst inside with Hannah close behind, her head lowered. John put his gun back into the cabinet, took off his hat, and flopped onto a chair.

Hannah folded her arms across her breast. "Don't try and beg me to stay."

Hannah's familiar brown face froze in determination. In a moment, Sarah recognized the depth of her love for this woman. How could one day change so much? Or perhaps nothing had really changed. Perhaps Hannah had always served her because she had to—because she was a slave. "I'll pay you wages. You know I'll treat you right."

Hannah blinked and sighed. "You always treat me right, Miz Browning. That's not the thing."

"The thing? I don't understand."

"The thing is, Miz Browning." Hannah had always called her *Miss Sarah* before. "The thing is if I stay, you be my missus and I be your slave no matter the wages or not."

"You've been talking to the others in town. I know some of them have been hurt by their masters."

"I never been hurt 'cept one thing."

Sarah remained silent, feeling the full impact of her guilt about sending Industrious to war. Even though he'd survived, the distance between them now might make it impossible for them to find one another.

Sarah's actions and their result seemed in many ways more cruel than the harshest beating.

"The thing is—now I free, I gotta find a new life somewhere else."

"Why? Why?" Sarah asked. "Even if you got a job with another family, they'd never care for you the way I do. The children—they love you, too. They'll miss you terribly." To Sarah, her words sounded hollow.

Hannah pinched her lips together. "The thing is, Miz Browning, now that the war's over, I really believe Dustrous gonna come back for me, so I ain't goin' far away. I get me a job with somebody 'round here. That the only way I be a free person."

Hannah turned her head toward the window. After a few moments, she faced her former mistress. Slowly, Sarah lifted her hands, then her arms, and Hannah, fear in her eyes, inched forward.

"You ain't gonna try and stop me?" Hannah asked as she allowed Sarah to hug her.

"No, Hannah." Then Sarah's tears started flowing. "I'm so sorry about Industrious. I had no right to insist that he go to war." In her guilt, she didn't believe she even had the right to ask Hannah to forgive her. "I'll be praying you'll see Industrious soon."

25

Woe unto them who call evil good, and good evil; that put darkness for light, and light for darkness; that put bitter for sweet, and sweet for bitter.

Isaiah 5:20

Spring 1865–Spring 1867

The day of the barn fire, Sarah had worried that their savings had burned. She recalled how she'd fallen on her knees in gratitude when they'd found their money wrapped in oilcloth under a charred grain box. But rebuilding the barn, even with the help of her neighbors, depleted their emergency money.

In April and May, heavy rain clouds teased with a promise of green pastures and tall corn stalks, then passed over and around Alligator Creek, leaving powdery ground with deformed corn ears and dried grapevines. Even root plants had shriveled in the arid soil. In a wry joke, Sarah claimed to be the only fruitful plant in the vineyard, her cynical announcement of her most recent pregnancy. When Sarah looked down from the bridge in front of her house, she saw only a trickle of spring water running through the creek bed.

After the Appomattox armistice and subsequent Confederate surrenders from April through June, defeated Rebel soldiers began drifting home from battlefields in Virginia, Georgia, the Carolinas, and Tennessee. Some came on foot, others by wagons, and still others on trains from Tallahassee, where Florida soldiers surrendered and took the oath of allegiance to the Union.

Whenever word came of a train returning with soldiers, Sarah and Frances waited at the depot. On a sweltering June afternoon, Sarah alone watched for a troop train from Tallahassee to arrive. Yelling men were crowded in open boxcars or hanging from the doors of freight cars. Some jumped off before the train stopped. Sarah scanned their faces. Following the healthy men, the sick and the amputees with empty sleeves, pinned up trousers, and crutches hobbled off the train.

Sarah finally recognized a boy who'd been in Alex's company. She called out, "Jimmy."

He turned a grim face her way. "Miss Sarah."

He attempted to smile, and she took his hand in hers. "Have you seen Alex?"

He shook his head. "Not since the Wilderness. Didn't know if he was killed or captured."

Sarah gasped, "That was a year ago. Have you seen him this spring?"

He shook his head. "We lost half the men we started with. We had a bare sixty at surrender."

What has happened to Alex?

Frances met her at the door when she returned home. "Did you find out anything this time?"

Sarah shook her head. "I'd prefer any news, bad or good, to this vacuum of not knowing."

Yet, no death notice came from the army. His absence from his company puzzled her, and his lack of communication confirmed her fears of abandonment. The rest of the summer, she haunted the post office at Bart's store, hoping for, though not expecting, a letter.

In late September, John and Sarah surveyed the fields. "We might as well chop down the stalks and stack 'em for fodder. That's about all they're good for," John observed.

Sarah sighed. "What's going to happen to us, Daddy John?" Hopelessness hung like a heavy curtain.

"We've still got last year's potatoes and onions in the root cellar." John counted on his cracked, swollen fingers. "We can kill the old hog and have enough meat to last us awhile."

"What, then?" she asked.

"I can't see that far ahead," he said. "Something's got to happen soon. Surely, we'll hear from Alex now that the war is over."

"I never thought Alex would abandon us," Sarah said.

"I tried to raise him right. But Alex changed. Those battlefields and prisons damaged his soul. There's never been a war as savage as this one in my recollection. I pray that someday he'll get over it."

Sarah blinked her eyes closed for a moment. She tried to remember how Alex had looked the last time she'd seen him eight months ago. "Even if Alex does come back, he may not be able to work. Maybe I could teach school."

John laughed. "How are you going to do that with the baby coming 'round October."

The memory of Lena's difficult birth haunted Sarah. "Next year, then. I could do it. I'm sure I could."

"I don't doubt it. There's nothing you can't do once you've set your mind to it."

He'll probably never see this baby. Work usually kept her mind off her worries, but she had only a few orders for dresses. Since the war ended, many formerly wealthy matrons who'd paid substantial prices for her dressmaking had moved away and abandoned their large plantations.

Except for her worries, she felt well during her pregnancy. Even in October, as her body swelled during the late weeks, her energy remained. One evening, as she knelt beside her bed and offered a prayer of thanks to God for her good health, she felt a small pain stab her abdomen. She made her way to Frances's bedside. "You may as well wake up. This one will come in the middle of the night, for certain." Minnie's birth came easily and relieved her concerns about her physical health. She grew stronger still as the child grew. Sarah often carried her baby along with her to town and for frequent visits to the post office, where she searched for the letter that never appeared. John also searched, but for rain clouds that never came to bring relief from the drought.

By January 1866, even the canned goods and smoked meat were running low. Sarah put on her bonnet. "Take me to town, John," she said.

"How come? We can't afford to buy anything."

"I'm not talking about buying. We need to go the bank for a loan. You'll probably have to sign the note."

That spring brought no word of Alex. The children's queries about him came more seldom now. Sarah didn't want them to forget him. She felt sad. All the children remembered of Alex was his dreadful visit the previous year. One evening, when she went into the girls' room to say prayers and tuck them in, Lula begged. "Tell us a story. Please."

Tommy tiptoed into his sisters' room and sat on the foot of Sallie's bed.

She decided to tell them the story of how she and Alex had met in Georgia, even though they'd heard the story many times.

One second Sunday, when I was barely thirteen, my mama had made her famous chicken potpie for dinner on the grounds after church services. According to Mama's instructions, I left the church just after the sermon to guard the pie from flies and also from greedy boys. Those boys often times came by during church and helped themselves to enormous servings, leaving none for the adults. Mama told me to stand by the table waving a fan. While I stood fanning the chicken pie, I saw a boy coming toward me, a tall, really handsome boy of about sixteen. I pushed my hair behind my ears, pinched my cheeks to make them rosy, and smoothed the ruffles on my best Sunday dress.

"I'm Alex Browning," your daddy said.

I had no idea what to say to a handsome older boy, so I just smiled at him.

"Have you ever been to the cemetery behind the church?"

"Sure," I said. "Lots of times. My grandparents and my daddy are buried out there."

"Have you ever seen the grave of the soldier who fought in the American Revolution?"

Since history wasn't my favorite subject then, I had no idea about the American Revolution, so I said, "No, I haven't seen that one."

"Would you like to see it?"

I told him I was supposed to stay there and guard my mama's chicken potpie.

"What are you guarding it from?" he asked me.

I waved the palmetto fan over the pie. "From flies . . . mostly."

So he said, "I'll bet the flies won't eat very much of it, if you went to the cemetery with me."

I really didn't think I should leave. "But I promised Mama . . ."

He interrupted. "We'll get back before church lets out. She'll never know you were gone."

He was very persuasive.

Sarah asked the girls, "What do you think happened while we walked through the cemetery?"

"He kissed you," Sallie said.

Lula said, "No, silly. The other boys came and ate the chicken pie, and when her mama came out of church, she was mad as a hornet!"

The girls giggled as they always did at the end of the familiar story. Even two-year-old Lena laughed.

"I'll bet he really did kiss her," Sallie teased.

"Did Daddy die in the war?" Lula asked.

"Your daddy was a very brave man." She told them about the battles he fought and his experiences as a prisoner. "He came home for a few weeks last year and told me he was going back to his infantry company. He never came home again. And he never wrote a letter."

"Why not, Mama?" Tommy asked. "Didn't he even love us?"

"He loved you with all his heart."

The bank loan, the sale of eggs, and a few crops carried the family through the summer. In August, Sarah decided it was time to act on her idea of teaching school. She tapped the office door of Josiah Mattox, the headmaster, who also worked as a bookkeeper in a lumberyard.

He removed wire-rimmed glasses and looked up from a ledger on his desk. "What can I do for you, Miz Browning?"

"I'd like to teach in the Academy," she said. Her own children attended the Academy, a school for white children.

Mattox frowned and tapped the edge of his pencil against the desk. "Hmm. What credentials do you have for teaching?"

"I made straight A's in high school, and I have a diploma. I've helped Tommy with his lessons enough to know the school curriculum. And I have much more education than the last man who taught," she said.

"It seems to me that you have your hands full with a batch of kids of your own in addition to taking care of the farm."

"I assure you I wouldn't let my family responsibilities interfere with my job."

He frowned again. "There's other considerations, Miz Browning, some issues I'd have to discuss with the board."

Such generalities annoyed Sarah, but she kept her voice calm and considerate. "I don't understand. What kind of considerations and issues did you mean?"

"Quite frankly, I'm speaking of the issue of the blatant Yankee sentiments exhibited by you and your family. You're as close to true scalawags as we've got in this county."

Sarah knew the derisive term for Southerners who supported the Union. "We're no scalawags," she said. "My husband fought five major battles in the War for Southern Independence."

"Nonetheless, you've kept that Yankee meddler in your home for three or four years. Why don't you apply to work at the school for Negro children since that seems to be your inclination?"

In her boiling anger, Sarah started to say something she'd regret later. She restrained herself to a quick "Thank you very much."

Mattox had already replaced his glasses and returned to his bookkeeping.

She walked out the door, fury heating her face. *Why not apply to teach at the missionary school? They'll likely pay me twice what the local school would.* She considered her frustration with some of the ladies from church and her devastation at the hands of marauding Confederate deserters. *Why not? Why not cast my lot with the other side?*

When Megan returned home that night from teaching an evening class of adult freedmen, Sarah waited in the parlor with freshly made tea.

"How lovely." Megan removed her jacket. "This has been a dreadful night. The Academy boys threw brickbats at the windows of the school."

"Good grief, Megan. They could kill you."

"They'll not go so far as that," she said. "They just want to scare me away."

Sarah delved into her inquiry. "What are my chances of getting a job with the missionary school?"

Megan's tired face brightened, and her words tumbled out in a torrent. "They're desperate for teachers. Oh my, what a godsend you'd be! Since the war ended, over a hundred children have flocked into the school. Now, our evening school is filling with their parents who also want to learn to read and write."

The next day, Sarah found the office of the Freedmen's Bureau, which had taken over educating Negro children in the county. The agent, a former Lake City slave freed before the war, sat behind the desk. Sarah had never dealt with a Negro except as a servant. She composed herself, determined to grant respect to this man. She held her eyes steady on his face and smiled.

"I'm Sarah Browning, and I'd like to teach at the children's school."

She expected him to ask about her qualifications. Instead, he gave her a wide smile and nodded. "Praise the Lord! You're an answer to my prayers. We have only three teachers. Mrs. McLoughlin is doing double duty. She teaches children during the day and adults at night. She's willing, but I fear we overwork her. Also, the Bureau needs her for other jobs now. She oversees voting, aids freedmen to get jobs in the city, and helps them find homes. We'll probably move her to Tallahassee soon. The end of the war has brought much work to be done. As the good book says, 'The harvest is plentiful, but the laborers are few.' I sincerely thank you for your willingness to be of service to our race, Mrs. Browning."

Impressed with the correctness of his grammar, Sarah cleared her throat. "I can't do this for free. I'd have to be paid a teacher's salary."

"Of course," he said. "We can only offer seventy-five dollars a month at this point, but perhaps next fall we could give you a raise."

Sarah sat in stunned silence as she compared his offer to the thirty-dollar monthly salary at the local school. She stood and nodded agreement. "Accepted. When do I start?"

In September, Sarah stood in a makeshift classroom with thirty children of varied sizes and various shades of brown. Lacking enough desks, some children sat on the floor with chalkboards on their laps. *Surely, the Freedmen's Bureau can find a better building for the school.*

She began by reading them "Little Red Riding Hood." When she got to the part about the wolf, one small boy interrupted with a story about wolves that had attacked some children.

Another child corrected. "Them wasn't wolves; them was boar hogs."

"One of them hogs ate their baby."

Sarah was horrified to hear children relate the appalling event with no more emotion than as if they'd lost a pair of shoes. Sarah also noticed their poor language skills and determined to teach them good grammar. Their clothes were patched and ragged, and many probably had head lice. While the children played outside, Sarah chatted with a white teacher from New York.

A scowl fixed the matron's face. "You're new here. You'll soon see how very ignorant and heathenish these children are. Even their parents are stupid—without the basic virtues of prudence, cleanliness, and diligence. It's my mission to help these people improve themselves."

Sarah disliked the patronizing woman and determined to instill hope and confidence in these former slaves who wanted so badly to learn.

By October, the Freedmen's Bureau assigned Megan to work in Tallahassee. She announced her departure at supper and tearfully hugged each of the children. She held out her arms to Sarah. "Thank you for taking me in. I'll never forget any of you."

Sarah held her close and kissed her cheek. "Be careful in Tallahassee, Megan. You are a good and trusting person, sometimes too good. I'll pray that God protects you."

One evening in December, Sarah sat at her desk after a particularly exhausting day with the children. She looked up from her books to see Bart Benedict grinning at her from the door. Since Alex had left, she'd frequently run into Bart in town. Claiming to be too busy or too tired, she'd refused his numerous invitations to take a carriage ride or to eat with him at the café. "What brings you here, Bart?" she asked.

"You, what else? Haven't you waited long enough to recognize the truth?"

"What truth?"

"Your husband isn't ever coming back. He's left you. In my opinion, a beautiful woman like you doesn't deserve that. You work hard. You deserve to enjoy life."

Sarah frowned. "I haven't time for courting like an adolescent girl. Besides, until I hear otherwise, I'm a married woman." She gave him a quizzical look. "I'm puzzled by your interest in me. Ruby is single and would adore your attention."

He gave her a slow smile. "Ruby is a lovely child. I prefer a mature woman."

Sarah shook her head.

"There's something else."

"And what would that be?"

"It's about this miserable job you've taken. Margaret told me that you and your family are hard up for cash. My friend Bill at the bank told me you'd taken out a loan. I'm sure you wouldn't have put yourself into such a position except for need."

She held her shoulders straight and smiled. "I didn't realize that my financial circumstances were the subject of so much speculation. The gossip you heard is true. We're having quite a difficult time, but, frankly, I enjoy teaching these children. I have spent most of my life doing things for my family and myself. I consider this an opportunity to help children who need it."

Bart laughed. "Come on, Sarah. I'm no fool. I know they're paying you a big salary to teach, but I'm warning you that many groups in this community object to what you're doing."

"What kinds of groups, Bart? Are you a member of one of them?"

"Your tone implies there might be something sinister going on. I'm a member of the Young Men's Democratic Club, an organization of some distinction here. Your friend Megan was observed by our committee before she left because of her meddling with Negro voters. We don't approve of giving the ignorant fools a vote. And we don't think educating them serves any useful purpose other than giving them grand ideas."

She frowned. "I can't agree with that."

"Look, Sarah, you don't have to degrade yourself. I can help you with money. I can give you a job in my store. I'm telling you this because I like you very much."

Sarah shook her head. "As much as I appreciate your concern, this is my decision."

When school resumed after Christmas, two of her older students told of some white men who had fired a gun into a house in their neighborhood and killed the thirteen-year-old brother of a friend.

"Why would they do that?" Sarah could hardly believe such a thing was true.

"Cause his daddy didn' do what the white men said. They tole him not to have meetins in his house. When he done it, they come back and shot bullets in the window and killed his boy."

"Sure enough," another boy agreed.

Later, Sarah learned that the story of the killing was true, the work of some who'd also killed a white Republican at his home in the middle of the night. Their handiwork included taking a Negro Republican leader five miles out from his house and torturing him until he revealed what he knew about the Union League and the Republican Party. Finally, they shot him and disposed of his body in Alligator Lake.

Sarah worked hard to educate and encourage her young pupils. She often visited their homes, counseled the parents, and helped them with their endless problems. She endured the rudeness of the small town's conservative Democratic faction and observed with dismay the influx of "carpetbaggers," the name tagged by locals for greedy northern speculators who came south with all of their belongings packed in a carpetbag. They intimidated citizens to sell businesses, plantations, or farms at huge monetary losses.

On the first day of school after Easter holidays, Sarah awoke to a beautiful spring morning. John hitched up the wagon to carry her to school along with Tommy, in his fourth year now, and Lula, in her first. Sallie, Lena, and Minnie remained home with Frances. First, John took the children to the Academy. Then, he drove the wagon to Sarah's school. "Be careful, Sarah. There's a lot of meanness in this world."

That afternoon, Sarah gathered her books and walked out to where John's wagon waited for her. The children sat huddled in the back. Lula was crying. Although Tommy's eyes were dry, his red face and puckered lips told Sarah her son was also upset.

John leaned across the wagon and touched her arm. "You'd better talk to the children, Sarah. I don't know what to say."

Sarah sat in the back with Tommy and Lula, held them close, and wiped their tears. When they reached home, she set a glass of milk in front of each of them around the table.

"Tell me what's wrong, Tommy."

"Barrett and Caroline started it. The teachers let us all go outside to play. I heard them singing a song they made up about us."

Sarah didn't understand. "About whom, Tommy?"

"About all of us," Lula said. "But you'll get mad at us for saying bad words if we tell you what they said."

"I promise I won't get mad. Tell me."

"Make Lena and Sallie go in the other room so they won't hear it."

Sarah sent the two younger girls out with Frances and turned to the two remaining children. "I want to know *exactly* what they said." She looked from one to the other. "Tommy, Lula?"

"You tell her, Tommy," Lula said.

"They said you were a nigger-lover," he blurted out.

Lula pressed her lips together and cleared her throat. "They said since you liked Negroes so much, you'd probably marry one."

"And we'd have a half-nigger baby sister or brother." Tommy lowered his head.

Sarah slumped back in the chair. From time to time, she'd heard people say such things, but she hadn't expected children to be so cruel.

She looked at each of the children. "OK, Tommy. You too, Lula. Listen to me. People say those things when they're scared. We know better than to be scared of the color of people's skin. The Lord made those little Negro children, and he loves them just as he loves you." She brought the Bible over to the table and opened it to Psalms. "Repeat after me, all of you: 'In God have I put my trust.'"

"In God have I put my trust," the children repeated.

"I won't be afraid of what others can say about me," Sarah paraphrased. They repeated her words until they'd memorized them. That night, Sarah wept in despair over her children's pain. *John was right. There's a lot of meanness in this world.*

26

What therefore God has joined together, let not man put asunder.

Mark 10:9

May 1867–March 1868

Sarah heaved a sigh of relief on the last day of school, not for herself but for Lula and Tommy. That afternoon, she took Hank out for a walk down the road. As she passed the old alligator, Hank slunk cautiously to her opposite side. Sarah welcomed this opportunity for some time alone with God. *Please allow my children to be happy this summer, and help them forget the pain they suffered from their classmates.* She prayed for the other children as well, that they would learn to show kindness to others. The temptation to abandon her job haunted her, but the continuous drought removed any hope for income from crops. She couldn't afford to give up teaching.

When she began walking toward the house, Hank ran back down the road. She turned and saw the dog approach a wagon driven by a Negro man with a woman sitting beside him. They came closer, and she recognized Hannah and Industrious. They stopped and climbed down from the wagon. Industrious approached with Hannah following him, her eyes cast down.

"Miss Sarah," Industrious's voice boomed. "You lookin' real fine. I see ole Hank's still kickin' 'round."

Sarah gasped and opened her arms. "Industrious, Hannah, I thought I'd never see you again. Come on in the house. The children will be thrilled." She ran across the creek bridge and opened the front door. "Children," she called. "Come see who's here!"

The children ran out on the porch just as Industrious stopped the wagon. Tommy recognized them first. He ran across the bridge and hugged Industrious around the hips. Hannah picked up Sallie. Lula came last, gripping Minnie and Lena's hands. Hannah greeted each of them with hugs.

Sarah stepped off the porch. "Come inside. We want to know all about you both."

Industrious removed his straw hat and walked forward; Hannah stood back and set Sallie down. Sarah put her arm around Hannah. "I'm really happy to see you." She led her onto the porch.

Hannah halted at the door, but Industrious firmly escorted her inside. He tilted his head toward his wife. "It's OK. We're free now. You can come in her house and sit in her chair."

Hannah ducked her head and spoke to the floor. "It's not that. She's probably mad at me for leavin'."

Industrious looked at Sarah. "She don't look mad." He followed Sarah to the parlor and directed Hannah by the elbow to a wing chair. "Sit down," he said in a firm voice. When she sat, Sallie crawled into her lap, and the other children huddled on the floor around the couple.

Industrious settled into a straight-backed chair and laid his hat in his lap. He began speaking in a low, resonant voice. "I been back here a week and asked around. I found my Hannah cookin' for Miz Pettigrew."

Sarah's eyes widened. "Mrs. Pettigrew?" She turned to Hannah. "Has she been good to you?"

Hannah frowned and shrugged.

Industrious answered for her. "That's the meanest white woman in Columbia County."

The children giggled.

"I don't know how come Hannah wouldn't have come back and worked for you, Miss Sarah. But no mind. I's here now, and she ain't gonna stay there no more."

Sarah turned to Industrious. "Alex said he found you working in a New York prison. Did you ever see him after he was released?"

Industrious bit his lip. "No, ma'am. I worked on the railroad up north after the war and saved up some money to come home. The government's been promisin' us forty acres for awhile now, so Hannah and me gonna find us some land. First, though, we're gonna get our marriage all legal-like."

Sarah furrowed her brows. "But you're already married. Alex told me Daddy John performed your ceremony at the old place right before you came with us to Florida."

Hannah finally spoke. "Mr. John married us, and it was better 'n most. At least, he say some words over us—'Do you, Hannah, take this man to be your wedded husband, then the same question to Dustrous. When we say, 'yes,' he pronounce us man and wife."

Sarah felt very sad. "You were married in the sight of God and certainly in my eyes . . . and Alex's . . ."

Industrious broke in. "In all our eyes . . ." Industrious leaned forward. "It *was* better 'n most. Some of my friends tell me all the marriage they had was jumpin' over a broomstick. Slaveholders never once said the most important words."

"What's that?" Tommy asked.

Hannah spoke again. "What God is joined together, let no man put asunder."

Industrious turned to Tommy and Lula. "You chillen might not understand all this, but maybe your Mama can explain it to you."

"I understand," Tommy said. "It's not right for slave owners to change what God did."

Sarah stared at Tommy and wondered how he learned such things.

"That's exactly right, Mr. Tommy," Industrious said. He turned to Sarah. "We been talkin' to some folks at the Freedmen's Bureau. They tell us ain't no slave marriages legitimate. They tell us—do it over. You see, I want Hannah to get my soldier pensions if somethin' happens to me. Also, we need to be legal married for the land they promised us."

Hannah raised her head. "Miss Sarah, we come here to ask you to witness our new wedding. Tonight at sunset, we going to the school-house, and the parson gonna do the ceremony for us and three other couples. Can you come?"

"We wouldn't miss it. Are the children invited, too?"

"Sure thing," Industrious's voice boomed.

After Industrious and Hannah left, Tommy and Lula made plans for a wedding present. They painted a clay pot, planted it with blooming marigolds, and tied a ribbon around it. Sarah ironed dresses for the girls and a white shirt for Tommy. She decided to wear a summer dress Frances had given her.

At sunset, the Browning clan entered the schoolhouse in their Sunday best. When they arrived, members of a Negro congregation ushered them to seats in the schoolroom. A thin Negro woman with a bright-blue-feathered hat played hymns on an out-of-tune piano as other guests were seated. The parson arrived, decked out in a white robe and embroidered stole. Finally, the couples entered in ill-fitting, but expensive-looking cast-off suits and dresses. Each bride followed several steps behind her groom.

The preacher began the service with the traditional words: "Dearly Beloved, we are gathered together here in the sight of God—and in the face of this company—to join together these men and women in holy matrimony, which is commended to be honorable among all men, and, therefore, is not by any to be entered into unadvisedly or lightly, but reverently, discreetly, advisedly, and solemnly . . ." Just before he pronounced the group husbands and wives, he spoke the critical words: "What therefore God has joined together, let no man put asunder."

After the preacher concluded the ceremony, Industrious and Hannah led the procession through an opening between the chairs and out the door. The other three couples followed. As they left, Sarah noticed that the brides had taken their rightful and equal places at their husbands' sides.

As Sarah and her children followed the procession into the lamp-lit street, she saw white people huddled in large groups on either side of the street. She overheard a woman say, "Look at them putting on airs like they think they're white."

Further on, a group of ten men sat on horses with rifles resting across their saddles. They wore the now familiar white masks identifying them as Regulators. When Sarah heard her name spoken, she turned her eyes straight ahead.

Even though few playmates joined the Browning children that summer, they entertained themselves playing "wedding" with one another. Each girl, even Minnie, took turns as the bride with Tommy as groom. They never mentioned missing their friends. Other times, as they were able, they helped their mother, Frances, and Daddy John with picking beans from the field, with canning, and cleaning the house.

Sarah rewarded them with a family outing. For the first time since Alex left, the family returned to Alligator Lake. The condition of the lake saddened Sarah. Most of the clear waters had drained out through sinkholes. Without rain, a smelly, brownish-green mat of compressed moss covered the dry lakebed, broken through by cypress knees protruding like buried bones of dead men. Returning home in the wagon through the dry countryside, they noticed brush fires reddening the sky.

The fall of 1867 arrived much too soon for Sarah. She watched her children jump out of the wagon, swinging their books by their straps. Sarah hoped to see a friend or two greet them as they walked across the schoolyard. With a fearful heart, she watched the other children huddle to the side as her three children entered the Academy alone.

On a typical afternoon that fall, after John brought them home from school in the wagon, Sarah sat the children around the table. She opened the hand-painted jar on the cabinet and set a cookie at each place. "What's the best thing that happened at school today?" she asked each child.

Ten-year-old Tommy grinned. "I made an A plus on the theme I wrote for English. I also learned some Latin words that Julius Caesar said after he won a battle—"Veni, vidi, vici"."

"My goodness, son. You even pronounced them correctly. Do you know what they mean?"

"Sure I do. 'I came; I saw; I conquered.'"

Sarah clapped her hands. "Excellent!"

"I got every single one of my arithmetic problems right," seven-year-old Lula bragged.

Five-year-old Sallie, who'd been learning at home, held up a chalkboard. "I can write my name." Sarah recognized a large S followed by an A.

Sarah hugged each in turn. "I am so proud of my smart children. Finish your schoolwork before you go play." If their teachers assigned nothing, Sarah gave them writing or reading to complete. She dared not ask about their classmates. They'd have told her if anything unpleasant had happened. Perhaps they'd followed Caesar's precept: "Veni, vidi, vici."

On a cold afternoon in early March of 1868, Sarah had gathered some small, dry sticks into a pile and taught the children to play jackstraws.

They learned quickly to remove a stick from the pile without disturbing the others. She left them playing in the parlor and walked outside. As she crossed the bridge, she looked for Agothos. Since she didn't see him, she assumed he'd not yet emerged from winter hibernation. She'd usually seen him by this time of year. On the far side of the bridge she saw buzzards circling. She walked over to investigate.

The odor of death overpowered her. She covered her nose with a handkerchief. Then, she saw the old alligator's massive body lying in a contorted position, his belly distended. She moved closer. At first, she thought Agothos might have died of natural causes. Soon, she thought differently. Three small black holes had punctured the side of his head, and two more had pierced his side. She knelt beside him. *Why would someone do this? Dear God, I know I'm supposed to forgive them, but I can't.* She knew that she and Daddy John would have to bury him soon.

She turned away and trudged toward the house, her eyes on the path beneath her feet. Nearby lay a burned-out torch and a box of damp matches. A ragged note nailed to a stake read: "Thers no reson to try and teach dum niggers or keep Yankee meddlers in yur hous. Be warned and stay safe. Next time, we hurt more than alagaters." She knelt on her hands and knees retching dry heaves until her nausea was spent. *The Ku Klux has been here on my property!* She stood and raced for the house.

27

Death, like birth, is seldom a peaceful thing.

March–May 1868

After school one afternoon in April, Sarah climbed up into the wagon next to Daddy John. A bandage covered his hand. "Dr. Taylor lanced it to let out the infection," he announced before Sarah asked. Two days ago, John had cut his hand while repairing a fence.

The next week, Frances and Sarah observed bright red streaks running halfway up the inside of John's forearm. Frances screamed, "It's blood poisoning, Papa. I'm taking you back to the doctor this day."

Sarah tensed with worry. Daddy John had become more than a father to her. "I'm going with you. I'll arrange for someone to take care of my class."

Dr. Taylor's nurse entered the waiting room and took John to be examined. Frances, gripping Lena's hand, and Sarah, holding Minnie in her arms, followed them. John winced when the doctor applied light pressure on his swollen hand.

Dr. Taylor frowned and traced the crimson streaks with his index finger. "You've got a serious infection here, John."

"What do you recommend, Doc?" John asked.

"There's only one solution—amputation."

John gritted his teeth. "No, no never. I plan on going out with the same parts I came in with."

"Think about it, Papa," Frances said as tears ran down her cheeks. "Living with one hand is better than dying. Lots of men have come back from the war with missing limbs. They live good lives. Don't give up."

John sat silent for several minutes. The sound of his heavy breathing filled the room. Finally, he asked, "How much?"

"I'm not going to charge you anything, John," the doctor said. "We've been friends for years. You can give me a couple of chickens sometime."

"No, Doc," John extended his left arm. "How much would you take off?"

The doctor examined the hand and arm again. "I could take off the hand, John, but it wouldn't help. With those red streaks, I'd recommend taking it off just above the elbow."

John cradled his left arm as though it were a baby, his face wrinkling into a grimace of anguish and tears welling in his pale blue eyes. Sarah knelt beside him and wrapped her arms around him.

"What do you think I should do, Missy?" he asked.

Sarah was not willing to make his decision for him. "I don't want to lose you, Daddy John."

He stood and shook the doctor's hand with his good one. "I'll let you know something this week, Doc."

Dr. Taylor's face became somber. "Don't wait too long, John. An infection like this can kill you."

By Saturday, John writhed in pain. While Frances and Tommy went for Dr. Taylor, Sarah sat beside his bed and bathed his arm and his steaming forehead with cool towels. It seemed an eternity until the doctor arrived with his black bag.

Dr. Taylor frowned when he examined John's arm, which emitted a distinct odor. Frances hovered over him. "What now? Can you amputate?" she asked.

The doctor shook his head and looked away from the family. He said in a barely audible voice, "It's too late. There's nothing I can do to save him."

Sarah cried, "It's my fault. I should have told him to let you take it off on Monday."

John raised his head. "It's not your fault, Missy. I'm the one who's scared of the knife. I thought I'd rather die."

Dr. Taylor put his arm around Sarah. "Don't blame yourself. Even if we'd amputated Monday, the infection still might have spread."

"What can we do?" Frances asked the doctor. He gave her several bottles of opium to administer when the pain became unbearable.

For the next week, John dropped in and out of consciousness. Sometimes, he screamed. At other times, when he fell into sound sleep, Sarah felt his chest to make certain he was alive. One afternoon, while Sarah sat beside him, he sat up, his eyes open wide. "I know I'm dying, Missy." His voice sounded husky but weak. "There's things you need to know."

Startled at his sudden awareness, Sarah leaned close to capture and memorize his final words.

"It's all there . . . in my will." His eyes closed and he began to breathe deeply.

"Where's your will, Daddy John?"

He lay still for several moments as though he'd not heard the question. Sarah waited without speaking. He stirred again. "Folded up . . . in the money box . . . write Walter."

Sarah knew she or Frances should have written John's brother earlier when the infection worsened. She'd post the letter that day. She leaned close to his face. "Is there anything else?"

"Make a new life, Sarah. This is too hard . . . too hard." He drifted into a fitful sleep.

When Frances entered the room, Sarah told her about John's words and went to her desk to write a letter to Walter. During the next three days, Sarah and Frances alternated sitting by his bedside while John lay on his back, his skin dry and pale and his lips open. His breathing became raspy, and at times he moaned and flailed his arms and legs in agitation. Whenever his face contorted, Sarah opened the side of his lips and Frances drizzled a spoonful of opium between his tongue and cheek. Each day, as Sarah witnessed the battle between the deadly poison in his blood and his strong will for life, she talked to Daddy John. Sometimes, she held his dry hand, told him how much she loved him, and how she couldn't have gotten by without his help. Other times, she read to him from the Psalms. Later, when he'd been unconscious for several hours, she began another monologue. "Daddy John, I know you can't talk to me, but I want you to know you've been like a father to me. You've taught me so many things—how to save money, how to care for animals, how to grow crops, how to live. Soon, God will welcome you into his loving arms. You'll be with him in heaven with your mother, your daddy, your wife, and Jacob. It's all right, Daddy John; it's all right to leave us and go into his arms. I can take care of myself and the children now. You don't have to keep struggling to live."

Suddenly, he lifted his head and looked straight into her face. He moved his mouth as though speaking silent words of good-bye to her. Then, he lay back, looked up, and lifted his arms toward the ceiling. Sarah knew he'd heard her words. His body relaxed as he rested on his pillow. His lungs sucked in air, four or five breaths in a row. He lay still for so long she thought he'd gone. She put her hand on his chest, and he resumed the labored breathing. Death, like birth, is seldom a peaceful thing. She prayed, "Dear kind Father in heaven, I'm ready to let him go now, to release him from this life of pain and struggle." Frances came into the room to relieve her.

The next morning, as Frances slept by his side, Sarah went into his room. He lay very still. She felt his face, kissed his cold lips, and breathed a heavy sigh. "Good bye, Daddy John. I've loved you so much." She touched Frances's arm to awaken her.

Four days later, during the last days of March, the rains began pouring in steady sheets on the dry earth. The lakes began to fill, and the fields became muddy with little rivulets in the ridges between the corn-rows. Under parasols, family and friends gathered at John Browning's graveside, a small plot he'd requested on a hill that overlooked Alligator Creek. Sarah looked out across the field at the road and saw two men with wide, white hats standing in the rain. They made no move to join the mourners. Since the death of Agothos, the appearance of strangers on her property alarmed her. *This is no time to worry. Surely no one, even the Ku Klux, would bother us at a funeral!* The minister said a few quick words and led the family and friends out of the downpour toward the Browning house. Sarah knew that John must be rejoicing in heaven at the answer to their relentless petitions during the past three years of drought.

Sarah turned just before entering and saw another wagon stop in front of the house. She waited on the front porch and smiled to see Han-nah and Industrious coming across the bridge. She ushered them in to join the others—Frances, Margaret, Ruby, and a few of Sarah's church friends—huddled around the sitting room fireplace drying their wet clothing. Walter and the Brownings from Georgia would probably pay their respects as soon as they could make the trip. Just as Sarah settled onto a long bench with her children around her, she saw a heavy-set, bewhiskered, white-haired man wearing a topcoat. He pulled at his la-pel and approached her. "Hello, I'm Adam Carothers, Walter's attorney. Could we talk? I need only a few minutes."

Sarah motioned Frances to watch the children and led him into the parlor. As soon as they sat, his expression became more serious. "Do you have a copy of John's will?"

Sarah rolled up the top of the secretary and removed the will from John's metal box. Carothers looked at it for a moment. "What about a deed to the Georgia farm?"

Sarah lifted out the document encased in an oblong blue envelope.

The attorney fingered his beard as he scanned the document. "Did John keep his correspondence from Walter?"

Sarah opened the metal box again and removed three letters. "I've never read these. Of course, I wouldn't have while he was alive." She passed the unopened letters to Carothers.

He scanned the first two and paused to reread the third. "This one's dated February of this year. Walter tells John he's had an offer on the farm for $5,000. Says he's getting too old to look after so much land and asks John to bring the deed to Georgia to complete the sale."

He lowered his bushy eyebrows. "John left the farm to you and Frances. What do you want to do with it?"

Sarah pondered. She saw no advantage in moving from Alligator Creek to Georgia. "Perhaps you can advise me. John planned to go back there after the war when Alex came back, but then . . ." Carothers patted her hand.

His kind voice comforted her. "Our lives often don't turn out as we intend. I know mine hasn't. This verse from Jeremiah gives me hope when I get discouraged. 'For I know the thoughts that I think toward you, saith the Lord, thoughts of peace, and not of evil, to give you an expected end.'"

Sarah smiled through her tears. "I'll discuss this with Frances, but I'm almost certain we'll want to sell. Can you help us?"

"I'll need to contact Walter right away. I'll send a letter by special courier. Let me take your documents to my office, and I'll let you know when I hear from him."

When Sarah returned to the living room, Hannah stood and hugged her. "Industrious and me so sorry, Miss Sarah. I loved Mr. John. He was always good to me."

Sarah nodded in agreement and squeezed Hannah's arm. "Thank you for coming to be with me on this miserable day." She looked across the parlor at her girls, who were having an animated conversation with Bart. "Come and see the children," she said to Hannah.

When Hannah began talking to the children, Bart took Sarah's hand in his. "I'm so very sorry about John. I know how close you were."

"John was more a father than my own." Bart's condolence touched something at her core. She gripped his hand between her palms as tears streamed down her cheeks.

He handed her a white linen handkerchief. She took a sad look at her children, apparently upset by her sudden tears. She enclosed them with her arms and led them to a bench by the fireplace.

Bart followed. When she and the children were settled, he spoke softly. "When you're feeling better, I have something to discuss with you."

"I'm sorry. I guess I lost control. Go ahead. Talk to me about anything." She wiped her eyes with Bart's handkerchief. "It will take my mind from what has happened."

"I don't want to be inappropriate."

She shrugged.

"I know of some land available in Texas. I'm leading a wagon train there as soon as I have enough people subscribed to support it."

"It sounds like a wonderful opportunity, Bart," she said, disappointed that he might be leaving soon. "I wish you the best."

"No, no. I want you and your family to go with us. I already have three families from here and another group to join us from Jacksonville."

"How much are they paying you to go along?"

"Different amounts depending on the size of the group. For a couple, $1,000."

"So larger groups would pay more?"

He nodded.

Hannah and Industrious stood nearby listening to Bart's words. Industrious cleared his throat. "Excuse me sir, I heard what you was saying about land being granted in Texas."

Bart turned toward him. "Yes?"

"Well, anyways. Me and Hannah here been wantin' a chance to get land of our own. Would you be needin' any workers on the trip?"

Bart paused and nodded. "Come by soon and talk to me at my office downtown, right behind my store."

"Are we going to Texas, Mama?" Tommy asked.

"Heavens, no. Mr. Benedict is taking some people there, but we have too much to do on the farm. Besides, I must stay here to wait for your father."

"How long has it been, Sarah?" Bart asked. "Two years?"

She sighed. "More than three."

"My daddy's been gone a long, long time," Sallie said.

Sarah stood. "Thank you for coming, Bart." When he pressed his arms around her shoulders, Sarah melted against his chest, savoring the warm comfort for a brief moment.

Industrious touched her shoulder. "Looks like the rain's let up. Me and the Missus better be making our way back."

Sarah put her arms around each of them before they left.

After the other guests had left, Frances admitted that going to Texas sounded interesting. "But I could never leave if you need me here. You know that."

"If you want to make a new life there, I won't stop you, Franny. I'll make out somehow." Sarah wondered if she were being honest. Except for the children, Franny was her last family member in her world.

During the spring, at school or at home, Bart visited Sarah frequently to describe the latest developments of the trip. Bart explained that $2,500 would pay for the wagon and food for her and her children. She was certain she'd need at least that much more to be able to build a house in Texas and to support the family until she could find a source of income. At this point, she didn't have enough money to consider the possibility. Even though she'd not heard from Alex, she still hoped for a letter or that he would walk in the front door and explain his long absence.

On the first day of May, Sarah's heart quickened when she heard a knock on the door. Adam Carothers, briefcase in hand, stood on the doorstep. "May I come in, Miss Sarah?"

Sarah called Frances into the parlor to join them.

Carothers unsnapped his case and withdrew a sheaf of papers. A wide smile creased his face. "I've got very good news for the two of you," he announced. "The Georgia farm sold for $6,000."

Sarah gasped. "Six thousand? I didn't expect more than $5,000. How did you manage that?"

"I made the trip to Georgia myself and met Walter. Walter's getting on in years, not well enough to make the journey here. He sends his condolences. We met with the buyer, who wanted that land more than we thought." He removed a stack of one hundred dollar bills from a heavy envelope and counted out sixty of them.

Frances stared at the stack of bills. "How much do we owe you, Adam?"

Carothers grinned. "If you'll give me a couple of jars of your preserves and bake me a pound cake, two hundred dollars will call it even. I know this money can make your life easier."

After he left, Sarah and Frances sat down at the sitting room table and counted their money twice more before putting it back in the envelope and into the box.

Frances sat up straight in her chair and smoothed her tidy hair. "I already know what I'll do with my part of the money." She took a newspaper clipping from the pocket of her apron and handed it to Sarah.

An advertisement announced a new certification for midwives available in Galveston, Texas. A doctor there offered apprenticeships for childbirth assistants. "What's this?" Sarah felt thoroughly confused.

"I've already applied and been accepted," Frances said with a proud smile. "But I'd have turned it down if the money hadn't come."

"How will you get to Galveston?"

"Now that I have money, I'll book passage on a ship out of Tampa later this month." A glimmer of excitement brightened Frances's face.

"You've never said anything about this."

"I was afraid they wouldn't accept me. You understand—I really must do this. I'll never be married. There's not much for an old maid to do as she grows older—a little knitting, crocheting, canning, and baking. I've loved helping you with your children, but they're growing up and soon you won't need me. I'd only be a burden."

Sarah put her arm around her sister-in-law. "You'd never be a burden, but I'll miss you terribly."

"You're a strong woman," Frances said. "You'll manage fine—I hope you'll take Bart's wagon train. I'll feel better knowing we're at least in the same state."

Sarah had pushed the idea into her mind's back corners. She'd use her money to pay off the debt on the farm, which she could sell to the carpetbaggers. Or not, depending on whether she decided to go to Texas. Either way, Frances would take the ship to Galveston. She felt as though she were losing her dearest friend. She knew if she begged Frances to stay, she'd forego her plans. But she understood Frances's need to pursue her own life. "I'm proud of you, Frances. I know you'll be the best midwife in Galveston." She bit her lip to hold back tears.

Frances stroked Sarah's hair. "Don't be sad. I won't leave for three weeks. We'll keep in touch and probably see each other again someday—either here or in Texas."

Sarah didn't feel so sure. When she stood back, she saw tears welling in Frances's gray eyes behind her spectacles.

Each Sunday afternoon after John died, Sarah laid wildflowers on his grave and spent a few moments talking to him about the cows, the crops, and problems with freedmen she hired to work the fields. Now, her conversations with John concerned what she should do with the money. Should she pay off the debt and keep the farm or uproot the family by moving to Texas? Without John and Frances, she'd be hard-pressed to manage the farm and the children. She prayed for a sign from God.

Sarah continued teaching her classes until the end of the term while Frances was still here to care for the younger children. On a warm, humid afternoon, after she'd taught class all day, she hitched Brownie to her wagon to pick up Tommy, Lula, and Sallie from the Academy, too tired and preoccupied to respond to their chatter. *What am I going to do?* Dark, gray storm clouds gathered on the western horizon, and a wicked wind snaked through the streets, shaking green leaves from the live oaks. When she made the last turn to Alligator Creek, a buggy parked at the bridge surprised her.

Frances met her at the door. A well-dressed young man stood behind her. "Sarah, this is Martin. He was Alex's friend in Savannah."

Sarah hurriedly removed her bonnet and offered him a seat in the parlor. "How kind of you to come, Martin. We have heard nothing from Alex in over three years. Please tell us what you know." She turned to Frances. "Has he already told you?"

Frances shook her head. "He wanted to wait for you."

A grim look on Martin's face told Sarah he felt uncomfortable with whatever he intended to share. A flash of lightning and a roll of thunder underlined the mood.

Tommy, Lula, and Sallie huddled on the floor around their visitor.

Martin took a battered box from his satchel and laid it on his lap. "Mrs. Browning, Alex sent me this, but I wanted you to have it. I received it three years ago. I apologize for my tardiness in coming, but I live in Jacksonville and I've been quite busy since the war, starting up a business, getting married . . ."

Sarah interrupted, "Don't apologize, Martin. Tell us. What is it?"

He opened the box.

Sarah's eyes opened wide and she gasped. "Alex's watch!"

The children gathered around and looked at it.

"I'm not very good at this, Mrs. Browning." He lifted out the watch and removed and unfolded a creased page. He handed the letter to Sarah.

She read the letter several times. Each time, her forehead wrinkled with more confusion. "What does this mean?" She pointed to the part where he said he hadn't touched the medicine.

"Alex broke his wrist in a terrible accident. He began taking too much laudanum, and I helped him quit."

"Then why would he say he didn't have long to live? Do you know whether he actually died?"

"He must have, Mrs. Browning. I never heard from him again."

Frances dipped a wad of snuff in her lip. "We've never heard from him, either."

Sarah was stricken dumb. Frances put her arms around her. "It's come home to you, honey. I know it's hard, but now you can heal."

Sarah continued to hold on to Frances. Finally, she looked at Martin sitting on the coach with the watch in his hand.

Martin stood solemnly and gave it to her. "You should keep this watch for your son."

Tommy came closer to examine the timepiece. Sarah took it in her hands and caressed its smooth surface. "I'd like to keep it awhile, Tommy. It won't be long before it's yours."

"I must be going, Mrs. Browning," Martin said. "I'm sorry to be the one to give you bad news."

Sarah stood. "Are you sure you won't stay until the weather clears?"

"My carriage is covered, and I really must go now."

Sarah felt relieved. "Thank you, Martin. I've needed to know this for a very long time."

After Martin left, Sarah examined a return address printed in tiny block letters on the outside of the cartridge box. A year ago, she might have made the trip to Savannah to find someone who could have more information about Alex before he died. At this point, she'd accept her husband's death rather than discovering more than she wanted to know.

Frances seemed to sense her thoughts. "Let it rest, Sarah. This is the sign you were looking for. Alex isn't coming back. You must plan a life for yourself and your children."

When Frances began packing her belongings for her trip to Texas, Sarah watched from the doorway. "I'll take you to your train tomorrow,"

Sarah said. She dreaded to say good-bye to her sister-in-law but determined to keep a cheerful demeanor.

The next day, she loaded the children into the wagon and waited at the gate as Tommy and Frances brought out Frances's bags. "Are you sure you've packed enough? Is there anything of mine you'd like to take with you?"

Frances hefted a large satchel into the wagon. "I think I've brought quite enough. I'll buy more after I'm employed as a certified midwife." She climbed into the wagon next to Sarah.

At the station, Frances hugged and kissed each of the children. She reached in her handbag and handed a thick envelope to Sarah. "Don't read this until after my train leaves."

Sarah slipped it into her apron pocket and wrapped her arms around Frances. "How could I have survived without you?"

Frances chuckled. "You could have, but I'll always treasure these years I've shared with your family." She released herself from Sarah's hold and carried her bags to the train.

As the train pulled out from the station, Sarah tore open the thick envelope and removed a sheet of paper covering a stack of paper currency.

At the top of the letter, Frances had printed an address in Galveston.

Dear Sarah and family,

I'm not good with fancy words and such, but I wanted you to have a thousand dollars of my inheritance. A spinster like me doesn't need much. What joy it gives me to know that my money will help you get settled in Texas, or keep the farm—whatever you choose.

With love always,
Frances

28

Fear not: for I have redeemed thee, I have called thee by thy name; thou art mine. When thou passest through the waters, I will be with thee; and through the rivers, they shall not overflow thee.

Isaiah 43: 1b–2a

May 1868

Sarah knew in her heart she'd seen a sign, perhaps several. The Lord was leading her to make a decision, but her grief rendered her oddly lethargic, unable to move forward or to make plans. She'd lost too much too fast—Daddy John, Alex, and then Frances. She spent most days sitting on the porch with Hank at her feet, looking out on the road just beyond Alligator Creek. She'd always envisioned Alex walking down that road, finally coming home to her. She scratched Hank's ears and noticed his labored breathing and the white hair in his thin yellow fur. For a week after Frances's departure, putting one foot in front of the other required all the effort Sarah could muster. She went to bed tired and awakened exhausted. When Tommy and Lula came home from school, they cared for the smaller children. Sallie, Lena, and Minnie left her alone and played quietly in their room during the day.

A week later, as if by miracle, the cloud lifted. She awoke early, clear-headed and focused, and fixed breakfast for the children. After dressing the younger girls, Sarah took her share of the farm money plus the other thousand Frances had given her to repay the loan on the farm. She sat the little girls on a wooden bench inside the bank. "You girls stay here until I finish my business." They nodded solemnly.

Mr. William McArthur, the bank president, led her into his private office and removed a heavy ledger from a low shelf. Licking his finger, McArthur flipped through the pages looking for Sarah's loan record. Certain of the loan balance, Sarah counted out three thousand dollars.

"Looks like eight thousand will get you out free and clear," he said.

"Eight thousand! I only borrowed six thousand, and I've been making payments for almost three years. How can that be?"

He ran his finger down a column and across a row on the ledger. "Well, it's like this. The Republican taxing agent has assessed your annual taxes at twenty-five hundred dollars a year. Since we have a lien against your property, they authorized the bank to collect the taxes."

"Why haven't I gotten notice of this assessment?"

"The tax office posted notices in the newspaper two months ago."

"It's not right!" Sarah said. "We've never had taxes over a few hundred dollars."

"I agree, but the new Republican legislature intends to punish us Southerners for our part in the war. They'll force us to pay their war debts and Union veterans' pensions, too."

"I don't have enough money, Bill. What can I do?"

"I don't know much you can do. If you don't pay the taxes, you'll lose your property."

Sarah put her money into her bag. "I guess the bank just got itself a farm." She gathered her children and proceeded to Bart Benedict's office behind his shop. There she learned from a stranger that Bart had recently sold the store. He directed her to Bart's place north of town.

She could tell right away which house belonged to Bart. Six prairie schooners stood in a field behind it. She stopped the wagon next to his house and left the girls in the back playing with some rag dolls they'd brought along.

"I've decided to join the wagon train," she told Bart. "Have you promised all these wagons?"

"One family changed their mind, so I have an extra."

She paid him twenty-five hundred for a wagon and food for her family. With Frances's money and what she'd saved from her teaching salary, Sarah felt she could afford to settle in Texas. A new and sturdy confidence erased her worries. God had provided thus far.

Bart interrupted her thoughts. "Go home and start packing. My men and I will bring the wagon and mules out later today. They'll help you get your things into the wagon. We'll be out to get you early tomorrow morning."

Tomorrow morning, I'll be leaving my home and everything I've known for sixteen years. It took her breath away.

"Will you be driving the wagon, Miss Sarah?"

"I'm sure I can. I've certainly had experience driving a wagon with a horse."

"Mules aren't much different. They're slower but stronger and don't tire so quickly. You can count on them to follow the wagon in front of them. In fact, most of the time, you won't even need to sit in the driver's seat. Those mules know what to do."

He stood, took her hand, and gave her a slow smile. "Sarah, you've made me a happy man."

By the time Bart and his men arrived, Sarah had written out a list of the furniture she wanted and the livestock that would follow the wagon.

First, she chose a small mahogany cabinet that had been her mother's and packed it with various kitchen utensils and a few chipped dishes the robbers hadn't taken. She included the dining room table, the bureau from her bedroom, several straight-back chairs, the hall clock, and a settee. Three beds that could be dismantled should be ample to sleep the family. She filled a wardrobe trunk and a smaller trunk with the family's clothes. As a last thought, she put in the girls' dolls and a few playthings. Then, she remembered her box of treasures: her diary, Bible, book of poetry, and a cameo that had belonged to her mother. Tommy packed a little box holding his personal belongings—rocks, seashells, his books, the horse his father carved, and Alex's watch.

Sarah went outside to choose livestock to take along. Brownie, their young mare, would be a good horse for the children to ride. She also picked out her two best milk cows, but she wasn't sure old Hank could make the trip.

Sarah met Bart and his men at the door and invited them in. The workmen stayed on the porch, but Bart removed his hat and came in. "I'd like to show you where we're going." He unrolled a large map on the table and traced the route they would take.

"We'll travel west following the railroad track to Tallahassee, then on to Mobile Bay. We'll head northwest across Mississippi and Louisiana toward Shreveport and catch the ferry across the Red River. Texas land grants are around here." He circled an area in eastern Texas. "These small towns are thriving with good crops, especially cotton."

Sarah studied the map. "Where is Galveston from there?" She wanted to know Frances's location.

Bart traced a line straight south. "It's on the coast—a long way from East Texas." He rolled up the map and took Sarah out to inspect the narrow, twelve-foot long prairie schooner hitched to three pairs of mules. With its brown cloth curving up over oval-shaped bows, the wagon stood about ten feet tall.

Bart knocked on the sideboards. "Hardwood. Won't shrink, and it's tarred so it's watertight. They say these wagons shelter almost as well as a house."

Sarah crawled inside and looked up at the heavy, brown bonnet. She climbed out and pointed to a box attached to the side of the wagon "What's this?"

"That's the jockey box. It's your tool box with extra iron bolts and parts in case you need repairs along the way." He touched a barrel next to the box. "This is your water barrel. Whenever we stop at a river, the men will help you fill it. On the other side of the wagon, you have a feed trough for your animals and a small chicken coop."

Sarah hadn't expected to be able to take her chickens but mentally added them to her list of livestock.

Bart and his men loaded almost everything from Sarah's list. She was amazed at how much the prairie schooner held. The wagon held all the furniture on her list except for the table. Sarah and her children caught a rooster and four hens and put them in the coop along with some corn.

Bart turned to Sarah. "We'll meet you at daybreak. Don't be late." With the wagon filled to capacity, the men drove it across the road and left it next to the barn. They put the six mules in the barn for the night and penned up Sarah's horse and cows. Sarah walked back to the house and watched the heavy cumulus clouds rolling overhead. As she crossed the bridge, she saw that the water of Alligator Creek had risen a few inches since morning and now it almost touched the bottom of the bridge.

Sarah put her children to bed early to rest for tomorrow's journey. Exhausted, Sarah fell onto the bed in John's room without even changing her clothes.

Sarah lay awake for a long time before dropping off to sleep. She awoke several times during the night and heard heavy rain falling on the roof. Finally, when dim light sifted through the window, she jumped out of bed and changed into a plain gingham dress. Then, she woke her sleepy children and helped the younger ones dress themselves. "Hurry, Tommy; we must be ready to leave when the wagon train comes." In the kitchen, she fed the children biscuits and milk and forced herself to eat a biscuit, not knowing when they'd eat again.

The children, dressed in their everyday clothes, waited for Sarah on the front porch. As she walked out the front door carrying a small canvas bag with a few last-minute belongings, Sarah heard the sound of rushing water cut through the stillness of the morning.

Tommy grabbed her arm. "Wait, Mama; we can't leave Hank."

"He's too old to make the trip."

"No," Tommy said and ran back to the house calling the dog.

When he returned with Hank, Sarah grasped Minnie's and Lena's hands. They walked together toward the creek with Tommy at one end, Lula and Sallie at the other.

Tommy noticed it first. "The bridge is out," he yelled.

The five stood by the bank of Alligator Creek transfixed by the vision of a stream, wider and wilder than anything in their memory. Sarah observed the rushing waters with a wary eye. "We have no other choice. We have to get across to the road. Our wagon will be here within an hour. Everyone, take off your shoes and put them into the bag."

Three-year-old Minnie began wailing, "I'm scared, Mommy."

Sarah summoned her courage. "Everyone hold hands and bow your heads." She began a prayer. "Still our fears, precious Father. Let us feel your mighty arms holding us as we pass through the water, protecting me and these precious children from danger. Give us strength and courage for this journey. Stay with us all the way."

"Amen," the children said in unison.

"Minnie, stay here next to Lula. You, too, Sallie and Lena. Tommy and I are going to swim across." Eleven-year-old Tommy had learned to swim at the spring where she'd taken the children on hot summer days. She'd have to carry the other children across.

"Hold onto my arm, Tommy," she said. She waded into the creek, her skirt swirling in the muddy water around her. "Wait a minute." Sarah pulled Tommy back, removed her shoes and long dress, and stuffed them into the canvas bag. Returning to the bank, she instructed him, "We'll wade as far as we can. Then we'll have to swim." The creek bed slanted down at a sharp angle, and, after a few steps, she sank to her hips in water. "When you're ready, I'm going to let go. Swim as hard as you can toward the other bank."

"I'm ready, Mama. I'm not afraid. God's going to protect us."

Remaining on the downstream side of her slight, eleven-year-old son, Sarah walked down the creek bed. Then, suddenly, the ground dropped away and she floated in rushing water. The current pushed against her. Tommy, dog paddling as fast as he could, slammed into her side. She took him under her right arm, kicking the water with all her power. "Kick your legs fast. Keep your knees straight." Finally, she put her arm around him and swam on her side. *Make me strong, O Lord.* After one final kick, she felt the current weaken. When she lowered her legs, her feet touched the slippery bottom on the other side. Tommy climbed up the bank in front of Sarah. *Thank you, Lord.* Tommy turned and grinned at her; then he closed his eyes and lowered his head. She watched Hank, soaking wet, drag himself out of the water and up the slippery bank.

Swimming back, she passed easily through the heavy current. She crossed to the other side to fetch Sallie, leaving eight-year-old Lula to care for the two youngest children. Sallie, who was much lighter than Tommy, would have an even more difficult time in the current. Sarah immediately swam on her side and pulled Sallie to the other bank to wait with Tommy.

She caught her breath on the bank before returning for another child. "Tommy, I'm bringing little Minnie next. You be ready to take her when I get her across."

Tommy patted her arm. "Don't worry, Mama. God will help you."

When she lifted her shivering three-year-old, Minnie wrapped her legs around her mother's waist. Sarah waded into the creek for the third time. Holding Minnie under one arm, she managed a desperate, flailing sidestroke with the other as she struggled across the current. As soon as she set the child down on the bank, Minnie scampered up the steep embankment with Sarah climbing behind her. When they reached the top, Sarah put her into Tommy's care. *Don't leave us now, Lord. Hold us safe in your arms,* she prayed.

When she crossed again to the bank where the last two children stood, Sarah turned and squatted on the ground with her back toward Lena. She allowed the four-year-old to wrap her thin arms around her shoulders with her legs squeezing her waist. "Hang on tight, baby. The current is really strong." Sarah stood with Lena on her back and walked down the muddy bank. When they reached the deep center of the creek, Sarah swam with the child gripping her neck like a vice. As the current hit them, Sarah struggled using her arms and legs to keep her face above the surface. The water's pressure grew stronger. Sarah's face went under. *I'm losing my strength, Lord. Just a little longer, Lord. Stay with us, please.* She kicked even harder to stay afloat. Her lungs burned, and her shoulders ached with the colossal effort. Yet, Lena hung on for dear life. Sarah's head went under again, and when she surfaced, she saw a huge tree limb floating toward her. She struggled upstream to avoid being hit by the branches, which brushed past and scratched her face. As the heavy part of the limb floated near, she grabbed for it, allowing the tree to carry her downstream. About twenty feet farther, the small branches caught on a root on the opposite bank. With Lena still stuck to her back like a leech, she climbed over the limb onto the bank where Tommy grabbed her hand and pulled her up.

Sarah caught her breath and went back for eight-year-old Lula. *Help me now. I'm getting weaker. I can't go much farther.*

"I can swim, Mama, I really can. Tommy taught me."

"Are you sure?"

"You can ask Tommy."

Sarah looked across the stream at Tommy, who seemed miles away. "I'm going to let you try, baby, because we'll have to carry the bag this time. I can't come back again." Sarah put the strap of the canvas bag across her shoulder and waded into the water with Lula. Sarah swam on the downstream side and Lula paddled through the current with a big grin on her face. Sarah thought perhaps that the pressure of the current had lessened before this last swim, but she never shared that thought with the happy child.

She gathered the water-soaked bag and offered a prayer of thanks that Bart had taken their packed wagon across the stream the day before.

At the top of the steep bank, Tommy sat holding Hank in his lap, with Lula, Sallie, and Minnie leaning over his shoulder crying. Tommy rubbed the dog's wet fur. "I think he died, Mama."

Sarah realized that they couldn't take time to bury their pet. "We'll leave him here by Alligator Creek. This has always been his favorite place." The children gave Hank tearful hugs and followed Sarah to the wagon. She opened one of the trunks to retrieve some dry clothes.

As the sun rose on a clear, steamy morning, four men on horseback approached. After stopping short of Sarah's wagon, Bart and his men opened the barn and hitched the mules to the wagon. One man checked the wheels and brakes while another loosed the horse and cows she'd chosen to take along.

A man Sarah had met the day before instructed her, "We'll take you to join the wagon train at the end of the road. Your animals will follow along with other livestock."

Sarah climbed into the driver's seat.

"Let us know if you need anything. Once we join the train, you won't need to drive. The mules will follow without any help."

As the wagon pulled away, Sarah looked back at her five children, already asleep cuddled together on a mattress. A great blue heron skimmed along the creek waters beside the road then soared high into the sky. Sunlight splashed the fields and the orchards. Sarah fixed her eyes on the two-story white clapboard house where she and Alex had moved soon after their marriage. The house had witnessed six births and two deaths. It grew smaller and with distance finally disappeared from sight as the wagon bumped down the road beside Alligator Creek.

29

Most of those who went to Texas were down to their last chance, and Texas was it.

Francis E. Abernethy
The Family Saga

May–June 1868

Sitting in the center of her wagon, Sarah held Minnie, who sobbed on her lap. Above her head, the shadows of tree limbs leapt in ghostly patterns across the taut, brown cloth.

"I'm scared, Mommy. I want to go home," Minnie wailed, her blond curls wet with tears.

Watching the silhouettes splay upon the ceiling, the child screamed again, "Look there! A bear's on the roof . . . with giant claws."

Lula laughed, "It's only tree shadows, you silly baby." Teasing Minnie, she held her hands, fingers outstretched, above her head and let out a fierce growl.

Sarah gave Lula a stern look. "Stop it, Lula! I remember a time when you were afraid of bears on the ceiling." She smoothed Minnie's hair out of her eyes. "Mama's here, darling. Look at me. I'm not afraid. We're on a wonderful trip to a new home. As long as we're all here together, we're safe."

"Why did we leave anyhow?" Tommy asked. "I'll really miss my home in Lake City. I'll never see it again."

The memory of her house and the treasures left behind also pained Sarah's heart. Each time she remembered something or someone lost in the past, she spent a moment of piercing grief. "You'll make new friends in Texas, Tommy. You're the kind of boy everyone likes."

"Yes, but what if they *don't* like us?" Lula whined. "I remember how the girls at school treated new students. I'd hate that!"

"Children! Don't worry about things that may never happen." Sarah wished she'd taken more time to talk to the children before they left. The last few months of sadness and confusion blurred through her mind. Now, she chose the simplest explanation: "We had to leave. We didn't have enough money without your daddy and granddaddy. I believe God intended us to leave the meanness behind to find a new life in Texas. Listen to me, children. The next few months will be difficult, but God will help us get through it. We're going to help one another."

They nodded.

"Say it then. Say it after me! 'We're the Brownings. Together we're strong. With God's help we'll make it through.'"

In one voice, strong and determined, they repeated Sarah's spirited chant.

Just then, Bart put his head through the back flap of their wagon, his white teeth glistening in a wide smile. "How are you feeling, Miss Sarah?"

"Much better now, thank you."

"We're asking able adults to walk behind the wagons for the next couple of hours. The mules are straining. We don't want the animals to give out before we barely get started."

When Sarah moved toward the rear of the wagon, Lena raised to her knees.

"We wanna go with you."

"Let me ride Brownie," Tommy said. "Please."

"Not yet, Tommy, maybe tomorrow."

Sarah and her five children slid off the wagon to join a growing throng following the covered wagons alongside the railroad track. Close to twenty Negro men, women, and children followed carrying their belongings in ragged satchels or flour sacks. Behind them, other groups followed in small farm wagons, some open, others rigged with makeshift bonnets to protect them from the weather. Behind the farm wagons, two men on horseback herded livestock.

For two hours, Sarah walked along the road. Ahead of them the wagon bonnets seemed to float down the road like billowing shirts on a clothesline. Some travelers had decorated their wagons with pictures, family names, or slogans like "Texas or Bust." Of eighteen prairie schooners in the train, Bart had organized his six wagons in a partnership with a group from Jacksonville who'd already been traveling nine days before they joined the group.

Sarah didn't mind walking. Contact with the earth gave her a sense of solid progress. She had no problem keeping up with the slow-moving wagons. Her children, in a complete change of mood, skipped, played, and sprinted with other children alongside the wagon train. For the first time in many days, Sarah felt happy in anticipation of the future.

Some travelers rode their horses. A couple walking beside Sarah pointed out a trio on horseback. "Their name's Larchmont. They were our neighbors in Baldwin—a very sad story." Kathryn Clements explained that the two young women were sisters, both widows from early in the Civil War. "The young man riding ahead is their brother. We call them the three L's—Lennie, Luella, and Lorena." The sisters rode astride their horses rather than riding sidesaddle, their skirts stretched high above their knees. Just then six-year-old Sallie ran past followed by a dark-skinned child about her age. Sarah turned and chased after them. She heard a horse's whinny and the stomping of hooves then a man's angry voice. She turned. It was Bart.

"What are you kids doing? Get away from those animals and find your parents."

Sallie, frightened and sobbing, ran to Sarah's side with the other little girl following.

"You girls mustn't play among the animals," Sarah said.

Sallie took her friend's hand. "Mama, this is Blossom."

Blossom looked up at Sarah, her eyes wide. "We didn't mean to do nothin' wrong, ma'am."

"Where are your parents, Blossom?" Sarah asked.

"Back that way."

Sarah followed her to the back of the group and delivered her to her mother.

"What you done wrong, Blossom?" her mother scolded.

Blossom ducked her head.

Sarah touched Blossom's shoulder. "They were only playing, but they should stay away from the animals. It's not safe." Sarah introduced herself and learned their names—Samuel and Charity Bishop. Charity told her they'd come along with the Clements, the people she worked for. She pointed out the couple Sarah had talked to earlier about the Larchmont family.

Samuel explained, "Mr. Benedict let us join up with the covered wagons train if Charity and me bring our own wagon and work for our passage. He's promised us some land at the end of the journey. We don't want to do nothin' to get him mad at us else he might leave us behind."

As they walked on, Sarah kept constant watch to see that her children stayed away from the animals. Then, she heard a familiar voice calling her name. In a wagon to her right, she recognized Industrious and Hannah. Thrilled to see them again, she walked closer. "Why didn't you tell me you were coming along?"

Industrious shook his head. "We would have told you, but we didn't know *you* were coming. We been signed up for a month now. Right after Mr. John's funeral."

Sarah summoned her children. "Look who's here!"

As the sun came directly overhead, the wagons turned off the main road, taking a path into a wooded area near a stream. A boy of about eighteen galloped astride a stallion shouting, "Nooning time; fetch your water cups and gather in the clearing."

Sarah and the children returned to their wagon. Locating three tin cups in her trunk, Sarah dropped them into her apron pocket and called Tommy to round up the other children. White travelers gathered in the center of the circle, and the Negroes clustered at the edges. Employees of the partners brought out pans of cold biscuits and bacon left from their early breakfast in Lake City. One man filled a clean bucket with water from the creek while others filled water barrels for the wagons.

Lula turned and pointed. "Look, there's Hannah and Industrious. Let's go sit with them"

"That's a fine idea," Sarah said. She and the children carried their plates with them to the outer circle where the Negro travelers stood.

While the travelers ate and quenched their thirst, Bart and his two partners from Jacksonville, Abner Dial and Caleb McIntosh, moved to the center of the circle. "Look around, folks," Abner said. "These people will be your family for at least three months, possibly four. I figure the distance to East Texas at over eight hundred miles. On a good day, we can cover fifteen miles if we aren't waiting out rainstorms or crossing rivers. Some of you'll get sick some hurt. Your family here will be your help."

Caleb McIntosh stepped forward. "Your new Texas home is about a week's drive from the Louisiana border, just across the Sabine River. Each family will have ten acres of your own to grow crops like cotton. The land is very fertile."

An older woman traveling with her grandson asked about hostile Indians.

"The place we're going is totally pacified," Abner said. "The government keeps the Indians on a reservation."

An adolescent boy, Willy McAllister, stood near Sarah with his pregnant wife. "My wife Mary here will be having a baby in a couple of months. Is there a doctor that can help her?"

An old man struggled to his feet. "I'm a doctor. My name's Frank Griffin."

Sarah stood and moved forward. "My sister-in-law was the best midwife in our county. She helped me with three of my births, and I've assisted her many times. Also, my friend Hannah is a wonderful nurse. We'll be glad to help Dr. Griffin."

A bearded man with intelligent hazel eyes turned to Sarah. "Ben Cole from St. Augustine, Florida."

"What brings you to Texas?" Sarah asked.

"The Texas governor appointed me judge in Harrison County. I got a letter in March asking me to take this job."

Sarah smiled. "That sounds interesting."

After a seven-mile stretch during the afternoon, the wagon train camped for the evening beside another stream. The men butchered a deer they'd shot, and the women fried the meat in large iron skillets over a smoldering wood fire. After sending Tommy and Sallie to feed the mare and the cows, Sarah helped the other women slice and fry potatoes. After supper, while the Negro passengers cleaned the dishes, white travelers gathered around the campfire to chat and listen to Caleb play his harmonica. Abner fiddled some lively tunes while the young people danced. Sarah, her hair loosened from the ribbon that held it behind her neck, sat on a quilt sipping hot coffee while she watched the children sing and dance. As the fiddles began another slower melody, Sarah felt someone sit beside her.

She turned to see Bart staring at her, coal-black eyes glistening, his faded-blue, cotton shirt opened onto his chest. "I wish you could see how your face glows in the firelight."

Sarah chuckled. "I had no idea you were so poetic, Mr. Benedict."

"So when is it 'Mr. Benedict' instead of Bart?"

Sarah started to rise. "I should get the children to bed."

He tugged her back down. "The children are enjoying themselves. Let them be." He put his arm around her. She squirmed against him and wondered if she should allow him to touch her like this.

"It's OK. Just relax."

She had not realized how tired she was. Her head dropped against his shoulder, and, for a brief moment, she nodded into sleep. Suddenly, she felt his lips pressed against hers.

"Sarah," he whispered. "Give me a chance."

Sleepily, she pulled away from him. "This is not a good time, Bart. I'm really tired."

He stood and leaned forward to kiss her forehead. She slipped away from the kiss. As she left, she heard Bart's soft voice, "I'm a patient man, Sarah. I'll wait."

She led her family off to bed in the wagon. As she lay beside her children, Sarah asked them to repeat the words of courage they'd learned earlier. Sarah said prayers with them, kissed their faces, and covered them with a light sheet. When their breathing became slow and deep, she knew they'd fallen asleep. Restless and wakeful, she contemplated how Bart had taken advantage of her fatigue. At the same time, she recognized her attraction to him, or perhaps it was her natural need for a man. Her mind wandered to thoughts of Alex. *Had he really taken his own life? Was he still alive?* Sometimes, she excused his chosen absence as a result of a change in his soul caused by the terrors that came after experiencing horrible brutality. *How can I blame a man with a damaged spirit? How did such a change take place? Was it a sudden thing, or did it evolve over time? Will I ever know?*

30

To be yourself in a world that is constantly trying to make you something else is the greatest accomplishment.

Ralph Waldo Emerson

June–July 1868

Two weeks later, the wagons stopped in Tallahassee to pick up more supplies. Would they never pass through Florida? They'd already crossed at least three rivers by ferry and forded twice as many streams.

The next day, they camped near the Ochlockonee River to fill the water barrels and allow the travelers to bathe and wash their clothes. Sarah ordered the children to stay in the wagon. She gathered the clothes they'd worn so many times, stiff with dust and mud. After tying dirty sheets around the laundry, she lugged her load down to the river where other women were already scrubbing clothes against smooth stones in the cold water. Using lye soap, Sarah set to work on a stained apron. Life had been hard at the farm after Alex had left, but nothing compared to the inconveniences of being a woman on a wagon train. At least at home, she had a private latrine behind her house—unlike squatting bare-bottomed in the woods in a cluster of vines, possibly poison ivy or, worse yet, a nest for a viper. The tasks she took for granted—washing her hair, attending to her monthly bleeding, eating, and washing—created major problems to be solved or indignities to be endured. She looked to her left and saw a young girl, profoundly pregnant, scrubbing her husband's dirty trousers. *Sorry, Lord; every time I slather myself with self-pity, you show me someone with worse problems than mine.*

"Hello," she said. "I'm Sarah Browning. How are you feeling?"

The girl looked up from her laundry "I'm Mary McAllister. I'm well, so far."

"When do you expect your lying-in?" Sarah asked, rubbing soap into a stubborn brown spot on Tommy's overalls.

"My doctor told me it would come near the first of August. He warned me about taking this trip, but Willy and I wanted to come. This was an opportunity to start over, and we had to take it." A determined but frightened frown crossed her face. "To tell the truth, Miss Sarah, I'm scared to the bone. I've know'd lots of womenfolk who've died givin' birth and some left maimed for life. Don't really know which is worse."

"If I can be of any help, please call on me. I'll pray for you, Mary. I still remember how frightened I was when my first child was born."

The hot temperature in June and July turned wagon beds into steamy ovens, and the travelers slept on their quilts in tents, the openings covered with netting. Tommy camped regularly with two boys his age. At night, the girls slept with Sarah in her tent.

"Where are we now, Mama?" Sallie asked.

"We're still in Florida, baby. It's not a big state, but it's a long way across. We're in the part called the panhandle."

In late July, the wagon train approached its first major crossing, the Tensaw River above Mobile. Most of the passengers walked behind the wagons except for the elderly and a few with intestinal problems that had passed from one to another. The next morning, the wagons lined up at the dock on the riverbank. Across the bay they could see Mobile, dark smoke puffing from the smokestacks of its factories and large ships moored in its vast ports. It would be a long wait before three ferries could load and transport eighteen wagons, fifty horses, and seventy-five cattle across the river. Sarah decided to check on Mary McAllister three wagons ahead. When Sarah and her children arrived at Mary's wagon, its flaps were turned back; Mary sat in the rear of the wagon next to Jesse Kuykendall, a young man whom Sarah had seen around the camp.

When he saw her, Jesse slid from his seat on the wagon. His sandy hair and thin features reminded her of a younger Alex. He grinned at her. "Are you the famous Sarah Browning I've heard so much about?"

Startled by his introduction, Sarah answered, "What might I be famous for, Mr. Kuykendall?"

"Your son Tom told me you swam a swollen stream with each of your children to get to the wagon train."

Sarah smiled. "A mother does what she has to do."

"You must have had powerful leading to endure such a feat."

Sarah thought back to her prayers for a sign, the horrendous events that made staying in Florida impossible, the moment she decided to cross the stream, and the power that took over her body. "You have a great insight, Jesse. Are you a minister?"

"No, ma'am." He dug his hands into the pockets of his worn denim trousers. "Not yet. But I've studied the Bible since I learned to read. I hope to find a church to pastor in Texas." He paused and smiled. "By the way, you have a fine son. He told me he'd like to be a minister. We've had some serious discussions."

Tom a minister? Sarah was happy her son had found a spiritual mentor. "You seem too young to be a preacher," Sarah said. *And too nice.*

When the train stopped for nooning in a thick grove of trees along the trail, the Larchmont sisters walked to the stream to get a drink of water. When Luella squatted by the stream and leaned forward to douse water on her gritty face, the waist of her pantaloons pulled downward, revealing the cleft between her buttocks. Several young men laughed and jostled one another as they leered at the young woman's hindquarters. While Tommy tethered Brownie next to the Larchmont horses, Sarah stood between him and the sight of Luella squatting by the stream.

Later, as they snacked on leftovers from last night, Sarah approached the sisters. "Luella, I'm sure you are not aware how much you reveal when you lean forward in those pantaloons. The young men notice it quite a bit. If I were you, I would be careful."

The two sisters laughed. "I wouldn't hardly think what we wear is any of your concern, Sister Sarah," Lorena said. "We're dressing cool for this hot weather."

Luella leaned on one leg and jutted a hip sideways. "As far as the young men are concerned, they have a choice to look or not. If anyone bothers us, our brother can take care of us just fine."

"Who are you to talk?" Lorena sneered. "I saw you out spooning with Bart."

Sarah's face grew hot. "Well, pardon my intrusion."

At dark, Sarah instructed all her children to sleep inside the wagon.

"It's too hot," Tommy complained. "I wanna sleep in the tent with my friends. Don't make us sleep in the wagon."

"We'll burn up," Sallie whined. "It's cooler in the tent."

Sarah put on a stern face. "Listen, children; I may be out all night helping Mary with birthing her baby. I don't need the extra worry of my children asleep under a tent in the woods. As soon as the baby comes, we'll all sleep in the tents whenever it's hot . . . Are we together?"

Grumbling, they agreed and crawled into the wagon.

"You girls may sleep in your short pantaloons."

They quickly undressed and threw their outer clothes into a jumbled pile.

Sarah's face became stern. "Fold those clothes and put them away in the trunk. Good night, children. Don't forget your prayers."

The successful birth of Mary's baby boy brought new joy to the travelers. Sarah noticed less complaining, less arguing, and more laughter as everyone shared in the young couple's happiness and hovered over the tiny baby in wonder.

31

We gain the strength of the temptation we resist.

Ralph Waldo Emerson

August–September 1868

In mid-August the wagons pulled into Natchez, Mississippi. The partners decided to cross the Mississippi River at Natchez rather than at Vicksburg, which still bore evidence of wartime destruction even after five years. By the grace of God, according to its citizens, Natchez escaped with only minor damage. The route to the river wound down a tree-lined boulevard between houses built before the war. Sarah admired a house with four Roman columns stretching two stories upward to the eave of a roof. Some houses had multiple chimneys designed to draw smoke from fireplaces that warmed living rooms and bedrooms of the privileged. The beauty of the Mississippi town stunned her. An even more stunning sight greeted her at the river.

As one by one the wagons stopped at the ferry landing, travelers crowded onto grassy plots to stare at the vast river. Several barges and a steamship inched north and south, crossed by ferries traversing east to west. Sarah called to her children to come see the river before they started across.

That evening, Abner and Caleb began fiddling a rendition of "Lorena," and several couples gathered around dancing. Jesse sang the lyrics of a lover's sad memory of his lost sweetheart. Sarah smiled at her children, who were playing tag with other children. She noticed Sallie's friend Blossom playing among them.

Bart approached Sarah and, facing her, pulled her toward him. His right arm circled her waist like a metal band, and he clenched her right hand with his left. "Let's dance."

She struggled against him, but the pressure of his strong grip forced her to follow his steps. "I didn't say I wanted to dance, Bart."

"Relax. You're as rigid as a cypress stump." When she allowed tension in her face and shoulders to loosen, he grinned at her. "You're pretty when you smile."

When the fiddlers began a polka, Ben Cole cut in and pulled her close then turned her out, stomping the three-step rhythm in wide circles around the seated travelers. Sarah smiled as they swayed, their extended arms pumping and feet galloping across the clearing. She followed the movements and steps with little effort although it had been at least sixteen years since she and Alex had danced the polka in Georgia. Ben's strong lead and the rollicking music carried her along until she felt like a young girl again, flirting with boys and dancing through the night. When the music stopped, Ben began to escort her back to her seat, but Bart intercepted them, took her arm, and led her away from the camp toward the river. She looked back to see her children still enjoying games with their playmates.

"Let's take another look at the mighty Mississippi while we are here. Who knows when or if we'll ever cross it again?"

As the sun sank in the west behind them, the mansions, the magnolia trees, and the waters of the river itself took on a rosy glow that reflected evening sunlight. Near the water's edge, a blue heron stood frozen on one leg, its neck crooked in readiness to spear a fish. Silently, she watched the bird until he uncoiled his neck like a spring, stabbed beneath the surface, and rose up, a fish impaled on his beak.

"That's amazing," Bart said.

She continued to watch. "Our heron often speared fish out of Alligator Creek." She turned toward Bart. "Did you want to talk to me?"

The heron extended his wide wings, lifting his heavy body skyward, and disappeared behind the trees. Bart slipped his arm around her waist. "There are not many opportunities to be alone with you." He turned his body toward her and pulled her close.

Sarah leaned into his embrace and returned his warm kisses with passion she had not known since Alex had left. She touched the hair at the back of his neck and pulled his face even closer. The pressure of his body caused a wave of desire to flash from deep inside, tingling every surface of her skin. He unbuttoned her blouse and she allowed it. She shivered as the humid air off the water touched her skin. He kissed her throat.

"Oh, my sweet Sarah, I want you so much. I don't think I can stand to wait much longer."

She gasped for air and swallowed, not thinking, only responding. Then she pulled away, her breath still rapid and warm. "We can't. Not here. Not now."

He nodded in agreement, interlacing his fingers with hers. "Meet me here later tonight after your children are asleep." They stayed behind a few minutes, watching the changing colors in the sky and on the water, and then turned back to the camp.

The next morning, after a light breakfast, Abner stood before the passengers and announced that the next river crossing would be the Red River between Louisiana and Texas. The wagon train should reach its destination by late September, he said. The travelers had been on the road three months now, rising in the dark of morning for a cold breakfast and leaving camp at first light. Twice the partners had traded their mules for new ones; four times a wagon had broken an axle requiring repair. Once, after a heavy rain, the wagon wheels sunk deep in mud. It took the physical strength of all the travelers to dislodge them.

During the next three weeks, Bart stayed busy making sure the wagon train continued its journey and found little time to spend with Sarah. She felt a degree of relief mixed with disappointment, but she was glad she had not returned to him that night by the Mississippi. When the train took a two-day rest in Alexandria, Bart sought her out after supper for a short walk into the town.

"You've avoided me since that night by the river. I waited for you, but you never came back." They crossed a railroad track and found a boardwalk leading into an area with several stores and businesses.

"I thought better of it," she said. She remembered with embarrassment how she had so nearly given into her desires. Fear of pregnancy coupled with scripture's warnings rescued her. "I've not avoided you. It's been the other way around."

He turned away. "I suppose you hurt my pride. I thought you'd come back." When she remained silent, he changed the subject. "We should be in Texas in two weeks," he said.

"Thank the Lord." She noticed his reflection in a store window, a handsome man in a western hat. She looked very small beside him.

"Have you made plans about your new home?"

Fear snaked across her heart. Sometimes the loss of Alligator Creek tore at her as much as the deaths of the people who had lived there. Imagining her new home saved her from belaboring her grief. "I have no idea what to expect. I supposed our new friends would help one another build houses in Texas. I saved back some money to pay for mine."

"I've already bought a two-story home near Jefferson. Last February, I made a railroad trip to Texas and visited Marion County—not far from our destination in East Texas. An older couple had built this house some time ago, but now they've decided to move in with their children in Marshall. It's quite a large home."

Sarah sighed. "I hope I can find an already-built house. I worry about living in the wagon with the children while we wait for our home."

"Sarah, don't worry. I'll take care of you. I have a wonderful plan."

She crossed her arms over her chest and stepped back. "What is it?"

"You may stay at my house—at least until yours is built or until you find a house to buy."

"Live with you, Bart? I hardly think that would be proper."

Bart reached forward and held her shoulders. "You and the children could have the whole second story, and I'll live downstairs. I'm not proposing an improper relationship."

Sarah shook her head. "Then, you must be looking for a housekeeper. Sorry, I'm not interested in that job, either." She turned her back to him. "Why are you offering me such a thing, Bart? I'm sure that either Larchmont sister would leap at the opportunity. One of them might even marry you if you'd ask. I've seen the looks they've given you." She faced him and gave him a mischievous smirk.

"I'm not interested in the Larchmont sisters. I'm interested in you." He stared at her with his amazing black eyes. "I'd marry you in a minute if you'd give me a chance."

Sarah laughed. "Even with five children? You must be insane."

"You'll have to marry someone. A woman alone would have a hard time out here. What will you do for money when your savings run out?"

Sarah had worried about that eventuality but had prayed the Lord would provide. She lifted her chin. "I'll think of something."

"Please consider my offer, Sarah."

She grinned, "The marriage or the house?"

"Both." A young couple passed them on the sidewalk. They walked close together holding hands. The man leaned over and kissed the girl's cheek. "Promise to think about it," Bart said. "I know you care for me, and I'm crazy for you." He put his arm around her waist and pulled her toward him. He smelled faintly of cigar smoke. A familiar shiver of passion followed his touch.

32

All that is necessary for the triumph of evil is for good men to do nothing.

Edmund Burke

September 1868

In late September, the wagon train crossed the Red River at Shreveport, Louisiana. A hint of fall cooled the East Texas air, and the moon that had followed them by day hid behind the earth during the dark night.

Sarah and the children were sleeping in the wagon again since the days had turned cooler. She did not know what to expect in Texas, but she felt excited that they were closer now—closer to having a home. Just after she relaxed into sleep, Minnie cried out, "Mama, I need to pee-pee."

Sarah roused herself and crawled to the back of the wagon, where she lit a lantern. "Come on, baby. I'll go with you." Sometimes, Lula accompanied Minnie, but the pitch black of the night would frighten the child this night. Sarah lifted her off the back of the wagon, and they followed a faint path into the woods to the area assigned to women. Myriad sounds surrounded them—cicadas chirping in a loud crescendo, a whistle of wind, something scurrying through dry grass, and trickling sounds as Minnie relieved herself. Sarah lifted the lantern while the child pulled up her pantaloons. Minnie clung close to Sarah as they turned back towards camp.

A nightmarish scream pierced the night. Sarah and Minnie halted just outside the clearing, and Sarah put her arm around her child. *What in heaven's name?* Loud voices piled atop one another in unintelligible cacophony, reminding Sarah of blackbirds migrating through Alligator Farm in the springtime. Finally, a shrill voice Sarah recognized as Luella's broke through. "It was that Negro man. He looked in our wagon."

As the travellers awoke, lanterns came alive in spots of golden light hanging inside and outside wagons, casting sinister shadows on the underbrush. As Sarah and Minnie ventured a few steps closer, someone ran toward them. Raising her lantern, Sarah recognized Industrious, wearing a straw hat, his eyes wide. She shot out her hand. "Industrious? Where are you going?" Her fingers touched his heaving chest.

"Miss Sarah, tell 'em I didn' do nothing wrong. They'll believe you," he said between heaves.

Sarah whispered, "Shh. Calm yourself and tell me what happened." Behind him people bustled about the camp.

Industrious stood, shaking and repeating, "Oh my Lord, oh dear Lord."

"Tell me. I can't help you if I don't know."

He sucked in an enormous gulp of air and exhaled. "I come out here to do my business. Didn' bring no light with me. It's so dark, Miss Sarah."

"I know, go on."

"Anyhow . . . when I finished and started back, I got turned 'round. Couldn't find my wagon. Stopped at the back of some white folks' wagons. The flap was opened. I just stood there a minute trying to see in the dark. Oh, my Lord."

"You must have stopped at the back of the Larchmont wagon."

"Just after I stopped, someone in the wagon lit a lantern and that lady started screaming."

Sarah swallowed hard. She believed the story, but she also knew the dire consequences of even the appearance of anything sexual between a Negro man and a white woman. If Lennie saw Industrious standing behind the wagon, he would accuse him of looking lustfully at his sisters.

"I'm runnin', Miss Sarah. If they catch me, I'm a dead man."

Sarah needed time to think. If he went back and told his story, the girls' brother and certain other members of the group would never believe him. On the other hand, running suggested guilt. She laid her hand on his arm. "Don't run, Industrious," she advised. "They'll surely catch you and kill you. Stay . . . I'll help any way I can. Mr. Benedict and the other partners will listen to me."

In the light of the lanterns, Bart along with five other men stood poised in the clearing holding guns. Abner and Caleb began to saddle horses. Sarah recognized Lennie and his sisters at the center of the gathering. Everyone talked at once in loud voices.

A female voice: "I nearly died of fright."

A male voice: "You can't trust them niggers."

Another male voice: "Industrious. His name's Industrious."

"Which way did he go?"

Another female voice: "We'll never be safe till you catch him."

Before Sarah could speak again, Industrious bolted into the dark.

During a fitful night calming her children, Sarah finally slept a few hours and awoke to the sounds of horses whinnying and stamping their hooves. She looked outside the wagon and saw two men arriving on horseback. Bart helped them tie the horses and led them outside the camp.

Thursday morning at breakfast, rumors spread like small pox, becoming more toxic as they passed around the camp. A large group clustered around the Larchmonts. Luella, hand over her heart and eyes rolling upward, told and retold the story of the Negro man in the straw hat who stood beside her wagon looking on her while she slept.

Sarah returned and sat next to the girls on the back of the wagon. Tommy along with his new friends, Carter and Legrand, approached. "Do you know anything about this, Mama?" Tommy said and sat beside her. The other two boys stood staring wide-eyed.

Sarah looked at her children from one to the other. "Don't believe all you hear. Industrious got up in the night. He didn't have a light and got turned around in the dark. He stopped at the back of the Larchmont wagon."

Carter frowned and narrowed his eyes. "How do you know that, Miz Browning?"

"He told me. I've known Industrious for a long time. I know that he is a good man. I also know because I saw him last night right after it happened."

Tommy gasped. "You saw him? We heard he raped someone."

Sarah grabbed Tommy's upper arm. "Where did you hear that word, young man?"

Tommy's face turned red. "This morning a lady came over and told Carter and Legrand's mother, but I don't know what it means."

All three boys shook their heads in pious ignorance.

Sarah pursed her lips, glaring at them. "Are you sure?"

The boys hung their heads while the girls leaned in closer. Blossom had come over as she often did to play with Sallie.

"Girls," Sarah said, "I want you to play hide and seek in the field. I see plenty of trees for you to hide behind."

"We don't want to," Lena whined.

"Go," Sarah said in her stern voice. "I mean it."

The girls and Tommy's friends scampered away into the field.

Sarah stood looking down at Tommy. "You boys listen well. I don't want to hear you talking about this to anyone. Tommy, you've known Hannah and Industrious for much of your young life. He's our friend.

Our family is always loyal to our friends, and we don't spread lies about them." She touched Tommy's shoulder. "You're in charge of the girls today. After they finish their game, take them back to the wagon and stay there. Do not come out. Don't let anyone talk to them. Do you hear me? Keep Blossom with you until her mother comes after her."

Tommy frowned as his friends scooted away. He trudged toward the field where the girls played.

With the children taken care of, Sarah decided to see Hannah. She located the Negro travelers' wagons and asked about her. Sarah peeked inside their wagon and saw Crystal sitting with Hannah. Hannah's eyes were swollen from crying. "I'm real scared those men gonna hurt Dustrous. The men on horses are chasin' him."

Sarah nodded. "I'm going to find friends in the camp who'll stand up for Industrious. We won't let them do anything bad to him." Amid deepening fear, she hoped her confident words would inspire courage.

Later that morning, as Sarah helped cut potatoes for the noon meal, she perceived a rift in the camp as clean as the twin white surfaces of the potato she'd just split. Jesse, Mary, and Willy were building a fire to cook the fish Ben cleaned. The four friends smiled across at Sarah. Four other travelers who'd joined the wagon train in Lake City caught her eye and nodded. Lennie and his sisters made an extravagant point of ignoring her. Sarah mentally counted the people clustered around the three L's and estimated almost equal numbers supporting the Larchmonts to those who believed in Industrious's innocence. Sarah or someone on her side needed to talk to those who seemed undecided to draw them to her side. Although unsure how to proceed once she assembled her allies, she had a gut feeling that the more friends Industrious had, the less likely the partners and the outside men who joined them would kill him without hearing his side of things.

After supper, Sarah, Ben, and Jesse made a plan. The men agreed to meet with an undecided couple if Sarah would convince the

Clements—Samuel and Charity's employers who were also friends of the Larchmonts.

Sitting outside their wagon, Robert and Katherine Clements were working at their crafts in the last hours of daylight. He shaved wood curls from the beak of a heron he was carving while she interlaced a length of red yarn between the strings on her loom. Robert wiped his knife on his sleeve. "We've been friends of the Larchmonts for over twenty years—friends of their parents longer than that. Those kids have had a rough time of it—losing their brother and their folks. It would be hard to go against them."

Sarah sat crossed-legged on the grass between them. "Industrious and his wife have been servants in our family almost twenty years. He went to war with my husband to protect and look after him. I would trust him or his wife Hannah with my life."

Robert interrupted, "He shouldn't have stopped at the open wagon to look at her. We are firmly opposed to miscegenation between the races."

"I don't believe Industrious intended anything of the sort," Sarah said. "Surely, you don't think—"

"I don't know what to think," he said.

"You know your slaves as well as your own family. I trust him the way you must have always trusted Samuel and Charity."

In a quick stroke, Katherine pressed the red yarn into the thick mat of the rug on her loom. "Samuel would never lay a hand on me."

Her husband stood. "This is different, Katherine. In my opinion, those girls have been flaunting their bodies around this camp more than I think is proper."

She nodded and rolled her eyes. "I'd say they brought it on themselves."

Sarah shook her head. "Listen; whatever those Larchmont girls did or didn't do has nothing to do with this. Industrious lost his way back to the wagon. I saw him right after it happened and he told me."

"What would you expect him to say?" he asked.

Sarah stood and shook her fist. "The truth. I know Industrious is a good man. Both you and Katherine have got to help him, or they're going to kill him. I don't think I could bear it."

Katherine gasped. "We can't let that happen. Just tell us what we need to do."

"Thank you, I will." Sarah explained the plan.

After the children were in bed, Sarah met again with Willy, Jesse, and Ben around a lantern just outside the camp. They told her right off that the Wakefields, the couple they talked to, had agreed to support them. "That gives us a majority," Sarah said; feeling less anxiety than earlier, she told them of her results with Robert and Katherine Clements.

"Let's make some quick plans." Ben extracted a piece of paper and a pencil from his pocket. "Those men may come back with Industrious any minute now. I only hope they haven't already strung him up."

Jesse scratched his head. "They wouldn't do that . . . I don't think."

"I don't think so," Willy said. "They know that a whole lot of us have taken a shine to him."

"You're a lawyer, Ben. What do you think?" Sarah asked.

"If we can get the partners to hold a hearing among us in the camp, it would help convince a jury in Texas to acquit him—if it goes that far. We may be able to settle the whole thing here."

Jesse shook his head. "I'd like to think my new friends would do the Christian thing, but folks get pretty agitated about race problems. I've seen church-going people kill a freedman with less evidence than this. Even with laws against it, Democrat officials look the other way."

Ben rubbed his beard and frowned. "Even the new Republican judges won't take a Negro man's testimony against a white man. I think we need to have an informal hearing at the camp."

"That's a wonderful idea, Ben," Sarah said. "You're a judge; you could set it up."

Ben shook his head. "They called me a scalawag in St. Augustine—I'm not so popular with the Democrats. I've also kept my distance from the partners. I think at least one has Klan connections. In fact, I suspect that the two men who came in this morning are Klan members from Shreveport or Texas."

Jesse turned and put his hand on Sarah's shoulder. "I've seen you talking to Bart. He seems to like you. If anyone could convince him about this hearing, it's you."

Sarah's throat tightened. She didn't want to see Bart now. "What if I can't talk him into it? I don't want Industrious to die because of me."

"You can talk anyone down, Miss Sarah. You must talk to Bart before something happens."

"I don't want the full responsibility. I'll arrange a meeting between the four of us and the three partners. Four folks of the same mind will have more power to influence them than I would alone." Sarah stared out at the dark pines around them. She wished the posse would return but dreaded the confrontation when they did.

She slept fully dressed near the back of the wagon so as not to miss the return of Bart and the strangers. *Maybe they won't find him. Maybe he'll escape.* She wanted to pray but didn't know what to ask for. Finally, in a vague prayer for Industrious's safety, she drifted into light sleep.

33

The white man's happiness cannot be purchased by the black man's misery.

Frederick Douglas

September 1868

Sarah awoke Friday morning to the patter of rain, which turned into a downpour accompanied by lightning and thunder crashes. She wrapped herself in a blanket and stared into the blackness broken sporadically by flashes that paled as the thunderstorm blew eastward. The tart fragrance of the earth, freshened by recent rain, quickened her nostrils. The slush of hooves slogged across muddy ground. Horses snorted and voices whispered muffled words just beyond the wagon where Sarah sat stone still listening.

"What're we gonna do with him?" a man asked.

Sarah recognized the next voice as Bart's. "I told ya; we oughta string him up by the river in Louisiana. Nobody's gonna give a damn about this nigger. I shouldn't have let you talk me into bringing him back here to the camp." Sarah pressed her knuckles against her lips.

Then she heard Abner's voice. "We owe it to Luella to have a part in his punishment."

"Yeah, she's not gonna get over this until he gets his just deserts," Lennie said. "Why don't we just tie him to the back of one of the wagons and wait until morning?"

Sarah heard the men grunting and shuffling in the wet leaves. She assumed they were moving Industrious.

Just after daylight brightened the sky, Sarah found Industrious outside the main camp behind the supply wagon, his knees bent with his arms bound around his shins. The men had inserted a heavy stick under his knees and over his arms. A dirty handkerchief gagged him, and a slipknot around his neck connected him to the back axle of the wagon. His face portrayed deep agony. She knelt beside him, talking softly. "We're going to help you, Industrious—Ben Cole, Willy, Mary, Jesse, and I. We'll try to get something started today. Can you nod your head?" Industrious bobbed his bound head.

"Good. Have the men hurt you?"

Industrious shook his head.

"Don't worry about Hannah. She's fine. Crystal is with her. I'm going now before they see me talking to you."

Later that morning, Sarah and her friends sat on a bench across from the partners and two new men. Bart raised an eyebrow at Sarah, his face for an instant exposing his desire. He composed himself. "I'd like you folks to meet our Shreveport friends—Jerry Mattingly and Morris Scruggs. They helped us hunt down the fugitive." The new men rose and shook hands with Ben, Jesse, and Willy. One of them kissed Sarah's hand in a chivalrous gesture.

Ben began with a straightforward approach. "We propose that you allow a hearing for Industrious Abraham."

"How come?" Abner asked. "There's no question of guilt or innocence. We caught the fool red-handed."

Sarah cleared her throat. "I was a witness the night it happened and talked to Industrious soon after. There are at least four of us who will attest to Industrious's character. It's only right to allow a hearing."

"It's the only fair way to deal with it." Jesse said.

"What do you think?" Abner asked Morris, one of the new men.

Morris shrugged at the partners. "A hearing can't do no harm. In fact, it'll probably help us. If the folks want to air their dirty linens in front of the whole camp, I say let 'em do it."

His friend Jerry nodded agreement.

Bart rubbed his chin. "We'll have to be quick about this. We're breaking camp tomorrow." He looked at his watch. "Be ready for the hearing right after the noon meal."

At one o'clock, the entire camp gathered within the circle of wagons. Sarah left her children with Hannah, who couldn't bear to be present. Someone contributed a table and three chairs for the partners. Industrious stood behind the three men, his hands bound, his eyes blinking, and his Adam's apple bobbing as he tried to swallow.

Bart stood, arms folded over his chest. He eyed the travelers one at a time until silence fell over the group. He stared at Sarah for a brief moment before he opened the meeting. "We are gathered here, my friends, to listen to your testimony concerning the guilt or innocence of Industrious Abraham." He tipped his head toward Industrious.

Jesse rose and handed a Bible to Bart. "I request that each witness place his right hand on this Bible and swear to tell the truth before God."

Bart laid the Bible on the table's corner and agreed to the swearing procedure. He called the first witness, Luella, who dramatized the event with histrionics one would expect from a second-rate Shakespearean actress. Finally, after several minutes of theme and variation based on assault against the honor of womanhood, Bart interrupted her, "Thank you, Miss Larchmont. Let's make this issue clear. On Wednesday, two nights ago, this Negro man opened your wagon and looked at you while you were sleeping. Is this correct?"

"He did, and, mercy God, I nearly died of fright."

"What did you do when you saw him?"

"What do you think I did, waking up to such a vision? I screamed my head off."

Ben walked forward. "May I cross-examine the witness?" Bart nodded assent and he began. "Miss Larchmont, let me get this straight. You were asleep in your wagon on Wednesday night?"

"I was."

"What exactly woke you up?"

"Well, I heard something rustling. I sat up and saw someone in a straw hat about to crawl into the wagon."

"Could you tell me who it was?"

She pointed at Industrious. "It was him. I'd know his black face anywhere."

Ben walked past Luella, his hands clasped behind his back. He snapped his eyes back toward her. "So you already knew Industrious Abraham?"

"Sure," she said.

"Do you know anything derogatory about him?"

She scratched her head. "De-roga—what does that mean?"

"Did you ever hear anything bad about Industrious, anything violent he ever did?"

She shook her head. "Nothing I can think of."

"Thank you, Miss Larchmont."

Lennie walked forward and related his version of Luella's story. "When my sister screamed, Industrious turned and jumped off the back of the wagon and ran off—a sure sign of guilt."

Ben stood. "I object. Industrious's fleeing does not signify guilt or innocence."

Bart looked at Ben. "Look here, Mr. Cole; this is an informal hearing, not a court trial. We can interpret things as we see them. The partners and I will make the final decision as to the disposition of Industrious." Ben's shoulders dropped, but he did not respond. "Go ahead; finish the questions," Bart said.

Ben put his hands in his pockets and walked closer to Lennie. "Have you ever heard anything derogatory about Industrious Abraham?"

"I never heard much about him one way or the other. He just minded his own business."

"Thank you, Mr. Larchmont," Ben said.

Bart called on each member of the posse who captured Industrious. One by one they related their recollections of Industrious's fear, which each in turn interpreted as a sign of his guilt. Abner repeated Industrious's verbal confession made in the wilderness before they returned to the camp.

Ben leaned toward Abner. "This confession—did Industrious offer it of his own free will, or did you coerce him—I mean threaten him with something if he didn't confess or offer him something if he did?"

Abner sputtered. "He wouldn't have confessed if he wasn't guilty."

"That's not what I asked. Did anyone threaten him? Please remember, Mr. Dial, that you have sworn on the holy Bible, the word of God Almighty, that you will tell the whole truth."

Abner swallowed and his eyes widened. "What was the question again?"

Ben repeated his question about whether the partners coerced the confession.

He flicked his eyes at Bart and Caleb, who gave him a cold stare. Abner swallowed again and rolled his eyes toward the heavens, perhaps asking God for forgiveness in advance. Looking at Ben, he blinked. "He just decided to confess and get it off his chest, I guess. We didn't press him or nothing."

Sarah watched Abner's eyes sweeping the crowd like a searchlight. "He's lying," she whispered to Jesse, sitting beside her.

Ben called the defending witnesses. He interviewed the Lake City residents and several other travelers who attested to Industrious's good character. Jesse and Willy told how helpful Industrious had been when some wagons got bogged down in the creek. Then, he called Sarah to the table. "Mrs. Browning, please relate for the members of this assembly the events as you remember them from Wednesday, September twenty-first."

Sarah stood in front of the judges' table and related her conversation with Industrious that night. "He told me he got confused in the dark and entered the covered wagon camp. He stopped by one of the wagons but didn't open the wagon or get inside."

"Confused, my foot!" Luella blurted out.

Ben turned and stared at her.

Bart stood. "Miss Luella, if you cannot remain silent during the testimony, I will have to ask you to leave."

Luella folded her arms and sulked.

Ben continued questioning Sarah. "How do you know Industrious wasn't lying?"

Sarah paused. "Wednesday was a dark night. The only light shone from a single lantern hung on a tree in the middle of the camp. It would be easy to get confused in the dark. I believed Industrious when he told me, and I believe him now."

"And why, Mrs. Browning, do you have such a strong belief in this man?"

"Industrious has been a servant and essentially a part of our family for almost twenty years. He's never paid attention to any woman except for his wife Hannah. He attended my husband Alex in the Confederate army as a body servant. My judgment about his character agrees with what other people have said, people who have also known him a long time."

Ben turned to the group gathered around the camp. "You have heard the testimony of many people of this group with only a few accusers and many who support Industrious Abraham. Even if he were so inclined, why would he purposefully enter a wagon where he would encounter the woman's brother? Furthermore, the darkness of the night caused him to lose his way back to his wagon. I can certainly understand why the woman became fearful, but her screams and the way Negroes are usually treated terrified Industrious. Of course, he would run." He paused and looked at each person in the gathering. "Let's have a vote."

Bart stood behind the table and avoided Sarah's eyes. "The lawyer Cole has requested a vote from the members of our group. Mind you; the partners and I will make the final determination regarding his guilt and punishment. All those who believe Industrious Abraham to be guilty, please say 'Aye.'"

The three Larchmonts, Frank Griffin and his wife, and ten other travelers responded with hearty "ayes."

Bart continued. "Those opposed—those who believe him innocent of a crime, respond with 'nay.'"

After thirty-four "nays" aimed toward the partners expressed the majority's solid determination, Bart led the partners back into his wagon.

"What do you think they'll do?" Sarah asked Jesse, her mouth dry and her pulse racing.

"Only the Lord knows," he answered.

A few minutes later, the partners emerged from the wagon with solemn, resolute faces. They took their places behind the table. Bart read from a sheet of paper. "It is the leaders' decision that the Negro, Industrious Abraham, performed a foolish but unintentional act to enter the Larchmont wagon. It is also apparent that the majority decision supports his character. Because of his action, as Miss Larchmont claimed, of entering the wagon and terrorizing an innocent white woman, Industrious Abraham will immediately receive twenty lashes and thereafter be released."

The crowd grumbled its dissent.

Sarah and Jesse walked toward the table. "You can't do that!" she yelled.

Bart sneered and returned to the wagon. Abner and Lennie led Industrious to a tree in the center of the camp. They placed a wooden box at the foot of the tree and lifted him onto it, binding his wrists around the slender tree. Bart followed, tapping a whip handle against his left palm. He shot a defiant glance at Sarah. Abner removed Industrious's shirt, revealing a broad brown back.

Sickened, Sarah turned from the group to retrieve Hannah and the children, determined to take them as far as possible from this camp until this unspeakable ordeal was finished. They walked along the riverbank and picked fall wildflowers.

While the children chattered and Charity put her arm around her, Hannah stayed quiet, nervously kicking small rocks into the river from time to time. She turned to Sarah. "What did they do to Dustrous?"

Tears formed in Sarah's eyes. She took both of Hannah's hands. "They whipped him. I'm so sorry."

Hannah exhaled a long sigh and pulled back her hands. "I was expectin' worse." She wiped her forehead with her apron. "Seems like there's still a lot of white folks that don't like us being free. Industrious and me come all this way so we could get some land to farm and start us a new life."

Sarah smiled. "You still can."

Hannah shook her head. "You think Mr. Benedict gonna give us anything after all this?"

Sarah hadn't considered this consequence.

"I'm going back to see about Dustrous." Hannah followed the river bend back toward the camp.

"Let's go," Sarah told the children. She left the children with Charity while she visited Industrious and Hannah's wagon. Ben and Hannah sat on either side of Industrious, who lay facedown on a mattress without his shirt and his back drenched with blood. He turned to face Sarah. His eyes, laced with red veins, bore into her and revealed a pain she'd never seen before. He began to speak in a low voice. "I guess I'm lucky I never got whipped before. Lots of slaves got whipped. It's curious. I never got beat till the war was over." He laughed without humor and turned to Ben and Sarah. "Thank you for standing up for me, Miss Sarah, Mr. Cole. I'd be a dead man without you . . . This thing's got me plenty worried."

Ben patted his brown arm. "What thing?"

"Mr. Benedict promised me ten acres at the end of the trip. Ain't no way he'll do that now."

Hannah's face contorted in an angry frown. "I wouldn't take it off him now if he begged me."

Ben patted her back. "I've been in these parts before. Marshall is the best place for you to live. There's a Union fort there and a Freedmen's Bureau. You two can work for me until you can find another job or some land. If anyone gives you trouble, come see me at the courthouse. I'll do my best to get your ten acres from that devil Benedict, and if I don't, I'll give you mine."

Sarah felt miserable, but she trusted Ben's advice. Hannah and Industrious nodded.

The next afternoon, the wagon train stopped in Marshall. Sarah and her children got out of their covered wagon carrying several large packages. Ben drove his wagon forward followed by Industrious and Hannah in their wagon. Sarah waved them to stop and get out. She and each of the children opened their sacks to offer their gifts to their former servants. Sarah gave Hannah a new bonnet that she'd bought in Alexandria. She folded ten dollars inside it. Tommy gave Industrious a small pocketknife. Lula gave them some fudge she made herself, and the other three children had drawn pictures. On her picture, Sallie painted figures representing her mother, the five children, and Hannah at their home in Lake City.

Hannah hugged each child separately and gave Sarah a long embrace. "How can we ever thank you?"

"You have already done more for us than I could ever repay."

Sarah turned to Ben and gave him a tin of sweets. "I'm leaving these two in your hands, Ben. Take care of them and make sure they're treated well."

Ben nodded his assurance and climbed into his wagon. "Follow me, and I'll take you into town."

Sarah and the children waved at the wagons until Abner gave the signal for their own wagon train to move on.

Three days later, the train finally reached the front of a long line of wagons and animals crossing over the Sabine River at Walling's Ferry in Camden. Most of the travelers entered Rusk County, the trail's end, in eerie silence. After Bart paid the fees for the crossing, he walked to where Sarah stood beside her wagon.

She turned her back toward him. "Don't even try to explain, Bart."

"At least, give me a chance to state my case."

Stone-faced, she stared at the ground.

He touched her hand and swallowed. "I know you're angry with me about the nigger, but that's over now, and we could start again. When we get settled . . . please say yes."

She jerked her hand away. "After that cowardly performance, nothing you can say would make me even like you again." The passion she had once felt for him fueled her outrage.

He walked around to face her. "I had to whip him. Anything less would have encouraged every buck in Texas and Louisiana to believe he could get by with unleashing his animal instincts on white womanhood. No woman in this area would be safe."

She shook her head, wide-eyed and unbelieving. "Where did you get such outrageous ideas? Industrious didn't try to rape anyone. The thought never entered the poor man's head."

Bart wrinkled his brows. "My God, you are naïve. Do you really think that sub-human animal can think like a white man? A beating is all his kind understands. Only because of you, I went easy on him. Any self-respecting white man would have lynched him, but I guess you can't appreciate that."

"You make me sick, Bart," she spat out. "Your evil ideas will send you straight to hell."

Bart's face turned red. "I've done everything on God's earth to help you." He pointed his finger at her face. "If you get in trouble, don't call on me. After today, you'll never see me again." He walked a few steps and turned back. "And you can forget about the ten acres."

"I've got a contract, and I know a very good lawyer!"

Bart stomped back to the wagon train.

Walking behind the wagons, she stared at dark shadows on the narrow road between thick groves of pine trees. She felt depressed. She'd placed her trust in the wagon train's leaders, and they'd betrayed her. Anger rose up like soured milk from inside her, spoiling her vision for the new home where she had thought she'd find refuge from the meanness she'd hated so much in Florida. Just hours ago, she'd watched Hannah sitting beside Industrious cleaning the split flesh on his back. Sarah squeezed her eyes shut in an attempt to erase the memory.

34

Where thou art, that is home.

Emily Dickinson

Late September 1868

A few miles farther, they came upon a small settlement called Harmony Hill. The name lifted Sarah's spirits. Soon, they reached a clearing with clapboard and log houses, a church, a small general store, a post office, and a building with a sign reading: "Harmony Hill School." Rope swings hung from branches of trees near the school. Men, women, and children emerged from the buildings smiling and waving at the newcomers.

"Is this the place where we're going to live?" Lula asked, solemn-faced.

Realizing that her sadness affected her children's attitudes, Sarah forced a big smile. "We're finally here, children." First, she took the children to the schoolhouse, a rectangular log building with windows on the long sides. When the heavy wooden front door creaked open, Sarah, with her five children following her, stepped into the stale air where dust and spider webs caught the sunlight pouring in through the windows. On one of twelve pegs next to the door hung a moth-eaten pink sweater abandoned by a forgetful child. Two rows of six benches, each long enough for three students, faced the front of the room with an aisle between them. Wooden tables, etched with overlapping initials, rested in front of each bench.

Lena raced down the aisle between the benches onto a platform where the teacher's desk sat in the front of the room. With her finger, she drew a circle in the dust on the desktop and frowned. "This looks like a poor people's school."

"It's a country school, Lena. There's a difference," Sarah said. The condition of the abandoned school dismayed her, too. While Tommy and Lula tried out the benches and tables, she examined bookcases behind the teacher's desk. Copies of *McGuffey's Readers* at various grade levels, Webster's spellers with ragged covers, and various books on arithmetic and geography filled the shelves. She scanned the wooden rafters across the ceiling where dirt daubers had built multiple nests in the intersections between the boards above the platform.

A deep voice boomed across the schoolroom. "Hullow." A youthful-looking man entered the room. He removed his derby and revealed thick, brown hair and sideburns. He wore a vest under his jacket with a bowtie on his shirt collar. Sarah smoothed the front of her wrinkled skirt.

The man strode up the aisle. "You must be the widow Browning. I'm E. C. Parr, a neighbor from down the road." His speech sounded foreign, similar to the accent Sarah had heard from Yankees she'd met in Florida but more drawn out.

"I apologize for our appearance, but we have been traveling for over three months from Florida." She introduced her children. "Children, say 'hello' to Mr. Parr."

E. C. gave each a warm smile. "I know you've had a difficult trip. We've all prayed for your safe arrival." He swept his arm around the room. "We haven't had a teacher since March."

Sarah tried to formulate an opening to apply for the job. She wasn't sure whether Mr. Parr was the person she should ask about it. While she thought, the children took up the conversation.

"In Florida, we went to school from September till May," Lula said.

"We went to the Academy," Tommy said. "It was a whole lot bigger than this school. We had three rooms. The older children and the younger ones had different teachers,"

"When does school start here?" Sallie asked.

E. C. laughed. "School starts as soon as we find someone to teach the students. Our usual term begins in November just after harvest and ends in March when spring planting begins."

Minnie walked closer to him. "You talk funny, Mr. Parr. Where are you from?"

"Minnie," Sarah scolded. "Don't be rude!"

E. C. put his hand on Minnie's blond head. "I'm from Canada, Minnie. It's another country a long way north of here. I've been living in Harmony Hill since I got out of the army after the war."

Tommy stepped closer to E. C. "My daddy fought in that war, too. He fought in Virginia for the Confederates. Maybe you would have met him. His name was Alexander Browning."

"Probably not, Tommy," E. C. said. "I fought in Tennessee and Georgia for the Union."

"He's a Yankee," Lula said in an audible whisper to Tommy.

"What brought you to Texas?" Sarah asked.

"Like so many other folks moving to the frontier, I headed west for land and new adventure. When I got to East Texas, the trees were so pretty, the weather so nice, and the people so friendly I decided to stay. I've been here buying land and raising cotton and cattle ever since."

"Are you in charge of hiring the new teacher for the school?" Sarah asked.

E. C. laughed. "I'm the Harmony Hill mayor, so I do just about any job from preaching at the church to being justice of the peace and head of the volunteer firemen—anything I can do to make this a good place to live. I'm not sure, but I'm probably the school principal, too."

"You seem young to take on so many duties."

E. C. grinned, "I'm not as young as I look. I'm twenty-nine."

Sarah had guessed his age at twenty-three, but he was only three years younger than she. "I'm sure your wife must help you in performing all your duties."

"You guessed wrong, again." He laughed. "You're looking at an old bachelor who's never found the right woman." He paused and looked at Sarah. "Mrs. Clements just informed me you've had experience teaching school."

"I taught in Lake City for two years."

E. C. sat on one of the benches next to Lula. "How did you like having your mama as a teacher?"

"She didn't teach at our school. She taught at the freeman school."

He looked surprised. "I'm familiar with freedmen schools. In fact, we have one near here in Harrison County for the Negro students." He stood by the table and looked steadily at Sarah with warm brown eyes. "Would you possibly consider teaching at our school, Mrs. Browning? We'd be much obliged to you. The pay's not much, but we'll give you a house to stay in, and the men of the town will add on more rooms for your children if you agree to help us out."

Her heart swelled with excitement. "I think you've just made an excellent offer, Mr. Parr."

He grinned. "Call me E. C."

On the way back to her wagon, Sarah considered the problem of finding someone to care for Lena and Minnie while she taught school and prayed that the Lord would provide an answer. A couple who appeared to be a few years older than Sarah approached her and the children with their arms full of clean clothes. "Hey there," the woman said, "we're mighty proud y'all moved here and hope we can make you feel at home. I'm Judy Jackson, and this here's my husband Kenneth. We'd shake your hand except we've got ours full."

Sarah smiled at the friendly couple. "My children and I look forward to knowing the folks here."

Kenneth walked toward the opening of the wagon, "Miz Browning," he said to Sarah, "Do you mind if we lay down these clothes?"

Without waiting for an answer, they stacked a pile of dresses along with shirts and pants and various sacks holding children's shoes into the back of Sarah's wagon. "First off," Judy said, "we need to let y'all know about supper at the church tonight. All us ladies are bringing food to the church every day for dinner and supper till y'all get settled in your houses. Tonight's the welcome party. We thought you might need some fresh clothes to wear after your long trip."

"We've got six children of our own," Kenneth said, "so we brought some dresses for your girls and some trousers and shirts for the boy."

"I put in one of my own outfits that'll most likely fit you just fine," Judy said to Sarah.

Sarah let out a happy sigh. "Thank you. You are very thoughtful. We hope we can return the favor. Tell these nice people 'thank you,' children."

The children were already looking through the stack of clothes.

"Y'all can come over to the house and wash up if you'd like," Judy said. "We live down the road catty-cornered from the church." She pointed to a clapboard house on the right.

"That would be lovely," Sarah said as the Jacksons turned to walk home.

"Thank you," the Browning children shouted after them.

After she had finished bathing the children and herself at the Jackson house, she dressed them in their new clothes. Half an hour later, Sarah led her entourage to the church supper. The rectangular wooden building had a steep shingle roof topped with a white wooden cross. Tall trunks of loblolly pines guarded three sides of the church. Behind it, enclosed by a picket fence, lay a little cemetery with white stones marking the graves. Bouquets of wild flowers lay next to the markers. Windows on the side of the church reflected the golden glow of the afternoon sun.

As the newcomers and the town folks pulled their chairs out of straight rows to make a large circle, E. C. walked around the room smiling and shaking hands with the new arrivals. Sarah surveyed the group, who'd made an amazing transformation. Apparently, many of the local families had taken in members of the wagon train, allowed them to bathe, and given them new clothes. Three young men crowded around Luella and Lorena. The Wakefields frowned as they lectured Carter and Legrand, sulky in starchy shirts and knickers. Jesse looked comfortable in his brown trousers and a soft plaid shirt. Old Dr. Griffin patted the hand of his tiny gray-haired wife. Kathryn Clements and her husband sat next to Willy and Mary, who was holding baby Will.

"Sit down, Sarah," Kathryn said, motioning toward empty seats.

E. C. marched up on the podium at the front of the room. "Good afternoon, everyone."

The crowd responded with "howdies" and a few "good afternoons."

"Before we partake of the food, I have a few announcements. First, I'd like to introduce our new teacher, Mrs. Sarah Browning." When Sarah stood, the group applauded. E. C. continued, "I've been leading this church for the past two years—as best I could with my lack of religious training, but I am happy to tell you that our new preacher has arrived on this wagon train. Jesse Kuykendall, come up to the front and lead us in a blessing."

"Let's bow our heads to give thanks to the Lord for our safe arrival and for the kindness of the people in our new community." Several "amens" came from the newcomers. Jesse spoke a long prayer of thanksgiving ending with a blessing for the food and the hands that prepared it.

As they were leaving, Judy invited Sarah to her house the next afternoon for a "quilting." She explained that the children played outside while their mothers quilted. Sarah knew that some groups admitted only expert quilters whose stitches would enhance the designer's pattern. Sarah worried that she might spoil someone's quilt since it had been ten years since her last experience.

At Judy's house the next afternoon, Judy introduced Sarah to Beatrice Heinz and her daughter, Erika. Sarah repeated the names to herself so that she would remember them. When Candice Wakefield, Kathryn Clements, and Crystal Bishop came in a few minutes later, Sarah felt more comfortable. The women followed Judy into a large room at the back of the house where long windows on two sides allowed sunlight to brighten the quilting area. In the room's center lay a quilting frame propped on four ladder-back chairs. The women took their places around the frame while Judy supplied needles, thread, and thimbles. Sarah recognized the intricate pattern on the quilt as the double-wedding-ring design.

"E. C. told us you'll be the new school marm." Judy leaned close to the quilt to push her needle through the layers. "When do you commence?"

Sarah smiled and threaded another needle. "As soon as the men complete the remodeling. E. C. said school would probably start by the third week of October."

"School opening can't come too soon for me," Candice said. "Those energetic boys of mine will likely drive me mad until that time."

"What did you think about E. C., our most eligible bachelor?" Erica asked Sarah.

"I liked him."

Judy smiled. "He's a Yankee, but folks here think he's nice. He's been a very busy man since he was elected a delegate in Austin."

"What kind of delegate?" Sarah asked.

"All I know is that they're working on a new constitution for Texas so the Yankees will let our state back in the Union. Most of it has to do with rights for the Negroes."

Crystal looked up from her stitching.

"That sounds like an important job," Sarah said.

Judy frowned. "I'm not smart enough to understand politics, but my Kenneth gets wrought up about the threat of a Negro rebellion."

While she and the children returned to the wagon, Sarah considered the new information about E. C. and about East Texas. Harmony Hill might not be as peaceful as its name implied.

As E. C. had promised, the workers completed the remodeling by the second week in October. The following week, Sarah busied herself moving into her renovated log house by the school. With the help of Peter Wakefield and Jesse, she placed her mother's mahogany china cabinet in the front room and lugged two mattresses up a ladder into the loft for the younger children. Sarah folded the children's laundered clothes into the wardrobe trunk and put her scanty supply of dishes into the kitchen cabinet. In spite of her excitement about a new home, the empty cabin saddened her. She longed for her mother's beautiful china and silver pieces, the linens and lamps, the things she had collected to make her home on Alligator Creek.

She heard a light tap and saw E. C. standing in the open door.

"You look sad enough to cry," he said. "I had hoped you would be pleased with the additions we made to the house."

Sarah forced a smile. "It's wonderful, E. C. I'm just a bit homesick. Truly, I am so very grateful to find a new home in this lovely town with all these generous people."

E. C. looked around. "It is somewhat empty. I can see you need a kitchen table, maybe a few chairs, and a couple of beds."

Sarah sighed. "I still have some money, but I don't know where to shop for things like that."

On Saturday, before the announced school opening, Sarah and the older two children rode with E. C. to Jefferson for a political barbecue. She left her young ones with Kathryn, Charity, and Blossom. E. C. had promised Sarah she could shop for some household goods at the stores there. After an eventful day, the carriage returned, several pounds heavier with Sarah's purchases. The children thanked E. C. for their delicious barbecue lunch.

E. C. opened the door of Sarah's house. She looked inside and gasped. Her kitchen held a long oak table with ten matching ladder-backed chairs, and a new settee sat in the living room. "Where did all this furniture come from?"

E. C. grinned. "I made it for you. Our neighbors put it in the house while we were in Jefferson."

Sarah felt overwhelmed. "When did you have time to do this? It's beautiful."

"I've been working on it ever since the first day I met you in the schoolhouse."

Sarah enclosed him in a huge hug and kissed him. He put his arm around her, and they walked inside.

The next day, Kathryn, along with Crystal and Blossom, joined Sarah as she walked home after church. "Crystal has something she wants to talk to you about," Kathryn said. "Would you mind if she came over this afternoon?"

"All of you can come in right now, Kathryn. I would love having company in our new home. The children are visiting with some of their new friends."

Kathryn declined, saying she must go home to her husband.

Sarah opened the door for Crystal and Blossom and waited for the woman to make her request. Crystal looked at her wide-eyed. "First of all, Mrs. Clements don't really need me to work for her, so I'd like to help you." When Sarah started to object, Crystal said, "You don't need to pay me. I'll work for free and keep your little children while you're teaching . . . that is, if you'll do just one thing for me."

"I'll do anything I can, Crystal."

"Blossom here is six years old, same age as your Sallie." Sarah nodded. "Could you to teach her some reading? Samson and me ain't never learned to read. We want her to do better."

"Of course I will, Crystal, and I appreciate your offer to keep Lena and Minnie during the day. I'll take Blossom to school with me tomorrow."

"No, no, Miss Sarah. You just teach her at night after school. She don't have no clothes to wear to the nice school."

"I think I can solve that problem." Sarah rifled through the drawer where she kept Sallie's dresses and found a yellow dress and a brown jacket she had sewn in Florida. Sallie, in a growth spurt, had outgrown the outfit, but Sarah felt it would fit Blossom, who was thinner and shorter than Sallie. She found a pair of Sallie's outgrown leather shoes she'd been saving for Lena and Minnie.

The next morning, Sarah's first day of class at the Harmony Hill School, she and Crystal helped Blossom and Sallie dress for school. Sarah overheard Lula and Tommy talking in the other room. Tommy said, "I'm glad we will all go to the same school."

"Me, too," Lula said. "Do you think we'll have friends at this school?"

"Sure," he said, "Lots of them."

Then Crystal took Minnie and Lena into the back yard to swing. As soon as Tommy and Lula were ready, Sarah opened the front door and paused for a moment. She wondered if the townspeople would object to her including a Negro child in the all-white classroom. Would this cause her a problem in her new community?

Then, she looked down at the excitement shining on Blossom's face and smiled. *I've dealt with worse problems before, and I can do it again. Besides, I have a strong feeling that E. C. will be on my side.*

She held Sallie and Blossom's little hands in hers as they left the house. Tommy and Lulu led the way. Halfway to school, Lulu turned and smiled at her mother.

"I think we've found our home, Mama."

Sarah nodded in agreement. *Indeed, we have, sweet children. Indeed, we have.*

EPILOGUE

And now without redemption all mankind
Must have been lost, adjudged to death and hell
By doom severe.

John Milton
Paradise Lost

La Porte, Texas: 1915

Tom Browning trudged away from the farmhouse with the white wreath on the door. He reflected on the gamut of emotions a minister might experience in twenty-four hours. He hoped his words and prayers had offered comfort to the family whose only child had died suddenly. Tomorrow afternoon, he'd transform his demeanor to ebullience for a wedding of two young people from a prominent family. As he crossed the streets through a section of town struck by a fire this spring, he winced at the mingled stench of charred wood, burned rubber, and scorched oil clinging to the burned-out hulls of homes and stores. He recalled the anguish of families who had lost all they owned. By the time he reached the seawall, a fragrant breeze off the Gulf of Mexico had replaced the foul odors. Waves dashed against the shore

339

and receded. He remembered God's promise of ever-present love and his own ministry to bring that promise to his flock. Sometimes, responsibility weighed on his heart—a heart never quite at peace. He headed for his church study, where he could return a few phone calls before going home for the evening.

He turned the doorknob and chastised himself for leaving his door unlocked. He hung his hat and jacket on the coat rack before turning on a lamp.

"Tommy." The cracking voice of an old man startled him.

He pulled the chain, and soft light haloed an ancient figure perched on a straight chair in the corner. "May I help you, sir?"

"Don't you know me?" the man asked.

Tom didn't remember meeting this old man, but he called him "Tommy." He must have known him long ago. The man's face bore strong resemblance to someone familiar—the creases in the sun-blotched skin, the slope of shoulders beneath a worn wool jacket, the blade of a nose, his parched, down-turned lips nearly obscured by a heavy white beard—an older version of himself. His father? Impossible. He died forty-seven years ago. Tom had read and reread the letter foretelling the death of his father. He winced as unwelcome memories overtook him.

The man spoke again in a shaky voice. "I'm your father."

Tom scrutinized the old man's features. He spoke slowly, enunciating each word. "I don't know what you're talking about. My father's dead. He's been dead nearly fifty years."

With his right hand, the man fumbled in his jacket pocket, then reached awkwardly across his body into the opposite pocket. He finally extracted a document and placed it between the index and middle finger of his stiff left hand. Tom now noticed that the hand bent at a right angle to the lower arm. With his good hand, the old man grappled for a walking stick lying against his chair and hobbled toward Tom, holding the document still between the fingers of his left hand.

Tom walked forward and took the document. The old papers granted freedom in an exchange of prisoners for Alexander M. Browning at Venus Point, Georgia, December 12, 1864, and the document gave the soldier permission to return home on a sixty-day furlough. Tom studied the old man and looked at the papers again. "This'll take a lot of explaining."

"I've gotten old. I've changed a lot since you saw me. I've grown a beard." Alex pulled at his whiskers.

"That's not what I mean," Tom said. Questions that had plagued his early years now flocked like vultures at the graves of exhumed memories: *Where have you been all these years? Why did we think you were dead? Did you ever try to find us?* The bitter gall of anger welled in his throat, but before he could frame even one of the questions, the old man began with queries of his own.

"Tell me about your mother. I want to know about Sarah . . . and the girls."

Tom pushed down his angry thoughts and began with his earliest recollections of his mother, expanded by what he later learned from listening to her stories and from entries in her journal. He told about Lena's early death and about Lula and Sallie's marriages and children. After he described his mother's last days, he stopped speaking. A poignant memory surfaced—her last words—"You must forgive your father, Tom." She'd said this many times before. He'd always answered, "I will," and he intended to—someday. The memory jolted him as though Sarah were speaking to him from the grave. He waited several seconds before speaking and continued by recounting his life during those terrible years when the war had taken his daddy away. He paused and clicked open his pocket watch. Perhaps he should call his wife, Helen, to tell her that he'd be late for supper.

"That's my watch," The old man pointed an arthritic finger at the timepiece.

Startled, Tom looked at it again. "Yes, this did belong to you. I remember when Mama gave it to me. It was after that man visited us, the one who told us you'd died."

Alex looked confused. "I don't remember losing it. I haven't thought about it in years."

Although he was only eleven at the time, Tom could never forget the day the stranger brought the watch to their home in Lake City, Alex's note foretelling his death, and his mother's despair leading to their decision to leave Florida. The memory brought back the turmoil of his childhood anguish.

"May I hold it a bit?" Alex asked

"Sure." Tom handed him the watch.

Alex opened and closed the case and examined the engraving on the back of the gold timepiece that had once belonged to his own father. He twisted the stem, held it to his ear, then handed it back to Tom.

Tom shook his head. "You keep it." Tom wasn't sure he even wanted it now.

"I always intended for you to have it, Tommy."

Tom shrugged and dropped it into his pocket. He moved his face close to Alex's and glared at him. "Tell me this. If you'd intended it for me, why did you give it to a stranger? What about the death message that came with it?"

"Such a long time ago. It was a low time. I couldn't think, couldn't sleep for the nightmares recalling the horrors I'd seen. I wanted to die, and I intended to take my own life."

"What changed your mind?"

"A kind doctor I met in Savannah helped me get over some of it—at least, the memories and nightmares."

"Mother would have cared for you. Why didn't you come home? You could at least have written a letter to let her know you were alive. Something else must have happened, something you're not admitting."

Alex hung his head.

"Another woman?"

He nodded. "It didn't mean anything. I was lonely."

Tom felt his anger rising. "I'm glad Mama didn't know." The telephone on his desk jangled. Tom welcomed the interruption that probably saved him from another outburst. He put the receiver to his ear. It was Helen. "I'm sorry, honey. I'm running late. Give me another thirty minutes. Can you put an extra plate on the table?" Helen, God love her, had grown used to his erratic hours and intrusive requests. He replaced the receiver.

"I'm old, Tommy. Don't have long to live. Not much time for making amends. Can't make amends to the departed, you know." He took a yellowed newspaper clipping from his pocket and smoothed it with his good hand. "Frances mailed me this in '89."

Tom knew the words by heart—his mother's obituary in the *Rusk County News*: a short message buried within a review of trivial community activities in a small town—bridge parties, luncheons, picnics, piano recitals. The only words noting the passage of an incredible life: "I went to Mrs. Parr's burying on Christmas day, the only burying I attended on that day," the reporter wrote. Tom smiled. "Always the renegade. Mother never followed the rules of her world."

Alex nodded. "You're right about that."

When Tom and his father left the church for the parsonage, Alex asked, "Was there a single moment when you knew without any doubt the Lord called you to be a preacher?"

"I always knew," he responded without pause. "My call was no sudden, earth-shaking moment. Mama taught me about a loving God while I was very young. The example of her absolute faith in darkest times stayed with me, her legacy of courage when she swam the swollen stream—Alligator Creek—carrying each of us children across to safety. I knew that God had called me before I was born."

The old man kept his eyes on the sidewalk in front of his cane. "The only thing I felt sure of in my long life was the call to fight. But I betrayed myself and many others following that call. Most important, I betrayed your mother." He stopped below a streetlight, straightened his body, and looked at Tom's face. "And now that I'm looking back, I don't reckon God had one thing to do with it."

"We all have our swollen streams to cross," Tom said. Growing up, Tom had many times said to himself: *My father betrayed us.*

"Did she hate me, Tommy?"

"Never. She should have, but she didn't. Even in her journal, she had only kind words for you. She blamed the war for your separation."

"She would." Alex stepped forward and stumbled.

Tom caught him by the elbow and steadied him. They ambled along, making slow progress, then stopped at the path leading to the neat brick house serving as a parsonage. From time to time, Tom had counseled older men who came to him to confess lifetimes of sin as they faced their own mortality.

"Why do you think you betrayed her?" He stopped by the gaslight next to the path to his home. Through the front window, he saw Helen and his fourteen-year-old daughter setting food on the dining room table.

"By my silence, my refusal to write to her, I led her to believe I died. I wanted to protect her. At that low point I felt unworthy."

Tom faced the man whose absence had tortured him, his sisters, and especially his mother. Anger rose up inside him again. "That's a sorry excuse. Why didn't you try to find us? Those years after the war my mother kept telling us you would return. No troop train arrived at the Lake City station that she didn't meet it with her hopes flying. She inquired about you from everyone who might have known you—to no avail." Tom turned his back to his father. "She wanted you; we needed you. She struggled to keep our home, to feed and clothe us."

Even today, at fifty-nine, Tom felt the pain as though he were eleven again, helpless to ease the burden his mother carried. He turned to face his father. "She never lost hope that you would return. Then, that man came and gave her your watch. You could have come back. You could have changed the course of our lives." Tom looked hard at Alex. "How did you find me?"

"I came back to Lake City a few months after you left for Texas. The farm had been sold. I visited my sister-in-law, Margaret, to find out where Sarah was. Frances had written Margaret from Galveston about Sarah."

Tom looked down at his father. He raised his voice as though he were in his pulpit driving home a point. "You knew where we were and didn't even try to find us then?"

Alex's shoulders slumped, and he stared at his deformed hand, rubbing it with the fingers of the healthy one. Tom knew he was torturing his father, but he couldn't stop the torrent of his unanswered questions any more than a human could stop the flow of a raging river. "You knew where Frances lived. Surely she wrote you telling you where we were."

He met Tom's eyes. "Yes . . . I did know. In fact, three months after you left for Texas, I purchased passage to Galveston and a train ticket from there to East Texas."

"What happened?"

"A bout of pleurisy. My time in prison maimed me, Tommy. You can't conceive of the pain—every breath was torture. The doctor put me to bed."

Tom didn't think he was still suffering from pleurisy. "But when you recovered?"

"Sarah deserved more than this pitiful man. I was maimed in body and mind." He averted his rheumy gray eyes.

Tom's annoyance with the self-pity exploded. "Tell me the truth! It's too late for lies, even to yourself." Tom waited in silence for a full minute for the old man to respond.

"Margaret nursed me back to health. She stayed by me every day, made strong broth and fed me, rubbed ointment on my chest."

"Our aunt Margaret? Good God, Mother couldn't stand the sight of the self-righteous bitch!" Tom stopped himself. He rubbed his forehead and shifted to a ministerial response. "The person who cares and touches you becomes dearer than a lost memory. Did you marry her?"

"I did. Then we found a land grant near the east coast of Florida and moved there."

"I suppose you needed someone to care for you." He looked at his father's pained face. "Where is she now? Did she die?"

"Yes, and the two little girls."

"I'm sorry." Tom meant it this time. He finally felt some compassion for this stranger, his father.

Alex looked down again. "Your mother and I never got a divorce decree, you know. You're a preacher. Tell me. Do you think God would ever forgive my adultery?"

"Mama remarried, too."

"But she didn't know I was still living. I knew she was alive."

In a moment, Tom recognized what his father needed was not pity but forgiveness. Perhaps it was what he needed, too. "Don't you know the Lord forgives you?"

"A preacher told me that long ago . . . I didn't believe it then . . . but I'd like to believe it now."

"It's true. God forgives you. Why don't you forgive yourself? Do you know more than He does?"

"Tommy." Alex bit his lip and shook his head. "I'm really sorry I caused my family so much suffering."

Tom bowed and spoke some silent words to Sarah. *OK, Mama, I'm about to do it right now. You'll never leave me alone until I do.* Tom enclosed the withered hand in his own. "Daddy." Tom took a deep breath and paused. "I forgive you."

When he heard his father crying, he put his arms around Alex's shoulders. Then, he felt his father's arm on his waist. "I love you, Daddy, and I'm glad you came back to see me."

Light poured out into the darkness from the windows of Tom's home. With their arms around one another, the two men made their way up the path to the front door.

Author's Note

Alligator Creek is based on a true story, or as a former professor called it, "a family legend." My ancestors told and retold the story of Alexander and Sarah Browning through at least five generations. Both born in Georgia, Alex and Sarah married June 1853 and moved to Lake City, Florida, where their names appear on the 1860 census. Alexander (I use the nickname, Alex, found on some letters he received) joined the Confederate army in 1862 and served in several major battles of General Robert E. Lee's Army of Northern Virginia. During the Battle of the Wilderness, he was captured and held first at Point Lookout, Maryland, and later at Elmira Prison Camp in New York. Sarah, believing Alex was dead, took her children to Rusk County, Texas. Their children included John Thomas, Lula Viola, Sallie, Helena (Lena), and Minnie. In Texas, Sarah married E. C. Parr, with whom she had three more children: Elizabeth, Maggie, and George.

Sarah died at 47, December 23, 1885, and is buried in East Texas at the Pirtle Methodist Church Cemetery. Alex came to Texas to visit his son, Tom, in 1915. He returned to Florida where he died February 6, 1917. Alex is buried with his second wife, Margaret, and their two daughters in Fort McCoy, Florida.

The family legend includes this story: A wagon train coming to Texas had camped across the creek from where Sarah lived. Recent rains had caused the creek to flow over its banks. Sarah swam across the swollen stream five times, each time carrying one of her small children to the wagon train.

As far as I know, I am the first to write an extended version of this compelling story. Writing in the twenty-first century about events that happened in the nineteenth involves tremendous research and some speculation. The Civil War caused horrendous suffering for both the North and the South; good and evil flourished on both sides.

In my branch of the family, Lula Viola married my great-grandfather, Jacob Solon King. My mother, Viola King Lipscomb, was named for her grandmother. I am also aware of several other relatives with the second name Browning. My grandfather's name was Asbury Alexander King. The prolific family now includes hundreds of descendants from Sarah and Alexander Browning, and I am proud to have their genes. *Alligator Creek* is neither a biography nor a genealogy, but the expansion of a compelling story of two ordinary people who lived through one of the most extraordinary periods in American history—the Civil War.

Bibliography

Ash, Stephen V. 2002. *A Year in the South 1865*. New York: Perennial.

Blackford, Susan Leigh, and Charles Minor Blackford. 1998. *Letter from Lee's Army: Or Memoirs of Life in and Out of the Army in Virginia During the War Between the States*. Whitefish, MT: Kessinger Publishing.

Browning, Alexander. Letters, 1909–1915.

Carter, Myrtle King. Letter to author, March 31, 1974.

Clark, Thomas D. 1944. *Pills, Petticoats and Plows: The Southern Country Store*. Norman, OK: University of Oklahoma Press.

Dean, Eric T., Jr. 1997. *Shook Over Hell: Post Traumatic Stress, Vietnam and the Civil War*. Boston: Harvard University Press.

Degler, Carl N. 1953. *At Odds: Women and the Family in America from the Revolution to the Present*. New York: Oxford University Press.

Eaton, Clement. 1954. *A History of the Southern Confederacy*. New York: The Free Press.

Fletcher, William A. (1908) 1995. *Rebel Private: Front and Rear: Memoirs of a Confederate Soldier*. New York: Penguin.

Foote, Shelby. 1958, 1963, 1974. *The Civil War*, Vols. 1–3. New York: Random House.

Haller, John S., Jr. 1981. *American Medicine in Transition, 1840–1910.* Urbana, IL: University of Illinois Press.

Keuchel, Edward F. 1996. *A History of Columbia County Florida.* Lake City, FL: Hunter Printing.

King, John. Interviews by Lottie Guttry, 1974.

King, Tom. Genealogy of King and Browning Families.

Leavitt, Judith Walzer. 1986. *Brought to Bed: Childbearing in America, 1750 to 1950.* New York: Oxford University Press.

Litoff, Judy B. 1978. *American Midwives 1860 to the Present.* Westport, CN: Greenwood Press.

Litwack, Leon F. 1979. *Been in the Storm So Long: The Aftermath of Slavery.* New York: Knopf.

Speck, Nancy Carter. Interviews by Lottie Guttry, 1974–2002.

Sutherland, Daniel E. 1989. *The Expansion of Everyday Life: 1860–1876.* New York: Harper & Row.

Trelease, Allen W. 1971. *White Terror: The Ku Klux Klan Conspiracy and Southern Reconstruction.* New York: Harper.

Varhola, Michael J. 1999. *Everyday Life During the Civil War.* Cincinnati: Writer's Digest Books.

About the Author

Lottie Lipscomb Guttry grew up in the small town of Kilgore, Texas, the site of the famous East Texas Oil Field. She attended Sweet Briar College, received a bachelor of music degree from the University of Texas at Austin, a master of arts from Stephen F. Austin University, and a doctorate from Texas A&M University at Commerce. She taught literature and composition at Kilgore College, the University of Texas at Tyler, and the University of Phoenix. She owned and directed Sylvan Learning Center in Longview. During her studies at Stephen F. Austin State University, a professor assigned her class to find and write a family legend. A cousin introduced Lottie to Sarah and Alexander Browning and their story—the basis for her historical novel *Alligator Creek*. Other publications include a musical, *Boom*, based on the history of the East Texas Oil Field; a play for children, *The Enchanted Swan*; a critical article published in the *Walt Whitman Review*; two devotionals published in *The Upper Room*; and numerous feature articles for *The Longview News-Journal.*

Lottie and her husband John, a retired dentist, live in Longview, Texas, near Kilgore, where they both grew up. She participates in the music program at her church, serves on several community boards, plays duplicate bridge, and travels. She has three grown children, eight grandchildren, and two great-granddaughters.